CONSENSUAL SCARS

© 2024 Ann Marie Huber

This is a work of fiction.

All of the characters, locations, and events portrayed in this novel are either products of the author's imagination or are used fictitiously. And any resemblance to actual persons, living or dead, businesses, events, or locales is entirely coincidental.

Consensual Scars. Copyright © 2024 by Ann Marie Huber. All rights reserved. Printed in the United States of America. No part of this book may be used or reproduced in any manner whatsoever without written permission except in the case of brief quotations embodied in critical articles or reviews.

Cover art and design by Jess McNeil-Estes.

For information, contact anniemariehuberauthoress@gmail.com

Library of Congress Control Number: 2024914921

To the girls who love too hard...

Consensual Scars

A Hippie in Lake City

When I was in high school, a boy once told me that attractive women fall into three categories: "sexy," "pretty," and "cute." He ranked the categories, leveling his hand at different heights to indicate the different tiers. "Sexy" was, of course, at the top. He then proclaimed that I fell into the third category, "cute." I felt like I lost a competition I never asked to join. I guess I should be glad that I made the cut for "attractive." But that's kinda fucked up too, right? That I would have any reaction at all to his insipid rating system.

Worse than his ranking of me, his description was probably apt.

I'm short (5'2"), with shoulder-length, wavy blond hair that I never quite know what to do with, so it usually ends up in a ponytail. My heritage is like a European mutt: a mix of German, Scottish, and Polish. But I don't feel a connection to any of that. I'm just your average, midwestern, middle-class, suburban white girl. I don't wear make-up other than the occasional lipstick (unless required to for the stage) and my clothes are made up almost entirely of jeans, t-shirts, and big flannel button-downs. I can't tell you where I got the flannel shirts; their origins into my life are a complete mystery. I can tell you *when* I acquired them: sometime during college.

One of the flannel shirts may be from a boy that one of my high school girlfriends was dating. This boy once told me that if my *friend* had turned him down, he would have asked *me* out instead. He shared this information in order to buck me up when I was feeling sad, meaning it as a huge compliment. (Was it really, though?) This off-handed comment, like the "cute" assessment, has haunted me for years. I just know that I'll be on my death bed somewhere, someday, hearing an echo of how I'm a third-tier, second choice kind of girl.

These experiences taught me early on not to be too impressed with boys. They are unwittingly cruel.

I'm now twenty-two years old and I have never dated anyone. Like, *anyone*. That's weird, right? It feels like it might be weird. I try not to think about it, but when I do, I like to think it's been my choice. The truth is murkier, however, since the disinterest appears to be mutual. How much is it my choice when there's no other option in front of me?

As for sexual history… well, I've spent my formative years in the theater so there's that. For the uninitiated, dressing rooms are delightfully indecent places. They may have gender-specific signs on the doors, but that stops no one. Sure, the boys would sometimes knock but it never mattered. We always let them in even in mid-dress. The girls wouldn't even bother to knock. If we did, they'd laugh at our decorum. In these spaces, I've had my share of make-out sessions. These instances, whether with guys (probably gay) or girls (definitely bi), were often spurred on by risqué games of Truth or Dare. (Though sometimes we'd get retro with Spin the Bottle.) These experiences, while perfectly pleasant, weren't reflective of any real desire on my part; I participated because I was expected to.

The only crush I've ever truly had was my Shakespeare teacher in high school, a man of around forty to my juvenile sixteen. His name was George Hamilton. The famous name just added to the allure of the brilliant and witty salt and pepper-haired man who would recite sonnets passionately, kneeling before our desks. All the girls in the class were smitten, huddling near our lockers to discuss the latest tidbits of information we'd learn about Mr. Hamilton. When we heard he spoke French, we were even more in awe. After our French teacher, spooked by the bombing of the Pan Am flight, refused to take the French club on our planned trip to Paris, we asked Mr. Hamilton to chaperone the trip. It was an unorthodox request that we made in desperation. After all, we had fundraised hard for this experience, selling pastries every morning for months on end, and weren't letting our European dream go so easily. Mr. Hamilton took the torch enthusiastically.

Don't get me wrong. Our debonair teacher never once acted inappropriately around us, no matter how much we may have wanted him to. No, he treated us with utmost respect, addressing us always by our surnames. "Ms. Fox," he would say to me as I walked by in the hall, nodding his acknowledgement, making my heart pound ever faster. On the trip, he let our small group run wild with little supervision in the strange city while he explored the landscape with his beautiful, much younger wife. ("She used to be his student!" we whispered. "She's sixteen years younger!") When I wasn't struggling to conjugate verbs or admiring global landmarks, I was watching this woman with acute curiosity and envy.

Since Mr. Hamilton, no man (or boy) has piqued my interest in that way.

At least, that's true of real people. There are plenty of fictional men whom I'm sure I would jump if given the chance (Special Agent Dale Cooper, for instance). However, that might just be the magic of media; maybe it's only the "fictional" part that makes these white knights so attractive. Maybe if Agent Cooper walked through the screen and was standing in front of me, he'd lose all appeal. In which case, I'm kind of fucked (or really, not at all fucked, as the case may be). Whatever my situation is, I know I'm missing out on something, some ancient knowledge and primitive instinct in the realms of love and relationships that other people seem to effortlessly possess. And unless I figure this stuff out, I'm going to be alone forever.

Okay, I'm being dramatic. I'm not *alone*. I have a few friends from both high school and college that have since scattered across several states. And I have Jonathan, my bestie, who is, I'm certain, a gazillion times better than any boyfriend could ever be.

I knew Jonathan was gay before he was ready to tell anyone, so for a while we just ignored the obvious. We watched movies (so many movies), did every school theater show together, and basically became inseparable from the time we met during our freshman year in high school through college graduation at Indiana University. Now that he's out and proud, he's making up for lost time. While I date no one, he dates everyone.

Since I've known him, Jonathan has had one goal: to be successful. And to that end, he earned a degree in the very practical subject of computer science. That degree, coupled with his networking prowess, landed him an entry level position right after graduation as a software developer for a burgeoning tech company in Chicago. If you don't look too closely, you would think that things come easily to Jonathan. But the truth is he works his ass off; the effortlessness is only a mirage, one that he carefully cultivates. His mantra: "If you look like you're trying, you've already lost."

Chicago is not that far (only about ninety minutes from my current location), but it's still too damn far. There's a hole in my life where Jonathan used to be, but I'm learning to deal. It's not the first time my life has experienced a deep and sudden loss. In my senior year of college, my mom suffered a cerebral hemorrhage and passed away. It was quick, and by the time I heard of anything happening, she was already gone. I try not to think about it, but now that I'm home, she's everywhere and nowhere, a ghost conjured of memories. My mom was my best friend, ever encouraging, ever loving, ever everything, and now… what? She's just gone? It's so fucking unfair that I want to scream whenever I think about it. So, as I said, I don't think about it.

I graduated college on May 6, 1995, and I was back home in my small hometown a week later. A little over four months have gone by and I'm still here with no plans to go anywhere. And while I'm glad I can be home for my father, I feel like I've entered some sort of purgatory, the space between college and "real life" (whatever that is). For the first time in my twenty-two years, I have no real game plan. Granted, until now, that plan wasn't more detailed than "graduate from college." And while I'm distraught over the lack of a new plan, I'm also not particularly motivated to come up with one. I figure the need for productivity will kick in at some point. I can't stay stuck here forever.

Meanwhile, my father is trying to come to terms with *not* being productive as he retired two years ago from his job as an engineer at the local public utility company. I've started to call my father "the narrator" in my head because he's constantly informing me of his upcoming actions:

"I'm going to read the paper." ("Okay, dad.")

"I'm going to get the mail." ("Okay, dad.")

Consensual Scars

"I'm going to make some lunch." ("Okay, dad.")

My mom mentioned this new phenomenon to me once, which began with his retirement. I think he needs someone, anyone, to know – to *care* – what he's doing moment to moment. He's like a man in need of a manager. I try to be understanding even if it is driving me slightly crazy. One thing is for certain: the man needs a hobby. Fishing, woodworking, gardening, stamp collecting, bowling… I really don't care what. Anything to get him out of his recliner and away from the television. But my dad has never been a "hobby" guy, unless you count watching sports from the living room. Of course, I don't have a hobby either. But hey, I'm twenty-two. My hobbies are drinking and hanging out.

My father's house is a white prefab dwelling with a small front yard and backyard. It sits nestled in a cul-de-sac on a country road, off another country road. The house has the basics: two bedrooms, one bathroom, a living room, dining room, and kitchen. It also has a slightly infamous basement. "Katie's Basement" was the home away from home for my high school group. The décor has remnants of the '70s like the wood panel walls and the mustard-colored sofa. Everything is well-worn and slightly tacky, making it the perfect place for my friends and me. My mom welcomed everyone, providing a wide range of unhealthy snacks for the constant stream of guests. My father tolerated them.

But all those people are gone now and it's just me and my dad. The house, once full of voices, now has an eeriness to it that confines me to my bedroom most of the time. This room, decorated with NKOTB and Bon Jovi posters, is a time capsule of another life and its nostalgia is like a suffocating film on my skin.

My father is good with taking on the chores that my mother once did. He takes out the trash, does the dishes, and pays the bills. But the deep cleaning my mom did isn't happening and there's a level of grime settling into the house that never existed before. Is that what a "woman's touch" really means? The absence of grime? Having lived with Jonathan, I've become accustomed to a particular level of order and cleanliness. So, I've decided to tackle the scrubbing. Which helps with the grime but not the ghost.

I've also taken over the grocery shopping, which I'm doing now in a big-box store that I despise. Maybe it's elitism but I'd rather not buy my underwear in the same place as I buy bread. I dream of living in a little village, where I can buy fresh pastries from a bakery on the walk home. This big box store, which gives me anxiety from the moment I step inside, is the polar opposite of this fantasy. My father and I don't cook so I pick up mostly frozen dinners and cans of soup. Anything that can be microwaved, basically.

This monstrosity of a store is now the center of my hometown, Lake City, Indiana. The name is misleading; it is nowhere near a "city," but a mid-size town bordering on Lake Michigan. It is a town that, with its beaches and mild summers, should be thriving but instead is shrinking as these types of stores come in, killing off everything in their path. The mall, where I spent much of my teenage years, is now mostly boarded up, though two of the three anchor stores stubbornly remain like tombstones in a concrete graveyard.

The mall, of course, had previously displaced the small shops in the "downtown" area. It's another misnomer; our "downtown" wasn't really a bustling metro area, but a single street filled with family-owned businesses leading to the public beach. While not New York, the area was, I hear, once quite quaint. But these storefronts have been boarded up ever since I can remember. Occasionally, a restaurant or shop will materialize and add a little charm to the area, but they always disappear as quickly as they arrive. Capitalism rolls on. Things get bigger and fewer, more generic, and just kind of sadder. I don't like to dwell on it, but I think it kinda sucks to be the first generation in a long time to do worse than our parents. And I'm not talking about money. I'm talking about towns. I'm talking about *life*.

Since I've been away, the town has shrunk in other ways too; the two movie theaters have consolidated, as have the two public high schools. My alma mater, located in the desolate "downtown" area, has been absorbed by the one that sits in the middle of a corn field. All the restaurants are chains. We don't yet have a Starbucks though we all have our fingers crossed. (For all my complaining, I'm not totally immune to the allures of capitalism. Especially when they come in the form of frothy caramel lattes.)

I don't want to be back here, in a town that feels like it's vanishing under my feet, but I don't know where else to go. After three years of

Consensual Scars

studying under an "undecided" major, I finally opted for the generic "liberal arts" degree, a fact my father finds woefully disappointing. He doesn't know what a "liberal arts" degree means. To be fair, I'm not sure I do either. I guess it means that I know a little about a lot. Which, come to think of it, is probably not great for launching a career. Oops.

My father had agreed to pay for my college as long as I attended a state school. If he could turn back time, I bet he'd add another condition: I study something practical like Jonathan. To his dismay, everything I'm interested in is decidedly *not* practical. (Philosophy: "How many 'wanted' ads in the paper do you see for philosopher?" Theater: "You want to be an out-of-work actor?") And so, in response, perhaps just to irritate him further, I dabbled in a bit of everything (psychology, English lit, journalism), never committing to any one thing.

Today, I remain still very much undecided.

As I carry the grocery bags from the car, our neighbor shouts a hello and waves to me. Mrs. Tucker has lived next door to us for as long as I can remember. She's a retired teacher, spending her days gardening and baking cookies. Some of the cookies go to my father, who started mowing her lawn and shoveling her driveway when her husband passed away about ten years ago. When I was younger, she would babysit for me. She was always kind but firm in the way the best teachers usually are. On the other side of our house is a property that's been sold multiple times over and I'm not quite sure who lives there now. Whoever they are, they obviously have small children as their lawn is decorated with Big Wheels and bikes.

After I put the groceries away, I go to work. Since returning home, I've taken a job as a bartender at one of the local chain restaurants. I don't have any real bartending talent but that hardly matters. Although the restaurant contains a full bar, 99% of the cocktail orders are either for beer, wine, or a proprietary concoction made with a specialty mix. I rarely get the opportunity to hone any real mixology skills.

And it's here, listening to that stupid piña colada song for the millionth time on the corporate-approved sound loop meant to drive all the workers crazy, when something extraordinary happens. Or maybe it just feels extraordinary because everything else is way too ordinary. I'm killing time by wiping down the bar in the post-lunch, pre-dinner hour. By now, I've worked enough customers service gigs to know the mantra of clean, don't lean. Which is fine by me. I'm not good at standing still even if all my motion is entirely directionless.

From the bar area, I can see a small portion of the restaurant where a solitary woman sits. But she's not solitary *sad*. She is vibrant and alive. Mid-thirties maybe? With her curly, wild red hair wrapped in a head scarf, handmade jewelry, bohemian skirt and sandals, she is an anomaly in this quiet, conservative-leaning town. She's talking with the server, laughing too loudly and gesturing too broadly. I instantly like her. I can't stop staring even as she gets up and travels to the bar. As she's walking, I half expect pixie dust to encircle her, traveling alongside her like the birds of *Snow White*.

"I'm supposed to meet a friend here but I just got a message that he's not coming. And I'm starving. Can I eat here?" Close up, I notice her freckles. Her smile is slightly crooked, and her voice has a hint of a Boston accent.

"Sure," I say. "Start with a drink?"

"Yes, please."

"Alright…" I say, waiting for more information. "What would you like?"

"Why don't you surprise me?"

If I may speak for bartenders around the world, we hate this. But her expression is so kind and encouraging, I'm not annoyed at the challenge.

"How do you take your coffee?" I ask.

"I don't want coffee. I want a cocktail!"

I have a theory about a correlation between coffee preferences and cocktail choices. It may be just nonsense but I'm not passing up an opportunity to test it.

"I'm asking about your taste preference. Do you like sweet drinks? Bitter?"

"Ah…. ahhhhh. Smart! I don't usually drink coffee. I'm a tea person. But I do like those caramel, frothy things. The hot milkshakes."

"Then we have something in common. I like those too."

While it's an opportunity to try my hand at creating something off-menu, I decide to make her one of our frozen rum concoctions. It seems less risky. I hand her the drink, and she tastes it.

"Yum! Tastes like pineapple. What do you call it?"

"A Tropical Fizz."

This sends her into a fit of giggles which causes me to join her. Her energy is infectious.

"I'm Matty, by the way. Matty O'Connell," she offers when the fit subsides.

"Matty. What is that short for?" I ask.

She glances side-to-side and leans in to whisper.

"Mathilda," she says. "But *please* call me Matty."

"Hi Matty. I'm Katie," I say, mimicking her formal introduction. "O'Connell. That's Irish, right?"

"Yes, but it's my married name. Oh, you'd love my husband."

Pronouncements like this normally annoy me. How do you know what I'd like? You don't know me! But instead, I'm charmed. We shake hands and I notice her wedding ring, a simple design of intertwining bands of white, yellow and rose gold.

"So, tell me about yourself, Katie," Matty says.

"I think the customer is supposed to confide in the bartender. Where are you from?" She can't be from here.

"Boston."

"What's that like?"

"Oh, I love it. Not as much as I love California though."

"You lived in California?"

"Yup. Before coming here."

"And what's here?"

"Well, my yoga studio for one."

Yoga. Of course, she's a yoga teacher.

After perusing the various fried appetizers, Matty settles on mozzarella sticks. I'm surprised. As a yoga teacher, shouldn't she be eating nuts and berries? But I like the contrast. A California spirit with a Midwestern stomach.

"I didn't know we had a yoga studio here," I say. I guess there are still some things you can't get at Walmart.

"The only one in town."

"You have a monopoly."

"Yes! A monopoly. I never thought of it like that. We have a monopoly!"

"Is your husband a yoga teacher too?" I ask.

"No, but he helps me run it."

She asks me again what my story is, so I tell her the grand sum of me: I'm in limbo, a college graduate, and living at home.

"Oh, that's exciting!" she exclaims. Her enthusiasm for my sad situation is so bizarre and at odds with my own perspective that I burst out laughing.

"Oh my god! It's so not! It's sad."

"You're young! The world is yours!"

I smile and shake my head in defeat. I'm not going to argue with her. Her joy is a powerful adversary that I have no will to fight.

While paying her bill, Matty exclaims, "You should come to a yoga class!" Before I can respond with all the reasons why I should *not* come to a yoga class, she takes a business card from her purse. She scribbles directions on the back and passes it to me. "We have one tonight. Come. And you can meet my husband! You'll *love* my husband."

"Yes, you've mentioned that." Either her husband really is fabulous, or I'm being drafted for a three-way.

"I have?" she asks, innocently. "Well, you will! Come tonight. Six-thirty. See you then!"

She leaves and the air seems different when she's gone.

Consensual Scars

Shane

I've never taken a yoga class before and I'm not an athlete. (My father really wanted an athlete.) But I want to see Matty again. And if I must humiliate myself in the process, so be it. After all, my social life is practically nil. Going to a yoga class – going anywhere different really – is wildly appealing. I find a tank top and a pair of biker shorts that aren't entirely unattractive on me. In fact, I look, probably, "cute."

Damn.

I follow the directions on the back of the business card, bouncing along the pot-hole ridden country roads in my ten-year-old blue Chevy Cavalier. I inherited the car from my parents in high school after I got my license and they upgraded to a new car. My mom was thrilled to hand over the keys, so excited that she no longer had to chauffeur me back and forth from theater rehearsals. I don't know how long this car is going to last, but if I had to guess I'd say, "after this next trip."

I'm not in entirely unfamiliar territory. Jonathan's family lives near here. But the specific street where the studio is located is new to me. I make the turn into a small subdivision and climb a hill, houses dropping off from the sides of the road. I reach the apex, where a lone farmhouse sits, at least a quarter mile from its nearest neighbors.

The house is surrounded on three sides by woods. On the remaining side, I pull up into a makeshift lot of dirt and gravel. I only see one other car and I know I'm early without looking at a clock. I tend to arrive everywhere early. My one recurring nightmare is trying, and failing, to make it to the airport on time. Which doesn't sound that bad but is completely harrowing and leaves me feeling anxious all morning. If I have good dreams, I don't remember them.

I park near the attached garage. A handmade sign ("Peace, Love and Yoga") points the way to a path of stone pavers leading to the back of the house. The sign is decorated with hand-drawn images of hearts and peace signs. Before I walk the directed route, curiosity gets the best of me. I stroll towards the front of the house which was hidden from view by trees on the drive up. There's no path from the driveway to the front of the house and in this way, the house is inverted. Guests are funneled to the back door while the front door leads to a private paradise.

This private paradise consists of an underground pool, hot tub, and pool house. Flowers and shrubbery are everywhere. Beautiful yet unpretentious, the house is a hidden wonderland in this otherwise unremarkable town. I wonder if they would notice a tent somewhere on the property.

I step away from the view of the front and start following the sign towards the back door. But before I reach it, I notice a pen about thirty feet behind the house in the massive, grassy backyard. The pen contains two sheep and one goat. Lake City is suburbia, but it's surrounded by rural farmland. So, maybe I shouldn't be too surprised to see these animals. But I am. I have never seen livestock in a non-farm, non-petting-zoo environment before.

I'm nervous and procrastinating. I'm not the best at meeting new people, doing new things, and I've been out of practice for a while. And yoga? I'm bound to fall at least once. But I can't stare at the sheep forever. I walk to the back door and knock, which prompts barking from, what sounds like, a very big dog. I'm fully expecting to be greeted by Matty, but instead the door opens, and a man is standing there, grinning ear-to-ear. I can see his dog between his legs and he's doing that dance that pet owners do when their animal is trying to get out.

He appears a little older than Matty, perhaps in his early forties. None of his features alone are striking but together they create a captivating composite. His black locks fall in unruly waves just below his ears, yet his facial hair is perfectly trimmed. His attire sits loosely on a solid, muscular frame. He's barefoot, wearing jeans that hang low on his waist and a beige linen top that's only partially buttoned, his dark chest hair peeking out. His fair skin is bronzed from the sun, and he has permanent smile lines around his green eyes.

More remarkable than the vision of him is his demeanor. He's relaxed, with no pretense or fear, exuding a comfort in his skin that is wholly foreign to me. His grin is a dare, challenging me to be entirely present in this moment. And it works. The contours of my reality slip away until there is only him. When he speaks, his voice is full of amusement as if this simple moment is warranting of great delight, an assessment that is disconcerting and mesmerizing in equal measure.

"You must be Katie! I'm Shane, Matty's husband. Welcome!"

His voice is magnificent. Deep and boisterous, with just a whiff of an Irish brogue.

"Hi," I manage, before thinking that Matty must be a sorceress.

"Come in, come in. This is Sebastian," he says, waving me inside and gesturing toward the majestic beast.

I enter a mudroom, with shoes and coats lined up along one side and a shiny, wooden floating shelf that extends the length of the opposite wall. It has a live edge and carries evidence of a grown-up life. Framed photos and little wooden bowls for keys and change are arranged on the shelf. The walls are a warm lavender. I expect to see other students gathered for class but it's just the two of us and Sebastian. I reflexively shift my focus to the animal, petting him with zeal. He's all white with a fluffy coat and I don't recognize the breed. While we never had a dog growing up due to my mom's allergies, I've always wanted one desperately.

"What kind of dog is he?"

"Great Pyrenees."

"He's beautiful."

Then I address the dog. "Hi, Sebastian! How are you? Are you a good dog? You're a good dog, aren't you?" He responds with a slobbery lick across my cheek. I'm so much better with dogs than people.

I turn my attention back to Shane. "Am I early?" I ask.

"Matty has been thinking it's Thursday all day today," he says, as a way of explanation.

I don't know what this means. Seeing my confusion, he clarifies. "She only thought she had class today."

"Oh," I say.

I don't know what to do with myself. Obviously, I should leave, but I just came in and that seems rude.

"Should I go?"

He ignores my question and asks his own.

"Want to hang out? Smoke some pot?"

I laugh because it's so unexpected and perfect. I absolutely want to hang out and smoke some pot. I nod.

"Cool. Follow me."

We walk through the first floor of the house, passing through a hallway with doorways on either side, presumably to bedrooms. The golden, hardwood floor is so polished and slippery, I have to fight the urge to run and slide across it *Risky Business* style. (I was raised on carpets, stained and flattened long past their prime.) We pass by the front door foyer, accented by a stone wall that leads into the living room, the centerpiece of an open-floor plan. Once around the corner, the stone wall reveals a fireplace nestled within it. The dining room and kitchen are in view, both bright with color and light. It's the light that takes my breath away. It's coming in from every direction, most spectacularly from the high sloped ceiling with its many sky lights. None of the windows that enclose the space have curtains, which makes the space feel like a solarium, the surrounding property visible from all angles.

The house is a contradiction, large and airy but with the rustic charm of a tiny cabin in the woods. The décor feels whimsical, a playground of colors and shapes, and the furnishings all look lovingly hand-crafted. None of it, I'm quite sure, came from the big box stores in town. The dining table easily sits ten and the kitchen has an island surrounded by barstools, with cookware hanging from wooden hooks above.

It's a home of artists, that much is obvious. The walls are decorated with abstract paintings and exotic sculptures are displayed on more floating shelves. An upright piano and a djembe drum take up one corner of the living room. Two faux leather white couches face each other instead of a TV, which is noticeably absent. Everything is

Consensual Scars

so strange and stunning that I actually gasp aloud when I turn and notice the loft. In the wide opening between the foyer and the living room stands a bamboo ladder, leading up to a small room with a daybed. The room has a backdoor and I wonder what lies beyond it.

We walk through the living room to the kitchen where he offers me a glass of water.

"Where is the yoga studio?" I ask, taking the offering.

"It's upstairs. I can show you if you want," he answers.

It must be behind the door in the loft. I do want to see it, but I also don't want to be a bother.

"No, no, that's okay. This is fine. Your house is amazing. Do you play?" I ask, pointing to the piano.

"A little. Do you?"

"I took lessons as a kid, but I'm no good. I can read music, but I can't play by ear. It's like with a foreign language. I took years of French, and I can read it and write it. But I can't speak it or understand it. Which is… kind of the point of language." I trail off as I realize I'm babbling. He doesn't seem to mind though. Instead, he's looking at me, studying me. His eyes are curious, not judgmental, so I don't feel uncomfortable under the warm spotlight of his gaze.

"You want to see something really cool?" he asks.

"Absolutely."

"Come on," he says, leading us out a door that takes us from the kitchen to the backyard. We turn a corner and we're on the other side of the house, opposite the driveway. Woods extend as far as I can see. Autumn is upon us, and the leaves are starting to turn their golden, mellow hues. I grew up with woods like these not far from my house. Memories of building forts and playing Capture the Flag come flooding back to me. We walk for a few minutes down a trail until we arrive at a clearing where there is a tipi.

I'm speechless. I've only seen them in books. Maybe cartoons too? The structure is at least twenty feet high and thirty feet in diameter. He opens the flap that serves as a door, and we go inside. There are blankets stacked in a corner and he lays them out on the wood flooring for us to sit. He pulls out a pipe, a baggie, and a lighter from his pocket. He fills the pipe, and hands it and the lighter to me so I can take the first hit. (Good pot etiquette is so important and he clearly has it,) I haven't smoked pot since leaving college. Not because I've lost the desire but because I don't have a local dealer. In fact, I've never had a dealer. Pot was always just around. Presumably, someone had a dealer. But I never had to manage the logistics of procurement.

I take the pipe and lighter, and we do exactly as he suggested. We hang out and smoke pot. Our conversation alternates between sounding completely profound and totally ridiculous, as stoned conversations often do. In the silences, I reflect on how much I miss the relaxed comradery that comes with this simple ritual of commonplace deviance.

"This is incredible," I say.

"The pot?"

"No... well, yes. The pot is good. But this..." I say, gesturing around me.

"Oh! Yes! My friend Kai helped me build it," he shares. "Traditionally, they're made of buffalo leather, but modern ones have a cotton tarp like this."

No leather. "Are you a vegetarian?"

"Vegan."

I reactively make a derisive noise. He raises his eyebrows. I'm relieved to see he's more amused than offended but I still feel the need to explain.

"I knew a few vegans in college who talked of nothing else."

"Ah. Judgmental."

"Yes."

"I try not to be."

"Does that work? The trying?"

"Not always," he admits.

A short silence is all I need for my brain to try to process what's happening. Because something is definitely happening. I don't have words for it but the molecules in my body are changing. Then again, maybe it's just the pot.

"Where did you come from?" I ask. Because, in some ways, he seems like a mirage.

"My mother's womb?"

"I meant..." and then just a trail of giggles. Now this is a reaction to the pot.

"I mean, are you from here? Are you a Hoosier?"

"What is a Hoosier?" he asks.

"Someone from Indiana."

"Yes, but what *is* it?"

"No one knows."

"Anyway, I *am* a Hoosier. I grew up here," he says.

"Really?"

"But I lived in California for a while."

So, he and Matty came here from California together. It's another piece of a puzzle I'm now devoted to solving. I've never been to the Golden State, but I want to go. From what I know of it, it's where all the liberal freaks are, and they could very well be my tribe.

"Los Angeles?" I ask.

"Yeah."

"What was that like?"

"It's a world in soft focus. Beautiful and… unknowable."

Whoa.

"But you came back?" I ask. "Why?" I can't imagine anyone coming here from somewhere as magical as Los Angeles. Visions of red carpets and palm trees flash through my mind.

"My father got sick. My mother asked us to come back and help."

"When was that?"

"About seven years ago?"

"1988?"

"Right," he nods. "Matty said you were smart." I'm not sure performing simple subtraction qualifies me as smart but I'll take it. The idea that these two people were having a conversation about me gives me butterflies in my stomach.

"Do you miss it?" I ask him.

"California?"

"Yeah."

"California is in my past. I try to live in the present."

"Does that work? The trying?" Did I just ask that? Am I repeating myself?

"Usually."

I wonder if I could live entirely in the present. And then I realize

I am. His presence is making the present quite extraordinary.

"What do you like most about yourself?" he asks.

The question takes me by surprise, which I'm sure was the intent. But I like the question because it's not something I think about often. Maybe I should. Maybe we all should.

"Well, I like math," I say, referring to my earlier calculation. I hope it's an answer that's just weird enough to be interesting. Because not many people like math, a fact that is almost instantly confirmed by Shane.

"I hate math."

"Everyone hates it," I tell him.

"Not you. Why do you like it?"

"I like that there's multiple ways to address a problem. You can use different methods to get the same answer."

"So, it's like destiny."

Whoa.

"And we also have pie on my birthday."

He stares at me, and I replay what I just said. I sound crazy.

"I mean, my birthday is March 14th. So, we always have pie… in addition to cake."

He still has no idea what I'm talking about. I start to sweat in a panic.

"Three point one four. March 14th. *Pi*."

And then the dots connect.

"Oh! *Pi*."

Relief floods me. I haven't lost him. So, I babble on.

"There's also something calming about absolutism. Math isn't subjective. Two plus two is four. It just is. It's not qualitative. Like art."

"Art is qualitative?"

"Sure. Isn't it?" Isn't that what the Oscars are for?

"You like things in black and white." He says it like a statement, and I immediately protest before he can judge me.

"No, no. I just think everything else is gray. I like that there's *one* thing that's, like, solid. You know what I mean? I love art though. I just suck at it."

"Impossible. Everyone is an artist."

"Well, if math is like destiny, maybe it's an art too. It can be elegant."

He nods his approval even if he can't see it. "I'm sure it is. But I'll take your word for it." He's still assessing me, and I'm as high from the pot as much as I am from his attention.

Before I can ask him what he likes best about himself, he moves the conversation elsewhere.

"Matty said you just finished college?"

"I just graduated with a 'liberal arts' degree," I say, making the little air quotes with my fingers.

"Why the…" He mimics me, making the same air quotes. I like his teasing.

"I don't know."

I do know, of course. It's been well drilled into me that I should apologize for my choice of studies. But no need to drop that bomb in here.

"A liberal arts degree sounds amazing," he says.

"Do you know what it means?"

"Do *you* know what it means? I think that's what matters."

"Not at all."

The lines around his eyes further crinkle as he barks a laugh so pure that it's my new favorite sound.

"I think it means that I'm not great at anything. Like, I'm good at a lot of things, but not great at anything," I tell him.

"Who gets to judge who's great?"

I'm stumped. All I can think of is the award shows in Hollywood.

"I guess… the other people who are great?"

"That's a lot of power."

He's testing me. I'm auditioning, though for what, I still have no idea.

"What would you like to be great at?" he continues.

"Oh, I'd love to be able to sing. Like, really sing. On stage. I love musicals, but I'll never get past the chorus. And even that's risky."

"'If you hear a voice within you say, "you cannot paint," then by all means paint, and that voice will be silenced.'"

I tilt my head, questioning the quote.

"Vincent Van Gogh."

"Yeah, well, ol' Vince never heard my ass try to sing."

He barks another laugh.

"What are *you* great at? Besides building tipis in the middle of the woods?" I ask.

"Oh, I'm great at everything!"

His grin tells me he's probably kidding. Nevertheless, I'd kill for the confidence to even make the joke. I realize he's also evading the question, so I try to be more specific.

"What do you do?" As soon as I ask, I wish I hadn't. I've grounded our theoretical conversation into the mundane.

"Do?" he asks. His left eyebrow raises, and I know he recognizes the shift too. "Oh, you mean for a *job*. A *career*." He does the little air quotes.

"Yes, those silly things."

He fills up the pipe again and takes a long hit before answering. "I'm a crop purveyor."

I don't know what this means. "Is that a fancy way of saying farmer? Is that why you have the sheep?"

Again, I regret the words. A sheep farmer would surely have more than two sheep. I suddenly want the ground to open and swallow me whole, but it stubbornly does not.

He chuckles but the laughter isn't derisive. "No, the sheep are pets. Loretta and Lucy. And the goat is Isabella." He pauses once again, before adding, "I grow weed."

Well, goddamn. I've hit the jackpot.

Having never met an actual drug dealer, I have so many questions. The one that comes out is simply, "Can I see?"

He gives me one last look-over. I must pass the test because he gets up and offers his hand to help pull me up from the floor. He leads me from the tipi, down a path that winds its way to an area behind the pool house where trees encircle, and quite effectively hide, a greenhouse. About the size of a one-car garage, it contains nothing but pot plants. I can't believe that he's trusting me enough to show me this and it's like he can read my mind.

"I don't normally show this off. For obvious reasons," he says. "So now..." He hesitates for dramatic effect, and I hang on his next words.

"… you're in the inner circle."

There's no place I'd rather be.

I explore the greenhouse and he introduces me to several of the plants. They all have names which I find adorable. ("This is Hank. Over here is Edna.") I'm fascinated to learn about the different strains and their various benefits. I discover that I know very little about pot before it goes into the pipe.

"There's two types of marijuana plant. Sativa and indica. Sativa is good for creative energy. I think of it as daytime pot. Indica is what you want if you're gonna zone out watching movies. Or need help sleeping."

"Nighttime pot."

"Exactly."

"So, most of the time I smoke pot, I get really chill. But a few times, I've gotten totally paranoid. Is that because it was sativa?"

"Definitely a factor. I mean, I'm not saying that you weren't part of the equation too. Maybe you were just in a panic-y place. But generally speaking, different strains give you different experiences."

"I never knew any of this."

"Well, you probably just buy what you can get, right? It's not like you're in a store with a display case and a helpful associate explaining the differences. Maybe one day."

"That would be so awesome."

"Yes, it would. But then you'd have to pay taxes on it."

"I'd love to pay taxes on it! Let me fund schools by smoking weed. Please. Just don't use it to fund the war machine."

He chuckles and I'm glad that he's not the type of hippie to go on an anti-government tirade. I've met a few of these types at college and they're never fun. They're exhausting.

As I move around the nursery in stoned awe, I feel a rush of adrenaline from the illicit beauty of my surroundings. I want to ask if he's ever afraid of such a risky occupation. But I don't want to be *that* person.

"What did you study in college?" I ask, realizing that I never asked him. "That is, if you went to college."

"I went for a year, but I bailed. I decided I'd rather be a student of life."

Considering I went for four years and can't quote Vincent Van Gogh, I don't think it's a bad decision.

"Where'd you go?"

"West Point."

"Oh, *shit*. That's real military shit." He was, like, *part* of the war machine.

"Yes."

I can't picture this at all and tell him so.

"I was a good little soldier. Until I discovered this," gesturing to the plants that surround us.

I have many more questions, but I don't want to annoy him.

"I should probably go," I say, not really meaning it at all. But the longer I stay, the more likely it is that I'm going to do or say something stupid. As it is, I'm going to replay endlessly in my head the comment about sheep farming.

As we walk back to the house, he asks if I'd like to come back Saturday night for a drum circle in celebration of the autumnal equinox. I've never been to a drum circle, but it sounds way more festive than my weekly trip to Blockbuster.

"I'd love to."

At that, he stops abruptly, causing me to crash into him. His body absorbs the hit, never losing balance.

"Oh! Sorry," I say.

He turns to me and grins. "Good."

It takes me a moment to realize he's responding to my answer to his invite rather my apology. He walks me to the door and hugs me goodbye. And maybe it's the pot again (and if it is, it's the best pot to ever come into existence), but I swear, I can feel his energy passing from him into me. This hug has a trajectory, a journey, and it leaves me feeling lightheaded.

When I get to my car, I don't start the engine right away. Instead, I close my eyes and take a deep breath. My body chemistry feels irreversibly altered. When I do start the car, I search the radio for an acceptable song. Jonathan has a theory that a good song at the start of a car ride ensures a safe journey and I've adopted this superstition throughout the years. (I've yet to get into a car accident so I have no evidence that it *doesn't* work.) I flip through the stations and find nothing but ads so I give up and switch to the cassette player. The song that comes on is *Ironic* by Alanis Morrissette, which is, frankly, fucking perfect.

Annie Marie Huber

Anchor

Saturday comes and, once again, I'm debating what to wear. I almost never think about clothes, throwing on whatever is around. I clearly didn't get the girlie gene so whenever I *do* think about clothes, I'm left feeling a bit helpless. I give up and dress in my regular uniform of slightly baggy jeans, an old concert t-shirt (*Slippery When Wet*, which feels downright retro by now) and my favorite flannel.

I wonder if I'm supposed to bring my own drum. What is the etiquette for a drum circle? I don't have a drum. Nor do I know how to play one. Hopefully, I can just listen.

When I arrive, Matty answers the door. She's all apologies for the mix-up earlier in the week but is thrilled that I've come back for tonight's event.

"No worries," I assure her.

She leads me to the living room where there's a small group of people, lounging on the couches and floor. They're all about the same age as Matty and Shane. They all have the same bohemian vibe. And they all have drums.

Matty does a quick introduction, but I know I won't remember any of their names. I need an actual one-on-one moment with someone before I remember their name and even then, I usually have to create a mnemonic device. I'm not great at remembering faces either. I'm too much in my own head to notice much around me, which I'm sure is some kind of fatal character flaw that's one day going to doom my fate.

However, there is one face I do remember. I scan the room looking for Shane, but I don't see him.

Conversations resume among the guests and Matty returns to host mode. Again, I'm struck by her unfettered joy. I watch as she moves among the guests with such ease and grace, I swear the woman has an aura. And I don't even believe in auras. At least, I didn't. Now, who knows?

"Katie! You're here! Have you met everyone?"

My head swivels toward the kitchen at the sound of Shane's voice, like a dog that hears the mailman.

"Hi. Yeah, Matty just did that. I'm sorry. I didn't bring a drum."

"No problem. We have extras. Or you can just listen."

He takes the small drum that's around his neck and places it around mine.

"There ya go," he says, satisfied. Then he addresses the group. "Shall we?"

Everyone gets up and makes their way to the door. We walk down the path to the tipi, enter it, and sit in a circle. There's quiet chatter among the group but I don't speak to anyone. Shane has found another, bigger drum. He starts playing and within seconds, the world changes. The sound is sudden and rousing, surrounding us and seeping into my soul. I find myself playing along with my little drum. Not with any skill, of course, not like the people around me. But a spell is being woven and I can't resist. And then Shane is singing but in no language I can understand. His voice is gravelly and deep, the type of baritone that has always given me goosebumps. The lyrics are clearly some sort of ancient chant. The group performs a call and response, repeating the foreign phrases.

I can only make out the words "Hare Krishna" and I wonder if I've inadvertently joined a cult. Isn't that what those folks in the airports are called? But before I can contemplate the idea much, the man on the right of me stops playing his drum to pass me a little wooden bowl. He has long, graying hair pulled into a ponytail and kind eyes.

I take the bowl from him and look at what's inside. Mushrooms. I'm pretty sure they're not just for snacking. I've never done psychedelics though I have a few friends that love them. Again, it's more about access than anything else. Pot was prevalent in my circle in college, psychedelics less so. Finding them felt akin to finding buried treasure. And *purchasing* LSD, I had come to find out one very disappointing evening, is not a sure way of actually *obtaining* LSD. That night, the white, useless tabs sat on our tongues to no effect at all.

Well, I figure, when in Rome. I take a mushroom, pop it in my mouth, and pass the bowl to the person on my left. It tastes like dirt, and I fight the urge to spit it right back out. Finally, after chewing for a solid minute, I swallow it. And wait.

Before I can feel any effects, I'm awash in anxiety. What have I done? I know alcohol lowers inhibitions but what about hallucinogens? I've done cocaine once before and all I can remember is talking nonstop, before wanting more and more cocaine. Presumably so I could keep talking. What if mushrooms have the same effect? What if I say or do something that I'll regret? I don't really have an anchor here if things go badly. I feel my heart racing and my body perspiring. I need air so I get up and leave the tent.

I walk the path to the backyard and stand near the pen where the animals are grazing peacefully. I don't know how long I've been standing there when Shane appears at my side. The shapes of things around me are starting to fluctuate. And whatever apprehension I felt before has slipped away into oblivion.

"Hey."
"Hey."
"Hey."
"Hey."
"Hey."
"Hey."

Each time we repeat the word my grin gets bigger. He laughs.
"You took some mushrooms," he says, stating the obvious.
"Yessssss..."
Words are fun.
"Have you ever taken mushrooms?"
"Nooooo..."
"LSD?"
"Nooooo..."
"Okay. So, I'm gonna hang with you. Make sure you don't die."
"Cooooooool."
I give him a thumbs-up.

"And you didn't? Take any mushrooms?" I ask.
"Nah."
"Why not?"
"Oh, I'm pretty sure I'm still trippin' from one particular night in '81."
"I was…" I count out the numbers on my fingers. "… eight years old."
"Are you saying I'm old?" he asks, teasingly.
"No! You're… experienced."
The look he gives me makes me blush. And then the world becomes dazzling.

Objects are amazing.
Sheep are amazing.
People are amazing.
Shane is amazing.
"I can't believe you have sheep."
Laughing forever.

Back to the tipi.
Music.
Happy place.
So, so good.
"You need water…"

Kitchen.
Water.
"Thank you."
People.
Wanting food.
Food everywhere.
"Ugh. No, no, no. I can't look at that."
"It's okay."
"No, no, no…"
Panic. Nausea.
Hands over my eyes.
Lips to my ears.

"Don't look."
Okay.
"Turn around."
Turning.
Falling.
"Fuck!"
Hands help me up.
"This way."
Walking.
"Sit."
Sitting.

Living room.
Man in the ponytail.
Holding court.
A prophet.
Surrounded by followers.
"… when you think about it, timing is *everything*."
Yes, yes, yes.
"I mean, what is luck? Good luck is just good timing. Bad luck is bad timing."
Whoa.
Shane now.
Talking.
To me.
What a beautiful mouth.
"Okay?"
"Okay."
Back to the man.
The man with the plan.
"… like the butterfly effect."
I know this.
One little thing changes everything.
Nothing is irrelevant.
Helluva burden on a little butterfly.
Shane?
No Shane.

Consensual Scars

Must find Shane.

The den.
Strange faces.
All the faces.
No Shane.
"Sorry."

Outside.
Tipi.
Drums.
So, so good.
But no Shane.
Must find Shane.

Outside.
Sitting.
Somewhere beautiful.
Clouds colliding.
Leaves swaying.
Better than any movie.
"There you are."
Shane.
Yay.
"Where'd you go?"
"I told you I'd be right back."
"No...."
"Yes."
"Oh. Sorry."
"You alright?"
"Everything is so real. But not *too* real, ya know?"
"No. Explain."
Sits by me.
"Not sure I can."
"Try."
"It's just a lot. Everything. Not just the sad stuff. All of it. Too much. Sometimes."

His hand,
Brushing the hair from my face.
"Yeah."
He's tired.
Or maybe sad.
Did I make him sad?
Don't be sad.
"So… why *sheep*?"
Smiling. Good.
"Ask Matty. She tells it better."
Matty.
Who floats like a butterfly.
Maybe *the* butterfly.
Changing everything.

Back to the kitchen.
No more food.
Matty cleaning.
People leaving.
Sitting.
Watching.

"How ya doin'?"
My fractured reality is coming back into alignment.
"I need to crash," Shane says. "Come on. I'll tuck you in. You can sleep in the loft."
"Tuck me in?" I ask, teasingly. "Ya wanna carry me too?"
"No."
"Aw. Come on."
"No."
"You're no fun."
"Babe, I'm *all* fun."
True.

He leads me to the stairs, not trusting me to climb the ladder. He hugs me goodnight. It's enough to fuck me up all over again.

I sleep but I don't, existing somewhere in between. When sunlight starts streaming in through the windows, I notice that the sounds of music and people have been replaced with morning kitchen sounds: the faucet running, the tea kettle whistling, and dishes being either set out or put away. The sounds are delightful, and I somehow find a rhythm in them. I close my eyes to enjoy the symphony. When I open them again, Matty is standing above me holding a glass of water.

"Hi. I thought you might be thirsty."

"Thanks," I say and take the glass.

"Was that your first time?"

"Yes."

"What'd you think?"

While the pieces of my world are now back in place, the full picture feels forever altered. Though how exactly, I can't possibly put into words. So, I simply say, "Amazing."

She smiles, satisfied with my woefully deficient answer. "I'm cooking breakfast when you're ready." She leans over me and, like a mother, kisses me on the forehead before leaving.

Annie Marie Huber

Pad Thai & Anger

While my salary at the restaurant is meager (and I should be saving for, well, a life), I start paying to attend Matty's yoga class regularly. The yoga is getting easier, and I always feel a little lighter after class. I'm still not in love with it but that's probably more about my own self-consciousness than anything else. I am, however, in love with Shane and Matty. They routinely ask me to stay after class and hang out, and I almost always accept. Throughout the month of October, they swiftly become the center of my world.

I have no illusions that I'm nearly as central to them, but they nevertheless are always inviting and enthusiastic about my presence. So much so that I start doing the "pop-in" even when there's no class. At first, I would come up with an excuse for my visit ("Here's the book I told you about…") but I've stopped. I keep waiting for them to get sick of me, to ask why I keep coming around, or for them to be too busy and kick me out. But they're always obliging. Perhaps it's because I'm not the first person to adopt them in this way.

Whenever I'm there, an endless stream of friends come to visit. No one knocks and the house sometimes resembles a commune, in spirit if not in appearance. (I imagine communes to be messier affairs than this always immaculate home but maybe I'm wrong. I've never been to a commune.) The friends that filter in and out are all artists, whether by trade or hobby. Painters, sculptors, musicians, and poets make up their inner circle. I'm intimidated by some of them and envious of all of them.

The kitchen is especially lively. It's the heartbeat of the home, where plans are made, ideas presented, and much of life is lived.

Consensual Scars

Being there is like dropping into a movie: Shane cooking, Matty holding court, wine flowing, friends coming and going, and bluesy rock 'n roll coming through the stereo. Whenever I'm there, I think about the cleaning-up-after-dinner scene in *The Big Chill*, and I can't believe my luck at having found this.

In this magical kitchen, conversation flows effortlessly. Shane and Matty are fearless talkers, with no topic taboo except politics. My original fear that they would be anti-government hippies has fallen away. Their aversion, however, isn't some genuflection to the altar of apathy. (A feeling I'm quite familiar with.) No, the topic simply bores them, especially Shane. He dismisses anything he deems not worthy of his – and by extension, anyone else's – energy. I find his reticence to engage on issues maddening and wonderful. Maddening because of the way he visibly loses interest when I talk of such things. (I watch his eyes wander away in the middle of whatever point I'm making and want to die of shame.) Wonderful because nothing bad out in the world can pierce this beautiful bubble. Which, I suppose, is a nice, privileged way to live if you've got the means.

I'm not terribly political but I try to stay moderately informed on at least the national issues. For the record, I think Clinton is fine even despite the recent revelations. Really, I don't give a shit about the sexual proclivities of our leaders. In fact, I'm happier knowing that the guy is getting some. I don't want the man in charge of the nuclear codes to be sexually frustrated. I mean, I had to watch *The Day After* in school and will forever be traumatized. I'll take a blow job over the end of the world. And really, how much of this shitstorm is about denigrating Monica's appearance rather than any moral high ground? I bet if he were fucking a modern-day Marilyn Monroe, nobody would give a shit. But alas, these thoughts I keep to myself.

Shane and Matty both cook but Shane loves it more, moving around the kitchen with confidence, loving it all. Cooking energizes him, as if food gives him strength even before entering his body. One blissful, post-class evening, when it's just the three of us, I watch as they gather ingredients to assemble dinner. We pass a pipe around as Matty makes a salad and Shane tosses spices and vegetables together in a wok. Their work is coordinated from years of experience. With no need to talk about what they're doing, they're free to engage on other pressing marital matters.

"Babe, did you pick up dog food?" Matty asks.

"Oh, shit. No, I forgot." Shane answers.

"That's it. It's over. Leaving you now," she deadpans.

He pulls her into his arms. "Oh, I don't think so," he says, before dipping her into a cinematic kiss.

My parents weren't openly hostile to each other; they just didn't *play* together.

"Ah, I know. You're leaving me for Greg," Shane says solemnly to Matty.

I wonder who Greg is but don't ask.

"Definitely. Have you seen him lately? Wow!"

"He looks great. Have fun. Let me know how it goes."

I'm pretty sure they're joking. My earlier fear (hope?) of a three-way invite has not come to pass. Of course, it's possible they *do* have an open relationship and I'm just not a desirable option. Shit.

"What are you making?" I ask, reminding them of my presence.

"Pad thai," Shane says.

"Impressive."

He shrugs. He doesn't think it's impressive. But since I make mostly ramen, anything not microwaved is impressive to me. Watching him cook is like watching the food shows on the Travel Channel; I'm always learning new skills and facts about exotic food that I try to file away so that I too can one day make pad thai.

"Can you hand me the rice noodles? In the cabinet behind you?"

I get off my barstool and open the cabinet. The interior is disorientating, stuffed as it is with mason jars filled with unfamiliar substances and not a Doritos bag in sight. After staring in a stoned haze for who knows how long, Matty takes pity on me and grabs the noodles, tucked in a corner in a tall glass canister.

"Sorry," I say. "I don't cook. Like, at all."

"Does your mom cook?" she asks.

I hate this type of question, not because it's rude or anything, but because it's in the present tense and I now have to clarify.

"My mom passed away last year," I say.

Her face starts to fall but before she can say the obligatory "I'm so sorry," I ramble on: "She cooked, but she hated it. Lots of Hamburger Helper and fried chicken from the deli. Nothing fancy. Certainly, no pad thai."

I hope she takes my cue, and we can continue talking about cooking. Or anything really. But the topic of my dear departed mom interests her more.

"How did she die?" Matty asks.

"Cerebral hemorrhage. It was quick."

"I'm so sorry," she adds.

There it is. Now my obligatory response: "It's alright."

As Matty peppers me with questions, Shane periodically locks eyes with mine. The empathy that radiates from his face is a salve for deep wounds that haven't yet scabbed over. Maybe they never will.

"You live with your dad?" Matty asks.

I nod.

"What's he like?" she asks.

"Angry," I say, more bluntly than I intend.

This gets a bark of laughter out of Shane.

"What's he angry about? About your mom?" Matty asks.

Her infinite curiosity, presented as an endless stream of questions, is so childlike, both adorable and annoying.

"Everything. Anything. He's always been a victim in his own mind."

They assure me they know the type and, of course, they do. It's a prevalent sentiment here. Of course, my father (straight, white guy on early retirement with a full pension) is clearly not as downtrodden as he believes. Nevertheless, he is perpetually disappointed. He rarely smiles and when he does, it's laced with irony.

"Are you two close?" Matty asks.

I reach for the wine and refill my glass. If this conversation is going to continue, I'm going to need more libation.

"Not really." Before she can ask anything else, I try to put the focus back on them. "How did you two learn to cook?"

"My mom," Shane answers. "The Italian side of the family. Lots of homemade pasta."

"I learned from him," Matty says, pointing at Shane.

I smile in response, hiding my jealousy. For a distraction, I grab three avocados from the wooden bowl on the kitchen island and begin juggling them. (This and flipping open a Zippo lighter are my only two parlor tricks.) Matty is delighted but Shane eyes me wearily.

"Don't drop my avocados," he warns.

"I'm not going to drop your avocados," I assure him, then immediately drop one of his avocados.

"You did that! You psyched me out!" I yell at Shane.

He shakes his head, entertained with my childish accusation.

"Where did you learn that?" Matty asks.

"Eighth grade gym class," I answer. "I don't know why but we did a few weeks on juggling. The trick is you have to start with scarves. Small, lightweight scarves that float down slowly after you throw them. That way you can see the pattern in slow motion."

"I have scarves!" She's not lying. I don't know anyone that has more scarves.

"Go get three," I direct her, and she whisks away to find them.

When Matty comes back with three scarves, similar in size and weight, I lead her to the living room. We start with one scarf then quickly move on to two. Within about ten minutes, she has her first successful throw with all three scarves, and she's elated.

"I never thought I'd be able to juggle! This is so cool!"

I leave her practicing, so I can sneak outside and engage in my occasional bad habit. Exiting through the mudroom, I step out to the backyard and light a cigarette. It's a sometimes-habit I picked up in college that I have yet to shake. Shane and Matty know my guilty pleasure. Matty, an ex-smoker, will sometimes join me, prompting disapproval from Shane. Shane's disapproval, however, is so lackluster that it feels more like tolerance. A roll of his eyes and shake of his head is all he can really muster. As if our bad behavior amuses more than disappoints.

So, I'm surprised when Shane, and not Matty, joins me in the backyard.

"Hey," he says.

"Hey," I say as I inhale and blow smoke away from him. "Is Matty still practicing?"

"Oh, yeah. We may have lost her for the evening."

"Sorry about that."

"No need to be sorry. I just wanted to see if you're okay."

"I'm fine," I answer quickly.

"Right. Well, if you ever do want to talk about it, you can. With me."

It's a tempting offer, if only to spend time with him.

"Thanks," I say.

He pulls a pipe from his pocket and offers it to me. I look at my cigarette and I know I can't smoke both at once.

"Trade you," he says.

I take the pipe and he takes my cigarette. But instead of holding it for me as I expect him to, he puts it out on the ground.

"Asshole," I say to his devilish smirk.

We smoke from the pipe for a few minutes in silence.

"I've never seen you angry," I say.

I can't even imagine him being angry, not like my father, and this feels like an important revelation. Freud would have a fucking field day with me.

He ponders this for a moment. "Well, I don't like being angry."

"Does anybody?"

"Maybe? Does your dad?" he asks.

"He might," I concede. "Why do you think that is?"

"Anger is easier than sadness. Fear too. If people could process what they're really feeling in a healthy way, I don't think they'd be so angry."

"So how do you do it? Process those things?"

"Meditation."

We haven't discussed meditation before, but I'm not surprised to find out he's a practitioner.

"How long have you been meditating?"

"About a decade."

"Wow. Every day?"

"Every day."

"Well, it must work."

"No idea."

"Really?"

"Kidding. It works. I can teach you."

"Eep."

"Eep?"

I smile instead of explaining. "Eep" is what my friends and I say to express dread or dismay, a perfect encapsulation of how I feel about meditation. While I'm fine with the yoga, I'm not ready to sit quietly with my own thoughts. Honestly, I can't think of anything more terrifying.

Internet Bugs

Noticing that I've wandered in for a visit, Shane calls me over from the living room where he's sitting with Sebastian. Usually, we'd exchange hellos and hugs, but he's distracted. I approach him and he points out a gumball-sized, reddish-brown bubble stuck to Sebastian's back.

"What's that?" I ask.

"A tick."

"Why does it look like that?"

"It's been feeding."

"Ew! Take it out!"

"I don't think I can just rip it off. They can carry Lyme disease. I need to think about this."

And that's what he does. He sits and he thinks, and I'm impressed, as always, with his patience. I would have just ripped the tick off Sebastian's back. But that's the difference, right? He sits and thinks, and I spin through an endless cycle of action and regret. Maybe meditation would be good for me.

"What about the Internet?" he asks, finally.

"You want to use the Internet to find out what to do about a tick?"

"I don't know. Can we?"

"I don't know. I don't have a computer."

"We have a computer."

"Yes, you do."

"And we have the World Wide Web."

"Well then, let's go," I say, gesturing for him to lead us onward. We go into their shared office space which, indeed, has everything one needs to conceivably access this new thing, this information superhighway.

"Do you know what you're doing?" I ask.

"I think so," he says, with a look that tells me he absolutely doesn't. "I actually haven't done this without Matty."

He turns on the computer and connects to the Internet through a series of high-pitched squeals. Eventually, a page appears (Yahoo) and he types in our query: "What should I do when a tick bites my dog?"

"Does that sound right?" he asks.

"Sounds perfect."

He clicks the mouse, and we wait for the results.

"This is really cool," I say. And it is, even if the results take forever to load. I haven't been anywhere near the Internet yet except to use email in the computer lab at college.

One of the results takes us to a page with text that outlines what we should do. According to this source, we need to take the tick out very carefully using tweezers, in a "straight and steady motion so as not to leave any part of the remaining bug inside, as this could lead to infection or Lyme disease."

Shane is reading the text to me and when he gets to the end, I congratulate him on his correct assessment of the situation.

"I'll get the tweezers. I'm gonna need your help," he says.

"I'm all yours."

Before we can start the minor operation, Carlos appears beside us. Carlos is Shane's best friend and the only person in their inner circle with whom I've really connected. I'm sure it's because, while the same age as Shane, he seems more of my generation. A little lost but game for anything. He's Portuguese, smaller in frame than Shane, and sports a clean-shaven head and face. He's a spoken-word artist with no obvious other job… except perhaps as a grifter. But, you know, the kind of grifter whose craft is so transparent as to be no actual threat. Instead, it's a joke we all share. He'll ask for anything one might be willing to give (a ride, a cigarette, a ten spot), with a smile that's clearly a confession. Usually, it works because he's persistent, charming, and utterly harmless.

"You figured this out on the Internet?" Carlos asks as we all take a task. Carlos shines a flashlight on the area, I hold Sebastian, and Shane gets into position to remove the tick.

"Yeah," I say.

"That's so cool!" Carlos exclaims.

"Right?" I agree.

Shane follows the instructions of the oracle, and the tick is removed.

"What did it say to do next?" he asks. "Should we disinfect the area?"

We all go back to the office to read what the web page says to do next.

"Clean the area with an antiseptic," Shane reads from the text. "If your dog develops any symptoms, make an appointment with your vet."

"Do you have an antiseptic?" I ask.

"We can use tea tree oil," he says. Of course. Tea tree oil. I once asked for a painkiller to alleviate my cramps and Matty gave me ginger tea. (It did not work.) Shane has *thoughts* about Western medicine.

He leaves to get the oil and Carlos sits down in front of the computer, mesmerized by what we've all discovered today. I join Shane in the living room with Sebastian. After we disinfect the area, Shane and I celebrate our success with a joint in the kitchen.

"Where's Carlos?" Shane asks.

"He's still on the computer."

"Oh. He'll come when he smells the pot."

"No doubt."

"You know, he asked about you. Asked if you're single," Shane tells me.

"What did you say?"

"I told him you've been hoping he'd ask."

I pick up an apple from the fruit bowl on the island and throw it at him. He effortlessly catches it and places it back in the bowl.

"I'm kidding! I told him to ask you," he admits.

"Good answer."

"You could have a lot of fun with Carlos," he tells me with a wink and not a trace of jealousy, which is both good and terrible.

"I'm sure I could."

"But no?"

"No."

"Not your type?"

"No."

"What's your type?"

"What's yours?" When cornered, fire back.

"I don't have a type. I like all women," he says.

"No men? We're all on the Kinsey scale, you know."

"I'm really, really low on that scale."

Hallelujah.

"Find anything interesting on the computer?" Shane asks Carlos as he joins us.

"Just some porn."

"Really?" Shane asks.

"No. I'm kidding!" Carlos laughs.

Shane and I share a glance, not sure whether or not to believe him. Carlos using Shane's computer to view porn isn't entirely inconceivable.

"I can probably find some if you want," Carlos adds.

"Katie? Want to see some porn?" Shane asks.

"No, I'm good," I say, while making a disgusted face.

I'm playing like I'm above it, but, of course, I've watched porn before. One of Jonathan's many summer jobs during high school was working at a video rental place, a mom-and-pop shop that didn't survive the arrival of Blockbuster. The shop had one of those curtained-off areas for the skin flicks. (This, of course, led to many stories of who was renting what in our town. In our defense, entrusting this kind of information with a high school kid is bananas.) Occasionally, Jonathan would bring one of these masterpieces home so we could watch it in the basement while drinking and critiquing the action. We even created an elaborate drinking game where each porn trope was worth a specific amount of alcohol. (Woman has sex totally naked except high heels? That's a shot. Woman has ordered some type of service and can only pay in sex? Chug a beer.) They were always straight movies with subtle titles like *Edward Penishands* and we always found them highly entertaining, as much for their terrible production value as for the illicit thrill of watching something we had to hide from our parents.

"Well, I just came by to see if you're going tonight," Carlos says to Shane.

"Yeah," Shane answers. "Want me to pick you up?"

"Yeah, if it's no problem. Okay, man, I'll see you later."

Carlos gives us both quick hugs and leaves, and I have to ask. "What's tonight?"

"Men's group," Shane answers.

"What's that?"

"Once a month, I get together with a group of men."

"Like a club?"

"Well, we don't have jackets."

Shane hardly drinks, doesn't care at all about sports, and isn't out picking up women. So, I'm really at a loss as to what this could be.

"And what do you do with this group of men? Because I know you're really, really low on the Kinsey scale," I tease.

"We talk."

"About?"

"Stuff going on in our lives. Problems, how we can work through them."

"In a bar?"

"In a barn."

Of course. In a barn.

"So… it's like therapy?" I continue to inquire.

"Sure."

"Can I come?"

"No. You're not a man."

"I can drag it up."

"Why do you want to come?"

"Because it sounds kinda crazy," I say. "Men voluntarily getting together to talk about their feelings? My father would rather die."

"Mine too. Or, you know, would have… if he wasn't already dead."

So, we have that in common. This tiny nugget of information is like a bump of cocaine. It only makes me want more.

"So… what problems do you have?" I say it in a way that lets him know that I know that I'm prying.

"Well, for starters, I have a very nosy woman in my kitchen."

He's joking but his evasiveness still stings. I'm jealous of these men in a barn that will know more than me about the secrets of his heart. I desperately want to be his confidante but it's not a position I can appoint myself to; relationships don't work that way. In fact, they probably work in the opposite manner. The more I try, the more likely I am to fail.

I make a promise to myself that I will never ask for more than he's willing to give. We finish the joint, and I leave him. Leaving him is always awful but not the hug goodbye. The hug goodbye is the only reason I can ever walk away.

Awakening

I'm sitting at my word processor trying to update my resume. Not because I want to but because I think I should. But instead of trying to find a way to make my restaurant job sound more impressive than it is, I just stare at the screen thinking about Shane.

Honestly, I'm not able to *not* think about him. I conjure his face upon waking and the image of him is the last thing I see before falling asleep. He's there when I'm working, driving, doing anything really, my mind toggling between memories I've already tucked away of him and imagined scenarios we've yet to experience (and most likely never will).

Like with Mr. Hamilton, I'm seduced by Shane's life experience, wanting to learn all that he can teach me. He's become bigger than a mortal man in my mind. He's a spiritual guru, a healer, and I'm starting to feel like I'm in his absolute power. Apparently, I have joined a cult, a cult with a lone follower: me. Ironically, I'm quite sure that Shane would be horrified by this narrative of his control and my powerlessness. And to be sure, he is innocent of all. I've done this entirely to myself.

I step away from my desk and call Jonathan.

"Hey, baby. How's it goin'?" he asks.

"Help me."

"Still obsessing?"

"Yes."

I've told Jonathan about Shane and Matty. He can't quite believe there are cool people in this town.

"How does he feel about you?"

"I'm sure he thinks of me like a puppy."

After all, I'm cute, just a wayward stray following him around. And honestly, it's not an unpleasant analogy. I would let him put me on a leash. More than that, I would welcome it. (In college, my girlfriends and I passed around *The Story of O* like contraband, delighting in its risqué power. Now I understand it.)

"You can always attack him and find out," Jonathan offers.

"No way!"

The idea is unthinkable. Not because I don't *want* to attack him but because his rejection would destroy me. I don't say that though. I just pretend that my hesitancy is about ethics.

"It would be wrong. He's married."

"Nah. Morally, you'd still be in the clear."

"How do you get *there*?"

"Well, *you're* not the one married. *You're* not breaking any vows."

"You sure that's not just one big rationalization for sleeping with married people?"

"Of course, it is. Doesn't make it less true."

I wonder how many married men Jonathan has slept with.

"You're gonna be okay," Jonathan assures me.

"Yeah." *No.*

No one who spends this much time in their bedroom touching themselves is okay.

The desire that has been dormant in me is awakening and it is exactly the kind of exquisite torture I've heard described by friends, movies, and literature my entire life. When I'm not at Matty and Shane's house or at work, I'm almost exclusively in my childhood bedroom where I explore my body with a frenzy I've never experienced before. I imagine my hands are his and my body aches for him. (Is this what being a teenage boy feels like? I now have a little more empathy for them.)

"Are you coming home for Christmas?" I ask Jonathan.

"Yup. You can introduce me then."

"Good. And you can help me figure out my life while you're here."

"Babe, I have figured out your life. Come to Chicago."

I should go to Chicago. I should go anywhere else where I'm not drowning in desire. Where I can't covet Shane.

Consensual Scars

I remember learning the word "covet" while watching *Silence of the Lambs*. And while I'm almost positive that I'm not about to make a suit of skin, it does worry me that the word I'm currently relating to most is used to describe a serial killer. That can't be good. But it's no doubt what I'm doing. I'm coveting him and Matty's whole life, and I know this situation isn't sustainable.

"I'll think about it," I tell him. We say goodbye and I'm left to ponder Jonathan's offer.

The truth is I'm stuck. I can't leave Shane. Even if I can see the flashing warning lights ahead of me, I know this want will remain unfulfilled and the inevitable destination is likely to be nothing but despair. I see all that. I just don't care. Because the pleasure of him, even in these most limiting of circumstances, outweighs exponentially the most certain of crashes in front of me.

I look at my half-finished resume and sigh in frustration. I get up and return to my bed, lost in thoughts of his body.

Annie Marie Huber

Sir Chamberlain & Lesser Men

In addition to hanging out at Matty and Shane's house, I start seeing Matty at the restaurant. She comes by the bar while I'm working, always in the mid-afternoon shift so I have time to chat. I think she comes as much to indulge in her guilty pleasures (cocktails and fried cheese) as she is there to see me. I've noticed that Shane does the "domestic" duties of cooking and shopping much more than Matty. So, cheese – while not forbidden – is a rarity in her house. Whatever the reason for the visits, I'm glad for them.

I'm sure Shane knows about her indulgences and I'm sure he shakes his head and rolls his eyes.

In these afternoons, I pepper her with questions as she so often does to me. I've learned that she's lived all over. First in New York for a short-lived college attempt, then a brief stint in Miami as a surf instructor, and then finally to California where she discovered yoga. She and Shane met when he started taking her class. He had recently arrived in Los Angeles on his own journey towards something bigger and better than Lake City. They shared a dream of building a house in the undeveloped lands a couple hours north of Los Angeles when they got the call to come help Shane's parents.

One afternoon, I finally get to the question I've had since meeting them.

"So… the sheep. Explain," I say.

She smiles broadly and launches into a story I'm sure she's told many times. "Shane got them for me as an anniversary present. It was our tenth anniversary and I asked for jewelry because, you know, a diamond is popular for your tenth. But he got me sheep instead."

"An obvious substitute," I say.

"Like, *of course*, sheep are better than jewelry," she adds with heartfelt conviction followed by laughter.

She knows how ridiculous this sounds and I love her so much in these moments. Regardless of my feelings for Shane, my feelings for Matty remain constant. She is an effervescent light. How can one not love an effervescent light? And as for their relationship, well, timing is everything, isn't it? Step into the right place and time and anything can happen. And what happened is she found him first. He is hers and she is his, and I accept that. Just like I accept the fact that I am undoubtedly, irreversibly in love with Shane. I don't find the two truths to be incompatible. Inconvenient, definitely. But can they both exist as true? Yes. Because they do.

I wish sometimes for a polygamous society where this could all be solved quite easily. I feel pretty confident that I'd make a great second wife to Shane and sister wife to Matty. Sure, the dynamic is another type of patriarchy but so is our current social structure. And I really like the idea of sister wives. Women should support women, a lot more than we do. And who knows? Maybe it does take multiple women to deal with one man's shit. The idea doesn't sound all that crazy to me.

I wonder often why they don't have kids. If any two people in the world should be reproducing, it should be these people who buy sheep instead of diamonds and never get angry. But it's not the type of question one can just ask without seeming like a judgmental asshole. Especially if you're a woman asking another woman. Whether we mean it or not, the question carries the implication that we *should* be having kids, that's it's the default position, and any deviation from it requires an explanation. And I'm definitely part of the problem because I want an explanation.

Fuck it.

"So… why no kids?" I ask.

Thankfully, she doesn't seem offended by the question. Probably because, like the sheep inquiry, she's fielded it before.

"It wasn't really our decision *not* to. It was more the universe deciding," she says.

"Ah," I say, understanding what little she's offering. "The Universe" being code for "shit you can't control."

I want to know more details. Is the issue a medical one? Did they go to a doctor? Is it him? Her? Did they ever try to adopt? Did the universe give them strict instructions not to reproduce so that they could pursue other more worthy endeavors? But I can't think of a non-terribly rude follow-up and the "the universe" is also a handy conversation closer. I mean, how can you argue with the universe?

"What made you want to teach yoga?" I ask, changing the subject to something less delicate.

"I got in a bad car accident when I was twenty-seven. I almost died. And yoga helped me heal. Physically and mentally. And, so, you know, I wanted to help others heal too."

A perfectly altruistic reason. If I didn't love her so much, I would most likely hate her, effervescent light be damned. (And again, I'm part of the problem.)

"Do you miss California?" I ask.

"So much," she answers. "But it was our destiny to come here."

Thank god for destiny.

"I want to start a teacher training," she says.

"What's that?"

"A program where I train people to be yoga teachers. It could be really lucrative. But, you know, I'd be creating competition."

"And ruining your monopoly."

"Exactly!" she concurs. "But I'd also be bringing yoga into the universe in a bigger way."

"Then you should do it."

"I think I will."

Why am I so good at sorting out other people's career problems but not my own? Then again, all I really did was push her in the direction she already wanted to go. My problem is I don't know where I want to go.

She asks what's going on in my life and I tell her that my friend Jonathan will be coming to town over the Christmas holiday.

"How exciting! Bring him by!" she says.

"I will," I promise.

"Are you guys…"

"Oh, no. He's gay."

"So many good ones are gay!" she exclaims.

"Gay, married, dead, or fictional. Or a priest," I say, counting down the list of men that are unavailable.

"Have you known any hot priests?" she asks.

"Just a fictional one."

"Oh, I *love* that movie."

"Me too."

I love the book also, but I don't say this because I know it sounds pretentious. My mom loved both the book and the movie. Even now, there's a dog-eared copy of *The Thorn Birds* sitting on her bedside table. It's been there as long as I can remember.

"And, you know, I think the actor that played him is gay," I say. "So, he could be, what, like three out of five?"

"Does that make him even more attractive? Is it, like, a point system?"

"Totally."

"To Richard, then." She raises her glass to toast the magnificent Sir Chamberlain and takes a sip of her drink.

"Whatcha toastin'?"

An obviously intoxicated man has joined us at the bar. He's a short, stocky man in a rumpled business suit, looking like he just got laid off. We don't answer his query; I instead ask him for his order.

"A dry martini," he commands.

Finally, a real drink! I haven't made a dry martini before but how hard can it be? It's just gin and vermouth. I take a shaker and pour some gin in with about a half shot of the dry vermouth. When he takes a sip, he makes a disgusted face.

"I said a *dry* martini," he says, admonishing my effort.

I don't know what this means. Less vermouth? I try again, putting a quarter shot of vermouth in the drink. He tastes it and again scoots the drink back to me across the bar.

"I said a *dry* martini," he repeats.

Matty clears her throat to get my attention. I walk over to her and lean in so she can whisper in my ear. "Just give him gin. No vermouth."

I follow Matty's advice, and the man is finally satisfied with the drink but not my service. He turns to Matty and says, "Can you believe this? Can't even make a fucking martini."

Matty doesn't take the bait; instead, she rolls her eyes. This enrages the man.

"Fucking cunts," he mutters.

I grab the removable nozzle from the sink and spray the man with water.

"What the fuck?" he screams as Matty cackles with laughter.

I know I'm only this bold because he's on the other side of the bar. But then he actually starts to climb over it. Fortunately, he's so ripped that he just manages to get on top of the bar on all fours. He's lacking the coordination to get down on either side, and the scene makes Matty laugh even harder. I want to laugh too but I'm almost positive I'm about to get fired. I'm sure there's some sort of company policy for dealing with this idiot. I'm also sure that I didn't follow it. Oops.

A manager comes over and helps the man back down to his side of the bar. The manager, whose name is Pete, is my age and cares way too much about this job for his own good. Pete apologizes to the man as he assists him. This, unsurprisingly, enrages Matty.

"Why are you apologizing to him?" she nearly shouts. "Did you hear what he called us? He was about to attack her!" She indicates me and I love her so much.

"She sprayed me! You should fire her!" the man demands. I can't deny it since he's dripping water.

Pete leads (drags) the man towards the exit, placating him with a promise to "deal with me."

Cool.

"That's bullshit," Matty says.

"It is, indeed," I agree. "I gotta go get fired. I'll catch you later."

"I'll wait," she says.

I go to the back of the restaurant and wait for Pete. When he arrives, he starts into me, reprimanding me in full view of all the cooks and servers. The public flogging makes my body go hot with shame. He ends the rant with a warning.

"I should fire you but I'm just going to write you up."

I wonder what "write me up" actually means. And do I even care? I should feel relieved. I'm not fired. But the shame has turned

Consensual Scars

to quiet rage. Fuck this. I don't want this guy's mercy. I want to walk out and never come back.

I calmly take off the apron around my waist and the corporate bowtie and hand them both to Pete. Without a word, I walk back to the bar to collect my things. Matty is still waiting for me. I tell her to hold her questions until we're gone.

Once outside the restaurant, she is furious again.

"I can't believe they fired you! We should sue them. That guy was a menace. You were just defending yourself. I'll be your witness."

"Slow down. I didn't get fired. I quit."

"Oh!"

"Yeah. That guy, my manager, is such an asshole."

"I got that."

"Oh well. Fuck this shitty job. I'm sure I can find another shitty job."

I pull out a cigarette and hand one to Matty. My hand is shaking but it's no longer from anger. I'm euphoric. No more piña colada song. No more asshole customers. No more pretending to be a bartender.

"Why does someone order a martini if they just want a glass of gin?" I ask.

"James Bond?"

"That guy was no James Bond."

"Not even close," she agrees.

"Ugh. I'm gonna need to find another job. Damn." The euphoria is already slipping quickly into the reality of being unemployed. And then Matty's eyes spark up and I know she has an idea.

"What if you *don't* get another shitty job?" she asks.

"I love that idea. Know of any non-shitty jobs?"

"Yeah. What if you come work for me?"

"Really?"

"If I'm going to do a teacher training, I'm going to need someone to help me with stuff at the studio. I can't pay you much, but I can probably match what you made here."

I have no idea what kind of work she wants me to do, much less whether I'm capable of any of it. But life is like improv sometimes. Sometimes you just say "yes" and figure out the rest later.

"Yes! I can definitely come work for you. Whatever you need."

"Great! Let's go to my place and figure it out. Follow me?"

I know she's asking if I'll follow her back to the house in my car, but I take the larger view.

"Girl, I'll follow you anywhere."

Teachable Moments

Matty has decided that she wants a website for her yoga studio and that I should build it. I have no idea how to build a website, but this doesn't seem to bother her. ("You'll figure it out!") Her confidence in me is contagious though, so I'm willing to try. I call Jonathan who knows way more about this stuff than I do. He's so excited by this development that he starts rambling off a bunch of letters (HMTL, FTP, PPP) and I have to ask him to slow down and start at the very beginning.

"Pretend I'm an idiot," I say.

"You're not an idiot," he reflexively replies.

"At this, I very much am. Now, start at the top."

He does and I'm able to grasp the concepts of these arcane letter combinations as he explains them.

I didn't realize how badly I needed a diversion, but I clearly did. I'm diving in, without thinking too much, and it's exhilarating. This project is the first actual goal I've had in months that isn't just "seeing Shane and Matty as much as possible." Fortunately, this job fulfills that goal too, as now I'm at their house way more than before.

Working with Matty is a dream job. More like a creative partner than a boss, we collaborate on everything, volleying ideas back and forth for hours. We take yoga breaks, snack breaks, and the occasional smoke break. We talk about the website and how to best market her classes (and upcoming first teacher training). I research and read so much that it feels like being back in college, only better. No tests or papers. Just learning and experience.

One afternoon in early November, while I'm at the computer

writing code, Shane enters. I had been waiting for Matty, but I welcome the change.

"Hey. How's it goin'?" he asks.

"Good. I love HMTL. A whole new language that's just reading and writing. I don't need to try to speak it. It's perfect for me."

"Unlike French," he says, and I'm touched that he remembers.

"Exactly!"

"So, Matty can't work today. She's not feeling well," he says.

"Oh no!"

"Yeah. But you can stay and work if you want."

And then, as if just to defy him, the computer shuts off.

"Or maybe not," he concludes.

There's no need for lighting in the office in the daytime with all the curtain-less windows. So, it takes us a moment to realize that the issue isn't solely with the computer. The house has lost power. We venture to the fuse box, but flipping the switches does nothing. It's up to the power company.

I love blackouts. I think it has something to do with control but I'm not sure what.

"Do you want to help me instead?" he asks.

"Yes."

"You don't care what you're helping with?"

"No."

"Cool."

We walk to the mudroom and through the door to the attached garage. He opens the garage door which brings in the chill as well as the light. I shiver and Shane goes back to the house, returning with a wool hoodie.

"Here."

The sweatshirt drowns me when I put it on. I wonder if I can keep it forever.

The garage is where Shane does his woodworking projects. Since meeting him, I've learned that he dabbles in almost everything. Music, painting, building, landscaping… if the activity has an artistic bent to it at all, he's tried it. And while he'll be the first to say he's a master of none, I've come to think of him as some sort of renaissance man. What he lacks in expertise, he surely makes up for with eager curiosity.

"So, I want to put a sauna next to the pool. But it's too cold to build it out there, so I thought I'd build the separate pieces here first. The walls, the floor, the ceiling. And assemble them out there."

"How big is it going to be?"

"Oh, not that big. About sixty square feet. Big enough for three people."

And with that, we get to work. I've done enough stagecraft to know my way around basic tools, so I'm confident that I won't completely embarrass myself. I haven't used a nail gun before though, so when he presents me with it, I ask him to walk me through it.

"Now, don't nail me," I say, as he's helping me place the gun.

"I won't... nail you."

He's clearly flirting with me. It's a new dynamic and I'm not prepared. I look at him, my eyebrows raised in surprise and my tongue too tied to function. I wish for all the world to come up with a clever retort, but I've got nothing, at least not until a little later.

"You're good at this stuff," he compliments me as we work.

"Thanks. I like working with my hands."

"Me too," he agrees.

"I bet you do," I purr, as flirty as I can manage.

He smiles broadly, nodding his head in approval.

We work together for the rest of the afternoon and the flirting continues. It's amazing the number of double entendres one can make around power tools. The flirting is light and fun with only the slightest hint of something more. (But maybe that's just on my end.) It's the kind of flirting that could be described as "innocent." I'm almost sure, if Matty was with us, she would be more amused than upset by our repartee. When we're done, he tells me that we're going to make lunch.

"And you're not just going to sit there and watch me. You're going to help. But first let me check on Matty."

I go to the kitchen to wait. The electricity has returned and soon, the sounds of Ramsey Lewis fill the house. A couple months ago, I had no idea who Ramsey Lewis is. Up until now, my taste in music has been mostly a product of Top 40 radio. This relationship is expanding my musical literacy as much as my palate.

"How's Matty?" I inquire. "Is it the flu?"

The flu is "going around" as it always seems to be once the weather shifts.

"No. She's just... having a hard day."

I don't know what this means exactly, and I want to ask for more details, but I let it go. We've all had shit days.

"So, what are we making?" I ask.

"California sushi rolls."

Like so many other delicacies, I've never eaten sushi. My understanding is that it's raw fish, but we'll surely be making some vegan version. I'm glad because it's the "raw fish" part that's steered me clear of the dish.

"Without fish?" I ask.

"No fish in these. Avocado, cucumber, seaweed."

"I think I'll cook better if I have some wine," I rationalize.

He rolls his eyes at me. I'm pretty sure he thinks I'm an alcoholic. And compared to him, I probably am. His body is a temple and mine is a wasteland. But out of kindness or pity, he searches for wine. He can only come up with an old bottle of Scotch.

"Want a shot of this?" he asks.

"If you do one with me."

"Oh, no."

"Come on. Just one. Please?" I'm like a child, begging him to play with me.

He sighs. "One," he says, giving in. He pours out two shots and hands one to me. I've only tasted whiskey once before and have never done a full shot of it. I didn't enjoy the taste but right now I want a drink and if it's all he has, so be it. (Hmm. Maybe I am an alcoholic?)

"To..." and he pauses while toasting, not sure what to celebrate.

I offer up the only Hebrew I know, thanks to *Fiddler on the Roof.*

"L'chaim."

"Yes, l'chaim!" he exclaims and we down the shots.

I now understand the appeal of whisky. My whole body is warm and I'm already half-way to tipsy. I immediately want more. But more than that, I want *him* to drink more. I want to see him drunk, see him lose control. Maybe then I'd get to know some of those secrets he's revealing in his men's group. But I don't know how to ply him with alcohol (and I doubt I even can) so I give up on the idea.

Shane moves about the kitchen, pulling out a container of prepared rice and a collection of veggies from the fridge. He gives me tasks to help ("stir this," "chop that") and I do my best, eager to please. When everything is prepped, the stereo shuffles to another CD and Joe Cocker's *You Can Leave Your Hat On* fills the kitchen. Shane whoops his enthusiasm for the song, one of his favorites (and one of the sexiest tunes in the world) and starts to sing along. Between verses, he gives me instructions on how to roll the sushi. I'm so inept that he circles around the island and stands behind me.

His hands slide across my arms. His fingers manipulate mine as he whispers "like this" into my ear. And then his breath is on my neck, his lips are grazing my skin, and oh my god I'm going to die right now.

But then Sebastian barks and suddenly Shane is back on the other side of the island. He's talking quickly to cover up the moment.

"You got it, you got it, just keep rolling," he says.

"Right, right."

I try to continue but my hands are shaking. I make a joke of it, to take us back to the land of innocent flirting. "I'm a little unsteady now. Wonder why."

He gazes at me, his face unreadable. I don't see any shame or guilt. For a second, I'm sure I imagined his lips. That is, until he smiles slyly and winks at me. And with that, the music changes again to something a lot less dangerous and we're back to whatever we are. We finish making the sushi and eat together watching TV in the den. I can't follow anything on the screen, of course. All I can think about is… what happened back there? And will I ever recover?

Night at the Casino

A week before Thanksgiving, I arrive at the house to work with Matty in the late afternoon. But before I can remove my shoes, she comes in and stops me. She's frustrated, near tears.

"Katie! Let's go," she says, grabbing her keys off the shelf.

"Oh... oh... okay," I stutter.

She takes my hand and leads me back outside and to her car. I don't know what's happening, but I feel like I'm escaping a crime scene. She gets into the driver's seat while I get in the passenger's side.

"You alright?" I tentatively ask.

"I just need a drink. Where can we go for a drink?"

I don't think a family restaurant is what she needs so I try to come up with a local dive bar.

"We can go to the Foxhole." It's one of the remaining small businesses in town. Dive bars and liquor stores are some of our longest lasting landmarks.

"Where's that?"

I love that she doesn't know. Our lives are so very different.

"Off of Franklin, near downtown."

We drive in silence until we reach the small, rustic establishment. We survey the space and take a table. It's early enough that there are only a few patrons. When the waitress arrives, Matty suggests Long Island Iced Teas which is a good indication of where this night is headed.

"So, why are we here?" I ask.

"We're here to drink."

"What happened?"

"Oh, he's just so goddamn stubborn."

"Shane?"

"Yes."

She doesn't expand and I'm dying to know more. I want their disagreement laid out in front of me so I can study it under a microscope. Who did what? Who said what? Before this moment, they've appeared to be the paragon of marriage. But I know this is foolish; of course, they have issues. Everyone does. Just what those specific issues are for Matty and Shane, I can't fathom.

"What is he being stubborn about?" I fish.

"Oh, it's nothing. It's dumb."

She's killing me.

When she finishes her drink, she tries to order us two more. I stop her, knowing that two of these deadly cocktails in less than an hour will make us both too wasted to drive.

"We'll call a taxi," she says.

"Where... do you think you are?" I ask. There are no taxis in Lake City.

"Ugh! This town!" It's the first time I've heard her express any disdain for our town. But then I remember, it's not *her* hometown.

"Well, let's get out of here then. Where should we go next?" she asks.

"We could go to the casino."

About an hour away, halfway between Lake City and Chicago, is a casino boat. Jonathan's mother works there as a cocktail waitress. I've never been there (or any other casino, for that matter) but I've heard it's fun.

Matty's eyes light up. "Yes!"

She pays for the drinks, and we embark on our new destination. When we enter the casino, the lights and noise are a jolt to my senses. Matty and I take in the lay of the land.

"Blackjack? Craps?" she asks.

"I have no idea how to play anything."

"I'll teach you. Come on."

We get some chips and settle at a craps table where two other women are also playing. Before Matty can make a bet, I see Jonathan's mother. She's a tiny woman, attractive but with slightly weathered skin from too much nicotine and sun.

"Emily!" I yell, to get her attention over the bells and whistles of the slot machines.

I've always been a little intimidated by Jonathan's mother, which contrasts with the intimate, first-name greeting. The greeting, however, has become habit, a social norm created and nurtured by Jonathan. I've never heard him call his mother anything other than "Emily," which may seem disrespectful but is said with love and affection. He calls my dad "Papa," which is both an endearing compliment to my father and an obvious dig at his own, whom he has labeled "the sperm donor." His dad, of course, is not actually a sperm donor in the technical sense. He's just an asshole. But what Jonathan's father lacks in paternal instincts, his mother makes up for; she's pure mama bear, fiercely protective and proud of her boy. According to Jonathan, his parents have finally started talking about divorce, a development that's long overdue.

"Ka-tie!" Emily responds, dividing my name the way she always does.

We hug and I introduce Matty.

"What are you ladies drinking tonight?" Emily asks.

"Long Island Iced Teas!" Matty answers.

"Oh. That kind of night," she responds knowingly. "You got it."

Emily hustles away and Matty gives me a short explanation of the game. We consistently lose so when Emily returns with our drinks, we get up to play something else.

"Let's try Blackjack," she says, and we venture to a different table where two men are playing. They're attractive, mid-thirties, and look like big city stockbrokers with expensive suits and loosened ties. They welcome us to the table.

"Bring us some luck, ladies!" yells the slightly taller man.

"We'll do our best!" Matty responds.

When she gets dealt in, I realize I do know this game. It's twenty-one and easy enough to understand. And unlike craps, the game is slow enough to enable conversation.

"So, what do you ladies do?" one of the gamblers asks.

"Sex therapist," Matty says, like bait on a hook, and I choke on my drink.

"Wow!" the shorter man says.

"I'm Willow," she says, holding out her hand to shake and I get the game. It's a dangerous game, to be sure, but the best ones usually are.

The two men put their hands out enthusiastically.

"Michael."

"Luke."

I notice the absence of Matty's wedding ring as she shakes their hands. The two men look at me expectantly with their hands still out.

"Sasha," I add, shaking their hands too, while trying to think up an interesting career choice. No need though because they're both stuck on "sex therapist." I can't blame them. I am too.

"So… what's that like?" asks Michael.

"Oh, you know, lots of people who don't know what they really want. Or just can't say what they really want. Tragic, really."

"Do you know what *you* want?" asks Luke.

"Always," Matty says, with a flirtatiousness that's so over the top, both men whoop with laughter.

I'm impressed that Matty can play two games at once. But on the next hand, we lose and Matty decides both are over.

"Well, gentlemen, it's been fun, but I think we're going to try our luck elsewhere."

The exit is so smooth and quick that we're on our way before they can protest. At the slot machines around the corner, we erupt into laughter.

"I can't believe you did that," I say. "You're a yoga teacher! Don't y'all have rules about lying? Or am I thinking of the ten commandments?"

"We do! But that wasn't lying. That was…."

"Improv?"

"Yes!"

We opt next for the slots which require no explanation, and thus, they quickly become my favorite casino game. When we run out of quarters, Matty declares we should eat. Since we're on our third drink, it's probably wise. We search and find a buffet where we make plates full of various cuisines that have no business existing side-by-side.

"How did you come up with sex therapist?" I ask.

"I don't know. Wouldn't that be fun though? Learn everyone's deepest desires?"

Girl, if you only knew.

"I want to go to Bombay," she says, as a perfect non-sequitur.

My geography is quite terrible, so I ask where that is.

"India," she answers.

"Ah." India is the birthplace of yoga, this much I know, so it's unsurprising she'd want to travel there. "You've never been?"

"No. And I just read about a doctor there. He's doing research on laughter as therapy. He leads a group of people that meet in the park, and they all laugh together. I think that sounds amazing."

"You should go."

She considers the idea for a beat. "Yes. We should go."

I think she means "we" as in "me and her" and I'm momentarily thrilled. But before I can respond, she continues.

"Will you housesit for us if we go?"

Of course, she means her and Shane. I'm bummed but then I think about living in their house while they're gone. The idea is seductive.

"Sure. I'd love to."

After eating, we go outside where she bums a smoke from me.

"Thanks for coming out with me tonight," she says.

"Anytime."

"I guess we should head back?"

"Probably. Want me to drive?"

"Please," she says, handing me the keys.

When we get back to Lake City, it's not terribly late. Our evening started early so it's only around 9pm. Nevertheless, I don't expect her to invite me in; unlike me, she finished her third drink and is clearly ready to crash. This is all good because, for the first time ever, I don't actually want to come inside. Whatever negative energy existed upon my initial arrival hours ago has most likely dissipated, but on the off chance it hasn't, I don't want to be in range. Seeing them argue would devastate me.

Consensual Scars

She hugs me tight, thanks me again, and disappears inside. I start down the hill from their driveway. Before I'm all the way down, I pull over to the side of the road. I don't know what I'm doing until I'm doing it, which is walking close enough to the front windows to see inside the main interior of the house. The lack of curtains gives me a wide view of the living room and the night provides me cover.

I see Shane reading a book on the couch and I see Matty enter. They talk. And then he rises, and they embrace. I'm thankful that whatever ugliness has transpired is now in the past. But as their embrace leads to a kiss, my gratitude turns to something else. His hands run down her back, and I'm flooded with a mix of envy and arousal. She drops to her knees, and I can't look away.

Annie Marie Huber

Adventures in Housesitting

"So, I'm a stalker now," I say as a way of greeting. I've called Jonathan to confess and to get some guidance because I'm obviously unwell.

"Oh, dear," he replies. "What happened?"

I give him the play-by-play of my evening with Matty. I end with, "but I didn't leave. I stayed to watch them."

"Well, everyone goes a little crazy sometimes. Everybody does the drive by."

"This wasn't a drive by, though. It was me, standing outside their window, wishing I had binoculars in my car."

"So, people go to jail for that. So, you're not going to do that anymore," he instructs me. "Tell me you're not going to do that anymore."

"I won't do that anymore."

"Good girl," he says. "Now what did you see? Tell me everything."

It only takes me a few weeks to break my promise.

Thanksgiving arrives and my father and I buy prepared food from the market rather than attempt to cook. We feel that my mom, who hated cooking but would try in vain to roast a turkey every year that would come out dry, would approve of this decision. We eat in front of the TV so there's no pressure to maintain a conversation. He watches football and I do crossword puzzles. But at least we're in the same room.

Matty and Shane spend the day with the family of Shane's sister. I haven't yet met his sister. As far as I can tell, they aren't particularly close. But Thanksgiving is for family, so I am with mine and he is with his. And while I think of him the whole day, I bet I never cross his mind. That's the thing about him being so *present*. If I'm not right there in front of him, I'm convinced I'll drop out of his consciousness entirely. So, I'm relieved when the holiday is over, and I get to re-join his world. Unfortunately, it's a short reprieve as they are both preparing to visit India to experience the healing joy of laughter. How quickly Matty's desire has transformed into reality is stunning to me.

Before leaving, Shane walks me through my various housesitting duties: feeding the animals, managing the compost, and – most importantly – caring for the plants in the greenhouse. Fortunately, pool season is over, or I'd need to do a lot more. For the first time, I start to see the work that goes into building this life. And while I'm sad that they're leaving, I'm excited to pretend that their life is mine.

They are gone for about three minutes before I begin snooping. I'm not proud of it but I rationalize any guilt away by clarifying my intentions to myself. I'm not doing this because I have some terrible motive. I'm not here to steal or blackmail; I'm simply curious about every single aspect of their lives.

I start in the cabinets in the long buffet in the living room and come up with photo albums that I spend hours examining. The wedding album is especially of interest. They got married in a private garden in California. Her bridal wear is a flowing, white dress and her head is adorned with a crown of flowers. He's in a white, linen suit. They're young and in love, surrounded by friends. Only a few of the photos are staged; most are candid, catching and keeping precious moments that would otherwise be forgotten.

Two albums reveal details of their lives before finding one another. Flipping through Shane's, I get stuck on a photo of him as a boy in a military school uniform. The contrast between this child and the man I know is striking. There's so much I desire to know, so much that I'll probably never know.

The remaining albums are of their life together, a life of adventure and travel, of yoga retreats and strange cities. From their stories, I know they've been to Mexico, Thailand, Costa Rica, and Indonesia. They tend to favor places where the living is cheap, and friends can put them up. (They seem to have friends from all over the world.) It's the kind of existence I desperately want and fear that I'll never have.

Nothing about what I'm doing feels good or right. The melancholy music on my Walkman, my constant companion while alone, surely isn't helping. But it's like picking a scab and I can't stop. I move into their bedroom, a sanctuary I've never entered before. I've peeked inside but crossing this threshold has felt too risky, like the room will somehow eject me of its own accord.

The king size bed sits low and has a frame of wooden logs with end tables on each side. I know that these end tables are where secrets will be and I'm not disappointed. In the first, I find pot paraphernalia and a vibrator. I wonder if it's hers alone or if they use it together. The other end table has a copy of the *Kama Sutra*. I wonder how many positions they've tried. Probably all of them. Having never seen this infamous text, I sit on the bed and begin paging through it.

With my headphones on, I don't notice Carlos until he's standing right in front of me. My face is undoubtedly reddening in embarrassment.

"Hey," he greets me. His eyebrows raise as he notices the book I'm holding.

"Oh, hey," I answer.

"Whatcha doin'?" he asks in a teasing tone.

Fuck it. I know Carlos well enough to know that he's not going to judge my bad behavior. In fact, he'll probably join me.

"Just lookin' at their copy of the *Kama Sutra*."

"Oh, cool. Can I see?"

And just I predicted, he sits next to me, and we flip through the book together. He appears to have no qualms about sitting on their bed, looking through their things. I suppose if one is going to get busted doing shady things, it helps to be caught by someone equally shady.

"You ever do any of these?" he asks.

"Nope," I say.

"Wanna try?"

"Nope."

He laughs. "Doesn't hurt to ask."
I shut the book and bop him on the head with it.
"Down, boy," I say.
"Where are Matty and Shane?"
"They just left for India. I'm housesitting."
"Cool. Mind if I hang out?"
"Not at all."

I do mind, a little, as I want to keep looking through the house for secrets. But hanging out with Carlos is probably healthier… which says a lot actually.

"Have any pot?" he asks.

I'm not about to raid the stash in the end table. Instead, I lead Carlos to the den where a little wooden box sits on the coffee table. We settle into the couch and smoke a bowl together, a bowl containing – what I believe – is Shane's best harvest yet. Two hits in and I'm completely baked.

"*Saudade,*" Carlos says through a haze of smoke and in a tone that suggests an important discovery, though I have no idea what the word means.

"What?" I ask.

"*Saudade.* It's a Portuguese word. It doesn't have a direct English translation. It means longing for something, a constant feeling of being incomplete. I feel like you might be experiencing saudade."

I'm captivated by this word.

"Wow. Yes. That's exactly it," I say.
"I know."
"You know?"
"Of course."
"You can't tell him."
"Who?"
"Shane."
"Okay. Wait, tell him what?"
"I… don't know."

We've lost the thread entirely. We burst into giggles. After a minute or so, Carlos finds it again.

"Wait… why Shane? Are you… in love with Shane?"
"Oh my god! *You said you knew*. You said that fancy word."

"Oh, I don't know anything. I just figured if you weren't into me, there had to be someone else. That and it's a pretty good pick-up line."

"Fuck."

"Are you guys…?" he asks, while doing that juvenile hand gesture that signals sex, with one hand forming a circle and a finger from the other hand poking through it. I really hate this hand gesture.

"No!" I deny as emphatically as I can.

"Oh, okay."

"You can't ever say anything. Like, ever. You have to swear to me that you're not going to ever, ever say anything," I plead.

"Wait… say what again?"

"Jesus."

Sometimes I'm just stunned by my own stupidity. I've just admitted my feelings to Carlos, Shane's *best friend*. When are the scientists going to come up with a time machine that just rewinds the world about fifteen seconds? Is that too much to ask? This life would be so much goddamn easier.

"You won't tell Shane," I clarify for him.

"I won't, I won't," he says.

"I'm serious."

"I won't," he says, with a little more conviction.

"Okay."

"Can you do something for me?"

Of course.

"What?" I ask, pretending I have a choice in the matter. He's got me on a hook, and he knows it. I either have to do whatever this favor is, or, obviously, I have to kill him.

"Well, it's for me but it's also for my girlfriend."

"You have a girlfriend? Weren't you just hitting on me, like, thirty-seven seconds ago?"

He does his signature shrug and smile.

I relent. "Fine. Whatever. Tell me what I have to do."

"Oh, come on! Don't be like that! It'll be fun."

"I'm sure it will."

"My girlfriend is in a band called Dead End. And I thought it would be really cool to get her a road sign that says 'Dead End' on it. There are all these dead ends around the lake just north of the public beach."

"So... we're talking about stealing a road sign," I say, cutting to the chase. Naturally, it's illegal. What is it lately about me doing illegal shit? Drugs, stalking, now stealing.

"Well, I don't like to think of it as stealing," he says. "We're reallocating public funds."

"Sure," I say. And why not call it that? I'm rationalizing everything I do lately so who am I to judge?

"And when do you want to do this?" I ask.

"Well, it's getting dark. We can go now."

So, we do. We exit the house through the back door and Carlos gets into Shane's truck. He must have commandeered it before Shane left and drove it here. I get in beside him and I ask about the game plan.

"How exactly are we going to get this sign?"

"I've got a shovel. But the ground might be too hard now. So, I also have a chain we can hook up and pull it out with the truck."

Oh yeah. We're getting arrested tonight.

"Man, I'm so stoned," he says.

I laugh because I am too. I turn the radio up and try to find an acceptable song. I find *Bombastic* by Shaggy and we groove together. Before long, we're driving through the curvy, hidden roads that make up an area on the fringe of our town where a few rich, Chicago commuters own property near the water. The homes aren't visible from the roads that wind through the deserted woods; they're behind gates and long, private driveways.

Carlos, having already staked out the area, pulls up to the mark. There's not a soul in sight so we get to work. It becomes obvious that I didn't need to be here as I do very little. The ground is too hard to dig so he uses the chain to remove the sign. The operation goes surprisingly smoothly and within minutes, the sign is freed, loaded in the truck, and covered with a tarp.

We get back in the truck and I turn to him. "You could have done this alone, you know."

"Yes, but that wouldn't have been any fun!"

He raises his hand to give me a high five for a job well done, just as we see flashing lights behind us. No siren though, perhaps a deference to the local residents.

"Shit!" I exclaim.

"Just follow my lead," Carlos says.

A policeman leaves his car and walks up to ours. The presence of police has always caused me serious anxiety. More than they probably should in a civilized society. Even in a checkout line, when an armed officer saddles up beside me, my entire body tenses. I used to just be bothered by the guns, killing machines that rest so casually against their hips. Now, it's both the guns and the fact that I, apparently, routinely break the law.

Carlos rolls down his window and gives a sheepish smile.

"What are you two doing out here?" the officer asks, confirming that he saw neither the sign nor the crime.

"Oh, we were…"

And then Carlos does that thing that men can do; with just a tilt of his head and a guilty grin, he manages to communicate non-verbally (and without the awful hand gesture) that the reason we're there is because we're having intimate relations. I put my head in my hands in horror at his plan. But this plays as embarrassment so it works for the part. It's a good plan. The officer is sympathetic and lets us off with just a warning.

"See?" he says. "I did need you after all! If you weren't here, I'd be heading to jail. The cops here aren't fond of folks who aren't white."

"So… misogyny trumps racism?"

"It does tonight!"

We shake off the narrow escape and revel in our victory by playing the radio even louder on the way back to the house. When we disembark, he thanks me for the help. I glance at the stolen sign once more and start to worry that Carlos will forget about it. I don't want to explain its presence there, but also, I don't want Shane getting busted for having it. I don't know how that would happen exactly, but I'd rather not test the universe.

"Hey, don't keep that in Shane's truck for very long," I tell him.

"Sure," he says, and then gives me a knowing smile, amused by my concern. I roll my eyes in exasperation.

"Seriously! You can never say anything."

"I won't, I won't," he says. And the more he reassures me, the less confident I am. When he leaves, I'm quite sure I've set the timer on a bomb this evening.

I decide not to sleep in Shane and Matty's bed while they're gone. I want to, of course. But the bed is made so well and I'm not sure I can replicate the hospital corners. I sleep in the guest bedroom, fitfully due to my recurring nightmare. It's the same as always. I'm heading to the airport to travel to some undefined destination, but I just can't seem to get there. At first, I can't pack fast enough. Then, the car has trouble, and the flight has changed. And on and on and on, one obstacle after another. As always, I never make it to the plane.

When I wake up, however, I'm not just flush with anxiety. I have a fever and a runny nose. This feels like karma for all my snooping. Shane and Matty rely mostly on holistic solutions of herbs, oils, and the occasional colonic so it's unlikely I'll find any familiar looking cold medicine in the house. I search the medicine cabinets anyway though and find a prescription bottle for lithium made out to Matty. I know enough about the drug to know that it's a treatment for bipolar disorder. Finding this feels like a bigger violation than finding the vibrator and I hurriedly replace it back in the medicine cabinet.

I go to the kitchen to make myself a cup of green tea. As I'm making it, I consider this new information. It casts a different light on our casino outing and reframes my understanding of Matty. I don't think any less of her; if anything, I'm comforted by the fact that she's not perfect.

I take my tea, curl up in the den, and watch TV. I'm falling in and out of consciousness when I hear the sounds of someone coming in the house, followed a few minutes later by the sound of the toilet flushing. I assume it must be Carlos. But then it happens again a few minutes later.

As the designated house sitter, I know I have a responsibility to figure out what the hell is happening. I'm feverish and exhausted, however, and I want to believe I'm just having auditory hallucinations. But no, it's becoming clearer. There's a repeating pattern every ten minutes or so: the back door opens and closes, footsteps in the hall, toilet flushes, footsteps in the hall, back door opens and closes.

I pull myself up from the couch and walk through the empty house. When I get to the living room, I see through the windows that a group of people are gathered by the pool. From the camera equipment and lights, I know it's a film crew. What they're doing here, however, I have no idea. Shane and Matty didn't mention anything about a film shoot.

I put on my coat and shoes, and venture down the stone path that leads from the front door to the pool area. There, a bizarre scene unfolds. The pool cover has been removed and three toilets have been placed on the floor of the pool. Five more are lined up, presumably to be placed in the water too. And various people are hanging about dressed in swimsuits and covered with robes to keep warm.

Miraculously, I recognize someone in the crowd who happens to be the man in charge. Ellis, a British video artist, with whom I once discussed David Lynch in depth, is holding court. (To be fair, it might not be the sparkling conversation that sticks with me but the British accent. I love a British accent. We could have been talking about anything and I would likely remember him.)

Ellis is a commanding presence. He's tall, lean, and impeccably dressed, with angled features that could probably get him a modeling contract should he desire one. I'm relieved that I've met him already or I'd never get the courage to approach him. I'd simply squirrel away back to the den and pretend I never saw any of this.

"Ellis," I say, after weaving my way to him. He snaps his fingers and points at me. He recognizes me but can't come up with a name.

"Katie," I say, helping his memory.

"Right! Right! Fancy seeing you here."

"Ah. Well, I'm actually housesitting for Shane and Matty…"

He peers at me, waiting for more information, and I don't know what else to say. I don't want to ask, "Do they know you're here?" because that sounds accusatory. Shane and Matty probably do know that he's here. I'm probably the one out of the loop. And really, if Shane and Matty don't know, would they even care? I'm at a loss.

Finally, I settle on just getting more information. Later, I can try the number I have for Shane and Matty to see if they know anything about this.

"So… whatcha doin'?"

The question elates him, as if he was just waiting to explain his artistic concept to someone.

"The world is a toilet," he declares, his arm stretching out so that I can see, more clearly, his grand vision.

"A meditation on capitalism and the environment," he continues.

"So… quite literal, then," I say, before I can stop myself.

"What?" he asks, having not heard my critique.

"Nothing, nothing. So… you'll put the cover back on after you're done?" I ask, gesturing to the pool.

"Of course, love! Don't you worry," he assures me. And it works. I stop worrying. Because, of course, this is fine. Why wouldn't it be fine? This is their friend. Matty and Shane probably know all about it.

And besides, my fever is spiking and I'm feeling queasy.

I go back to the den to lay down, wondering if all that really happened or if I'm in a fugue state. But a few hours later, I get my answer when another person walks into the house. The footsteps don't stop at the bathroom like the others. The footsteps come right to the den. It's a woman I don't recognize.

"What's going on down by the pool?" she asks in a decidedly unfriendly tone.

Fuck.

I don't respond right away. Partly because I'm groggy as hell. Partly because the only thing I can think to say ("the world is a toilet") is not going to fly. But mostly, the reason I sit there in silence is because this woman kinda sucks. And rudeness always seems to shock me mute.

"Are you housesitting?" she follows up, even though I haven't answered her first question.

I nod because I might as well take the bullet that's heading my way. I'm too tired to move.

"I'm going to call Shane and Matty and see what's going on," she says before turning and leaving. It's not quite a threat but it feels like one and now I don't know what the fuck to do. I feel like I've done something wrong even though I'm quite sure I haven't. (At least, not in regard to *this*.) Nevertheless, it's like I'm being reported on for my very bad housesitting skills. And really, what if this woman, while clearly awful in demeanor, is correct in her assessment? Surely, someone housesitting should know all about a video shoot happening at said house. It doesn't seem like too much to ask. If someone else was housesitting for them, and I walked in and saw what she saw, would I be just as concerned? Just as protective? Maybe.

My thoughts are spinning. I lay down and try to breathe.

After a few minutes, I return to my original plan. I'll call Matty and Shane and try to explain my side before this woman gets the chance. I get up and go to the fridge, where the number has been placed. I try it from the kitchen phone, but I'm rebuked. They've forgotten to write down the country code. I could probably find it on the Internet but I'm too tired. I go and lay back down, planning to wait for them to call me.

That evening, Matty phones. She launches right in: "Hi, Katie! I just heard from Vicky. She said that there's a film crew down by the pool. What's going on?" The question is all bemusement and no hostility.

"It's Ellis," I say, hoping that will be enough and miraculously it is.

"Oh, Ellis!" she squeals, pleased that the mystery is solved, and all is apparently well.

"Yeah, Ellis," I repeat, because it feels good to say it again, to know that I'm not in trouble.

"What's he filming?"

"Something with toilets."

"Ha! Awesome. I'll call Vicky, let her know everything is fine. Everything else is fine, right?"

"Yeah. Everything's good. How is India?"

"Oh, it's amazing! I can't wait to make you laugh!"

"More than usual?"

"So much more! Alright, we'll talk soon. Love you," she says.

"Love you, too."

The film crew is there late into the night. I expect to see them (or least remnants of them) in the morning but there's no trace they were ever there. The covering on the pool is back in place, the toilets are gone, and everything is back to normal. Well, as normal as this

Consensual Scars

strange and wonderful place ever is.

Annie Marie Huber

Snowed In

Not long after Shane and Matty's return from what is now called Mumbai (RIP Bombay), we're cleaning up in the kitchen after dinner. Which I'm happy to report I helped to make, chopping vegetables as instructed. The more time I spend at their house, the more comfortable I'm becoming. I mean, I'm still on fire when in Shane's presence, don't get me wrong. But I'm not as anxious about taking up space.

This mild bit of confidence is tested when two of their friends burst through the kitchen door. They are opposites in appearance. He's at least sixty, tall, and skinny; she's in her thirties, shorter, and plumper. I don't recognize them, and it quickly becomes clear that we're foregoing any introductions. After the briefest of "hellos," they get to work as if on a mission from god.

The couple transforms the living room. They move the couches to make space for a card table and four chairs that they've brought with them. Their movements are so quick and efficient that they remind me of a well-executed scene change between acts. I don't know what's happening and no one tells me. I'm sure we're not going to be playing games as we never play games. (Shane finds them trivial.) I only begin to realize what's about to happen when the man starts lighting candles, and the woman starts burning sage. And then when the man places a board on the table, I know for sure. We're going to be connecting with spirits. Apparently, they have no interest in connecting with the living as they haven't acknowledged my presence at all, a fact I find a little offensive. Or maybe I'm just jealous that my time with Shane and Matty is now going to be shared not

Consensual Scars

just with the living but the dead as well.

In college, we played with Ouija boards on occasion. And while I think I have a normal balance of curiosity and skepticism, I'm not actually normal at all. As everyone walks to the table, my eyes start to water uncontrollably. Here's my quirk: Whenever I think or talk about the paranormal, I start to cry. It's like a weird allergic reaction to the topic, more a physical reaction than an emotional one. At least I *think* so. I can't explain it and I definitely don't want to try right now. I wipe the waterworks away and pretend that I'm fine. Fortunately, no one notices.

I haven't participated in a seance since my mom died and I don't want to now. The couple notices my presence. They're disappointed by it, their shoulders slightly slumping, but they dutifully look for another chair and rearrange the ones already set up. Matty pulls me along, trying her best to make me feel included. And because I can't voice any of my reticence, I sit down along with the others.

The board on the table isn't the Parker Bros. version. It's older and heavier with symbols I've never seen. We all place our fingers on a heart-shaped device. The man and woman take turns firing off questions and the device answers. (Is it moving of its own accord? Or is someone pushing it? Who knows?) If someone is pushing it, they're doing a lame job. Because it just lands, again and again, on the affirmative "Yes" on the top right of the board.

"Is someone here?"

Yes.

"Are you here for Matty?"

Yes.

"Are you a friend?"

Yes.

Then, Matty, somehow:

"Is it Audrey?"

Yes.

"Do you want to tell me something?"

Yes.

"Is it about the bridge?"

Yes.

Now, the man, somehow, "She's gone."

And then, without missing a beat, he begins again.

"Is someone here?"

Yes.

"Are you here for Shane?"

Yes.

And so, it continues. I'm wondering why there are any other symbols on the board other than the word "yes." I'm also wondering how the man and woman seem to know exactly who the spirit is here to see. Either they're gifted or the spirits are all there and are just politely taking turns as their names are called. I have no idea. All I know is that everyone else seems to know exactly *which* spirit is there to see them and what *exactly* they want to say. Which is either amazing or a great parlor trick and I can't decide. What I do know is that my turn is coming.

"Are you here to see…" and, of course, the man has no idea what my name is.

Matty assists. "Katie."

"… Katie?" he finishes.

Yes.

"Are you a friend?"

Yes.

I know this is my cue. I'm supposed to ask. Matty knows too, so she does it for me.

"Are you Katie's mom?"

Yes.

"Do you want to tell Katie something?"

Yes.

Again, it's my cue. I'm supposed to know what she wants to say. I'm not convinced it's real but what if it is? What if she's really here? But if she's here, shouldn't I know what she wants to say? What does it mean that I don't? I have to say something. Something innocuous that sounds deep, like "the bridge." (What the fuck is that about anyway?) But before I can think of anything, the man has moved on.

"She's gone."

And he's off and running again onto the next spirit in line. But those last words just hang in the air in front of me. She's gone. Yes, she's gone.

Tears sting my eyes, and my heart starts to pound. Invisible needles prickle across my body and my ears are ringing. I've got the cold sweats like I just came down with the flu this very second and everything is slipping out of focus. I'm vaguely aware of Shane taking my hand and leading me away from the group. We're walking down the hall and now I'm in the den on the couch with him at my side. I close my eyes.

"Focus on my voice," he softly says.

He sounds far away, but I do as he says. His voice, always the anchor.

"Nod if you can hear me."

I nod.

"Focus on my hands."

He's holding my hands. I can do that. I can focus on his hands.

"Squeeze them if you can feel me."

I squeeze his hands.

"Focus on your breath."

I don't want to switch my focus from him to me, but I do as he commands. I would do anything he says. I don't know how long we sit there but he never moves.

"When you're ready, open your eyes."

I open my eyes. His face is inches from mine and I'm not ready for that. I shut them again.

"It's alright. When you're ready," he repeats.

Another few minutes pass and I open my eyes again. This time, I'm prepared. Well, as prepared as I can be. We stare at each other for a moment and then he puts his hands on either side of my face, kisses my forehead, and says, "You had a panic attack."

I've never had a panic attack before. I'm not sure how to feel except embarrassed.

"I'm so sorry," I say.

He seems to be considering whether or not to say something. Choosing to proceed, he takes both my hands in his and says without reproach, "You apologize a lot. You don't need to do that. Please stop saying you're sorry. You have nothing to be sorry about."

I reflexively want to say "I'm sorry" for all my apologies but I manage to stop myself. Instead, I smile and agree to try to stop. And then I almost apologize again for keeping him from his friends.

"Have you had these before? A panic attack?" he asks.

"No."

"Hmm."

I feel like his patient, and I don't hate it. *Heal me.*

He's still holding my hands. I imagine bringing them to my lips. Maybe he can sense my desire because he looks down and lets go.

"You should go back to your…" I almost say "party" but that's obviously wrong. But he hears it too and picks it right up.

"… party?" he asks.

"Sorry."

"Hey."

"Right. Not sorry."

"Good. Want to hang out and watch TV? We'll be done soon."

I turn on the TV when he leaves. But after flipping through the stations, I realize I don't really want to watch anything. I want to try that breathing thing again. It's what I'm doing when Shane joins me.

"Nova and Ash just left."

So those are their names. Fittingly odd. I doubt I'll ever forget them now even if I don't know which is which. We've had a moment. Not a good one but a moment, nonetheless.

"I should go," I say. As always, it's just something I say.

"About that…"

"Yeah?"

He gestures for me to follow him, and I do. We walk into the garage where he opens the door. We can see my car in the pool of the exterior lights, and it's buried under, at least, eighteen inches of snow. I've been here much longer than Nova and Ash were, and it shows.

It's the first snow of the season, which is always a little wondrous. By February, we'll all be sick of it but not yet. The first snow is a baptism.

"You're not going anywhere," he says.

"Yes, sir."

He leads me back to the den. Matty joins us and we all watch TV together. Shane flips through the channels, eventually landing on an unfamiliar action movie. I never quite get the plot before falling asleep.

A little bit of snow is annoying. Too much snow can be incredible, provided you're in a place you can enjoy it with nothing on your docket. You can't plan for a snow day and that's part of its charm. Schools and businesses close and everything just kind of stops. As a child, I remember listening intently to the radio, waiting for the announcement that my school was closed for the day. Whenever it happened, it always felt like a mini-miracle, a gift from the universe, a day to play. It feels that way, even now.

I wander to the coffee-less kitchen. One day, I'm going to buy them a coffee maker. Or, at the very least, bring over some instant and hide it in the cabinet. It's a bright morning and the snow is still falling. I don't see anyone else up, except Sebastian who has come to me for attention and a chance to go outside. I let him out through the patio door and watch as he frolics in the fresh snow.

After I let Sebastian back inside, I leave the kitchen and quietly ascend the steps to the yoga studio. The studio has windows on three sides, giving an expansive view of the entire property. I can see Shane before reaching the top step, sitting cross-legged in front of one of the windows, facing east towards the sunrise. He's still and serene, clearly meditating. And I do what I do; I watch him. I wonder what secrets the universe is telling him.

I realize this is still a kind of stalking, which I'm trying to cut back on (along with all my other crimes), so I turn to leave as quietly as I can. Also, interrupting someone's meditation practice, I imagine, is not very cool. But the stairs squeak as I make my way down, ruining my stealth exit. I stop and cringe before squirreling away back to the kitchen. I feel like I've done something wrong. So, I look for something to do, some way to be a benevolent presence instead of a meditation-interrupting idiot. I decide to wash the dishes. That's helpful, right?

They have a dishwasher, but I have no idea how to use it. (We never had one growing up.) I don't mind the handwashing though because I like the comforting feel of the hot water on my skin. And the window above the sink is a vista of snow and barren trees. The activity calms me and before I can finish, Shane enters the kitchen.

He's rejuvenated and his voice is boisterous.

"Good morning!"

I try to match his enthusiasm in my greeting, but I can't. I'm not sure anyone could. Anyone without coffee, anyway.

"Want to go in the sauna?" he asks.

"You finished it?"

"Got it goin' a few days ago. Come on."

He leads me to the hall closet where he hands me a guest robe and a towel. I'm about to go find the swimsuit I've tucked into a corner of the guest room when he stops me.

"You can just wrap a towel around yourself. You don't need a swimsuit."

"Oh."

"I'm just saying…" – and here he must know he's flirting with me because he's got a wicked smile – "… it's gonna be really hot."

I go the guest room, get undressed, wrap the towel around me, and cover it with the robe. When I come out, he's dressed the same but with snow boots. The look is ridiculous but necessary. I retrieve my own boots and we walk down the snowy path that leads to the outdoor menagerie. The sauna is freezing at first but the small space heats quickly. Soon, I'm sweating and wondering about the appeal of this obvious torture device. I start feeling dizzy and tell Shane.

"Close your eyes."

I do.

"Focus on your breath."

I do.

After a few breaths, the dizziness passes, and the heat feels less oppressive.

"How do you do that?" I ask.

"*I* didn't do anything."

"So, what is this supposed to do for me?"

"The sauna?"

"Yeah."

"What do you want it to do?"

"Come on."

"Well, it can do a lot of things. For me, I like it because it feels good."

I'm dizzy again though not from the heat. I love his hedonism so much.

"What should we do today?" he asks.

"If I were a kid, I'd go sledding."

"Pass. I bet Matty would go sledding with you."

"Do you have a sled?"

"No."

I laugh. "So… sledding is out. What else can we do?"

I want him to say something flirty, something suggestive, but he doesn't.

"We can watch movies," he offers. "We can watch all the *Godfathers*. Or the Tarantino films you lent us that we never watched."

Be still my heart.

The day is spent in the dark den, watching ultra-violence that Matty shrieks at throughout. Every disgusted response elicits eruptions of laughter from Shane and me.

"I don't know how you guys can like this," she says.

"You need to be more stoned," I say, passing the pipe to her. "It'll help."

She's game. It seems to help as she starts to find the funny. We watch three movies (*Reservoir Dogs*, *Pulp Fiction*, and *True Romance*) before moving to the kitchen to make dinner.

"What are we making?" I ask.

We. Life is good.

"I thought we'd try to make that curry we had in India," Shane answers, already pulling out ingredients.

"Oooh, good idea," Matty says.

I realize I should call my dad and let him know where I am. One of the inconveniences of living at home as an adult. I borrow their phone and make the call.

"Hey, dad. Just wanted to let you know I'm fine. Not sure when I'll be home. Kinda snowed in with my friends."

"Oh. Thanks. Damn snowplow's blocked me in again."

"I'm sorry." Why am I apologizing? I didn't plow the damn snow.

"That asshole does this every time," he continues.

"I know."

<disgruntled grumble>

"Well, I'll probably be home tomorrow."
"Okay."
<awkward silence>
"Bye."
"Bye."

My mom and I would have talked for twenty minutes. And I'm pretty sure we would have laughed too.

"Tell me what to do," I say to Matty and Shane.

Shane puts a peeler in my hand then places a few sweet potatoes near the cutting board. "Peel and cube these."

I do as I'm told, chopping a little aggressively.

"You alright?" Matty asks.

"Yeah. My dad is pissed off. He's been having a feud with the city for at least a decade. The snowplow dumps all the snow right at our driveway so we can't get out."

"What started the feud?" Shane asks.

"Our house is at the end of a cul-de-sac. It's just over a quarter mile from the road where the school bus stopped. My dad didn't want me walking all that way to the bus stop, so he researched the city ordinance and actually measured the distance. I remember him out there with a tape measure. He complained and the school bus had to come closer to pick me up. Someone at the city was obviously annoyed by his tenacity."

"That's pretty great," Matty says. Shane nods his agreement.

"It was a little humiliating."

"But it was to keep you safe," Shane counters.

They're right, of course. How annoying.

"We should enjoy a fire tonight," Matty suggests as she opens a bottle of red wine.

"You want me to make a fire?" Shane asks.

"Hon?" she asks him in a sweet voice.

"Yeah?"

"Can you make us a fire tonight?"

"Yes, dear."

They're so fucking cute. I love their cuteness even as it kills me.

After dinner, Shane makes the fire while Matty and I bring our wine glasses to the living room. We sit on the opposite couches, facing each other. I ask Matty about the laughing yoga in India.

"What was that like?"

"Oh, it's amazing. Want me to show you?"

"Yes."

And then, like a magician, she makes me laugh. Softly at first, then so hard that I feel like my chest is going to burst. How does she do it? By simply laughing. A false chuckle quickly turns into genuine roars that are inescapably contagious. I'm amazed.

"That was crazy," I say, still gasping for breath, tears streaming down my face.

"I know! I love it. I need to teach a class in it."

"For sure."

Once the fire is going, Shane joins Matty on the couch.

"Do you have holiday plans?" Matty asks, now calmer and sipping her wine.

"Jonathan is coming."

"That's right!" Matty remembers. "I can't wait to meet him."

"He'll be here during the quiet week," I say, using the term that Jonathan and I coined ages ago.

"The quiet week?" Shane asks. I almost clarify but he's already figured it out.

"You mean the week between Christmas and New Year's."

"Yeah."

"I love that. The quiet week."

His approval delights me.

"And what about your dad?" Matty asks.

"What about my dad?"

"Will you two be doing anything for the holidays?"

"I don't know. My mom did all that stuff, you know? The tree, the presents, the food."

"Do you want to do any of that?"

"No."

I answer so fast, so honestly, that we all laugh.

"What are your plans?" I ask, hoping to be invited to some kind of festivity at their house. They don't have any holiday decorations up though so maybe they don't even celebrate.

"We have some parties we usually go to," Matty says.

I'm jealous, of course. Not of the party invites but of their friends who get their company.

"Oh, you should come along!"

If I go, I will probably stand in a corner by myself, too intimated to speak. But it's a sacrifice I'll make to be near them. And then Matty has another idea.

"Oh, she can meet James!" she says enthusiastically to Shane.

Oh no.

Shane smiles because, obviously, they've had this conversation before.

"James is so gorgeous," she continues. "You have to meet him."

I know there are a lot of terrible things in the world. However, having the wife of the man you covet try to set you up really must be high up on the list.

"James is great," Shane says, looking directly at me. I can tell he's teasing me, reveling in my discomfort which, ironically, comforts me.

"At least come to the New Year's Eve party," Matty insists.

"Sure," I say, just to get out of the conversation. I will come up with some excuse later.

As the wine gets drained, Matty gets frisky. I watch as she squeezes Shane's knee, hinting at what awaits him in their bedroom tonight. He gets the hint quickly and soon we're all saying goodnight.

Matty leaves to get me some pajamas and toiletries I can use tonight. When she's out of the room, Shane gives me a hug and a fleeting, friendly kiss on the lips before retreating to their bedroom. Then Matty returns with the items. She hands them over and does the exact same thing as her husband: hug, kiss, retreat.

Once I'm alone, I get a cigarette from my bag and open the sliding patio door. I position myself in the entryway so I can blow the smoke outside while staying warm and dry. Shane would be horrified by this, insisting I get my ass all the way outside. But I do it anyway, channeling my bad girl. A naughty girl with naughty thoughts.

The snow has finally stopped, and the world is so quiet. I try to appreciate it because I have a sense that things are about to change. Nothing this good can last. I put out my cigarette, discarding the stub in the kitchen trash can. I take the pajamas and toiletries to the hallway. I stop and listen, but I only hear the faintest of indecipherable noises.

Standing here between their bedroom door and the guest bedroom door, I feel like I'm in a demented game show:

Behind one of these doors are treasures beyond compare!
Behind the other is a night of aching desire!
Choose!

I know which one I'll pick but it doesn't make it any less agonizing when I step inside. It's a lovely room with all the amenities a guest could want. It's a room I'm grateful to occupy. Now, if I can just get rid of the feeling that I'm being punched in the gut repeatedly... well, that would be fan-fucking-tastic.

Annie Marie Huber

Jonathan

As the holidays barrel towards me, I think a lot about my response to the question Matty posed. Do I want to do any of the things my mom did? My blunt response ("no") is absolutely true. But is it *right*? I mean, shouldn't I at least try? What would my mom want? Shouldn't that be a consideration too? I respect the hedonism but there's also karma to consider, right?

I end up trying a little.

I venture to the garage and retrieve the boxes of holiday decorations. When I was little, we'd go as a family to cut down a Christmas tree. But my father's steady stream of swear words throughout the process was finally enough for my mom to invest in an artificial tree. I manage to put up the tree and decorate it by myself while my father reads the paper in the kitchen. (Decorating was never part of his domain.) I put on *A Charlie Brown Christmas* because it was my mom's favorite. He comes into the living room and nods his approval before retreating to his bedroom. I'd feel better about my effort if I couldn't see the tears in his eyes. Lately, his sudden bursts of rage have been replaced by a consistent melancholy. Or, maybe, like Shane theorized, the anger was just a disguise all along.

On Christmas morning, my father and I exchange a few gifts, continuing our custom of buying each other presents we will most likely never enjoy or use.

Shane and Matty are busy with their own holiday plans, so I spend a lot of my time at the Foxhole, meeting friends from high school that have returned home for the holidays. The scene is strange as we're

Consensual Scars

all finally old enough to drink legally together. We catch up and reminisce but it's clear nothing is the same as it once was. Our lives have veered down different directions, theirs punctuated by milestones like engagements and career advancements. By just being here still, I feel like the loser of the group. (No one would *say* this, obviously. I know it's all in my head. As Shane would say, "it's a story you're telling yourself.") I don't mention Shane and Matty to my old friends except in reference to my job. I don't want to share them with anyone except Jonathan.

The day after Christmas is when Jonathan arrives, bursting through the front door of my father's house. I thought I'd have to pick him up, so his sudden entrance surprises me. I run to him, and we bear hug. He picks me up off the floor and spins me around, my legs twirling. We're both yelling our greetings.

"I missed you!"

"I missed you too!"

"I thought I was gonna have to pick you up!"

"Emily's not workin' tonight. I borrowed her car. I *miss* driving."

"You could get a car."

"Fuck that."

Jonathan turns to my dad who's sitting in his recliner. "Hey, Papa!"

"Hi, Jonathan." My dad smiles. He can't help it.

"Ready to go?" I ask Jonathan, who rolls his eyes at my eagerness.

"Down, girl. Yeah, I'm ready."

Jonathan and I leave and get into his mother's blue Pontiac. I don't recognize the thumping beats that blare out from the speakers. I give him directions to Matty and Shane's house, shouting over the music. He parks the car in their driveway next to Shane's truck. Before we go inside, I give him a tour of the property like it's my adopted homeland. I show him the sheep, the pool, the recently added sauna, and the hot tub.

"Tell me we're going in there," he says, indicating the hot tub.

"Sure," I say, as if it's my right to do so.

"Do I need a bathing suit?" he asks.

"Not at all."

As for me, I always wear a swimsuit. Shane and Matty always go in the hot tub brazenly naked while I try to nonchalantly avert my eyes, looking for the line between pervert and prude.

In high school, Jonathan would have wanted a suit too. But since coming out during his first year of college, he has discovered his tribe's true religion. Which is to say he goes to the gym. A lot. And all the insecurity he harbored in his youth has since fallen away as has any leftover baby fat. His 6'2" frame is now lean and muscular. And the curly, blond locks atop his flawless face could rival the cutest member of a boy band. Traveling with Jonathan now is like hitching a ride from a unicorn. People notice.

We go inside without knocking and I announce our arrival on the way to the living room. It's a perfect tableau; Shane and Matty are lounging on a single couch facing one another. He's rubbing her feet, the fireplace is lit, and ethereal music plays in the background.

Jonathan and I sit on the couch opposite Matty and Shane. I make quick introductions, which aren't really necessary as I've talked them all up to one another for the past few months.

"That's a gorgeous sweater. Is that cashmere?" Matty asks Jonathan.

"Oh! Thanks! Yeah."

I hadn't noticed the cream-colored sweater.

"Let me guess. Was that a Christmas present from Fat Cat Jack?" I ask Jonathan.

"You know it."

"Who's Fat Cat Jack? Your sugar daddy?" Matty asks, eyes wide with interest.

"Ha! No, my sugar daddy is Paul, but we're kinda over. Fat Cat Jack is Jack Monroe the third. My grandfather."

"He's well-off?" Shane asks.

"Very."

"What's he like?" Matty asks.

"No idea. Never met him."

"Really?"

"Really. There's a bit of a family feud between my dad and my grandfather. I just assume it's because the sperm donor is a dick."

I know it's more than that. The reason the wealth is skipping a generation is because Jonathan's father, though very much an asshole, had the audacity to marry a cocktail waitress. Jonathan knows this truth too but if he acknowledges it, he'll have to take off the sweater in solidarity with his mother.

"Anyway, when I got to college, I started getting gifts." He turns to me and asks, "Did I tell you he gave me a Rolex for graduation?"

"And you're not wearing it?" I tease.

"Oh, honey. It's gold and hideous. What do you think I could get for it?"

I laugh. "Like I'd know."

He turns to Shane. "Wanna buy a Rolex?"

"I don't wear watches. I don't want to be tied to time like that, you know?"

Jonathan pauses to take that in, and I have a brief flash to a memory. A discussion about timing. What was that all about? Oh yeah. Timing is everything.

"Want some wine?" Matty offers us.

"Well, actually, I brought us a little something," Jonathan answers, indicating me as the other part of "us." He digs around in his messenger bag and produces two brown bags, each one containing a bottle of Boone's Farm, the cheap and terrible alcohol choice of our college years.

"Oh my god! Strawberry Hill!" I shout, pointing out the flavor we drank the most. "But we're not really going to drink these, are we?"

"I thought we'd take a few sips for nostalgia and then switch to something better." We unscrew the tops (fancy!), toast, and drink directly from the bottles. Shane and Matty watch the ritual.

"Oh, wow," I say. "That takes me back. Now can we have real wine?" I ask Matty. She insists on tasting the cheap stuff first, declaring it tastes like a "lollipop."

"Ew," Shane says, rightfully horrified.

"No, it's good!" Matty argues. "I might have to put some of this in a glass."

"That bottle is all yours," I tell her.

We all move to the kitchen where Matty distributes red wine in ornate stemware, the kind I vow to own someday, while gamely holding onto the Boone's bottle. We toast and Jonathan launches into a story.

"I was planning to be here yesterday for the actual holiday, but my roommate decided to throw a party last night. I had to stick around to protect my stuff. Lock my room, you know, because whenever he has a party, it's mayhem. He works at a restaurant and yesterday, I hear that he's handing out food along with our fucking address. Like, 'here's your tuna melt... *and* there's a party tonight!' So, I've got all these random people at my place last night. And this morning, they're all still there! Half-naked, hungover strangers everywhere."

"Sounds like a great party!" Shane interrupts.

"Getting them out is like herding cats," Jonathan continues. "But I *finally* get them out. Then I need to clean up cause shit is a mess, right? My CDs are everywhere, and they were using them as fucking *coasters!*"

"I think you need a new roommate," Matty says.

"Oh, I definitely do," he says, while directing a look at me.

"What?" I ask, as if I don't know where this is heading.

"Come *on*. Move to Chicago. Get out of here! I can float you until you get a job!"

Surprise registers on Matty's face. "You're not leaving, are you?"

"I have no plans at all," I say. Inside, I register just how depressing that fact is. I should have *some* plans. Jesus. But before I can slip into internal dread, Jonathan interrupts my thoughts.

"So, when do we get in that hot tub?"

Minutes later, we're all soaking in the hot tub and as expected, I'm the only one in a bathing suit. But that's not what's making me uncomfortable. No, it's the questions that Matty is asking Jonathan about me. And, in particular, my nonexistent love life.

"She won't tell us anything," Matty explains.

"There's nothing to tell," I say for what feels like the millionth time.

"There's really not," Jonathan confirms.

If it's possible, I'm both humiliated and relieved at his confirmation. Humiliated because of the general population's collective lack of interest in me and relieved that there's no dirt to share. Matty can't let it go.

"Wait... are you a virgin?" she asks.

Kill me now. I close my eyes and hope to disappear.

Jonathan saves me. "So, you're a yoga teacher?" he asks Matty.

Consensual Scars

As they engage in conversation, their voices get lower and drowned out by the jets. I look at Shane who is staring at me, one eyebrow raised ever so slightly. It's not a lecherous gaze but a curious one, as if I've just unveiled a bizarre hidden talent. All I've really done is be unattractive to others. Not really a skill set there, I think. But boys (and apparently men) see the situation differently. The primal need for discovery is alive and well in them. I try to tune back into Matty and Jonathan.

"And what about you," Matty asks Jonathan. "Are you seeing anyone?"

"Not seriously, no."

"But you're dating?" she continues.

"Oh, sure. We can call it that."

Shane laughs but Matty is confused. "What do you mean?" she asks.

"It means he's fucking," Shane clarifies.

"Really?" Matty asks Jonathan.

"Pretty much," confirms Jonathan.

"Be careful, love," I say.

"I'm always careful, baby." I don't need to say it. He is always careful. We used to keep a candy bowl of condoms in our apartment right on the living room coffee table.

Matty and Jonathan decide we need more drinks. They get out of the hot tub and head to the kitchen, leaving Shane and me. In all the time we've spent in the hot tub, we've never been in here alone. Every cell in my body is suddenly alert. After all, most of my fantasies start just like this.

I'm really hoping he doesn't say anything because I'm not sure my mouth will work. But, of course, he does. And he does so in a voice too low to hear over the jets. I look at him and shake my head, trying to indicate in a non-verbal way that I have no earthly idea what he's said. So, he moves closer, taking the seat right next to mine.

He leans toward my ear. "Hey," he says.

"Hey."

"I would miss you if you went to Chicago," he says. "But it's a good offer. Chicago is definitely more exciting than here."

My body begs to differ.

"Would you two make good roommates?" he asks.

"We were roommates in college. So, yes. Even if he is really persnickety." Oh man, did I just say that? He's not going to let that go.

"Persnickety?" he teases.

"Shut up. I'm a Hoosier." He laughs.

"And he practically lived at my house in high school," I continue.

"Was his house… safe?" It's such an insightful question and I'm impressed.

"Safe, yes. Happy? Sometimes. His mom tries. She doesn't care that he's gay. But his dad…"

"The sperm donor?"

"Yes! The sperm donor."

"And your dad? If he was staying at your house, was your dad okay with it?"

"Jonathan charmed his way in."

"I can see that. It's wild he's never met his grandfather."

"Right? These gifts make me a little nervous."

"Why?"

"I feel like Fat Cat Jack is making some sort of trail, you know? Tempting him."

"Tempting him to do what?"

"Who knows? Rich people are weird."

"How many rich people do you know?"

"None."

We laugh. "'He is richest who is content with the least,'" he quotes.

"Ghandi?" I ask, offering up my best guess.

"Socrates."

"Damn. One day, I'm gonna guess right."

"But fuck Socrates. I'd be good with being rich," he declares.

"Oh, you'd be great at being rich," I agree, thinking about his propensity for pleasure. "You'd probably build a zoo or something."

"No, no. Zoos are bad."

Shit. *Of course*, zoos are bad. Why did I say that? He doesn't seem to care about my political incorrectness though as he's still lost in the possibilities.

"I would build *something* though."

No doubt.

"What about you?" he asks. "What would you do if you were rich?"

"I guess… whatever I want."

He winks at me. "Good girl."

Annie Marie Huber

Small Town Strike

The next day, Jonathan and I take our customary drive around town down memory lane. We drive by the abandoned building that was our high school. ("Remember when Donna was dancing during *Anything Goes* and her shoe flew off into the audience?") We drive past our favorite teacher's house (Ms. Jenkins, our appropriately dramatic drama instructor) where we used to leave notes to amuse her. And finally, we drive past the greatest landmarks of our youth, the sites of the "massage parlors."

I don't know if it's a quirk of Lake City or a feature of many places across America, but our little town had six of these establishments. Six! That seems like a lot in a place without a single café. I sometimes wonder what the ratio was of massage parlors to churches.

We knew they weren't just giving massages. We'd try to confirm this theory for own petty amusement by periodically daring one another to gain entry. It wasn't easy. The stoned woman running the front desk (there was always a stoned woman at the front desk) wouldn't let just anyone pass through the beaded curatains. (Not until recently have I felt any empathy for these women, who may or may not have chosen to be there.)

One restless teenage night, we dug out a Halloween costume to see if a disguise would help our mission. Could I get past the curtain in a nun outfit? With my friends waiting in the car, I walked through the front door into the tiny lobby. The woman behind the desk, dressed in a flowered kimono, looked at me in a familiar haze.

"Please, ma'am. May I use your bathroom?"

"Uh... uh..."

Usually, she'd shoo me out, but the costume has her hesitant.

"Please?" I beg.

She gives in, waving her arm. "This way, this way..."

"Bless you." I hold my hands together in prayer and do a little bow.

She lets me into the inner sanctum and walks me down a hallway of many doors. The only open one is to the bathroom. I walk in and close the door behind me. It's surprisingly clean. I do a cursory search that turns up a half-used bottle of lubricant. Ew. I wrap it in paper towels. Then, I lift the disguise and slide the lotion into the pocket of my hoodie. I flush the toilet and walk out. The woman escorts me back to the front. When I join my friends in the waiting car, I lift the tube in victory as if it's a trophy.

Since we've been at college, the spas have all quietly closed and are now vacant storefronts. This tends to prove our suspicions though we were never privy to any legal actions taken.

As we drive around today, Jonathan critiques the barren surroundings of our youth.

"This town sucks."

"Yup."

"We should drink."

"Yup."

We go to a chain restaurant for drinks where we order fruity concoctions like the ones I made while bartending. And one second after the drinks are set in front of us, he stares at me with eyebrows raised as if waiting for an explanation.

"What?" I ask, pretending I don't know what's coming.

"Well, I think your obsession might be getting worse."

"Is it that obvious?"

"Yes. I mean, Matty can't see it because she loves you."

"I love her."

"Complicated shit," he says with a shake of his head.

I raise my glass in a toast. "To complicated shit," I say, clinking my glass to his.

"But you should be careful. You do look at him like Mary looks at Jesus in *Superstar*."

"Of course, I do. I worship him."

"I worship her," Jonathan says, referring to Matty. "Well, not worship. But she's cool as fuck."

"Matty's great," I concur.

"Really great."

"Really, really great."

"You're fucked."

"I know."

"Maybe you can be their concubine?" he suggests.

"What exactly is a concubine?"

"I'm not sure but I'm pretty sure you'd get to fuck him."

I close my eyes and shake my head in defeat because that's exactly what I want.

"But I don't know. As a concubine you might have to fuck her too," he continues, unabated. "I'm not sure about the rules."

Something to think about.

"Or you could just be the other woman. Less eccentric, more conventional," he continues.

"So how was your time with the fam?" I ask, changing the topic.

"The usual. My mom tried to make it special, and my dad did the opposite."

"Ah, dads."

"Your dad's not so bad. He's just not warm and fuzzy."

He's right. I'll take my dad over his any day of the week.

I haven't drunk much since coming home and while I keep up with Jonathan drink-for-drink, I'm losing when it comes to sobriety. We start down another road of "remember when's" and before long, we're laughing so hard that tears are streaming down our faces. We're loud but Jonathan has already charmed our server enough that we can probably dance on the table without reproach.

When I catch my breath I ask, "Don't you think it's a little sad to be so nostalgic about events that happened just four years ago?"

"No. Those were good times. We should remember them."

I nod because he's right. We should remember for as long as we can.

"I don't think those two guys over there are having a good time," Jonathan says, looking over my shoulder. Jonathan is a people-watch-er, always noticing everyone, which might be a trauma-informed response. Me on the other hand? I never seem to notice anything not within a three-feet radius around me. Which also might be a response to trauma. Who knows?

"Now don't look over there too obviously…" Jonathan says, teeing me up to do what he knows I'll do, which is immediately look over my shoulder in the most obvious of manners. It's an old joke but one we do well; when I turn abruptly to stare, Jonathan puts his head in his hands in mock horror.

The two people he's pointed out, however, are not as amused by our behavior as we are. Two guys our age, dressed in preppy polo shirts, white ball caps, and baggy jeans, are scowling at us.

"Ignore them," I say, because that's what we do with fools.

"The jocks that never left home," Jonathan says.

"Hey, I haven't left here either."

"You went to college. You're just taking a break right now. You're not gonna live here forever. I simply won't allow it. Even if you have met the two coolest people in this shitty, little town."

"I can't move to Chicago with you."

"Why not?"

"Because what would I do there exactly?"

He scoffs. "You'll get a job."

"You should live alone. No one can fuck with your stuff if you live alone."

"I don't want to live alone. I want to live with you."

I take a moment to sit with that, the idea of being wanted.

The two guys walk by our booth as they leave the restaurant. Once they pass us, Jonathan shakes his body to rid himself of their negative energy. We finish our third cocktail, which has left me tipsy, and ask for the check. The check arrives and Jonathan picks it up before I can say a word.

As soon as we walk outside, we break into hysterical laughter. While we were in the restaurant, the light snowfall became a winter storm. Cars are buried under at least a foot of snow, with more still coming down. The wind is whipping around us.

"Holy shit!" Jonathan yells. "That happened fast."

I'm a little unsteady, the icy road exasperating the effects of the alcohol. I grab his hand and we venture toward the cars.

"I don't even know which one is mine!" I exclaim. This makes us explode into more giggles, doubling over.

"Hey, faggot!"

And then two figures, made blurry by the storm, approach us. One of them has a baseball bat. I'm knocked on my ass, his boot in my face. Screaming, laughing, then nothing.

I'm lying in a hospital room. I wake up with a doctor attending to me. Tubes are connected to my arm. Thoughts are slippery and I can't catch them. Something happened. Something bad and… what was it? When I try to remember any details, I get nowhere. It's like I've blacked out, but I never black out. My memory, while terrible with names and faces of other people, is usually excellent when it comes to everything that *I* say and do. (It's an unfortunate curse since what I remember most are the things I'd most like to forget.)

I conclude that I must have been knocked unconscious.

The doctor is talking, and I'm trying to make sense of his words.

"You're in the ER. Do you know what happened?"

"Not really…"

"You were attacked. Right now, we have you on a morphine drip for the pain."

Pain? I don't feel any pain. Well, that's probably *because* of the morphine drip. The doctor asks me about my vision. I assure him it's fine.

"You may have a concussion. You've got some bruises and we're going to do a few x-rays to see if anything's broken."

And with that, the doctor leaves. I want to stop him. There's a question I need to ask. But I can't get it out, can't piece it together. If only I can remember. And then another wave.

Jonathan.

Oh god, Jonathan! My eyes well up as possibilities race through my mind. I close my eyes. Breathe. Just breathe. Time passes but I can't tell if it's hours or minutes. When a nurse returns to my room, I ask the question.

"Jonathan? My friend? How is he?"

"I don't know," she says reflexively. Seeing my face, she softens.

"But I can find out for you. Now let's get some x-rays. Are you able to stand and get into the wheelchair?"

I realize again that I'm not in any physical pain. While my brain is lagging, my body can move. I get up from the bed and sit down in the wheelchair. While she wheels me to the x-ray area, I look around and search for Jonathan. I don't see him, only curtains that protect the patients from curious eyes.

I'm still trying to focus on my breathing but now all I can think about is the smell. I know this odor, this aroma of disinfectant mixed with terror, and it's everything bad. I want to be anywhere else but there is nowhere else. This ER is suddenly the whole world, where the best of us try to solve the problems caused by the worst of us.

The X-rays are negative. I'm bruised but nothing is broken. I know I should take a moment for gratitude, but I have a sole focus now. Where is Jonathan? Is he alive? As I lie in the hospital bed, waiting for discharge instructions and paperwork, my father walks into the room. I'm briefly amazed at how, while everything is so obviously spinning out of control, someone, somewhere, managed to contact my father.

He settles into a chair next to the bed.

"How ya doin'?" he asks in a way that wants to sound unserious, and by doing so, will make the situation unserious by the transitive property.

"I'm okay, I think. I just want to know about Jonathan. I was with Jonathan when…" I trail off, not sure how to put into words what happened. My father craves ways to feel useful, especially in time of crisis, and jumps at the task.

"I'll try to find out," he says and almost runs from the room. He's only gone for a moment when two policemen take his place.

"Hi. Katie, is it?" The older officer is talking, a man with silver hair and a sizable gut hanging over his belt. His tone is one of disinterested boredom, like he's got one foot into his pension. The other officer is much younger, likely just out of the academy.

"I'm Officer Taylor. This is Officer Carter," the older officer continues. "Can you tell us what happened?"

"I was hoping you'd tell me," I say. I'm not ready to commit to anything. Everything is still too fuzzy.

"You were attacked," the older officer says. It's a statement but sounds a little like a question, like he's just not sure whether such a thing can be believed, no matter the evidence of my bruises right in front of him.

"We were attacked," I correct.

"Right, right," he acknowledges. "Do you know by who?"

Fuck. I hadn't even considered this. But of course, the police didn't show up during the assault. They showed up after. Which means these assholes are still out there somewhere, a contingency that has me suddenly feeling nauseous. I get up and kneel in front of a trash can just in time for the rising bile to leave me. I vomit whatever's in my stomach, which I'm grateful isn't much at all. When I return to the bed, I try to tell them what I know.

"There were two guys. One had a baseball bat."

"Yeah, that's what you told us at the scene," the younger officer says. This is news to me. I was talking at the scene? I wasn't unconscious?

"What did I tell you at the scene?"

"You don't remember?"

"No."

"Well, you were pretty upset before you got into the ambulance," the older cop shares, because apparently my hysteria is the real story. I try to put my frustration with the obvious misogyny aside and instead grab another piece of the puzzle.

"I got in the ambulance... on my own?"

"Yeah."

"I don't remember that." The officers shrug as if this is no big deal. But it feels like a huge deal to me, that my body and brain can act so independently of one another. Apparently, my brain can just defensively decide not to process specific events because they are just too much. It feels like a superpower, one I wish I could harness and apply at will. It would have come in handy at my mom's funeral. Unfortunately, right now, it's doing more harm than good.

"Let us know if you remember anything else," Officer Taylor states while handing me his card. And with that, they're gone and I'm doubtful that I'll ever see them again.

I'm released from care, but we don't leave. My father and I both sit in the ER waiting room. The staff won't share anything with us as we're not officially family, so we're waiting for Jonathan's mother to arrive. She's probably being tracked down in the casino, in that same magical way the staff tracked down my father.

When her petite frame comes through the automatic door, it's like a bullet-train. Her body is all determined energy. It's only when I get close enough that I can see the panic in her eyes.

"Emily..." I say to let her know we're here.

"Katie... Gene..." she says, acknowledging me and my father. "What happened? Is he okay?"

I try to find the words to answer at least her first question, but I can't. My father leads her to the front desk while I sit back down to wait for answers.

"They're getting someone," Emily says, returning with my father.

They sit on either side of me. Finally, a doctor walks through the interior, electric doors and walks to the front desk. He's tall and lean, with a ponytail that makes him look a little younger and a little hipper than he probably is. The receptionist points us out and he approaches.

"Mrs. Monroe?"

Emily nods and he sits next to us. He takes a deep breath and dives in. "I'm Dr. Hayes. Your son has two cracked ribs, a fractured tibia bone, and a head injury. It's the head injury that we're most concerned about. It's caused a subdural hematoma. Do you know what that means?"

Emily nods and responds. "His brain is bleeding."

"There's a buildup of blood in the brain caused by the injury," he nods while explaining further. "It's a slow bleed, which means it could stop on its own. We're monitoring him now. If it gets worse, we'll have to go in to relieve the pressure. The good news is he's young, strong, and healthy."

"And the bad news?" Emily asks. She's fearless. I don't think I've ever asked anyone for the bad news. In fact, I try to widen that gap between knowing and not knowing for as long as possible. My life is one long Schrodinger's cat experiment.

"We'll cross that bridge when we come to it," he answers.

"Can I see him?"

"Not yet, but we'll let you know as soon as it's possible."

Emily nods. The doctor takes her hand and squeezes.

"Hang in there. I'll be back as soon as I can."

And with that, the three of us continue to wait. I'm convinced that the ER is a level of hell. The interminable waiting, the uncertainty, the fear, that terrible smell. All thoughts and no distractions. Thoughts that tend toward memories. I've been in this ER a handful of times before. Once when I was twelve and broke my wrist. Another time when my dad had chest pains that were determined to be caused by a mix of stress and indigestion. And the last time, when I came through the entryway to find my dad waiting for me. Just a little too late. Tears are starting down my face and I try to focus my energy on anything else. Not long after I've counted the number of floor tiles (1685), Emily tells us that she needs a cigarette. "You want one?" she asks.

I nod and we leave the waiting room together to find a smoking section outside. It's dark out and I realize I have no idea what time it is or even what day it is. She tries to light her cigarette, but her hand is shaking too much. She hands it to me to help. We lock eyes and I realize I still haven't answered her question. She still doesn't know what happened. But our shared look is like telepathy.

"How did this happen? How did he get hurt? I don't understand. You were with him?" She fires the questions at me, and I'm momentarily stunned.

She's angry though I can tell not at me. Still, I step back and tell her what I can remember which isn't much. Parking lot, two guys, a baseball bat. Everything is still just flashes in my mind so my retelling, I'm sure, sounds as jumbled as my memories.

"But why?" she asks again.

It's a fair question to ask and I know the answer because I can hear an echo of the word "faggot." But I can't repeat this to Emily. Saying it aloud will make me nauseous again. Fortunately (or unfortunately), I don't need to. She reads my expression, and a sickening understanding takes shape across her face, like a curtain closing across a stage. She knows why it happened. And now there's a line in her life, between knowing and not knowing, between before and after.

"Do you know who they were?" she asks.

"No."

"Do you remember what they look like?"

Not only do I have no idea who they are, I can't even picture them. Nameless, faceless boys in hats, that's what I have in my useless memory. When am I going to stop focusing on myself and start paying attention to the world around me?

I haven't answered her yet, but she takes my silence as the "no" that it is.

"It doesn't matter. I'm gonna find them. And I'm gonna kill them," she says.

I believe her.

Annie Marie Huber

Branded

Doctor Hayes finds us in the waiting room a few hours later. The bleeding hasn't abated, and Jonathan is being prepped for surgery. Jonathan's father arrives and the vibe shifts from just devastating to devastating and awkward. His once-thin-frame is now defined by a beer belly. He's scruffy with a two-day old beard like he's been in this crisis much longer than the two minutes he's been here. He nods an acknowledgement to my father and I, then sits and talks in hushed tones with Emily. My father, ever practical, sees his arrival as an escape for us and convinces me to go back home with him for a few hours to eat and rest as the doctor has recommended. We won't know anything for hours. I tell Emily that I'll be back soon and to call me at my father's house if she needs anything.

The events of the night have felt endless but the clock in the car is telling me it's 2am. The snow has stopped falling and the main roads have already been plowed. For a moment, I feel bad for the kids that won't get a snow day. But then I see the holiday lights on the houses we pass and remember that it's Christmas break. Every thought feels like a re-orientation of sorts.

The house is dark and quiet when we arrive. I go first to the bathroom to wash my face and brush my teeth, to do something that feels normal. I go to my room and lay down on the bed.

Rest doesn't come. Instead, flashes of memory keep dripping in like water though a broken roof, slow but insistent. I want to stop them, but the effort is futile. They feel like visions more than memories, like premonitions I should warn myself about if I could travel back in time. There's no context, no chronology, no dialogue. Just moments. Flashing lights on a police car. Medical equipment in the ambulance. Jonathan bleeding. And with this flood of disjointed visions is a gnawing sensation that what I should be remembering (what I *need* to be remembering) is outside my grasp.

My heart starts racing and I give up on sleep. My father has gone to bed and the house is quiet, so he doesn't notice when I take his car keys and leave. It's the middle of the night and there's nowhere to go, which is fine since I only want to drive. At least, that's my conscious thought. But my body clearly has other instincts as I arrive at Shane and Matty's house. I park far enough away so they won't hear the car. I don't intend to go in as I don't want to bring any of this to them. But I want to be near them.

I start to feel dizzy, probably due to exhaustion. I get out to feel the cold, to wake me up. The house is completely dark, encircled by a vista of fresh snow. I want to see the sheep. I want to be *like* the sheep. A thick protection of wool to deal with the elements, with the world. As I trudge up to the pen, I trip over my own feet and land in a deep pile of snow. The cold seeps right through my jeans and soon I'm soaked. And then Sebastian starts barking.

Fuck. I get up and start back to the car but not before the back door opens.

"Who's there?" Shane asks, while shining a flashlight in my face. "Katie? Is that you?"

I stop and look up. This is not what I wanted. Or maybe it was. I walk toward him. He's in nothing but a robe.

"Get in here. What's going on?"

"I'm sorry," I say, walking in, forgetting my promise to stop apologizing.

The mudroom is lit by a single candle and reality is nothing but shadows. "Sorry," he explains. "The power's out again. I was just heading to the fuse box when Sebastian started barking."

He's more amused than annoyed by my arrival but his expression changes as he takes in my state. I realize what a mess I must be. I know I brushed my teeth, but I wonder when I last brushed my hair. And then, because the thought is so irrelevant and stupid, I start to laugh. It's a scary kind of laughter, the kind that makes other people slowly back away rather than join in.

"Are you okay?" he asks.

Clearly I am not. Bad hair is one thing, but I've come to him broken and beaten.

"What happened?" he whispers.

"Me and Jonathan. We were attacked."

I can barely get the words out. Saying them aloud makes it all too real.

"Attacked?"

He's incredulous, not because he doesn't believe me, but because evil like this doesn't have a doorway into his world. He acknowledges it but it never makes impact. He's a man that carries no emotional burdens. It's what I love most about him, and I don't want to lie mine at his feet. It's not a fair thing to do.

"I should go. I don't wanna bother you." I start to leave but he grabs my arm.

"You're not bothering me."

I narrow my eyes at him, certain he's lying to protect my feelings. But then I remember. He doesn't do that.

"I was watching a movie when the power went out. Come on," he instructs me, leading me up the stairs and through the yoga studio. The house is so quiet.

"Where's Matty?" I ask.

"She went to see her sister in Boston."

"You didn't go?"

"Her sister makes me crazy."

Ha.

We arrive at the loft. "You can sleep here. I'll get you something dry to wear." He leaves and I take off my damp clothes and wrap myself in a blanket. He takes long enough with the task that my thoughts turn back to Jonathan and my throat closes up. When he returns, tears are streaming down my face. I wipe them away.

"I'm sorry," I apologize again. "Jonathan is not okay."

He puts the clothes down and walks to me. He takes me in his arms and the hug is like home.

Before he can let me go, I do exactly what I've sworn I would never do. All those promises I've made to myself, all those lines I said I'd never cross, disappear. My lips, so close to his neck, make contact and before I know it, I'm kissing him there. I hear him sigh and I become emboldened. My hands reach behind his head, and I pull his lips to mine. And to my eternal relief, he kisses me back. Slowly, deeply, he brings me closer, arms tightening, a lightness, a joy, a desperation. I need him. I need this. Somewhere in my head, I know it's wrong, that I'm crossing a Rubicon. But everything is wrong, so nothing is right, and I can't care anymore. I can only feel, and I only want to feel him.

We stop kissing and I slide his robe from his shoulders, revealing all that I've been thinking about for months. I want to kiss him everywhere, touch him everywhere. I can see in his expression an internal struggle. The line that has vanished for me is still there for him though I can feel it fading. He has to decide.

Time stands still.

Miraculously, he brings his lips back to mine. The blankets that are wrapped around me fall away while his lips find my neck and my shoulders. I want to make him feel how he's making me feel, but my experience is limited. His is not. He takes my hand and guides me.

"Touch me here," he whispers, and I do. I'll do anything.

His arms are strong, and I want them to control me. His body leans into mine and soon I'm laying down with him above me. His hands run up my arms, placing them above my head. And then it's like he remembers something.

"Are you sure?" he asks.

"Yes."

His palms press into mine as he enters me. It hurts but I don't want him to stop. I bite his shoulder and he moans in response. But my face must betray me because he stops.

"Does it hurt?"

"Yes."

"Should I stop?"

As an answer, I grab him and pull him deeper into me. I breathe, knowing that this pain is just a prerequisite to pleasure. He groans again and our eyes meet. And I know that in this moment I've somehow been branded. Whatever comes tomorrow, I know this unescapable truth: I am his. And for the moment, just this one moment, he is mine.

The pain fades. As he moves, I begin to move with him. My body is a magnifying mirror; every response in him elicits a greater one in me. When I feel his body start to shake, I pull him to me, urging him to stay inside me. Anything else would be sacrilegious and I can't bear it. This is my communion.

I fall asleep in his arms, but I wake up alone. Morning has finally arrived, and the room is awash in sunlight. I put myself together as best I can which isn't much. I take a moment to assess whether I feel differently now that I'm no longer a virgin. I do and it feels like relief. But the feeling is short-lived as I remember the other events of last night. I wonder if I can escape without notice and avoid a most infamous walk of shame. But the stairs squeak and ruin my getaway.

"Katie?" his voice rings out. "Want some tea?"

Tea? The offer feels absurd but like a puppet on a string, I walk towards the voice into the kitchen.

"Tea?" he asks again, holding up his own mug as an example as if this is any other morning.

The silence is deafening as he moves about the kitchen fixing me a cup of tea. I don't want it. I want Jonathan to be alright and for this man before me to say the right words. I don't know what those would be exactly but surely they exist. Words that will reassure me that what happened was real and important. I have them, these words of love that have been bubbling inside me since the day we met. Last night felt like an unlocking, an opportunity to let them finally fly free from my heart. But this morning, the ground has shifted and what felt possible just hours before again feels inconceivable.

As he hands me the cup, our eyes meet.

"We shouldn't have done that. I'm sorry."

He doesn't speak with malice but instead with a serious matter-of-factness. It's a tone I've never heard from him before. It makes me feel foolish and small, like a child being reprimanded for bad behavior. The words he's chosen gut me. He's sorry. I am a regret. If I could have any superpower, it would be to disappear. Just, poof.

It turns out that boys don't shed the cruelty of their youth; they only just perfect it. These are the words I'll hear on my deathbed. Forget those silly assessments from high school boys that haunted me before. No, this is the one, the phrase that will echo in my ears for eternity. Before I can fully digest this horrible new paradigm, he continues with a confession.

"Matty cheated on me. A little while ago. I think I wanted to get even."

This information throws me even more off balance. Not because he used me in a game of revenge. He can use me all he wants. It's the fact that she cheated. For a moment, I want to take the fruit bowl off the kitchen island and smash it on the floor. She has everything and it's not enough. But then I think about the medicine in the cabinet, her missing wedding ring at the casino, and I wonder if all these things are connected. And, of course, admonishing her behavior, considering the moment I'm currently in, feels wildly hypocritical.

My thoughts are everywhere, and I can't respond in any meaningful way to his confession. No need though because he has more to say, more ammunition to fire.

"We need to keep this between us. Forget it happened," he says, as if such a thing were remotely possible for me.

"Right," I answer because what other answer is there? No? I wonder what he would say to this refusal but I'm afraid to find out. Would I finally see him angry? Anything feels possible at this point. I'm paralyzed, surrounded by land mines.

He smiles then, a small one of satisfaction indicating that all is again well. By agreeing to his terms, we've solved the problem of… well, me, I suppose. And I can't help being amazed at his ability to compartmentalize, like there's a switch inside him that can turn his emotions on and off with ease. Is this the same man that was, just hours before, inside me? How can that be?

The thought makes my throat tighten and tears start to pool behind my eyes. I'm not going to make it through any more of this conversation without falling apart. While he seems perfectly fine, I'm tumbling into the abyss that I've been avoiding for months. Except it's so much worse than I could have possibly imagined. To be welcomed and rejected within a few hours adds a sense of whiplash to the pain.

I put the tea down, having not tasted it. I try to focus on anything else to keep myself from crying. And that's when I remember the other tragedy unfolding in my life, Jonathan. Fuck. It's like making a broken leg feel better by smashing an arm.

"I should go. I should get back to the hospital."

"Jonathan? That's right. How is he?" While obviously concerned about my friend, he seems a little relieved to be talking about anything else.

"I don't know. Not good," and with that I'm out the door, racing my tears to the car.

Requiem

When I get home, I immediately take a shower. I don't want to wash him off me, but I know I never truly will. I go to the kitchen in search of coffee and am relieved to see a pot already on. My father is there too, sitting at the table with a newspaper. He shifts in his seat when I enter. Obviously, he's been waiting for me.

"Emily called. Jonathan is out of the ICU. He's awake." I sink into a chair and tears stream down my face. This, understandably, confuses my father.

"I'm just relieved," I assure him.

"Oh. Alright."

"What else did she say?" I ask.

"The pressure's gone down. It started going down on its own right before they operated. He's not out of the woods, but it's good news."

"Oh, thank god, thank god, thank god," I repeat to help the news sink in. And then when I regain my composure, "Thank you."

"He's family."

His words are unexpected and so earnest that I'm touched beyond measure. I instinctively get up and hug him. He's still sitting so it's awkward but not much more awkward than any show of affection between us.

I know my father is fond of Jonathan, but I never thought he considered him "family." Who is this man who sits before me? My father has softened around the edges and it's weird and wonderful. I can't help but think his transformation is all for the worst possible reason but man, talk about making lemonade. (That's so trite. I'm sorry, Mom. But I think you'd agree. It's a wild sight to behold.) It sucks, of course, that he couldn't be this way when she was here. I wonder if it's a karma thing, a balance in the universe. Like, I'm only allowed one or the other. (And let me just say, that if that's the case, it's a shitty choice and I have some words for the universe.)

"I need to go back to the hospital," I say. "Can you take me to get my car?" I'm assuming my car is still at the restaurant. I don't want to go back to the scene of the crime but what other choice do I have?

"Sure."

My dad drives me to the restaurant and drops me off at my car. But before going back to the hospital, I find myself heading towards the beach. I have to clear my head before facing more people. The beach is deserted which is just what I want. I trudge through the snow and stare out at the Great Lake, where there are no boundaries and the sky and water meld together into one blue-gray hue.

My mom used to bring me here all the time when I was a kid. It wasn't until years later that I discovered she hated everything about the beach. She feared the water because she couldn't swim, and she loathed the mountains of sand that followed us home. She even disliked the sunshine that caused her fair skin to burn unless she used gobs of sunscreen. But she tolerated it all for me, never letting on her distaste of the whole experience. Quite the opposite. She was, in my eyes, as delighted as I was to be here. This is what a "woman's touch" actually is, I think. Making sacrifices that no one sees.

I watch the relentless waves and soon my thoughts become relentless too. The ones I've been trying so desperately to keep at bay are flooding in now. The crash is finally here. I wonder again about karma. Does every good thing have to have some unknown cost? Jonathan is going to be okay and I'm so thankful. (He is, right? He is. I simply won't believe anything else.) At the same time, my heart is being ripped out of my chest. Because while Shane seems quite willing and able to just move forward as if nothing at all happened, I know that I can't. I can't pretend like that; I'm not that great of an actor.

And then, of course, there's Matty. Matty! How can I ever look her in the eyes again? Fuck. I close *that* Pandora's Box as soon as I open it. Because thinking about Matty means regretting what happened. And I don't. Regret touching him? Regret the best moment of my life? As ridiculous as it is impossible. The bottom line is I made a choice last night whether I meant to or not. One experience and a lifetime of its memory in exchange for any future ones. (Frankly, it's another shitty choice, universe. You are not impressing me today.)

For a moment, I think about how brave and beautiful it would be to walk into the icy water, and to just keep walking until the pain and confusion stops. But I am neither brave nor beautiful, so I just walk back to my car.

When I get to the hospital, I'm walking in as Emily is walking out. She grabs me and hugs me.

"Did you talk to your dad?" she asks.

"I did."

"Come on."

She leads me into the hospital where we find a place to sit.

"The pressure started going down on its own before they needed to operate."

"That's what my dad said. How is he?"

"He's awake but on a lot of painkillers. So, he's groggy. He's having a little trouble talking but the doctors think that'll get better."

"Thank god."

"He might have some other shit to deal with, but we just don't know yet."

"Right."

"I think he should move back in here with me. Until he's better."

I'm not sure how to respond to this because I know Jonathan and I know he'll never agree to this. Getting out of this town was imperative to him. Which, given what has happened, was a pretty good instinct.

"Can I see him?" I ask.

"Come on."

She leads me through a corridor that leads toward an elevator, where we ride up to the second floor. We travel another hallway until we reach Jonathan's room. The hospital is not as awful as the ER though it still feels oppressive and cold. When we reach his room, I'm unprepared. IV tubes are pumping liquid into his veins. His head is bandaged, and his left leg is elevated and covered in a cast.

He's awake but highly medicated. Nevertheless, he's able to turn his head and acknowledge me.

"Hey," he whispers.

"Hey."

"I'm gonna run home and take a quick shower and come back. You'll stay?" asks Emily.

"Yeah, yeah. Go," I tell her. She leaves and I turn all my attention to Jonathan. I want to hold his hand but that's where the IVs are so instead I gently touch his shoulders.

"I love you, baby," I say.

"Love you too, baby."

With Jonathan, these words have always come easily.

"You're gonna be alright," I continue.

"So are you."

This is our refrain no matter who needs comforting. Because, in reality, in this world, we all need comforting. I kiss his forehead and say what I need to say.

"You have to be okay. We've got some shit to do in Chicago." It takes a moment, but the message arrives.

"We?"

"We."

A satisfied smile settles across his face.

The next week is made up of more hospital visits until finally Jonathan is released to finish the rest of his recovery at home. He and Emily have many semi-heated discussions on just what this means. Emily thinks it means staying in Lake City where she can supervise his care. Jonathan thinks it means returning to Chicago with me. I try to stay neutral. I want to leave but in truth, I'm not crazy about changing bedpans. They settle on staying in Lake City for another six weeks until Jonathan is able to navigate on crutches and his ribs have healed.

During this time of negotiations, Jonathan and I learn that Emily has been on a mission to find out more about our assailants. She calls the police station every day asking for progress on the investigation and every day she gets the same response: nothing.

One day when I arrive, she's at the dining room table with newspapers spread before her.

"They never printed anything about the assault. Nothing," she says to me.

"Oh. What were you expecting?"

"I don't know. Something. It's *news*, isn't it? I'm going to call the paper."

I excuse myself and go to Jonathan's room. "Your mom's on the war path."

"I know."

"She's calling the paper."

"Emily!"

Emily comes in holding the phone receiver. "What do you need?"

"Are you calling the paper?"

She holds her fingers to her lips to shush him. Then she turns her attention to the receiver. "Yes, I'm here." She leaves the doorway.

Jonathan rolls his eyes in frustration. "I've been telling her to move on," he says.

While Jonathan and I would love to see the assholes held accountable, the process of getting there feels both insurmountable and intolerable. Jonathan's not comfortable with being seen as a victim and I'm not comfortable around the criminal justice system (for obvious reasons). Emily, however, is not deterred by our arguments.

"She's also talking about hiring a private investigator," he says.

"Does Lake City have private investigators?"

"I doubt it."

Later, I look for private investigators in the yellow pages and come up empty. I also look for therapists, which I do find. I don't call any of them, but I do keep the knowledge of their existence as a balm. Because right now, I'm definitely falling apart.

While I pack, I find myself torn by two different realities. In one, I'm celebrating Jonathan's recovery and my attempt at a new beginning. I've been to Chicago many times via school field trips (the art museum, the Brookfield Zoo, a French club outing to *Les Misérables*), but I've never spent a significant amount of time there. I don't know the lay of the land and I look forward to the moments of discovery ahead of me. In the other reality, I am dying. At least, it feels that way.

The idea of never seeing Shane again is like a weight that sits on my chest at all times. I have to remind myself constantly to breathe, which reminds me of him, and the cycle continues. I can't count the number of times that I find myself on the bathroom floor sobbing. I don't eat much and when I do, food has no taste. My sleep is fitful, more exhausting than not even trying. There's a hole in my body and in my spirit and every time I close my eyes, it drops deeper and deeper, sucking out everything until there is only blackness. In this reality, I am alone. There are no support groups for the other woman, and I can't burden Jonathan with any of this.

Of course, the people I want most to talk to are the people that I can't talk to. The push-and-pull is still there, which is why I don't say goodbye to Shane. I'm only strong enough to leave him if I'm, somehow, already gone. My plan is simply to disappear from his world, which I fear will be woefully easy. I'm positive he won't try to contact me; he never has before. I don't think he even has my phone number. I'm the one who came to him. Every moment I've spent with him has been in his world. He's never stepped one foot in mine. (This isn't an accusation. Why would he? What could my world possibly offer him?) Worse than never contacting me, I don't expect him to think of me either. Thinking about the past is stealing from the present.

With Matty, I know I can't just disappear. We're entangled via work, and I don't want to leave her in a lurch. I care about the website. (I'm pleased to find that I care about something still, something that's productive instead of destructive.) I use Jonathan's computer to write Matty an email which is the height of cowardice but it's all I can manage. I explain how I need to go to Chicago to help with Jonathan's care. I refer her to some names that Jonathan has given me of people that can help her continue the work on the website. And I tell her that I love her.

I hit send on the message and vow to get a new email address. I'll never be able to read the reply.

As I pack my things, I think a lot about the stages of grief. It's a thought that, at first, gives me hope that there's a finish line somewhere out there and I just can't see it yet. But they're not really stages, are they? They're just unwieldy emotions that blindside me at random and, usually, at the most inopportune moments. I'm not getting any better at hiding my sudden crying jags, but my father is getting better at pretending not to notice. For all I know, he thinks they're the result of the assault. I guess if you're going to have a personal crisis no one can know about, try to have a public one too for cover. Helpful.

As for the stages of grief, I skip right over denial and just waffle between bargaining and depression. Bargaining feels like I'm an animal trying desperately to claw its way out of a trap. The only obvious way out of this dark tunnel is to get him back. This thought inevitably leads me down another spiral because how can you get "back" something you never had? But I'm clawing toward *something*, nonetheless, even if it's just an imaginary space and time. This clawing takes the shape of ridiculous ideas I cling to if they offer even a shred of hope for a new circumstance.

This is all to say, that if I knew how to dabble in some voodoo right now, I absolutely would. Or maybe some type of reverse hypnosis where instead of using it to remember pertinent events, I could use it to forget them. But do I want to forget? Could I just selectively slice out the uncomfortable moment in the kitchen and keep the memory of his body on mine? Or should I forget everything because the memory is torture?

The depression overtakes me. I think about cutting myself which I never understood before, but now seems to make some kind of sick sense. I want equilibrium; I want my outside to reflect my inside. I want a physical release, a distraction, a replacement, something, anything to stop these endless tears. I sit on the bathroom floor, holding a knife, and just the threat of it is seems to be enough. I've always found thoughts of suicide soothing (sounds quite terrible, I know), but what could be more calming than an escape hatch? Ironically, thinking about suicide always makes me less suicidal.

I crave numbness so I try getting drunk. I consider going to a bar, but the idea causes me a mountain of anxiety. (I wonder if I'll ever be able to go out drinking again.) So, I search and find an ancient bottle of vodka in the freezer which must have belonged to my mother since my father is solely a beer-man. I take the bottle to my bedroom and do shots. With each shot, I imagine Shane's disapproval and part of me wants to drink to oblivion just to spite it. But drinking alone is quite awful and it only takes the one time to rid me of this self-destructive notion. Misery and drinking only go together if you have someone to tell your sad story to and I clearly do not. And anyway, what I really want is pot. But the pot I normally would smoke is not here; it's at Shane and Matty's house. I never bothered to keep my own stash and I regret this decision deeply.

Another part of me wants to run around and sleep with a dozen or so other guys. Dilute his memory with all new ones. (I wonder if this is why some women sleep around. Not because they have any carnal desire for lots of lovers but because they're trying desperately to erase one in particular, whether that one was wonderful or traumatic or somehow both.) I never try to sleep with anyone else though. Picking up men is so alien to me and I can't do it from my bedroom. And the thought of leaving it is exhausting.

The quiet is what's going to drive me crazy but music, which I always could find salvation in, has become like kryptonite. The Walkman that was my constant companion has been tossed aside in frustration and now lives buried under a pile of clothes in my bedroom. While the silence is terrible, music is so much worse. Every song, no matter how jovial in nature, is somehow about him.

He is everywhere and nowhere. I have no photos of him. Nothing physical for me to remember him by at all and I kick myself for not only failing to scam some pot, but also never grabbing something of his. I have girlfriends in college that always took souvenirs from lovers. It would have been so easy to take a shirt, one of his linen pullovers that smells like him. But at this point, I'd take any tangible souvenir that I could hold and feel like the past three months weren't just an illusion.

I dig through the old *Sassy* magazines I've kept in my closet, looking for advice on heartbreak. I don't find anything useful but it's a good mindless distraction. (The magazine is far too feminist to acknowledge this kind of lame pain.) And then, I remember how in college, whenever a girlfriend had a broken heart, she'd dye her hair. We'd joke that the chemicals contained healing powers. I decide to try it. Standing before the selection of colors in the drugstore,

Consensual Scars

I choose the blackest of blacks. I have a feeling it will look awful against my fair skin and the thought is thrilling. Make me a monster. Once home, I follow the directions on the box. While the dye takes hold, I shave my legs. And maybe the dye does have mystical ingredients because I don't think seriously even once about cutting myself with the razor.

I assess the result in the mirror, and I'm satisfied that I no longer look like me. He never looked at this girl, never touched her. This girl can be free.

Of course, Emily is properly horrified when she sees me.

"What did you do?!" she exclaims. "Your blonde hair!"

Em is blonde, so her affection for my hair isn't one of envy but genuine love of her own hair color. I wonder what that's like. To love what you have.

"I just needed a change," I mutter.

She shakes her head in disapproval, which only makes me want to do more. I walk past her into Jonathan's room where he's resting on his childhood bed.

"Well, that's a look," he says.

"I was bored."

"Right? Oh my god. I'm bored as fuck."

"I'm bored enough to pierce my nose."

"You're finally gonna do it?"

"Yes."

"Yourself?"

"Yes."

"Badass."

"Wanna help?"

"You can't do it here. Emily would freak. But I can tell you what you'll need. Get ice, a needle, and something to stick up your nose. So you don't damage the septum."

I'm impressed with his knowledge, and I tell him so.

"Just common sense," he shrugs.

"What should I put up my nose?"

"A carrot?"

"Ha! Alright."

"What did Emily say about your hair?"

"She did not approve."

"I can imagine."

On my way back home, I go to the grocery store and pick up a single carrot. Once home, I find my mom's sewing kit and locate a needle. Then I get ice and wrap it in a washcloth. I sit in my bedroom trying to psych myself up. I've wanted a nose stud for a while, and what better time than now? Certainly, it's better than playing with knives.

I hold the ice against my right nostril. When I think I'm numb enough, I stick the carrot up my nose and push the needle into my flesh. I can get it in far enough that when I let go of the needle, it remains, dangling. I take a deep breath, and as tears stream down my face, I press the needle down as hard as I can. I hear a small "pop" and I know that I've done it. I feel high, triumphant. I go to the mirror and laugh at how ridiculous I look. I take out the carrot, which I'm not sure I even really needed. But better safe than sorry. My septum is fine.

And then I realize I forgot one important detail. I don't have a stud to put in place of the needle. I look through my old jewelry box, but I've long stopped wearing earrings. My relationship to jewelry is much like that of makeup. Great for the stage but just too much work to bother with most days. My mom's jewelry box is still in her bedroom closet, but she never pierced her ears. She has a few pairs of clip-ons but that's not going to work.

Well, this is a pickle. Should I pull it out and forget it?

No. Fuck it. I've come this far.

I grab my keys and venture to the giant box store, finding the jewelry department tucked between groceries and shoes. I've got the needle through my nose, and I wait for someone, anyone, to toss the most obvious of insults my way. But no one says anything. I'm a little disappointed by the lack of interest. When the check-out woman eyes me oddly, I explain my predicament in the way I've practiced in my head. I expect a laugh, or at least a smile, because surely this situation is amusing if not hilarious. But she just stares at me blankly as she rings up a pair of silver studs. And with that, I know for certain now, if I was trying to turn into a freak, I have succeeded. Awesome.

Also, I need to get the fuck out of this joyless town. Not one "Needle Nose?" I mean, come the fuck on. It's *right there*.

When I get back home, I replace the needle with the stud and step back to admire my work. The physical transformation does the job. At least, enough for me to keep moving and packing. A new me. A new city. Just a few weeks away. I give up my embargo on music because this look needs a fitting soundtrack. I dig out Nine Inch Nails' *Pretty Hate Machine* and turn up the angriest song I can find. I dance around my room, desperate for more distractions.

Annie Marie Huber

Laundromat Confession

My father is simultaneously relieved and pained to see me go. He wants me to have a bigger life and is thrilled to have a reason to visit the city. But I know that he's lonely and will be lonelier with me gone. As for Emily, she's made me promise to keep a watchful eye on Jonathan to be sure there's no lingering effects from the head injury. Though she needn't have bothered.

I find myself watching Jonathan intently of my own accord. He does experience headaches and dizziness on occasion, and he has trouble concentrating for long periods of time. But all these symptoms seem to be improving. He's doing physical therapy for the fractured tibia bone and is still on crutches, though that injury also seems to be recovering at a rapid rate. The company he works for has been understanding to an impressive degree, allowing him to take a paid medical leave for three months. Of course, I'm sure if they weren't, Emily would sue them to high heaven. Lord knows, she's ready to sue *somebody*.

Instead of booting out his roommate, Jonathan has decided to get a new place just for him and me. He seems determined to make this a fresh start for both of us. He opts for a three-bedroom apartment in the South Shore neighborhood. It's a sublet from a friend and sits just a few blocks from Lakeshore Drive. It's close enough to public transport and I consider leaving my car in Lake City, but Jonathan (who has never had a car) insists I bring it for road trips.

"Take my parking spot."

"The apartment has a parking spot?"

"Yup."

"How much is this apartment?"

"Twelve hundred."

I almost choke but he brushes it off. I have about fifteen-hundred saved, the most I've ever had and the result of living at home with few expenses.

"I'll cover us until you're working. And then we can figure something out. I can pay a greater share. You know, since I'm raking in the bucks."

I can't tell if he's kidding or not. I really don't know how much he makes from his job, but I'm starting to assume it's a lot. Up until now, money hasn't been an issue in our relationship. Probably because neither of us really had any. In college, we split the bills down the middle and took turns picking up the restaurant checks. And we've always covered each other if necessary. So, his stance isn't a surprise. Still, I don't know how I'll ever keep up.

We officially make the move to Chicago on Valentine's Day, which we properly vilify by wearing all black. The apartment is on the top floor of a brownstone. It has a small galley kitchen that's next to a brightly lit dining area just large enough for a table and four chairs. The front door opens to a living room, featuring a leather sectional sofa and big-screen TV. Everything in the apartment that's nice belongs to Jonathan. I'm sleeping on an air mattress and my furniture consists mostly of milk crates. My only contribution to the décor is a giant, framed poster of Mr. Blonde from *Reservoir Dogs* that I acquired in college. I hope to upgrade my space soon but right now, I don't even really care.

Although the shadow of Shane lingers, distractions are in abundance now. I have a whole world to learn and a new life to build. The city is cold and blue and gray, and that feels a lot like me. But even in this state, the city is alive and thriving. I suck in the cold air and feel it cleanse me despite the accompanying fumes. Or maybe because of them. (Shane would be horrified by this thought and that makes it all the better.)

The locals are feeling quite done with the slushy season and the more I hear them swear about it, the more I love them. I love how everyone is talking all the time, words flying about in a symphony that is chaotically charming simply because I can see the love. It's written all over their faces even as they complain. They love this place. And so do I.

I love rounding corners and seeing the landmark buildings that ground me, like the Sears Tower and the Diamond Building (made famous in *Adventures in Babysitting*). I love the sound of the "L" traversing the landscape, enabling me to go places without my car. I love the signature lakefront winds that whip around the buildings, blowing away everything in their path. I love seeing Wrigley Field and thinking of my mom who adored the Cubs. I love the food, especially the deep-dish pizza. (Jonathan and I try various delivery options, searching for what will be our eventual favorite.) I love the little shops that haven't yet been devoured by big corporations. I love the yellow cabs that are everywhere, announcing the fact that yes, this is a *city*. You have places to *go*. Chicago is seductive, sad, and hopeful all at the same time. And I'm so here for it.

Upon arrival, I search out the nearest bookstore to replace my copy of *Coding for Dummies* that I left behind at Matty and Shane's house. I don't have a project to work on anymore, but I had discovered something in that book, a new possibility and I don't want to give it up quite yet. Maybe I have a future in this strange, new digital world.

While in the bookstore, I realize that I haven't read anything other than textbooks in ages. (Even the *Coding* book feels like a textbook.) As a child, I was a voracious reader, riding the familiar trajectory of girls my age: from the innocence of Beverly Clearly to the sometimes-scandalous Judy Bloom to the downright shocking incestuous stories of V.C. Andrews. But once I got to college, I did all the required reading. (Yes, I was *that* student.) Ironically, all that homework left no time to enjoy books for pure pleasure. I want to get that joy back, so I pick up a few fiction books. I don't know what I like anymore so I trust the rest of society by choosing titles marked as bestsellers.

The stereo in the living room is constantly playing, always upbeat club music that energize us as we set up the apartment. Jonathan has no patience for my angsty faves, banishing the grunge and Lilith Fair headliners to my bedroom. I don't mind. After all, I now know every word to RuPaul's *Supermodel* album and, I have to say, I think I'm a better person for it. (Jonathan talks incessantly about an electronica revolution in music and he's waiting impatiently for it to take over the airwaves. I don't think it'll happen but what do I know?)

I want to fill my mind with the culture all around me: the museums, the restaurants, and the shops. But all of that takes money and my funds are minimal. So as soon as we move in, I make an appointment at a temp agency. As a college graduate who can type eighty words a minute, I surely have some employable skills. (Thank you, high school typing class.) The woman I meet with agrees with this assessment and immediately starts sending me on random jobs throughout the city. Most of these are in the corporate world where I'm answering phones, sorting mail, and other menial tasks. I don't mind the work though the dress code is a pain, forcing me to invest in some business attire.

And then, two weeks into this new life, just as things start to have a rhythm, everything changes. My breasts are tender and I'm feeling nauseous all the time. Not one to keep a watchful eye on my period, I don't know exactly how late I am.

(Are there really women that keep track of their cycles in a little journal? Or is that just in movies? My period surprises me every month. I'll cry over something trivial one day, then the next day start bleeding and think, "Oh! That's why that broken glass made me have an epic breakdown." Amazing that something that has happened no less than one hundred times in my life should still be so unpredictable but that's the truth. Maybe I just don't want to think about it. Or maybe I'm just mentally disconnected from my own body.)

Even without knowing exactly how late I am, I know what's happening. I count back from my night with Shane. It's been ten weeks, plenty of time to know for certain. (And plenty of time to make a run for the clinic.) When I break down and buy a pregnancy test, I'm relieved to be in an anonymous city, away from the prying eyes of my hometown. I take the test back to the apartment, unwrap the package, and read the directions. It seems simple enough and about three minutes later, I watch as the pink plus sign appears.

I feel the desperate need to run away. But I've already done that, haven't I? No worries. There's always someplace new to run. I grab the laundry basket from my floor and throw detergent and some dirty clothes into it. I find a handful of quarters on my dresser and put them in my pocket. And then, I walk to Jonathan's bedroom door. It's early in the day but not too early and I hear him moving around. I knock.

"Come in."

I open the door and he sees the basket.

"You know I can't drive," he says.

"I know. I'll drive."

"Okay. Give me a minute to get ready."

"Cool."

I get my wallet and car keys and wait by the door. Together, we walk to my car, slowly as he's still using crutches. He gets into the back seat, sitting sideways with his leg up on the seat. I've brought a couple of pillows for him, and we arrange them to give him the maximum amount of comfort. I get into the driver's seat. Suddenly, I feel guilty. Maybe this isn't a good idea.

"Is your leg alright back there? Maybe we shouldn't do this."

"Go," he commands.

I start the car and dutifully choose a song for our soundtrack, flipping through the radio stations. I settle on *Run Around* by Blues Traveler.

"This okay?" I ask him.

"Tape deck still broken?"

"Yeah."

Lately, when I put a cassette into my car stereo, it gets stuck. I listened to No Doubt for two months straight before I jimmied the tape out with a screwdriver. Even though I know I shouldn't, I'm tempted to put another tape into the player. I'm sure this is an allegory somehow for my life.

We have no destination in mind, except to find a Laundromat, somewhere away from here.

Ever since I got my driver's license and inherited my mother's old car, Jonathan and I have been taking road trips. Sometimes short ones just across the state, sometimes much further. The destination never matters, just that we are going somewhere, anywhere. And just to prove that point, we came up with a ridiculous excuse for our routine excursions. It started simply enough before our inaugural trip:

"I can't go anywhere. I have laundry to do."
"Bring it."

So, that's what we did. We threw our dirty clothes in a sheet, tossed the bundle in the car, and drove a few hours to a Laundromat somewhere in Ohio. Since then, we've done our laundry in a number of places across the Midwest. Once we even took our dirty clothes all the way to New Orleans. Of course, we didn't just do our laundry while there. We also drank too many Hurricanes in the streets of the French Quarter and made friends with the various street performers in hopes of securing a place to crash. (Our charm was not in vain. A beautiful guitarist welcomed us in for the night.)

We haven't taken a trip like this since leaving college though, so it feels good to be driving aimlessly. Aimless or not though, when I get to the freeway I have to choose a direction.

"Hey, what's west of Illinois?" I ask Jonathan. One of the greatest things about having a bestie is being able to ask stupid questions without hesitation.

"Iowa, Missouri…" he answers. "Or we could go north to Wisconsin."

I head west following signs to Des Moines. Jonathan falls asleep and I'm left alone with my thoughts, which are a jumble.

I have no qualms about abortion though I have trouble saying the word aloud. (No one says the word aloud. Even when I took a girlfriend to get one in college, it was a "procedure" to deal with an "unplanned event.") So, it's an option, one that I can easily take. As I often do, I say a thankful prayer for Roe.

The issue is the father. If this were the result of some sloppy one-night stand, I would be racing to the clinic. But this life inside me is an extension of him and in that way, it feels like a gift. I mean, I wanted a keepsake of our time together. And this is certainly that. Oh man, is that a terrible analogy? Comparing a baby to a stolen sweater? Am I already sucking as a mother? Oh god, *mother* is such a heavy word.

Then I think about the night when it happened. I wasn't careful.

After years of telling Jonathan to be careful, I acted in the opposite manner. I was deliberately careless, which is a contradiction in terms. I had intent that night, in that moment, whether consciously or not. And suddenly, I'm acutely aware that something has changed in me beyond the physical. The hole that I've been trying so hard to fill is gone. This life is giving me life.

I roll down the window and let the wind blow through my hair. I turn up the music. I try to just be in the moment, afraid that things around me are getting too real again. Since leaving the city, we've been hugged on both sides by corn fields. Billboards assure us there are many things not too far away. Specifically, shops that specialize in guns and fireworks. Ah, the Midwest.

Hours pass and eventually I take a random exit that appears promising. The turn jolts Jonathan awake.

"Where are we?" he asks.

"Cedar Rapids, Iowa."

"Cool."

I look in the rearview mirror and I can see Jonathan holding his head.

"Ugh. I have such a headache."

"Oh, baby. Hang on. I have some Tylenol."

"Do you have water?"

"I'm gonna have to stop for directions. I'll pick you up something to drink."

I pull into a gas station. Inside, I purchase a Gatorade and gas. I ask the clerk for directions to the nearest Laundromat. He obliges, directing us to a spot just down the street. When I get back to the car, I give Jonathan a couple of pills and the drink.

"How bad is it?"

"It's okay. I'll be okay."

I'm sure this would be his answer even if he was dying.

When we arrive, I help Jonathan out of the car and grab the basket from the trunk. We make our way inside to a nearly deserted coin-operated establishment. I start a load of laundry and we both settle into the cheap, plastic chairs provided for our comfort.

(I'm not judging. The cheap, plastic chairs are an important part of the ambiance for these adventures. I like to think we chose these particular establishments for a reason even if the thought was never voiced. There are no rich elitists in Laundromats.)

"So... how are *you*?" he asks, cheekily.

While we don't need a reason for a road trip, he can sense that there is one this time.

"I'm pregnant."

He sits there, looking at me. He's speechless and I've never seen him speechless before. I wave my hand in front of his face to make sure he's still with me. I can only imagine what he's thinking. As far as he knows, I'm practically a monk. He's noticed my melancholy, of course, but he's been attributing it solely to my obsession. I never told him about the night with Shane.

He has every right to chastise me, but he doesn't. Instead, he stretches his arms out, inviting me in for a hug which I accept.

"It's going to be alright," he says. "Do you need money? I can go with you," he says.

I'm not surprised that we've leaped right to "the procedure." He knows my stance on the issue and, honestly, I can't argue that it's not the most rational path.

"I think... I might not do that." I make the decision at the same time I'm forming the words.

"Oh!"

"Yeah."

"Really?"

"Yeah."

"Who's the father?"

I look at him with a grimace, hoping that he'll put it together without making me say his name. Saying his name always hurts.

"Oh, shit," he says finally.

"Yeah."

I can tell he's struggling to not say what he clearly wants to say.

"Go ahead," I say, granting him the permission that he doesn't need but wants.

"Doesn't that make it, I don't know, more complicated? More reason to..."

"You would think."

"I know he was your first, sweetie. And that's gonna leave a mark.

But he's just a guy." And then because he can't resist, sings "He's a man, he's just a man" from *Jesus Christ Superstar.*

I don't have an answer for this. I hear the logic in his argument, understand it, but it never reaches my heart.

"Are you gonna tell him?" he asks.

"No."

"Really? Just no? I thought women used pregnancy to trap guys?"

"Ugh. I don't want him obligated to me. Do you know how awful that is? To have someone in your life just because they *have* to be?"

He regards me stone-faced.

"Oh, shit. Of course, you do. The sperm donor. Sorry. But it sucks, right? Like, so much?"

"Yes, it does."

"The thing is… I can think of a million reasons *not* to tell him."

"Give me three."

"Three? Alright. Well, there's the one we just talked about. We can call that the pity one. And then there's the fact that it could blow up his life with his wife."

"Very altruistic of you."

"And let's face it. No one wants to be the pregnant other woman. If he doesn't know, this can just be the result of a one-night stand. I mean, technically, it *is* the result of a one-night stand."

"Oh, man. You didn't even get a whole affair? Just one night? And you got pregnant?"

"Right? I swear, I'm never having sex again."

"Those are all sound reasons. Any others?"

"Well, you know, he doesn't want me."

"So… spite?"

"You say that like it's a bad thing."

He laughs. "Not at all. I've done plenty of things for spite."

"It's not spite though. I mean, I don't want to punish him. It's just that, right now…" and here I struggle to put in words what I'm feeling. "We're a package deal, at least right now. And I can't have a relationship with him. Before, when it was just a fantasy, we could be friends. But now that I know… that we've…"

"Now that you have carnal knowledge of him…" he helps.

"Yes! Exactly! Damn, I never thought I'd need that phrase. Yes, now that I have *carnal knowledge* of him, I can't go back. I can't. I'll want him even more. And I swear, the wanting is bound to kill me. I mean, I was fucking stalking him. I'm gonna go Glenn Close on him."

I've just begun to heal here in Chicago. Any relationship with him feels impossible. It would be taking a giant step backwards. And then there's another fear. The fear that I'll lose this too. Somehow. Just like I lost my mom and Shane. I know it's irrational, but I can't get it out of my head, the image of a happy family, one that doesn't include me at all.

Jonathan interrupts my thoughts with a fair question. "So, a reminder of him every day for the rest of your life? Is that gonna help?"

Of course not. I have no doubt it's gonna hurt like hell.

"I guess I'm gonna find out."

He gazes at me, assessing the situation, here in a Laundromat in some random town where my world (and his world, by extension) has been irrevocably altered.

"You're really going to do this?" he asks, finally.

"Yes."

"Do you know anything about babies? Like, I don't know, anything at all?"

"I guess I'm gonna find out," I repeat.

"We will find out."

"We?"

"We."

And with that he takes my hand, squeezes it, and tells me, again, that everything is going to be okay. I'm not sure I believe him, but I want to and that's enough. We finish our laundry and head back home.

Annie Marie Huber

Problematic Preference

Over the next several weeks, I do what I'm supposed to do. I stop drinking and smoking. I visit the doctor and get a prescription for prenatal vitamins. I pay out-of-pocket for both because I'm still on my father's insurance. I don't know how these things work; what sort of paperwork would land in his hands. I'm going to have to tell him at some point, but I dread that conversation more than the actual birth. I think it would be easier to just show up with his grandchild and tell him then.

I need to know if a man coined the term "morning sickness" because I have to assume that one did. It's such an effective way to trivialize a woman's pain. Because this nausea is all damn day. Honestly, I've never felt so crummy in my life. I'm also worrying constantly about everything.

I worry that I'm not the kind of person Shane would want raising his child. Like, should I be getting a doula and having this child in some sacred space blessed by a shaman? Or should I go to the hospital and get a proper epidural because, you know, I can?

Maybe it doesn't matter because he doesn't know and maybe will never know. This is the quandary I can't work out. Is it morally unethical to keep this secret? The weight of it isn't trivial. I'm deciding life-defining circumstances for two other people. And while I can rationalize not telling him (as it would surely destroy him and Matty), I can't help wondering if I'm making an epically bad decision.

But there's more nagging at me than questions of right or wrong. I have selfish concerns too. This decision will seal my fate with Shane. Sure, our fate was arguably already sealed, but that's the thing about unrequited love. There's always a sliver of hope, yes? And I would be lying if I said that I didn't harbor such hope. Hell, I don't just harbor it. I caress it lovingly at night when I'm falling asleep. I play the "what if" game in my head, carving out wildly improbable scenarios where he ends up in my arms. Those scenarios will go from improbable to impossible with this lie of omission.

I'm also constantly worrying about what I will tell my child. I know I have some time on this one, but it's there, always, waiting for me. And I have no idea. I'm going to have to come up with an answer that, while not an outright lie, isn't the play-by-play of what happened. Here, I pray for enlightenment, the perfect phrase that encompasses all that I need it to.

And then there's Jonathan. He's making everything easier which ironically is making me worry too. He's finally off the crutches and is helping me turn the third bedroom into a baby room. As we put together a crib, I try to explain my weariness.

"I'm so grateful that you're cool with me staying here. But, come on. You can't tell me it's not gonna crimp your style. How will you explain all this to your conquests?" I ask, gesturing around me for emphasis.

"I don't need to explain anything to anyone."

He says it with such conviction that I take note of the change in him since the attack. His confidence has an edge to it that it never did before as if he's daring others to take issue with him.

"But one day, you might need to. If, you know…" I trail off.

"If I fall in love?" He mockingly stretches out the word "love." Jonathan has never been in love, not the way I am with Shane. He's not opposed to the concept but he's also not sure if it's worth the trouble. Maybe it's a product of being a child of two people determined to stay together even if doing so makes everyone miserable. No matter the reason for his reluctance, I'm definitely not helping to dispel the idea that love isn't a big pain in the ass.

"It could happen," I say.

"It could. Anything could happen. But I promise you this. If I choose to have a relationship with someone, it will be, in part, because they're cool enough to understand what we are."

"A fag and his hag?" I joke.

I don't find the term "fag hag" to be derogatory. I probably should. I mean, "hag" isn't a term of endearment. Of course, neither is "fag." But I find it useful shorthand in explaining my relationship with Jonathan. And since it's a term that applies to me personally, I feel like I can reappropriate it as a positive. Nevertheless, I haven't used the word since the attack, and I can see Jonathan wince when he hears it.

"Sorry," I say.

"It's okay. I was gonna say 'family.'"

"Babe."

But before things can get too mushy, he adds, "And, you know, I can always kick you and your little bastard out."

"Ha! Uncle Jonathan would never."

"Uncle Jonathan, eh?"

"Yup."

"I like it. Implies affection with not so much actual responsibility."

"I'm also grateful that you paid for the crib. But that's another thing. Money."

"Ah."

I'm not referring just to my own finances that are about to get a lot more challenging. I've noticed the credit card bills that have been coming to Jonathan. I know he's spending way beyond his means even if his means are much greater than mine. He's also started receiving bills from his hospital stay. While he's still getting checks from work during his medical leave, I know it's not enough for us to coast like this for very long. So, I'm surprised when he tells me he has no interest in returning to work.

"It's not that I don't want to work," he clarifies. "I just don't want to work there."

"Okay," I say. "Where do you want to work?"

"I want us to start a business together."

I can't imagine what skills I have to put towards a business, but I bite anyway.

"Alright. And what kind of business are we starting?"

"Well, I see you reading that coding book a lot. I see you writing things down. I think we could build websites."

"You know, I'm just a beginner," I warn him. "I'm not that good, yet."

"You can learn. Everyone is learning. Now is the time."

"You know anything about running a company?" I ask.

"About as much as you know about having a baby."

"Ha! Fair," I admit. "And where are we getting startup money?"

"No idea. But I bet I can charm some investors."

"I bet you could."

"So, let's start a company. Yes?"

"Yes."

Because if he can get on board for my crazy, then I certainly can for his.

A few weeks later, Emily comes to visit. She doesn't know yet about the pregnancy and my baggy t-shirt still effectively hides the baby bump. She's carrying a heavy box that she immediately drops on the kitchen table.

"What's that?" asks Jonathan.

"I want you to find them," Emily answers.

Jonathan and I walk over to the box and peer inside. The box is filled with yearbooks from the two Lake City high schools. "How did you get these?"

"I put an ad in the paper and bought them from people."

"I told you I want to forget it."

She ignores his comment. "The reporter that I've been talking to has been getting threats about this. There's something going on here."

"What kind of threats?"

"Middle of the night phone calls. The voice just says, 'Drop the story. Or you'll get beaten with a bat too.'"

Jonathan and I both stare at Emily in disbelief.

"What the fuck?" he asks.

"Is she going to continue investigating?" I ask.

"She was... until they smashed up her car window. Now, she's too scared."

"She should be," Jonathan responds. "She should drop it. You should drop it."

"But don't you want to know what the fuck is going on?"

Jonathan sighs and sits down. I can tell he's torn between *absolutely* wanting to know what the fuck is going on – and wanting to put all this in the past.

"I don't want anyone else to get hurt," he concludes.

Emily doesn't have a good answer to this, so she turns to me for help. After a moment of staring, she says, "You look different."

"I'm pregnant."

I'm not sure I would have said anything if not for the desire to change the topic so definitively.

"Oh, shit!" she says. We sit at the table. And because she doesn't know if this is good news or bad news, she waits for a clue as to how to react further. But I'm not sure how to qualify it either, so we end up just looking at one another dumbly.

"I didn't know you were seeing anyone," she says, finally.

"I'm not."

"Oh."

"Yeah."

I wish there was some shorthand for "I slept with a married man. I'm in love with him. But I also love his wife lots and don't want to fuck up their marriage and so here we are." But there really isn't, is there? So, I don't elaborate and let her assume what she's most likely assuming: a reckless one-night stand has landed me here. Which isn't entirely off base. It just omits a lot of context. But maybe the context only matters to me. And maybe it doesn't matter at all.

"But you're keeping it."

"Yeah."

"Then we'll call it good news," she decides. "Congratulations."

"Thank you."

"Does your dad know?"

"No. Want to tell him?"

"Ha! No, thank you," Emily answers, before asking bluntly, "Who's the father?"

"No one. Nameless," I reply.

"I assume you knew his name at some point." It's a joke but then she realizes it could have darker implications. "I mean... unless you didn't."

I immediately pick up on what she means.

"No, no, no. I know his name. It wasn't that."

"Oh, good," she sighs with relief, and I wonder if she's been victimized.

Because we don't know, do we? We never know. Like when I was at a bar with a group of two girlfriends and one man, a stranger who had joined us. The conversation turned, somehow, to rape and I shared a statistic that I had recently learned: one of every three women are sexually assaulted. The man challenged it, asking – because there were three women right in front of him – if any of us had ever been assaulted. We all said "no" and he smugly confirmed the statistic as bunk. But when he left us, one of my friends said that she had been lying. She had been raped. And that's when I realized that what we truly know about people is only what they are willing to share. Never assume anything.

Emily stays for coffee and takes me aside before leaving.

"Make Jonathan look at those yearbooks, please? And you look at them too."

I tilt my head hopelessly, knowing I can't make Jonathan do anything.

"What if it was your baby?"

Well played, Emily.

"Okay. We'll look at them," I relent. But when I turn around, Jonathan has already moved the box out of sight, and probably, out of mind.

"Want me to come with?" Jonathan is watching me from the kitchen table as I get ready to leave for my ultrasound appointment. "This is the big one, right?"

By "big one," he means the appointment at which I discover the sex.

"Would you? That would be great." I'm nervous though I don't want to say why. I desperately want a girl and I know that hoping for any particular result is bad form. I should only be hoping for a healthy baby. But I can't help it. Boys (and men, apparently) are wildly alien to me. Then again, so are many women. Fuck, what if I suck no matter which it turns out to be? I'm starting to spin, and I have to remember to breathe.

"Sure, I can come along."

Jonathan and I ride the 'L' to the doctor's office. He hasn't been to any of my appointments, and I can only guess at the assumptions about to be made. The sonographer doesn't waste any time. Once I'm hooked up to the machine, she asks Jonathan in that blunt, yet not unkind, Midwestern way, "Are you the father?"

"Oh, no. No, no. Just the gay best friend."

"Don't say 'just,'" I say. "You're, like, everything."

"Aw, well," he demurs, waving his hand.

"Well, it's great that you're here," she adds. "You want to know the sex? I can tell you."

"Absolutely," I answer.

"If you look here," she says, pointing to the image on the screen. "You can see it's a boy!"

I know I'm supposed to respond in some grandiose way, but my hormones are rolling over me like a tidal wave. I start crying and she interprets my tears as ones brought on by joy.

"A boy!" she cheers again.

Jonathan can read me like a book, however, and saves me.

"Can we have a minute alone? Just, you know, to... celebrate?" He's reaching, after having already declared himself "not the father." And what we would do to "celebrate" is a mystery. But she nevertheless leaves us, promising to return with images of my son.

My son. I have to get used to saying that. It sounds crazy. I'm too young to have a son. Surely, there are rules against this. My throat is closing up in panic and I squeeze Jonathan's hand in terror.

"Fuck. What the fuck am I doing?" I ask him.

"So, I take it you wanted a girl?" If he's judging me, he's hiding it well.

"Yes. But not because I think girls are better! It's just... I don't know anything about boys. I don't know anything about anything!"

"You'll learn."

"Yeah?"

"Yeah. And, you know, maybe you'll get lucky. Maybe he'll be gay."

"God, wouldn't that be great?"

Fat Cat Jack

I'm sitting on the couch looking through a book of baby names, trying to find a boy name that I don't actively hate. The intercom rings out in the apartment and Jonathan runs over to answer it.

"Hey."

"Is this Mr. Jonathan Monroe?"

"Uh... yeah. We don't want any."

"Excuse me?"

"If you're selling something. We don't want any."

"I have a message for you from your grandfather."

"Oh... okay." He presses the buzzer to unlock the front door to the building.

Jonathan and I exchange curious glances. He watches out the peephole to get a look at the man as he approaches.

"He looks harmless," Jonathan shares as the man knocks on the door. Jonathan opens up to a short, wiry man in glasses and an expensive suit.

"Mr. Monroe?" he asks.

"Yeah. Come in."

The man enters. "My name is Mr. Anderson. I work for your grandfather. You've been summoned to see him. I can take you now."

"Excuse me? I'm sorry. Summoned?" Jonathan asks, incredulously.

"Yes."

"What if I have something else to do right now?"

"Do you have something else to do right now?"

"Well, no."

"Okay, then. Do you need a few minutes to gather your things?"

"Yeah. Can you give me a sec?"

"Certainly, sir."

Mr. Anderson stands at attention while Jonathan retreats to his bedroom, motioning for me to join him. He shuts the door behind us and asks, "What the fuck?"

"I don't know, man. This is definitely weird."

"I'm too curious not to go."

"You shouldn't go alone."

"Great. Come with me."

"Oh, I'm definitely coming with you." I'm curious too. We grab our things and join Mr. Anderson in the living room where he hasn't moved an inch.

"My friend is going to come along," Jonathan tells him. I expect some push-back but there's none.

"As you wish, sir," he replies and all I can think of is *The Princess Bride*. But this guy is no Westley.

Westley. Now there's a name.

We leave the apartment together where a black limousine is double parked at the curb waiting for us. I've ridden in a limo once before for senior prom when Jonathan and I attended as friends. The sight thrills me. The three of us climb into the back of the vehicle and settle into the luxurious gray leather seats. I take note of a bar with a bottle of brown liquor and think of the Scotch I drank with Shane. I shake the memory loose and try to focus on the present.

"What do you do for my grandfather?" Jonathan asks our escort.

"I'm his attorney."

"Ah." Jonathan turns toward me. "I didn't know attorneys did kidnappings."

"I don't think kidnappers usually use limos," I say.

"Good point." He turns back to our Mr. Anderson. "And where exactly are we going?"

"To Mr. Monroe's home."

"Let's assume I don't know where that is."

"You never checked the return postage on the gifts?" I ask.

"They came directly from the stores."

"Ah."

"Madison, sir," Mr. Anderson replies.
"Wisconsin?"
"Yes, sir."
"And how far away is that exactly?"
"About three hours."
"Ugh!"

Jonathan gives me a conspiratorial look like we're back in high school. He's gonna fuck with this lawyer a bit. The great thing about hanging with Jonathan is that we could have fun at a tax seminar. So, a three-hour ride with this guy in a fancy limo should be easy.

"Can we drive through McDonalds? I'm hungry."

Exactly what we did in high school.

"Sir?"

"And can I have some of whatever this is?" he asks, indicating the liquor.

"I'm certain your grandfather would prefer you sober."

"Fair enough. Oh! Is that a sunroof?" Jonathan continues, almost jumping out of his seat like an eager toddler.

"No."

Jonathan eyes him suspiciously, not sure whether or not to believe him.

"And a phone!" Jonathan points out the car phone sitting near the Scotch. "Can I make a call?"

Mr. Anderson eyes him wearily but nods.

Jonathan picks up the phone and dials a number. He rattles off quickly the much-practiced prank the way he's always done.

"HiThisIsBobFromBaskinRobbinsIfYouCanNameThirtyOneFlavorsInThirtyOneSecondsI'llGiveYouThirtyOneDollars AndThirtyOneCentsNowGo!"

He waits a moment and then hangs up the phone.

"They didn't name any flavors?" I ask.

"No, they hung up."

"Bummer."

Mr. Anderson clearly wants to chastise us. But before he can, Jonathan asks for some music. Any second, he's going to ask, "Are we there yet?" and I'm going to lose it.

Mr. Anderson pushes a button that lowers the barrier between us and the driver, whom he instructs to turn on the radio. Jonathan loudly vetoes every station ("Next!") until the driver gives up, turns it off, and raises the barrier again. Jonathan releases the most exasperated sigh in history, and it sets me off into a pile of giggles. Mr. Anderson shuffles in his seat uncomfortably like he wants to be anywhere else in the world. The more uncomfortable he is, the funnier everything is. Soon, Jonathan and I are both hysterical, tears streaming down our faces.

"Stop!" I yell. "I'm gonna pee!" This only sets Jonathan off more.

Eventually, we calm down and talk amongst ourselves, ignoring Mr. Anderson completely, who has taken out papers from a briefcase to read.

"So, I never asked. Do we hate him?" Jonathan asks.

"Hate who?"

"Your baby daddy."

"You have *got* to stop calling him that. I feel like I'm on *Ricki Lake* when you do that. And no, we don't hate him."

"You never told me what happened," he says.

"Well, let's see. I'll recap it. We had sex and when I woke up, he said it was a mistake."

Mr. Anderson's eyes raise up from his papers, widened by the turn in conversation.

"Excuse me. This is a private conversation," I say with a sarcasm that fully acknowledges the absurdity of the statement. Mr. Anderson returns to his papers.

Jonathan laughs. "Damn. No wonder you wanted to get outta dodge. And I thought you came to Chicago just for me!" he decries dramatically.

"Shut up," I say.

"It seems like we *should* hate him. Cuz that sounds pretty fuckin' cold."

It was cold. And yet, not? I don't know. When I try to see it through his point of view (or, let's be honest, a *male* point of view), I come up with this: Shane never lied to me. He didn't lead me on. I pursued him and he... acquiesced. That's the worst I can say, isn't it? And I can't be mad about that. Would I rather he hadn't? Would I rather he pushed me away? Not at all. But, of course, that's not what Jonathan is asking. He's talking about *Shane's* regret, not mine. Should I be angry about that? It would be so much easier if I could be. But no. His regret just makes me sad.

"I don't hate him," I say, definitively.

"Alright if I hate him?"

"Sure."

While I can't get on board, I love the loyalty. I reward him with a few more juicy details.

"There's more. He told me the reason he… was because Matty cheated on him."

His eyes widen in surprise. "No way! What did you say?"

"Oh, I was perfectly articulate. I ran out of the room."

"Well, that's understandable," he assures me. Then, "Wow. Matty cheated too. Damn. I don't know why people are so attached to monogamy. Seems like it causes more problems than it solves."

"Right?"

Talking about Shane exhausts me, so I lay down across the seat to nap the rest of the way.

I'm disoriented when Jonathan shakes me awake.

"What?" I ask. "Oh, right. You ready?"

"Not at all. Let's go."

We climb out of the limo and we're standing on a circle driveway inside a gated property in front of a huge three-story colonial-style house. I try to do a quick count of the windows I can see and come up with twelve. As we walk to the front door, I realize this is the first time I've been in a rich person's home. I'm suddenly wildly uncomfortable. I feel like I'm naked and I look down to make sure that I'm wearing clothes. I am, of course, but they feel terribly inadequate for the time and place. I look at Jonathan who, while dressed casually, nevertheless looks fabulous. Of course he does.

Mr. Anderson rings a bell beside a door that surely costs more than the house I grew up in.

"I have a coffee stain on my shirt," I whisper to Jonathan. "I should have changed."

He considers my shirt, and I can tell that he agrees with this assessment, though our friendship code requires him not to be too harsh.

"Babe," he says, a response both sympathetic and amused.

"Why'd you let me leave like this?" I whine.

"The next time I get summoned, I won't. Promise."

The door opens to a delicate, fiftyish woman in a traditional maid's uniform. I thought they only existed in movies.

"Jonathan Monroe and..." Mr. Anderson says and pauses to glance my way. "... *guest* are here here to see Mr. Monroe."

"Certainly, sir," she says. "He's waiting for you in the drawing room."

The drawing room! As out-of-place as I feel, I can't help but be excited by the words. I've never been in a drawing room. I don't even know what it is except that rich people have them in their mansions. I lean into Jonathan and say under my breath, "I wonder if this house has a library with one of those ladders that move around the bookshelves? Can you ask? Cause if so, I want to see."

"Be cool."

Easy for him to say. He doesn't have a coffee stain.

We follow Mr. Anderson to an ornate room with a high ceiling and cathedral windows. A chandelier hangs down, illuminating a circle of antique seating options that all look equally uncomfortable. The furniture sits atop a massive rug of muted colors, the same colors on a painting that covers almost the entirety of the back wall. The painting is of a woman and could either be a queen or Jonathan's grandmother.

Fat Cat Jack is nowhere to be seen.

"You can wait here," the maid says. "Make yourselves comfortable and I'm sure he'll be here in a moment." She turns and leaves. I look at Jonathan and I realize that we're alone. Mr. Anderson has slipped away as we made our way here.

"Dude," I say, hoping to convey everything I'm feeling.

"Dude," he responds, in agreement.

We're still whispering, like we're in a church.

"Should we sit?" I ask.

"I guess so." We pick two chairs that face each other.

"This is such a power play," I say.

"Making us wait?"

"Yeah."

"Yeah."

We settle into a silence, and I wonder what happens if I start to giggle again. Luckily, a booming voice stops the possibility.

"Jonathan!"

Jonathan and I turn towards the source of the exclamation and see, at long last, his grandfather.

He's the opposite of frail; he's tall and built like a bear, ready to overpower and intimidate all those around him. He has a full head of short, dark brown hair and a thin matching mustache. He's wearing a light gray suit tailored to perfection and his face is full of purpose.

"Well, stand up, young man." he barks, and Jonathan pops up on cue. Jack stands in front of him, assessing his grandson for the first time. Suddenly, he smiles approvingly. He grabs Jonathan's shoulders and pulls him into a tender-less hug with strong pats on the back.

"Have a seat," Jack commands. Jonathan sits and Jack walks over to a buffet to take a cigar from a wooden box. He brings it over with him, settling into a chair between Jonathan and me. He clips the cigar with a gold-plated clipper and lights it with a gold-plated lighter. I wonder if he has a gold toilet too.

Only once he's settled, does Jack take note of me. "I see you've brought your friend. Katherine, is it?"

I can't talk. My voice is gone. How does he know my name?

"Yes... this is Katie..." Jonathan responds for me. "She came with me to make sure I wasn't being kidnapped."

"Ha!" Jack yelps and the sound reminds me a lot of Jonathan.

"And you're pregnant," he announces.

"Uh..."

"Is it a boy?" he asks me. I'm surprised he doesn't know since he seems to know everything.

"Yes."

"Good."

I want to be mad about the comment but it's just so perfect in this setting that I let it go. Also, I'm a little terrified of this man.

He turns to Jonathan, dismissing me.

"I've summoned you here because I would like to have a relationship with you. I regret not making more of an effort with your father. I don't want to make that mistake again."

"Ok. But you could have tried before now."

"Your mother and I are…" he hesitates, searching for the perfect words. "… socially incompatible."

He really did find the perfect words. Not just for him and Emily but to describe how I feel right now. I am socially incompatible with this world. It's fascinating but I don't belong. Everything about me is wrong here.

Jonathan nods in response to this judgment.

"I heard about the violent incident on your person," Jack continues. "I'm very glad that you've recovered."

"Oh. Thanks."

"And I'd like to make sure that something like that never happens again. I'd like to make sure that you're protected."

"How exactly are you going to do that?"

"We'll get to that. First, what I want you to know is that I would like an heir. Your father was an only child as are you. I've worked hard for all I have, and I would like to leave it to family. Which means you."

"Dude." I exhale the word without thinking.

Jack glances at me. "Indeed." He turns back to Jonathan. "But before I update my will, I'd like to ensure that my name, your name, is going to continue once I'm gone."

We all think about that.

"Are you asking me to…"

"I know that you're… I'm not interested in your proclivities. I am interested in heritage." He glances my way before continuing. "I realize now that my standards in the past may have been too exacting. I won't make that mistake again."

I'm pretty certain I've just been insulted but I'm not quite sure how.

"You're trying to start a business, yes?" he asks Jonathan.

"How do you know…?"

"If you're starting a business, you're going to need seed money. What I'm proposing today is a deal. I want to help you. I will invest

Consensual Scars

in your business if you meet my provisions. Mr. Anderson can talk you through the details of the agreement on your way back. He'll walk you through the next steps should you accept my proposal."

Jack rings the bell that's been sitting next to the ashtray in what I can only assume is a call to a servant somewhere. He stands up. "I am so glad that we've had the chance to finally meet. We have some catching up to do. But right now, I need to get back to work." He holds his hand out to Jonathan, perhaps deciding the earlier hug was too awkward to repeat.

"Mr. Anderson can escort you back to the car as well." Mr. Anderson appears in a manner so choreographed I almost laugh.

Mr. Anderson leads us out of the house and back to the limo. Once inside, he opens his briefcase and pulls out a stack of papers. "I'm to go over the contract with you."

Jonathan nods.

"It's really very simple," he says, in direct contrast with the inch of documents in his hands. "Mr. Monroe has set up a living trust fund for you, which you can access as soon as you meet his provisions. Specifically, his assurance that the family name shall carry forth."

"Can you say it in English?"

"Marry this woman. Give the child your name. Get lots of money."

His blunt response makes us both laugh and it's a little like a spell has been broken. Jonathan leans into Mr. Anderson and whispers, "So, you're a lawyer. Is this shit even legal? I mean, it's crazy, right?"

Mr. Anderson puts his briefcase and the papers aside and gestures toward the bottle of liquor. "Shall we?"

"Oh, I definitely think we should."

I'm jealous that I can't indulge too but I'm eager to see where this is headed. They pour out two glasses and take sips.

"This is an open trust fund. Which means that it can be changed infinitely to meet Mr. Monroe's requirements. If this were a closed trust, you could certainly contest it. But if you contest this, he'll simply dissolve it."

"A closed trust means he's…"

"Dead. Yes."

"Got it. Just how much money are we talking about?"

"The trust fund, which is intended to fund your venture, is $250,000. The assets in the will total much, much more than that."

"You can't tell me?"

"No."

"What if I guess?"

"No."

Jonathan turns to me. "I still don't get how getting married is supposed to ensure my *safety*. He never explained that."

"I think it's like with my dad," I say. "Remember when he thought I was dating Jeremy and freaked out? I accused him of being a racist and he kept saying he was just worried about *my safety*. You know, from *other* bigots. It's weird parent logic that just reinforces the bad shit."

"Or a giant rationalization."

"Yup."

"Okay, but I was *already with you* when it happened," he says, referring to the night of the assault. "I wasn't making out with a guy on a street corner."

"I bet he doesn't know that," I say, referring to Jack.

"Why the hell not? He apparently knows everything else! What the fuck is that about?" Jonathan asks, turning to Mr. Anderson for more answers.

"Mr. Monroe has many contacts in many places."

"So, he's spying on us?"

H doesn't answer which I'm taking as a definitive "yes." Jonathan and I look at each other, both of us wondering just what all his grandfather knows. Not that our lives are filled with dark, deep secrets. Just the one growing inside me… as far as I know.

"I just want to be one hundred percent clear about something," Jonathan says to Mr. Anderson. "My grandfather doesn't actually expect me to *be* straight. Like, he knows that's not possible, right? This is just about appearances?"

"Not even appearances, really. It's about paperwork."

"What do you mean?"

"I mean, your grandfather doesn't care about illicit affairs. As long as they're discreet. If your grandmother was here, she could confirm that." The comment surprises Jonathan.

"I don't know anything about my grandmother."

"I shouldn't have said that."

"Said what, exactly?"

Mr. Anderson stays silent. I think "what he said" is that Fat Cat Jack is quite the cad, but I stay silent too.

"What do you think?" Jonathan asks me.

"About getting married?"

"Yes."

"It's fucking crazy." And it is. I'm almost certain.

"Totally," Jonathan agrees. "Except…"

"What?"

"This trust is enough to start our business. And the will? I mean, that's gotta be, like, 'fuck you' money." He turns to Mr. Anderson for confirmation of his estimation. "Right?"

"It is definitely 'fuck you' money," he confirms.

"Who do you want to say, 'fuck you' to?" I ask Jonathan.

"Shit. Everyone. But mostly the student loan people."

Good answer. We're both in their sights.

Mr. Anderson picks the contract back up and hands it to Jonathan. "You can take this copy of the contract and read it over. When you decide what to do, give me a call. Please note the non-disclosure agreement that's included."

"What's that?" I ask.

"It means we can't tell anyone about this," Jonathan explains. "Right?"

"Correct," Mr. Anderson affirms.

Cool. Another secret.

Annie Marie Huber

The Game of Life

When we get back to the apartment, Jonathan and I flop onto the couch.

"Well, today was a weird day," he says.

"Indeed," I agree.

"I'm hungry."

"Pizza?"

"Yes."

I order pizza from our favorite place. While we wait, we continue to debate the proposal, now sitting on the coffee table in front of us.

"It's just paperwork. It can be like a green card marriage," he says.

"Would I have to take your name?"

"I assume so. He wants an *heir.*"

"So, my son would be an heir. Gotta say, that sounds kinda amazing. Considering I have, like, nothing to give him. *Katie Monroe.* I don't hate it. But we really should read this contract." Ugh. Legalese gives me a headache.

"We need a lawyer to read this contract," he corrects.

"Do we have a lawyer?"

"I know a lawyer."

"Are you fucking this lawyer?"

"No!" he says, feigning offense. Then, "Well… not yet."

"Ha!" I respond, before asking, "Does it break the non-disclosure agreement to have a lawyer read this?"

"That's a really good question. But, we're not *really* not going to tell anyone. Right? I mean, there are gonna be questions."

"Emily?"

"Of course, Emily."

"But if it's like a green card marriage, then why does *anyone* need to know?" I ask. "I mean, if it's just paperwork?"

"Weird that he cares *only* about paperwork. And I don't give a shit about that."

"I think that's what he's counting on."

"I wonder what the penalty is for signing the non-disclosure agreement and breaking it?"

We both look at the stack of papers and sigh.

"I bet a lawyer could answer that," he says.

I give in. "Fine. Call your friend. What's his name?"

"David."

"Is he hot?"

"So hot."

"How did you meet?"

"He's volunteering with Pride. Helping with the parade."

"Ha! Perfect."

"Why?"

"How covert. We're enlisting an activist you met at Pride… that you're dating."

"Who said dating?"

"Okay… hunting? Is that better?"

"More accurate. Not sure it's better. But I can be discreet."

"Babe," I counter, incredulously.

"I can!" he protests. "Besides. He doesn't care about 'illicit affairs.' Cuz apparently, my grandfather was a horn dog."

"Right?" I concur. "So, you'll have David look at the contract for us?"

"Yes."

With that, we turn on *Seinfeld*. We dig into the pizza when it arrives. I'm so happy I can finally enjoy food again, the nausea of pregnancy finally having subsided. During the first commercial break, Jonathan turns down the volume and looks at me.

"You know, I'm in. That is, if you're in."

"You don't want to talk to David first?"

"I want to fuck David. This might…"

"… make things awkward?"

"A bit."

"So, we'll read the contract ourselves?"

"Sure." He says it with such confidence that I can't help laughing. I know better. He won't read a page of it. And he knows that I will try and give up after three pages.

But fuck it. What do we have to lose?

"I'm in too."

And with that, we're engaged. I have a small worry that I've sold my soul (and possibly my baby?) to the devil. I shake the thought away.

I have to decide how to tell my father about the pregnancy. While I have no plans to see him, I live in fear that he'll stop by the apartment on a whim. Not that he ever has but I'm not feeling particularly rational right now. My emotions are all over the place lately.

I settle on writing him a letter, which I know is cowardly. But I can't bear to see the look of disappointment on his face. And really, how do I answer the inevitable question about the baby's father? I mean, I don't want to imply to *my* father that *all* fathers are irrelevant. And, of course, I don't think they're irrelevant at all. In fact, in my case, they're everything. But I can't say any of that.

In the end, I keep the letter simple and short. I tell him that I'm pregnant and I'm keeping the baby (cue Madonna), I'm not involved with the father, and that I hope he can find a way to be supportive of this decision. I tell him that I'm financially secure and healthy, and that he needn't worry. I tell him that I love him and will visit soon, after he's had time to digest this news.

As I struggle with the letter, Jonathan makes calls to figure out the logistics of a simple, civil ceremony. He makes the appointment for March 14th.

When the big day arrives, I tell him that we should go out for pie after we're hitched.

"To celebrate?"

"Yes. My birthday."

"Shit! It's your birthday! Fuck!"

"It's alright."

"Our anniversary will fall on your birthday."

"Our *anniversary*?"

I look at him and we laugh at the very idea.

"You should have told me," he says. "You know I forget that shit."

"Take me out for pie and I'll forgive you."

"We could have a party!"

"Do I look like I want a party?"

"No. You look ridiculous actually."

He's not wrong. I'm dressed in a too-tight t-shirt that accents my baby bump and jeans that sit low on my hips, barely buttoning up. I've been treating our nuptials like a scene in a show, picking costumes and props. Since it's going to look like a shotgun wedding anyway, I'm leaning into the look.

"Come on," I tell him. "Get into the spirit with me. Dress the part."

"You want me to look... *trashy*?" He's horrified.

"It's not *real*. I mean, it is. But not really. We should have some fun with it. I dare you."

He laughs at the juvenile remark.

"Fine. Since you *dare* me."

He goes into his room and comes out wearing a white tank top with a flannel shirt over it, jeans slung low, his underwear fully visible, and a blue Cubs hat placed sideways on his head.

"Perfect," I say. "Now what about rings?"

"Do we need rings?" he asks.

"Maybe just for the ceremony. We can take them off after."

"Cool. Do you have any?"

I have a small collection of costume jewelry and we pick out terribly tacky, plastic, colorful atrocities. After a few more minutes of hair primping (for Jonathan, not me), we head out to the Cook County Clerk office. We take the 'L' there. As we ride, Jonathan is tugging his pants up and I can't stop laughing.

"I don't know how straight boys do this."

"Aw. You look cute. Like a skater boy."

When we get to the building, we are sent to a hallway to wait. The building is boring bureaucracy itself: functional furniture, neutral colors and stale air. We sit on a bench opposite another young couple. They're holding hands and I presume they're also waiting to get married.

Once seated, we drop character.

"I feel like we should be drunk and in Vegas," he muses. "At least that place is fun. This is… tragic."

The couple across from us gives him an admonishing look that only makes me want to make them more uncomfortable.

"So, how are things with David?"

"They are progressing. We've got a date tonight."

The other couple gets up and moves to a bench slightly farther away, which makes us both laugh.

When it's our turn, the ceremony is brief and completely surreal. The justice of the peace is a no-nonsense man of about fifty with thinning hair and glasses that set low on his nose. I resist the urge to push them up further on his face. He rolls his eyes at our appearance, and I suddenly regret our costumes, wishing we had both worn more conservative attire. I wonder if he can refuse us service, but he doesn't. He proceeds, starting our ceremony in a low monotone. I can barely hear him and my mind wanders.

As a little girl, I never fantasized about getting married. A fortunate circumstance given this generic ceremony. We may as well be the stick figures in the game of *Life*. That was such a weird game, wasn't it? Well, now my little car has two pieces in it. And soon there will be a third. How did I get here? My mind is spinning when I realize that both Jonathan and the justice are staring at me. I've missed my cue.

"I do."

The words have a weight I don't expect. I remind myself to breathe, that this is just a legal thing. Just paperwork. We kiss chastely on the lips because that's nothing new between us. And before I know it, I'm a married woman.

We walk from the government building until we find a diner with an acceptable pie selection. We sit across from one another in a booth, and I ask about the next steps.

"We have to wait for the certificate. Should take about six weeks. Maybe eight? Then I'll call Mr. Anderson."

"Cool. Do you feel any different?"

Consensual Scars

"No."

"You sure? You don't feel like you've betrayed your brotherhood?"

"Ha."

"You know what I mean."

"I know what you mean. But I don't need to respect an institution that doesn't respect me."

"An institution?"

"Marriage."

"Ah."

"What about you?" he asks. "Do you feel different?"

"I mean… I do feel safer if that makes sense. But that's about the money and not, you know, *this*," I say, indicating the tacky ring still on my finger.

"Right. That makes sense."

"We need to be smart about the money."

"Oh, for sure." He says it with such ease that I'm immediately uneasy.

"We can't, you know, blow it all on drugs and clubs."

"Hey!"

"I'm just saying."

"A little trust, Mrs. Monroe."

"Man, that's weird."

"You have to do me a favor," he says.

"Another one? Geez, I just married you!"

"Ha. Don't let me turn into a rich asshole."

I look at him. He's serious and I'm touched by his concern over this.

"I won't."

"For real. Check me."

"I will. I promise. If you start actin' a fool, I'll drive you to a faraway Laundromat. That'll bring you back down to earth."

Annie Marie Huber

And David Makes Three

The second trimester is way better than the first. The queasiness is gone and now I'm just exhausted. And I guess that makes sense. I mean, I am growing a *person*. (Oh, what did you do today? I grew an *arm*. Women are amazing. No wonder men are always trying to compensate. I would be too.)

Jonathan goes out to bars and clubs regularly with a posse of friends he's met out here. I would join them if I wasn't pregnant. Even if I wasn't so tired, going out and not drinking while watching everyone else drink sounds terribly tedious.

I fill my days with building our business website between naps. I go to bed early and sleep late.

On one of these lazy, late mornings, I stumble into the kitchen to find a stranger, beating eggs. I'm shocked because I almost never meet Jonathan's conquests. They're usually shuffled out the door too quickly. This one is about 5'8" with dark skin and cornrows that fall to his chin. He's in a sarong with flowers on it and pink-colored sunglasses. Despite his youthful outfit, I can tell he's older. Early-thirties perhaps. He grins broadly when he sees me.

"Hey," I say.

"Katie?"

"That's me."

"David," he says, offering his hand to mine. I take it and smile.

"David! You're working on the Pride parade."

"Oooh. You've heard of me. That bodes well for me. Want an omelet, dear?"

"Hell yes."

"Awesome. Cheese good?"

"Cheese is perfect." I sit down at the table and watch him in the galley kitchen. It's an anomaly, someone cooking in there.

"Jonathan in his room?" I ask.

"He went for lattes."

There's a coffee shop two blocks away that he's been frequenting since being off the crutches.

"Lattes. Yum! Oh man, I love this town."

"From Indiana, yeah?"

"Yeah. You?"

"New York."

I'm not surprised. He has a confident, no-bullshit quality about him that I associate with New Yorkers, even though I've never been there. I'd love to visit one day and I tell him that.

"Oh, you should go! New York is amazing."

"Why did you leave?"

"Job offer. And you Midwesterners intrigue me."

"No!"

"Truly."

"We're *boring*."

"You're *nice*."

"Ick."

"Ha!"

He talks as much with his hands as his mouth and I'm taken by his charisma. He's electric, and I can't help but think that Jonathan might have met his match.

"And how does Chicago compare? To New York?" I ask.

"New York is like jazz. Frenetic, unpredictable… *beautiful*. Chicago is like…"

"… the blues," we say together.

"Yeah," he says, nodding enthusiastically, pointing at me. "You get it."

"Yeah."

I want to know everything about David now.

"And what do you do?" I ask David.

"I'm a lawyer."

I don't know any lawyers or doctors, not even future ones that would still be getting their degrees. My friends are mostly aspiring actors and screenwriters, with a few techies and teachers in the group.

"Wow. That's, like, a real job," I say, and I know I sound stupid.

"Ha! Yeah, I guess so. Just don't say, 'you don't look like a lawyer.'"

"You know, I was about to."

"Why?"

"Lawyers wear stuffy suits."

"Well, I'm a non-profit lawyer so my suits aren't all that stuffy."

"Really? That's cool."

Jonathan arrives with the lattes and hands me the decaf. We all eat breakfast together and discuss the upcoming Pride parade.

"Will you be coming?" David asks me.

"I would but I hate going out in public right now. Everyone thinks they can touch my stomach."

"I get that. Everyone wants to touch my hair," David says.

"You have excellent hair," I tell him.

He assesses me. "You want to touch it, don't you?"

"No! Well, kind of," I admit. "I don't know why."

"Fuckin' white people," he says, shaking his head.

"But I won't! I promise. Don't touch my stomach and I won't touch your hair."

"Deal."

We shake on it, and I like David very much.

While I'm not a gatekeeper, having a relationship with me makes a relationship with Jonathan easier, and David – to his credit – instinctively understands this. Nevertheless, our relationship develops organically and quickly the way relationships sometimes do. Right away, we find common ground in our shared love of Billy Joel. I'm playing *An Innocent Man* on the stereo when he comes by one evening. He immediately starts singing along.

"You like Billy?" I ask.

"What? I'm only supposed to like hip-hop?" he retorts.

"Oh, shit. No, no, no..."

He breaks into a teasing grin. "I'm kidding. God, you're so easy to fuck with."

"It's just... I know he's not 'cool.' I mean, my *dad* likes Billy Joel."

"Fuck 'cool.' *New York State of Mind*, baby. And remember, I'm from Long Island. We're, like, required to love him."

I point to Jonathan and say, "He hates him."

"I don't *hate* him. I just don't *love* him. And you've had that tape of his stuck in your car forever."

He's right. My *Greatest Hits Vol. 1* tape is currently jammed in the cassette player of my car. I recently slid the tape in when I decided I just had to hear *Pressure* even though I knew the cassette would reside there indefinitely.

"I've got two tickets to see him later this month. Wanna go?" David asks me.

"Um... *yes*."

Jonathan shakes his head at both of us. I can tell that this development (David and I bonding) makes him a little weary, a feeling he expresses when the two of us are alone.

"I just don't want you getting too attached," Jonathan tells me, as if I'm a child and he's my single parent.

"Well, he has my endorsement. And I think I might keep this one even if you don't," I tell him. It feels a bit like breaking a cardinal clause of the "fag hag" contract. But I like David and I'm not in a rush to push him to the curb.

"I just don't want it to get weird," Jonathan says.

"Why would it get weird?"

"What if he wants to be monogamous and I don't? And we stop seeing each other but he's still coming around, hanging out with you but pining after me. That could be weird."

"Wow. That's a pretty specific scenario."

"I can see it happening. Let's face it. I'm a heartbreaker." He's only half-joking and I admire his confidence.

"I'm so glad I don't ever have to worry about your self-esteem," I tease him.

Regardless of Jonathan's initial reticence, David becomes a fixture in our apartment in the evenings and weekends. I now find him making breakfast in the morning more often than not and that's when we talk most.

"So, my non-profit needs a website," he tells me, handing me a toasted bagel with cream cheese.

"Yeah?" I ask. "I'm surprised you're touching these," I say, indicating the bagel. If television has taught me one thing about New Yorkers, they have very high bagel standards.

"They're trash but I'm hungry. Anyway, I want to hire you guys."

"Fuck. That's amazing. Wow!" I run up to him and give him a hug.

"Now, I expect y'all to build a kick-ass site. I'm going to have high expectations as your client."

"We have a client!" I giggle at the word. "Sorry. This is a first."

He's grinning at me, amused at my delight.

"Well, congratulations."

"How..." I trail off because I don't even know what questions to ask. I've never done anything in the world of "business" other than customer service, usually the lowest rung on the corporate ladder. I've never had a *client*. I'm so excited.

"How do we get started?" he asks, rescuing me.

"Yeah."

"I can email you and Jonathan the specs of the project, what we need. You guys will put together a list of deliverables, some mock-ups, and a quote."

"Damn. You're smart."

"I already talked to Jonathan. That's what *he* told me."

"Ha! Phew!" I dramatically wipe imaginary sweat from my forehead. "Well, it's good that one of us knows what the fuck we're doing."

"Don't worry. Y'all will figure it out. It's really great what you're doing."

"Thanks. It would be cool to have, like, a career."

"Yeah, well, I've found it useful. Hey, have you changed your mind about Pride? The parade is this Sunday. I promise I'll keep your stomach safe from strangers."

"I don't know, man. I'm so tired!" I answer.

"Come on. It'll be fun."

"Fine. But you guys better not ditch me."

"Why would we ditch you?"

"I don't know. To go somewhere a vagina isn't wanted."
"Like?"
"I don't know. A bath house?"
"This ain't San Francisco in the '70s."

He seems pained when he says it, like he's lost something he'll never get back.

Annie Marie Huber

Ménage à Trois

On Sunday, the weather is gorgeous when we arrive at the parade. We're navigating through the crowds, and it's been forever since I've been around this many people. My anxiety ratchets up, my hand gripping Jonathan's like a child at Disneyland. I take a deep breath to calm myself. I'm not a child, I remind myself. I'm just creating one. And I know my way home.

Relaxing my grip, I take in the sights and the energy which is all positive and electric. Everywhere I look, I see rainbow flags and feather boas. The crowd is diverse, from men and women in military uniforms to elaborately dressed drag queens. So far, I've seen tributes to Madonna, Cher, and Dolly. Joyful music from the passing floats fills the air.

After walking for about an hour, I can feel my ankles start to swell. I ask the guys if we can take a break and sit somewhere. Anywhere.

"We could go to The Eagle," Jonathan suggests, referring to the city's most prominent leather bar. "They're having a retirement party today for the bartender."

"I don't think I'm dressed for The Eagle," I tell him. I've finally had to give in to maternity wear, and it's not exactly club clothes.

"You're fine. We're not wearing leather either." He waves his hand to indicate the matching attire on him and David: cut-off denim shorts and tank tops. "But we can hang in the front bar. We just can't go in the Pit," referring to the back bar.

"Okay," I agree, desperate to rest.

We head to The Eagle. When we arrive, our timing is perfect. A group is leaving, and we squeeze into their table. As soon as we've secured our spot, David joins the packed bar to get us drinks. He returns with two beers and a soda for me.

"If I'm this tired at five months," I tell them, sipping my soda, "I might not be able to move at all soon."

"You should exercise!" Jonathan says, always the gym evangelist. I grunt in response.

"You could do yoga," David advises. "Isn't that a thing? Prenatal yoga?"

The word "yoga" has weight. I've missed doing yoga but every time I get into lotus position, I start to cry, flooded with memories of Shane. It's a real barrier to inner growth.

"There's a guy staring at you at the bar," Jonathan tells me.

I look up, and it takes a minute to recognize the man, who is dressed in not much more than chaps. It's Ellis, the British filmmaker, whom I last saw while I was housesitting for Matty and Shane.

Apparently, the word "yoga" has manifested more than memories.

"Oh my god," I respond.

"You know him? He's gorgeous. Introduce us!" Jonathan encourages.

I don't have a choice because Ellis is now walking towards us. He's snapping his fingers, trying to place me.

"Katie," I help him.

"Right, right! How are you, love?" Noticing my pregnancy, he continues, "Ah! It looks like congratulations are in order!"

Shit. There's a trail now, a way for the truth to get from me to Shane.

"Oh… thanks," I stammer, my mouth dry with panic.

Jonathan, taking the initiative, introduces himself and David. Ellis joins us at the table.

"How are Matty and Shane?" I ask. "I haven't seen them in a while."

I can't help but touch the hot stove.

"They're splendid, love. Just splendid. As always."

My heart sinks. It shouldn't, of course. I should want him – *them* – to be doing great. But in my fantasy world, Shane's been terribly distraught since I left.

My three companions start talking, their conversation flirty as sexual innuendos fly. Soon, I feel like a third wheel (well, technically, a *fourth* wheel).

"I think I'm gonna take off," I tell them. "I'm really tired."

"Alright, baby. We'll see you back at the apartment," Jonathan says. I give kisses to him and David and lie to Ellis, telling him that it was great seeing him again. His British accent and delightful demeanor can't make up for reminding me of Shane. I take the train home. When I get there, I cry myself to sleep even though the sun hasn't even set yet.

The next morning, I prep a smoothie in my effort to eat healthier for the baby. Before starting the blender, I check the time to make sure it's after 10am (our agreed-upon start time for noisy appliances). Nevertheless, the sound of the blender wakes someone up. I'm sipping on my fruity concoction when Ellis stumbles out of Jonathan's bedroom.

I shouldn't be surprised but I am.

"Oh, hey," I say.

He's wearing Jonathan's robe and I'm grateful. Chaps are a lot to take first thing in the morning.

"Hi..." he says, snapping his fingers *again*. This man will never remember my name.

"Katie."

"Right, right! Sorry."

He seems a little sheepish about it this time though, so I immediately forgive him. I ask if he wants some coffee, and he accepts. I make a pot and we sit at the table while it brews.

"You boys have fun last night?" I ask.

"We did. You?"

"The parade was fun," I answer.

"I think I had more fun after the parade."

"Ha! I bet you did. I'm so fucking jealous of gay men."

"And why is that, love? Because of all the shameless sex?"

"Yes!"

"Who says you can't have lots of shameless sex?"

"Oh, I don't know. All of society?"

"Ah, fuck society."

I agree with the sentiment even if I have trouble living it.

"Society is just constructs," he continues. "Constructs that are created by humans. If we constructed them, we can destroy them. Like marriage, for instance."

"Go on."

"Why is there so much divorce? Because we force people to live their lives in discordance with their very nature. To desire is human. We're all sexual beings, just... *energy* really. Some energies attract, some repel. Energy matters more than specific body parts. At least, that's how I see it. We're so focused on putting people in boxes when all it makes us wanna do is break out of 'em."

"You're against labels."

"Exactly, love. Just don't label me as anti-label."

"Got it. So, how are your film projects?"

I want to know about the toilets. Please tell me about the toilets.

"I've got a few in the can." (Hee!) "I'd like to put them online, but I need a bloody website."

My ears perk up. "I can help with that. Well, we can. Jonathan and I."

"Jonathan?"

I shake my head, laughing. "Yeah. The guy you just spent the night with. Lives here. The blonde?"

"Ah, yes! Gorgeous bloke. So was the other one. What's his name?"

"David."

"Right, right."

"So, you can't remember anyone's name. How do you expect to make it in the entertainment industry?"

"I'm an artist, love. Fuck the industry."

I'm sensing a theme. The coffee starts gurgling and I get up to get him a cup.

"Cream? Sugar?"

"Black as midnight on a moonless night."

I grin at the *Twin Peaks* reference and remember our late-night Lynch theories.

"Here you are, Coop," I say, handing him the drink.

"Cheers," he replies, before taking a sip.

Are Ellis and I becoming friends? The idea is a little crazy as the line that connects him to me goes straight through Shane and Matty. But if he's cool enough to quote Agent Cooper, surely he can be trusted to keep my secret.

"Can you do me a favor? It's going to sound weird."

"Oooh. I like weird."

"Can you *not* tell Matty and Shane that you saw me?"

His eyes widen with interest. "Why, love? Are you on the run?"

"No, no. I just..." I'm searching for some kind of plausible reason for my odd request, but I come up empty. "I can't tell you why."

"Oooh!"

I have just become one thousand percent more interesting to him.

"Please? Just don't mention me."

"I had no idea you'd be such a mysterious maiden! Well, now I'm dying to know why. But it's good. Mum's the word. I mean, just think of how *boring* things would have to get for us to start talking about you."

My mouth drops open, but he smiles and winks to let me know he's joking. The buzzer in the apartment rings, alerting us to a visitor. I get up and answer.

"Yeah?" I ask.

"Mr. Anderson to see Mr. Monroe."

Shit. "Yeah... yeah... come in."

I push the button that unlocks the door downstairs. I turn to Ellis. "I need you to go back in there," I tell him, shoving him towards Jonathan's room. "And send Jonathan out. Now!"

Ellis, wildly amused at this development, laughs the entire way. "Girl, what is happening? And Jonathan...?"

"The *blonde* one!"

"Okay, okay!"

I get him in the bedroom. Then I walk to the front door to let in Mr. Anderson. I'm still in my pajamas. I really hope we're not being summoned again.

"Mrs. Monroe. Good morning," he says.

"Hi. Come in."

"Thank you. Is Mr. Monroe available?" He walks in but doesn't move more than a few feet from the front door. He's, again, a soldier at attention. I was hoping we were beyond this façade after the limo ride but apparently not.

"Sure, sure. Just one sec," I say before walking to Jonathan's room. He opens the door just as I'm about to knock. He's wearing sweatpants and nothing else. His JBF hair is properly messy, and his eyes are barely open.

"Mr. Anderson is here!" I whisper-yell.

"Oh, shit. Yeah. Give me a minute." He shuts the door before I can stop him. I grunt in frustration and go back to Mr. Anderson.

"He'll be out soon. Really. You can sit down if you want."

"I'm fine."

"Okay." I consider excusing myself, but I feel like I should be standing here awkwardly. Finally, Jonathan joins us. He's now a little more presentable in jeans and a t-shirt, his hair combed out.

"Hey, Mr. Anderson! Good morning! How are you?"

"Mr. Monroe." Mr. Anderson isn't sharing in the bon amie. Instead, he reaches his arm out for a polite handshake. Jonathan takes his hand and shakes it enthusiastically.

"What brings you by?" Jonathan asks.

Mr. Anderson walks over to the kitchen table where he places his briefcase. He takes out a newspaper and hands it to Jonathan. I come over to look at it. It's a copy of the *Chicago Tribune* and the page features a photo of Jonathan and David celebrating at the Pride parade. They're on the street, looking adorable among the celebration, and kissing for the camera.

"Awww!" I say, automatically.

"Hey! We made the paper!" Jonathan says.

Mr. Anderson clears his throat.

"Oh," I say.

"Oh," Jonathan repeats.

We exchange a guilty glance.

"Let me guess. My grandfather saw this and isn't too happy?"

"Correct."

"I said I wasn't gonna live in the closet."

"You also said you could be discreet. This isn't discreet."

"Right," Jonathan says with slightly clenched teeth. I can see the struggle in Jonathan. On the one hand wanting to shove this guy and his grandfather right out of his life. And on the other hand, a deep, deep desire for "fuck you" money. I'm having the same, exact struggle.

"Hey, guys! What's going on?" It's David and all our heads turn to him. He's dressed in his signature sarong of rainbow colors and nothing else.

A long, uncomfortable silence follows.

"Your grandfather would like your discretion in the future."

Jonathan tersely nods and Mr. Anderson makes his exit.

"What the fuck was that?" David asks.

Jonathan shows him the newspaper photo. "We made the paper," he explains. "Fat Cat Jack is not happy."

"Awww!" David says, looking at the photo.

"Right?" I say. "Fuck Fat Cat Jack."

"Who the fuck is Fat Cat Jack?" David asks, looking from me to Jonathan.

"My grandfather."

"Ah," David says. "And he doesn't approve of 'your lifestyle' I take it?"

"You could say that," Jonathan says. "Don't worry about it, baby. Now, come on. Make us some eggs."

David gives me one last quizzical look before letting himself be dragged to the kitchen.

A New Mantra

At six months, my recurring airport nightmare gets more harrowing. Instead of just trying to get to the airport on time, now I feel like I'm being chased. What I'm running from is never clear, no clearer than what I'm running towards. All I know is that I wake up in a cold sweat and it takes me hours to recover from the anxiety and fear. I'm sitting in the living room doing just this one morning when Jonathan bounds into the apartment.

"Good morning, baby!" he says, cheerily.

"Ugh."

"Oh no. Let me guess? Airport dream?"

"Yes."

He joins me on the couch and gives me a goofy grin.

"Well, if you want a therapist to figure that shit out, you can probably pay for one soon."

He produces a manilla envelope, holding it up for me to see.

"Oh shit. Is that…?"

"Yup! Our marriage certificate."

We open the envelope and gaze at the form. Seeing it there, so official, is weird.

"I'll call Mr. Anderson and find out what to do next," he says. "Before I leave."

"Leave?"

"I'm going to New York with David for a few days. To meet his family."

"Oh, wow. That's serious."

"It's… something."

"Come on. It's a good thing."
"I know. It's just... ah! Meeting the parents."
"You're great with parents."
"Sure, parents of *friends*. Not *boyfriends*. This is new territory."
"Good territory."
"Sure, sure." He nods, doing his best to let himself be convinced. "Unless you don't want me to go? I can cancel if you want me here."
"I'm not an invalid, baby. Go to New York with your hot man. Meet his mama. I dare you. Besides, it'll give me a chance to nest."
"Is that, like, a pregnancy thing?"
"Yeah. It means getting everything ready."
"Everything is ready."

Physically, everything is ready. I've got the crib, car seat, changing table, diaper bag, and about a dozen onesies. The AOL message mommy boards are coming in handy, prepping me for my son's arrival. I've paid for all these things on a credit card that I have no way of paying back until the money comes from Fat Cat Jack. But I'm not going to think about that now.

Anyway, I'm not talking about the physical.

"I mean getting *me* ready. Mentally ready. I want to find some prenatal yoga like David suggested. And try meditating again. I'm going to be pushing a person out of me. I should have some, I don't know, mental strength? And I can work on the website for David. Really, I could use some alone time."

Jonathan has never gravitated to the mystical, but he can respect the pursuit. And while I'm almost certain I'll end up crying in a fetal position when I attempt any of this, I still feel like I should be at least *trying* to better myself. Lord knows I'm not ever going to the gym with Jonathan.

"Besides, I need to go home. Visit my dad," I continue.
"Biting that bullet, huh?"
"I'm so fucking scared."
"Trade you? I'll go tell your dad. You go to New York."
"Ha! Yes!"

My father hasn't responded to my letter. And while I'm fine continuing to hide, I know my mom would want me to try.

Consensual Scars

The next day, I drive Jonathan and David to the airport, the whole way plagued by the Billy Joel tape that's still jammed in the cassette player. Jonathan, sitting shotgun, digs out a pen in the glove box and uses it to pry the tape out. Unfortunately, the magnetic strip remains caught. He pulls the strip out, creating a black blob of tape.

"Now you've done it," I tell him.

"I'm sorry. I just couldn't anymore."

"I get it."

After dropping them off, I head to Lake City to face my father. The two-hour drive is nothing but dread. When I arrive, I see that he's home, but I sit in my car for a full twenty minutes before finding the strength to go inside.

"Hey! It's me!" I call out.

There's no answer but I can hear the TV playing in the living room. I go there and stand next to his recliner where he's doing his best to ignore me. I wait for an acknowledgement of my existence, but he just stares straight ahead at the TV. My father isn't a big man, only about 5'9", but he's big to me which I'm assuming is quite normal. So, the silent treatment, while immature, is devastating. Whatever soft edges had been forming around my father when we lived together have hardened again. Suddenly, I'm sixteen again.

That was the only other time my dad employed the silent treatment with me. That was when he thought that Jeremy and I were dating. We weren't. We were just friends, but the truth didn't seem to matter much. I was hanging around a *black boy*. The *audacity*. That was the day I discovered something ugly about my dad. (I shouldn't have been surprised. My grandfather's overtly racist comments make me cringe still.)

But I don't write my father off. He's not beyond hope. I've seen him change. I saw it after years of me bringing home friends from college of all races. I see it through his affection for Jonathan. My generation isn't marching in the streets, but we are doing the hard work in the living rooms with our Boomer parents. I don't think we'll ever get as much credit as we deserve for this. It's way fucking hard.

And if my dad can let go of all that baggage, surely he can get past this too. I just need to give him some time. But I try one last tact before leaving.

"Mom would want you to know your grandson."

I see him twitch ever so slightly but that's all the reaction I'm getting today.

"I don't have a name yet," I continue. "But I'm thinking of Mr. Mistoffelees."

I know he won't let this go.

"The hell?" he asks, looking over at me for the first time since my arrival.

"I'm just kidding," I confess.

"Oh." He turns back to the TV, not quite ready not to be angry yet.

"But if I think of a name… should I let you know?"

He grunts a non-committal response. But it's something and I take it.

"Okay," I say, turning to leave.

When I get back in my car, I feel accomplished. I've fulfilled my daughterly duty. The moment calls for celebratory music but all I have is a mangled tape deck. I sigh and start the car.

I promised myself that I would drive straight back to Chicago, but I head to Shane's house instead. Before I turn on his street though, I manage to pull over. I can't go any further. And really, I shouldn't have come this close. The closer I get to him, the more I hurt. I'm torturing myself, wallowing in the missing of him.

I wonder what he's doing right now. Is he cooking? Do they have friends over? Or are they alone, trying Kama Sutra positions? Are they even together? Did their respective affairs have any kind of lasting impact? And what would happen if I just walked in the door and revealed myself?

I do a quick gut check. Nope. I would rather die.

I start the car and head back to Chicago. In a few months, my life will be something different and all my focus will be on the baby and the business. And then maybe, maybe, I can get over him.

When I return to the apartment, everything feels a little different. I realize that while certainly lonely, I have never been physically alone much at all. I went from my parents' house to living with Jonathan to my parent's house and back to living with Jonathan. And while I always had my own room where I could close the door, it's not the same as this. I could walk around naked in the apartment. I don't, but I could, and the thought is a little thrilling.

My first night alone I order takeout, watch a Lifetime movie, and cry about all the things that can't be. I let down whatever gate has been holding all my anxiety and grief at bay. It's wonderful and painful and glorious and awful. By the time I turn in, I've gone through two boxes of tissues. I feel numb and my sleep is dreamless.

The next morning, I try to start my day with meditation. Shane taught me the basics. Just sit and breathe. Focus on the breathing. Allow thoughts to come and go. I close my eyes but all I see is my father's disappointed face. When I shake the image away, it's replaced by Shane's judgmental face. I'm drowning in the disapproval of men. I give up.

Meditation is a bust but that doesn't mean yoga will be too. I get out the phone book to start calling various yoga studios in search of a prenatal class. Surely in a city like Chicago, there has to be one somewhere. As I dial the first number, I notice an incessant beeping coming from Jonathan's room.

I go in his room and find his pager on his dresser. He must have forgotten to bring it. I can only imagine how annoyed he must be about that. I check the device and recognize Jonathan's home number. I must have dialed it a million times in high school.

David left a New York number on the refrigerator, and I call it. A woman answers the phone.

"Yes?"

"Hi. My name is Katie. David gave me this number. I'm a friend of Jonathan's. Is he available?"

"Ah no, child. They're out right now. But I can leave a message for him."

"If you could tell Jonathan to call his mom, that would be great. He left his pager here, and it's going off like crazy."

"Oh dear. I'll let him know. What was your name again?"

"Katie."

"Alright. You have a good day now."

I say goodbye and hang up. The pager starts going off again and I go back to Jonathan's room to see if I can shut it off before it makes me crazy. This time, I notice something else on the dresser: one of the yearbooks that Emily brought over. I haven't seen them since that day. I just assumed Jonathan had stuffed them in a closet.

I pick up the yearbook, sit on his bed and page through it. It's not from our high school, but the other one, the one in the middle of a corn field. I page through the student pictures, and I find two photos that Jonathan has circled. They're in the senior section and their names are Josh Owens and Nick Rivas. It's a 1989 yearbook, which means they're two years older than us. I study the images, but I can't be sure of anything.

I've tried many times to recall what happened that night, but the holes in my memory are still there. Everything is just flashes and sounds: the snow piled high in the parking lot, the slur yelled out by one of the boys, the sirens, the inside of the ambulance. I've thought about trying hypnosis, but that assumes there actually are memories in my mind to recall. I feel like my brain just opted out of processing stuff, like a full email box that rejects any new input. I can't unearth buried memories that were never formed in the first place.

I stare at the photos. I want to imprint their faces and names, commit the neural pathways that I didn't before. I look for any distinguishing marks that would make them easier to identify but they just look like two generic white boys to me. So, I recite their characteristics in my head. Josh: blond hair (parted down the middle, landing in waves just below his ears), blue eyes, slightly chubby cheeks, a wide nose and thick neck, and perfect teeth. Nick: dark hair (in a crew cut), brown eyes, high cheekbones, a gold earring in his left ear, and a dimple in his chin. I stare and stare until I'm sure I can recognize them.

I'm tempted to call Emily and arrange to give her the yearbook. But Jonathan would probably kill me. If he had wanted her to have it, he would certainly have already handed it over. I decide it's best to talk to him first. Maybe he can talk to David about it? I mean, the man is a lawyer. He would have insight on what we should do. That is, if he even knows about the assault. I've heard Jonathan explain away the crutches as the result of a car accident. When I asked him about the lie, he just said that it was easier than the truth.

"Sometimes the truth just makes people uncomfortable and

Consensual Scars

weird."

He's right, of course, but I wonder if we're both getting a little too comfortable with lying.

Before I put the yearbook back, I find my coding notebook and write down the names of the boys. Now that I have this vital information, I feel a pull to do something more. So, I locate a phone book for Lake City in the kitchen and page through it, looking for the name Owens. There are three listed, none with the first name of Josh. I take a deep breath and dial the number of the first one listed. I listen to a perky answering machine message and hang up. When I try the second number, a gruff voice answers.

"Yeah?"

"Hi. I'm looking for Josh," I say.

"Josh is my son, but he lives in Muncie now. Went to Ball State!" he brags, pausing for a reaction, as if I care about the boy's college credentials.

"Oh."

"But, you know, if you give me your name and number, I can give him a message."

I hang up. And then I panic, praying he doesn't star69 me. But he doesn't, so I continue to the second name. There's two Rivas listings, one with the first name of Nicholas. I want to call to confirm this is the right number but I'm not sure how to do it. How can I specify which Nick I'm trying to find if his father answers with the same name? ("Hi. I want to talk to the Nick that assaulted me and my friend." That's not going to work.)

I write the numbers and addresses on the sheet of paper alongside their names. I don't have a plan for this information, so I just stare at it. Jonathan and I had both agreed to put the event behind us but it's a little harder to do now. Then again, do I want to go the police station and get into this? Not remotely. Especially now. My focus should be on my son and not that horrible day. I try to channel Shane. I need to sit and think. Not be so impulsive. I need, in fact, to not do anything. Why is that so hard?

I need a distraction, so I return to my quest for a prenatal yoga class, finally finding one downtown. The studio offers it once a week and lucky for me that day is today, this afternoon. I get directions from the woman on the phone, then I work on the website until it's time to go to the class.

Jonathan and I have converted the dining area into an office. It's working for the moment, but I suspect Jonathan will want to upgrade soon. And why not? If things go according to plan, we'll have the money to get something bigger. Although, for the first time, I'm thinking about getting my own place. After experiencing just one night alone, I can see the benefits of having a place where I can cry in peace. Of course, I'm not sure that really works for a marriage façade, so I tuck that idea away for now. Maybe, one day, when we're happily divorced? Hell, maybe by then, he can actually marry for real.

My yoga mat is buried in my closet, covered in dust. I take it out and wipe it down, my hands unsteady, nervous at the thought of attending this class. Whatever skills I had amassed during those months in Lake City have long since atrophied. I feel about as flexible as a lead pipe. Add to that my protruding belly and I have no idea if I'll be able to do anything without falling over.

Go, I tell myself. Just *go*.

I breathe a heavy sigh but manage to leave the apartment. I take the 'L' and walk a few blocks to a small studio on a busy street, sandwiched between a juice bar and a gym. This block must be for the healthy people. I enter the studio and approach the front desk.

"Is this the prenatal class?"

"Yes! Welcome!" A beautiful red-headed woman takes my money and helps me sign in. I discover moments later that she's also the teacher and her name is Chrissy. She's a little younger than Matty but her energy is the same and I think about running out.

I'm glad I don't though because the class is amazing. Only three other people show up but that just makes it better with the personal attention we all get. The yoga is gentle and self-affirming and makes me feel better than I have in a long time. At one point during the class, Chrissy creates thrones made of pillows for each of us. I feel more relaxed than I have in… maybe ever? She treats us, and our bodies, with such reverence that I'm euphoric when we're done.

As I'm putting on my shoes after class, I tell her how wonderful the experience was. She's delighted to hear it.

"Thank you! I hope you come back. Do you have a birth plan yet?"

The euphoria swiftly swings to anxiety. I don't have a birth plan. I've only been focusing on what to do *after* the baby is here.

"No," I say. And then I start crying. It's so sudden that she's taken aback.

"Oh my! Are you okay? Can I get you anything?" she asks.

"No, no. I'm sorry. I'm just… no, I don't have a birth plan. I don't know what I'm doing really." Whatever was blocking this particular anxiety has been dislodged by the stretching. I'm an open wound now. Cool.

She leads me to a bench, and we sit together. I can tell that she's going to offer me some wisdom and I'm thirsty for it. Please tell me what to do, kind yoga lady who reminds me of Matty. I promise I'll do it.

"I'm gonna tell you a little secret. There's gonna be a lot of people telling you what's right or wrong for you and your baby. But you only have *one* goal right now. *Healthy baby*." She pauses to make her point. "That's it. Whether you do a home birth with a doula or go to a hospital and get an epidural, the goal is still the same. Healthy baby. All the rest is crap. Tune it all out if you need to."

She takes my hands in hers and squeezes. I love this framing of pregnancy and I immediately make it my mantra. "Healthy baby." Nothing else is going to matter. I thank Chrissy and tell her that I plan to come back for another class. We hug and I feel like I've been blessed.

I keep the mantra in mind as I walk to the 'L,' thinking about this "birth plan." While a natural childbirth sounds wonderful (in theory), I want a doctor. And really, I want *my* doctor.

In the past couple of months, I've developed a little crush on my OBGYN, Dr. Adler. It's an inevitable development as I feel terribly unattractive and here's a nice man who resembles Richard Gere. He has kind eyes, salt and pepper hair and is wholly interested in me and my body in a way that absolutely no one else is – not even me. I mean, how could I not swoon?

As for the epidural question, I just don't know. Chrissy is right. People have lots of opinions about everything. The AOL Mommy message boards are constantly lit up with advocates on both sides of every issue. And nowhere is the vitriol stronger than in debates over natural childbirth and breastfeeding. The longer I spend anywhere near those topics, the more confused and upset I get.

And then there's Jonathan. I really don't want to subject him to this whole experience. If it's anything like what I see on TV or in the movies, childbirth is fucking terrifying for everyone involved. Men fainting, women screaming. As a gay man, he could conceivably avoid this kind of thing forever. And really, shouldn't that be one of the perks?

But being without a friend in the delivery room would be awful.

Really though, I don't have anything to *decide* when it comes to Jonathan. He will do what he wants to do. That's what Jonathan does. All I need to do is ask him what his intentions are and plan accordingly. What I need to do is find a back-up. David has already told me that he'll be in the waiting room, smoking a cigar if it was allowed. (Which I respect. I'd be there too if I could.) My dad isn't an option, obviously. I try to picture Shane in the room with me. Him telling me to breathe and to push. But the picture is all wrong, made of Jigsaw pieces that won't fit together no matter how much I bang on them.

Fuck. Maybe I can kidnap Chrissy? I really need some girlfriends.

Before reaching the entrance to the 'L,' a scent hits me. Warm, cinnamon sugar. I turn and see the bakery that I'm walking past. Without breaking stride, I walk inside and almost faint from the olfactory pleasure. It's a small shop, with little more than a display. I walk up to the fortyish woman working and she asks for my order. I gaze across the line of desserts and stop at the ones with the most chocolate per square inch.

"Give me one of the… no, wait. Give me three… no, wait. A half dozen. Of those chocolate eclairs."

I expect her to make a cravings comment. She doesn't, though she does give me a knowing smile as she hands me my change. As I walk back onto the busy street, I take a moment for gratitude. A spontaneous pastry purchase at a small shop while walking on an unfamiliar city street. This is the dream. I'm giddy the rest of the way home as if the sugar high has already taken hold.

The next day as I'm working, Emily shows up at the apartment on her way to the casino. She's panicking because Jonathan hasn't answered her pages. I wonder if he got my message. I probably should have called Em myself, but I didn't think to do so until right this moment. Damn. Maybe I can blame "pregnancy brain."

"He's in New York," I tell her. "He didn't call you?"

"No. Asshole." She says it with equal parts irritation and affection. "Is he with David?"

"Yup. Meeting the parents."

She raises her eyebrows at this development.

"We like him, yes?" she asks.

"We do!"

She smiles in agreement, but it fades when I ask about her pages. She takes a deep breath before sharing her news. "His dad is in the hospital."

"Oh, shit."

"Liver failure."

"Oh, shit," I repeat.

The days and nights on the bar stool have finally caught up with him.

"How serious is it?" I feel like it's a dumb question. I should have watched more *ER*.

"It's serious."

"Jesus. I'm sorry." I don't know how sorry I am, really, but I know that's what I'm supposed to say. My only concern is Jonathan. No matter how damaged their relationship, the man is still his father. Maybe this will break through the wall between them. Or maybe it'll just solidify it. Who knows?

"Do we know when he'll be back?" she asks, referring to Jonathan.

"In a few days. But he can change his flight. I can try to reach him."

"No."

"No? You sure?"

She thinks for a second and then confirms her decision. "No, let him have this time with David. I'll tell him when he gets back."

I know her choice is about protecting Jonathan, about not letting his father ruin this moment with David. But I don't really want custody of another secret. Then again, what's one more? I sigh but agree to her terms.

She starts to leave but I stop her. I have a woman to talk to and I'm not letting her out of my sight just yet.

"Hey, did you get an epidural? When you had Jonathan?"

"Oh, hell yes." She takes my hand in a sudden panic. "Wait. Are you thinking of *not* getting an epidural?"

"I don't know. I haven't decided."

"Girl, get the epidural."

"Did you breastfeed?"

"Nah. It wasn't really fashionable then. Everyone did formula."

"Right." A time before the "breast is best" campaign cry that I find all over the message boards.

"If I were to do it today, I'd definitely breastfeed."

I nod again. "I found out it's a boy."

Her face lights up. "Oh! That's great!" She hugs me.

The reticence I initially felt about having a boy has faded. I think it's the clothes. The little boy blues, with their bulldozers and trains, have melted my heart.

"And I told my dad."

"Yeah? How'd he react?"

"Silent treatment. Until I told him that I was thinking of Mr. Mistoffelees as a name."

"As in… the cat?"

"Yes."

"And that got him talking?"

"A little. He's still pretty pissed."

"I'll talk to him."

"Really?"

"Yes. Now that you've done the hard part. Now, get some rest."

"Yes, ma'am."

"And you're not really thinking of naming him Mr. Mistoffelees, right?"

"Not at all."

"Good."

Dante

I don't speak to Jonathan until he and David return. It's obvious that he still has no idea that his father is in the hospital, and I'd rather not be the one to break the news. I rationalize that I'm only following Emily's lead. I do tell him to call his mom though. After he does, he finds me in my room.

"I've gotta go to Lake City. My dad's in the hospital."

It's the first time I've heard him refer to the man as "dad."

"I can come with you," I offer.

"No, no. That's alright," he says.

"Are you sure?"

"Yes."

"Can David go with you?"

"I don't want anyone to go with me," he says.

"Okay." I get it. Family stuff can suck and sometimes you just don't want a witness.

Jonathan leaves for Lake City on Monday and by Thursday he calls to tell me that his dad has passed away. David and I both offer to attend the funeral, but Jonathan insists on going alone, again. David fights him on it via speaker phone.

"Why don't you want me to go?" he asks Jonathan.

"It's not what you think."

"What do I think?"

"That I'm ashamed of you? Of us?"

"And that's *not* why?"

"It's not why. I'm ashamed of *him*."

I, on the other hand, don't fight Jonathan on his decision. I've been to five funerals so far in my life, each one worse than the one before as my cognitive understanding of what was happening developed. The first four were for my grandparents (both sets) and then my mom's funeral. I remember everything about *that* day, though I wish I didn't. Most of all, I remember the weather. I wanted gray skies and black umbrellas but instead got a beautiful, sunny day that felt impossibly at odds with reality.

Over the next several weeks, I look for a change in Jonathan, something that hints at such a pivotal event having occurred. What I see is not only a jaded acceptance of death – but also of life and all the ways it can disappoint. The cynic in him has been strengthened. I don't know if he harbored hope that his relationship with his father could change but now it never will. I say a silent prayer that my own relationship with my father can forge a different path.

Jonathan's mood improves when we get a check in the mail. The $250,000 investment check from Fat Cat Jack is finally here.

"We need to go shopping," he announces.

"Babe."

"I'm kidding! Sort of."

"We need to open a business account."

"Right! Of course."

So that's what we do. We spend a day running errands, from setting up a bank account to ordering business cards. After much debate, we settle on the name JK Productions. All this productivity makes me nervous. Like I should know what I'm doing.

When I share this with Jonathan, he responds confidently. "Hey. I don't know what I'm doing either. We just fake it till we make it."

"Sure, I know. I just wish I wasn't faking it on so many fronts."

"Word."

The last weeks of my pregnancy drag on, and every day becomes more uncomfortable. While I dread childbirth, I also look forward to the possibility of feeling normal again. I don't make it to any more prenatal yoga classes. I'm too lazy and too embarrassed by my crying jag. I really only leave the apartment for various appointments and quick shopping trips. I'm in the tedious process of changing my maiden name so I visit the DMV, the bank, and the social security office. Ironically, if I was marrying for love and not money, I most likely would keep my maiden name. Think of the most horrible, boring, bureaucratic places to be when very pregnant and I've been there.

I also go to numerous OBGYN appointments which become ever more frequent the closer I get to my due date. Here, I also have to change my name so that the medical forms will be accurate. I try to be casual about it but, of course, there is nothing casual about announcing your marriage when you're this pregnant. My nuptials are a Hail Mary, saving me from my shameful single state.

"That's wonderful! Congratulations!" Dr. Adler exclaims when I tell him the news.

"Thank you," I say. "But, you know, he's really busy. With work. I'll probably be coming to most of my appointments alone."

His response is one of compassion and I soak it up.

At my final ultrasound, one week before the baby is due, it's determined that the baby is breached. I sit in Dr. Adler's office, and we discuss his recommendation for a cesarean section. While I hadn't decided yet on getting an epidural or powering through the pain, I'm a little miffed at being cheated out of a choice. Any hope I had of making the birth as natural as possible is gone. Instead, my son will arrive via surgery. I wonder what Shane would think of this development. Would he be disappointed in me? Would he think I'm defective? Maybe I am.

"Don't worry," he consoles me. "You'll still be a woman."

Sure. A defective woman but still a woman. Cool.

Healthy baby, I remind myself and as I do, I become defensive at his comment. It really is a weird thing to say.

"What does that even mean?" I ask.

"Some women get upset that they can't go through labor," he explains. "They feel like it makes them less of a woman."

While I can understand the disappointment because I feel it too, I would never equate a cesarean section with *losing my womanhood*. Jesus. Are we that singular in our purpose?

"That's absurd," I tell him.

His lips twitch up in a smile and I know he agrees.

"So, let's schedule the procedure. How is tomorrow?" he casually asks.

While I have a bag semi-packed for the hospital, the thought of having the baby *tomorrow* is wild. Like, is tomorrow good for you to change your life forevermore? Sure. Why not?

"What's the date tomorrow?"

"September 19th."

I want to know the astrological sign for September 19th, but I know I'll sound like a flake if I ask. I don't know how much I believe in astrology but still. It would be nice to know. I do know that nineteen is a prime number and that feels kind of rad. And if nothing else, that will help me remember the date.

"September 19th it is," I agree.

As he begins explaining the low-risk procedure, I realize that a c-section does have one advantage.

"Since you're going to be, well… *there*, anyway… would it be possible to tie my tubes?" I ask him.

"I don't usually perform tubal litigation on women as young as you," he tells me, clearly surprised by my request.

"Why not?"

"Well, you might change your mind and it's difficult, if not impossible, to reverse."

"Right. But what if I'm certain?"

I feel certain. While I would never voice it to anyone (except Jonathan and David), I really hate being pregnant. It's like having an alien inside me. Only that one time during the prenatal yoga class have I ever gotten close to feeling like the radiant goddess I've been conditioned to believe all pregnant women are. Mostly I just feel like a blob. I can't imagine ever being desired by anyone ever again. Why not just tie them up and never think about this again?

"What about your new husband? What does he think?"

I should have expected this question. I've heard of doctors refusing the procedure without the permission of a spouse or father. Legally, I know I'm able to get it done without such a thing. I just need to have a doctor willing to do it. And there's the rub.

"He's fine with it," I assure him but to no avail. He's not going to budge on this. "If I were a man my age getting a vasectomy, would you feel differently?" I ask him.

"Well, that's easier to reverse but not always successfully so."

"Right. But that's not what I'm asking."
"I would have reservations about that too," he admits.
"So, it's just the age thing."
"Yes."

And then he smiles that incredible Gere-like smile and I let it go. I'll have to go on birth control instead. Not because I plan on having lots of sex but because I don't trust myself.

The next morning, Jonathan and David escort me to the hospital for the procedure. Jonathan decides to accompany me into the surgery. I'm grateful because I'm terrified. Nothing is what I expected. I had imagined ambiance for this event: soothing music, candlelight, maybe some flowers. Instead, I'm sitting in a brightly lit surgery where an anesthesiologist injects me with medicine. As he does so, he asks if I'd like some music and points to a boom box in the operating room.

"Yes!" I answer enthusiastically, imagining the ethereal sounds of the prenatal yoga class. Anything to make this experience less sterile. But instead of a carefully chosen CD, he just flips on the radio. The room is filled with the familiar sound of C+C Music Factory's *Gonna Make You Sweat*. The contrast makes me giggle as the lower half of my body goes numb. Welcome, baby boy. Are you ready to get your groove on?

Jonathan, standing next to me in a gown and mask, starts dancing.

"Everybody dance now!" he sings, and I beg him to stop so I can stop laughing.

Dr. Adler tests that I'm completely numb. I lay back as he places a sheet over my knees so I can't see anything. After a moment, I turn to Jonathan and ask if the procedure has started. Jonathan leans over to see behind the sheet, makes a horrified face, and turns back to me.

"Um. Yes. He's holding your uterus."

"Really? Wow. I can't feel a thing." Maybe c-sections aren't so bad.

Another few more minutes pass and Dr. Adler is holding my baby up for me to view. He's a bloody mess but the most beautiful bloody mess I've ever seen. The nurse takes him away to clean him up. When she's done, she asks Jonathan if he would like to hold him. He's resistant, unsure of how to hold an infant. She helps him. When he has the baby in his arms, he comes closer to me so I can see him fully. Dr. Adler sews me up while I marvel at the little miracle before me.

"Wow," I say.

"He's so cute," Jonathan says and it's the first time in a long time that the word doesn't sound like a veiled insult to me.

I'm sent to a post-op recovery area where I lay behind a curtain. I won't be able to hold my son until I'm taken to my hospital room. My whole body starts itching as I wait. I'm scratching everywhere when a nurse appears in front of me.

"Why am I so itchy?" I ask.

"Oh, that's from the anesthesia. It'll go away in a few minutes."

I try to stop scratching and focus on the nurse.

"I have some bad news," she says.

My heart sinks. My baby had looked perfect. What could be the problem? What terrible thing has happened? I can't breathe as I wait for her next words.

"We don't have any private rooms right now," she says.

"Oh! I don't care about that!"

So, I rarely want people to get fired for incompetence. I figure everyone has a bad day now and then. But this nurse should be ousted immediately. Really? She thought that was a great thing to say to a new mother just minutes after a c-section? Then again, maybe she's encountered people who really do pitch a fit at such news. I remember all the crazy people I've encountered serving others and I let it go.

After about an hour of itching and scratching, I'm finally taken to a hospital room where there are two beds, both empty. It may not be "private," but it is currently "empty" and my annoyance with the nurse resurfaces.

Not long after settling into a bed, my baby boy is brought to me. He's swaddled in a blanket with a tiny blue hat. I've only seen him for about a minute up until now, but I swear I could pick him up out of a lineup of a million other babies. Apparently, my trouble with faces has one exception and this somehow feels like ancient, universal knowledge. Everything you hear is true. The moment he's put into my arms, I'm changed.

He has a few wisps of dark hair and green eyes just like his father. The eyes don't stay open long as he drifts in and out of sleep. Jonathan and David enter the room and join me bedside.

"Does he have a name yet?" asks David.

Westley, the name I've been considering, doesn't feel right. Maybe if he had my blonde hair. But the dark hair makes me want a darker name.

"I'm thinking about Dante," I tell them.

"Like in *Clerks*?" Jonathan asks.

David laughs. "*That's* your reference?"

"What?" Jonathan protests.

"*Dante's Inferno?*" he asks.

"Oh, sure. That too," Jonathan retorts, rolling his eyes.

I was ready for references to fire and brimstone. I was not ready for the indie movie reference. I'm bummed because that character is such an epic weenie. Jonathan and David notice my disappointment and assure me that it's a great name, but it's a little hard to believe now.

"The problem is that names that work for babies don't work for grown men and names for grown men don't work for babies," I complain.

"He'll grow into it," David assures me.

"What does the name mean?" Jonathan asks.

"Dante?"

"Yeah."

"Something... good. Shit, I can't even remember now. My brain is mush. My baby naming book is in my bag over there. Can you get it?"

David finds the book and searches the name. "It means 'steadfast' and 'enduring.' Also, 'everlasting.' It has an Italian origin."

Jonathan smiles at me and nods, knowing why I've chosen it.

"I have another problem. And I need input from you two. I need to decide on whether or not to have him circumcised."

They both cross their legs as if in a bad sitcom.

"Come on! Help me! I don't have one of those... things."

I'd love to have Shane's input. Jonathan has the same thought.

"Was Shane?" Jonathan timidly asks as if his name is forbidden now that Dante is in earshot. Never mind that he won't understand a word. At least, not yet.

"Yes."

"Then, yes. Right?" he asks David to back him up.

"I'm staying far away from this," David responds, literally taking a step back.

"Fair enough," I say.

I tell them about the scary nurse, and they agree that she should not be allowed near people of any kind. And then we're in suspended animation in awe of tiny fingers. A nurse enters and begins talking of breastfeeding and that's enough to break the spell.

"We should go," David says.

"Daddy can stay," the nurse says, nodding to Jonathan.

"Oh. Well…" Jonathan answers.

David stares at him quizzically, expecting him to correct the nurse. But Jonathan is watching the nurse as she writes on a whiteboard displayed prominently in the room. She writes her name (under "attending nurse") and my name (under "patient"). My *married* name.

"What the…?" David asks, reading the name on the board.

I try to save the situation. "You two go get some food. I'll see you later."

Jonathan takes David's hand and leads him from the room.

"We'll be back soon," Jonathan says before they're gone.

I can only imagine the conversation that's coming.

The nurse asks if I'm planning to breastfeed. I tell her that I am, having read all about the health benefits. She's elated with my response.

"Wonderful! When he's awake, call me with that button and I'll come help," she says.

Once I'm alone, I do what all the new mothers I've seen on TV do. I talk to Dante.

"Hey," I whisper, so as not to wake him. "Welcome to the world. Just so you know… I don't really know what the fuck I'm doing. Shit. Ah! By the way, I curse a lot. I should probably try to stop. But, then again, everyone in this city curses so you should probably just get used to it." I'm off on a tangent, thinking about the inventive cursing of Chicago cabdrivers, one of my favorite things about the city.

"Anyway," I continue. "About your dad. The thing is… the reason he's not here…. It's not because I don't love him. I do. Too much, actually." That truth makes me tear up, so I start again. "And it's not because he doesn't care about you. I'm sure if he knew about you, he'd care. Probably a lot. But we don't belong in his world. I'm pretty sure we'd blow it up. So, you know, we're gonna have to build our own. Which I know we can do. I'm going to make sure you're surrounded by people that love you. And I'm never, ever gonna let anyone hurt you."

The maternal love is fierce, and I can imagine slaying dragons for him.

When he starts to stir, I press the button and the nurse returns. She helps me into position for breastfeeding, but Dante won't latch on. We try the other side but have no luck there either. Soon, he falls back asleep, apparently exhausted by the effort. The nurse assures me that we have time to figure this out without resorting to formula. I'm relieved because I've read that once a baby takes a bottle, they're less likely to take a breast. I had been so excited about this beautiful bonding experience that I hadn't ever considered the possibility that I would lack the skills. How fucking unfair.

About an hour later, Dr. Adler enters the room. My son is out of the room, getting tests. He has the exact opposite advice of the nurse, which makes me want to scream.

"It's normal for babies to lose weight after the birth but the amount he's lost is just a little more than I'd like. He's lost twelve percent of his body weight. Five to ten percent is considered normal. We need to bring it up and I'd like to do it now by giving him formula."

"Will he still be able to breastfeed after I give him a bottle?"

He appears annoyed at the question as if this concern is of no importance. And maybe it's not. I don't know. "We'll see. But we should give him the formula."

I don't argue. After all, he's the doctor. But I'm secretly crushed. My body is defective. Again.

When my son is returned to me, the doctor gives me the formula and I feed him. He's wide awake and drinking it quickly as if he'd been starving. And now I know the doctor was right and I feel better.

First rule of motherhood: feed a hungry baby. I thought that rule was fairly obvious but apparently not. I'm a little shaken. How many minefields are in store for me when the first hours are this fraught?

Dr. Adler leaves and the nurse checks in on us. She makes a face when she notices the bottle. Her disappointment is palpable. I feel like I've betrayed the sisterhood, and my cheeks redden in shame.

"The doctor made me," I try to explain.

"He won't take your breast now," she admonishes me, and I'm taken aback by her tone.

I hold in the tears just until she leaves. I'm still crying when Jonathan and David return. They have a giant pink bear and balloons.

"Oh no! What's the matter?" Jonathan asks as I wipe away the tears.

"I'm already a failure. Formula," I say, nodding toward the bottle.

"And that's bad because…?" David asks.

"He won't breastfeed now," I explain.

"Oh."

"Fuck it. Healthy baby, remember?" Jonathan says. I had shared my mantra with him, making him promise to remind me of it whenever necessary. "I was bottle fed and look at me. Perfection." He twirls around to showcase his flawless body.

"Right," I agree, laughing through the tears. "Sorry. I'm just way emotional."

"I think that's normal," David says.

"I can't believe you guys brought a pink bear."

"Well, I thought we'd indoctrinate him early," Jonathan says.

"I love it. Hey, can you do me a favor? Find a phone and call my dad? Just, you know, tell him the basics. He has a grandson named Dante. And that he was born at nine-thirty this morning and weighed seven pounds, eleven ounces?"

"Sure," he says.

"Thanks, baby."

Jonathan leaves to find a phone and I let David hold Dante.

"Wow," he says, when he's settled into his arms.

"Right? He's so fucking amazing. I can't take it."

"Things still fucked up with your dad?" he asks.

"Yeah. We haven't spoken since I went to see him, and he gave me the silent treatment. I'm hoping the actual reality will, you know…"

I trail off because I don't want to say what I'm thinking, which is that he should, simply, stop being an ass.

"Speaking of dads…"

Shit. Jonathan must have told him the truth about our marriage.

"I swear it's just a paperwork thing."

"What the fuck did you guys sign?" His tone is more amused than angry.

"I wanted you to read it! I swear! But Jonathan didn't want to ruin things with you."

He sighs. "So, you two are actually married. And Jonathan is the father of Dante in every *legal* respect. Is that correct?"

"It's just paperwork."

"Right. Legal paperwork."

"He's not *really* going to be the father."

He sighs again and I really want to know what he's thinking.

"He explained about the money?" I ask.

"He did."

"So, then you know why we did it."

"I do."

"Don't be mad. Please don't be mad."

"I'm not *mad*. I'm… I don't know what I am."

I nod. I can relate. But as much as I want to keep talking, I can't. The adrenaline rush of the day is over, and I can barely keep my eyes open.

"You look tired. I should go and let you sleep."

I grab his hand and squeeze it. "I love you."

"Same."

David leans in to give me a quick kiss on the forehead before leaving to find Jonathan. Dante, now fully satisfied with the formula, is asleep again. We snuggle together, and I join him in a state of blissful gratitude and the lightness of one less secret.

I stay in the hospital for three days recovering from the c-section. My room remains empty of other patients the entire time. I'm so thankful because I don't know how well I would react to the site of a healthy, perfect nuclear family next to me. While I'm deliriously happy, I know the state is fragile. Looking at Dante, I can see Shane and I miss him even more, a reality I would have thought impossible. But now, it's like I'm wanting him for both of us. The desire I have for him to hold his son, to share in this, is overwhelming. My resilience is slippery enough that the sight of a proud new father would surely push me over the edge.

Nevertheless, the days in the hospital are amazing. The nurses have stopped looking at me like I'm the devil and I'm allowed to revel in motherhood. I know everything will change once I leave this safe space so I hold onto the experience as best I can.

Jonathan was only able to leave a message on my father's answering machine. So, I'm surprised when they arrive together as I'm preparing to be released.

"Look who I found! Papa!" Jonathan says enthusiastically, leading my father into the room.

Thank god for Jonathan. His ability to grease any uncomfortable situation is unparalleled.

"Hi," my dad greets me, tentatively, walking in behind Jonathan.

"Oh! Hi," I answer, matching his careful tone.

Dante is in the bassinette, swaddled but awake. I ask my dad if he'd like to hold him, and he accepts. As I hand over Dante, Jonathan walks briskly to the whiteboard and effortlessly wipes away my married name with his fingers. I give Jonathan a quick thumbs-up as my dad gazes down on his grandson. I can see the love but it's a love twinged with sadness.

"You can't do this alone, you know," he tells me.

"I'm not alone."

"No. You're not."

I realize I had played it all wrong. In the letter I wrote my father, I wanted so much to reassure him. I was so adamant that I was fine, that I needed nothing from him. But my dad expresses his love through actions, not words. He needs to feel useful, and I made him superfluous. And the worst part of this mistake is that it's not even true. I'm going to need all the help I can get. I try to convey this message, but I couch it in Dante's needs rather than my own.

"He's going to need his grandpa, you know," I tell him.

Still gazing down at Dante, he nods.

"Grandpa," he repeats, taking in the new title. "And I guess I'm not supposed to ask about the father?" he asks.

I sigh because I can see a fight on the horizon if I evade the question. But vague is all I can manage.

"It's complicated," I say. This irritates him and I don't blame him.

"*What's* complicated?"

"You say you want to know. But, trust me, you don't *really* want to know."

"Yes, I do," he protests.

"Fine. He's involved with someone else," I say, omitting the whole marriage detail.

"Does he know?"

I shake my head and he echoes the motion, expressing his disappointment. Obviously, he thinks Shane deserves to know. And maybe he does. For not the first time, I wonder again if omitting the truth is akin to lying.

"He needs to step up," he states. "Financially, I mean."

Ah. The moral quandary is not what's concerning him. His concern is about money. Responsibility. I should have guessed. I have the answer to that, of course. But that would mean explaining my marriage and that might push my dad right over the edge. On the other hand, maybe he'd just be happy that I'm married. Maybe that would help cover up the sins of his daughter? We've already broken the non-disclosure agreement by telling David. Would it hurt to tell my dad too? I can't decide and it's too much to figure out right now.

"I'll tell him… when the time is right," I say to placate my father, wondering if it's true or not. "And you don't have to worry about the money thing. Jonathan and I are starting a company. And we have an investor." This much is safe to say.

He raises his eyebrows and turns to Jonathan for confirmation.

"Yes, Papa. You don't need to worry."

"What kind of company?"

"We're building websites," I tell him. I direct Jonathan to show him our business card.

My dad scrutinizes the business card and smiles approvingly. But he's not entirely persuaded of our financial security.

"So, what do you need?" he asks me.

I almost answer "nothing" but I stop myself. He needs to be needed. Surely, there must be something I require.

"I think we've got it covered," Jonathan says.

"Formula!" I nearly shout, grabbing onto the one thing I didn't buy. The hospital is sending us home with a few bottles but those won't last long. After trying a few more times to breastfeed, I've given up the goal. I'm still disappointed but at least I'll be able to comfort myself with a cocktail once I'm off the painkillers.

"Did you drive here?" I ask him. I always worry about my dad driving in the city. It's so different than the country roads he's used to.

"I took the train and a cab."

"Oh, well then come with us and you can see the apartment. We can get formula later."

"How about I just do this…" he says, handing Dante off to me, so he can take out his wallet. He removes an envelope and hands it to me. It's full of cash.

"It's two thousand dollars. Just, you know, to help with things," he says, his chest puffing out with the pride of providing.

"This is really helpful. Thanks, dad."

He declines our offer to see the apartment and we drop him off at the train station to head home.

"Call me if you need anything," he says, hugging me goodbye.

I'm so happy to hear this that I start to cry.

"Thanks, dad." And then, I say what I almost never say to him. "I love you."

He nods, unable – as always – to say the words.

In Defense of Soap Operas

I'm making a list of the benefits of being a young mother. So far, I have two. The first is the assurance from my OBGYN that my body will "bounce back" with greater ease due to my younger age. I'm not particularly concerned about that, but I do want my old clothes to fit. Mostly because I hate shopping. The second benefit is that I'm almost certain to still like roller coasters by the time Dante is able to ride one. I'm sure there are more benefits but I'm too tired to think of them.

As we travel to the apartment, I already miss the hospital and all the people that helped me take care of Dante. They didn't let me leave until they knew I was able to do what I need to do. But the reality of no supervision is terrifying. Add to that the fact that I'm on strong painkillers for the next ten days to heal from the c-section. While I can move about without too much discomfort, I have to do so slowly that it's like like moving through water.

Fortunately, when we return to the apartment, Em is waiting for us.

"Surprise!" she stage whispers since Dante is sleeping in his carrier. "Oh, wow! He's so cute! Congratulations!"

She tells me that she's arranged her work schedule to have a few days off so she can stay and help. I'm so grateful I could cry. As we take care of Dante, I can't stop thanking her.

"I'm happy to do it," she tells me. "I don't think I'm getting a grandchild. So, I'm adopting Dante."

I want to tell her that, legally speaking, he actually is her grandson. But I don't. Em stays for three days and crashes in our living room.

By the time she leaves, I feel a lot better about my abilities. And really, none of the infant care is rocket science. Feed him, change him, let him sleep. It's not difficult but it is hard. I tell this to Jonathan when he asks how I'm doing.

"It's exhausting. Maybe because it's so redundant."

"Redundant," he repeats in our long-standing joke to always say the word twice.

But it's not just the redundancy that makes it all so tiring. It's the constant attention that must be paid. The fact that a part of my brain will always – from now until forever – be focused on this little person. I'm overwhelmed but not depressed and I'm thankful for that. It would be so easy to find myself there. Like, I can *see* it from here. After all, I barely got the chance to be a reckless "legal" adult before having Dante – a thought that hits me whenever I see Jonathan and David preparing to go out. Nevertheless, I know how fortunate I am. I'm a single mom, sure, but I have the privilege of this time with him. Time without having to find outside childcare while reporting to a job. Time to focus only on my baby.

(David, who backpacked across Europe between his undergraduate and law studies and who has been seemingly everywhere, tells me that this time with Dante wouldn't be considered a "privilege" in some other more progressive countries. Apparently, the United States is at the bottom of the barrel in terms of social programs that allow for parents to actually spend time with their newborns, a fact I find genuinely horrifying. These weeks are so precious that I never want them to end, even as I'm dragging myself around the apartment looking like a vagabond.)

Jonathan has decided that we should take a three-month hiatus from the company so that I can find my footing and so that he can "blow off some steam." Since he's been working nonstop since the age of fifteen, I think his desire is valid. And lord knows, I'm not about to argue with any plan that allows me the opportunity to do less right now. While Jonathan helps with Dante in a pinch (like watching him for a few minutes so I can grab a shower), he stays true to himself. For the next three months, he spends most days at the gym and most nights at the clubs. I barely see him and when I do, the encounters are usually bizarre. I'm sleep-deprived and he's on a perpetual ride, either on his way up (primping for the club in the evenings) or on his way down (returning home in the early morning hours).

On Halloween, I talk Jonathan and David into pre-gaming in the apartment so I can join in at least a couple of cocktails. I'm desperate for just a small break in what seems an endless cycle of eating, sleeping, and diaper changing. And I've always loved the pre-game ritual even more than the eventual destination, anticipation always outdoing reality.

Once Dante is asleep, I pour out cocktails. Jonathan and David present their costumes to me in a dramatic catwalk across the living room. I immediately lose it, doubling over in hysterics.

"You *didn't!*"

"Oh, we *did!*" Jonathan retorts.

They're both dressed as Michael Jackson. David is sporting the *Off the Wall* afro and suit. Jonathan is wearing a wig of straight black hair and dark sunglasses. It's an obvious play on the pop star's ever-lightening skin color.

"You sure that's not politically incorrect?" I ask, gasping for breath.

"Ah. Fuck 'em if they can't take a joke," David says.

We drink two martinis each, relatively quickly. Unfortunately, after so long without alcohol, my tolerance is completely shot. When I stand up, the room starts to spin. The sensations are all the worse because they're mixed with motherly panic. I can't be drunk and do the things I need to do.

I weave to the bathroom on my unsteady feet. After throwing up, I call out to them.

"Don't leave yet," I plead.

"Oh baby, we won't," Jonathan calls back to me. His voice is empathetic, but I can hear them giggling. Fair. Who the fuck gets this drunk off two martinis?

Nothing else comes up so I move to the couch. I breathe deeply, trying to steady myself while cursing my bad judgment. I look over at the baby monitor, grateful that Dante is still asleep.

"I'm such a bad mom," I cry into a throw pillow.

David joins me on the couch and talks me down from my self-flagellation.

"You are not a bad mom," he says, handing me a glass of water and a Tylenol. "Now, drink this and take this."

Jonathan and David stay with me another hour until I'm sober enough to function.

"Thanks, guys. Have fun tonight," I say.

I kiss them both as they leave, off on another adventure, one that I can't even imagine. Apparently, the club scene has transformed in my absence. When Jonathan and David return (along with the sun), they're not drunk or high on coke. They're on ecstasy, lovey-dovey and grinning car-to-car. While I'm a little jealous of their experiences, that emotion is tempered by how annoying they can be.

One night, I'm sleeping with Dante at my side when they wake me to tell me some Very Important News.

"Katie!" Jonathan is trying to whisper and failing spectacularly.

"What?" I mumble, my eyes trying to focus. Jonathan sits on my bed and David is standing next to us. Jonathan's eyes are dilated.

"I have to tell you something."

"Okay," I say. I know what's coming but there's no point in stopping him.

"I love you!" Jonathan exclaims in a joyous reveal.

I want to both hug him and throttle him.

"I love you too. Now go away before you wake him," I whisper back.

David grabs Jonathan's arm, dragging him from my room.

"Let her sleep, babe."

My last thought before nodding back off is that Dante and I really need to get our own place.

The city is awash in autumn colors and the cool air revitalizes me whenever Dante and I leave the apartment. I quickly become adept at taking Dante places, even if those places are just the park, the pediatrician's office, and the grocery store. The stroller is his favorite place in the world, and I get tons of exercise walking around the neighborhood.

When I'm inside, I live in sweatpants and oversized t-shirts, drinking coffee all day and night. Days flow into one another with little delineation among them. If it weren't for the shows on television, I would have no idea what day of the week it is.

My desire to live alone comes and goes. The more Jonathan and David stay away, the lonelier I get and the more I crave interpersonal communication. As amazing as Dante is, he's a terrible conversationalist. He is, however, a great listener. A fact I remind myself of often.

I keep the television on throughout the day just to keep me company. My mom and I used to watch *Days of Our Lives* when I would get home from school, and I've picked it back up again. I even tape it so I can watch it at night if I'm unable to catch it during the day. Jonathan follows it just enough to offer commentary and ask questions as he passes through. ("That Sami is a schemer!" "Is Jennifer back with Jack yet?") But David doesn't get the appeal at all.

"Why do you watch this? It's so silly," he asks me.

"Hey!" I retort.

"Uh-oh. Now you've done it," Jonathan warns him.

"What?"

"She's gonna get on her soap box… pun intended."

I do just that. "Soap operas are rich tapestries woven over literal decades. They're only derided because they center the female perspective over the male one, a total anomaly in the early television landscape. Hell, *all* media landscape, even today."

He stares at me blankly and I continue unabated. "Plus, the storylines have been passed down through generations of women, not unlike the oral traditions of Native Americans."

David laughs. "Someone wrote a paper."

"Guilty."

"Women's studies?"

"Television theory."

"Nice."

"Besides, you watch *Melrose Place*. What's the difference?"

"Amanda."

"Yeah, okay. I'll give you that," I admit. Amanda (aka Heather Locklear) is the best of soap opera divas.

The show is a great distraction but when the "secret pregnancy" storyline inevitably appears, I watch intently. I wonder if my reticence to tell Shane the truth is because I want the drama, the soap opera. But that's not right. Telling him would cause drama. I convince myself that what he doesn't know can't hurt him. Even if my heart breaks with each new milestone, knowing he's missing everything.

Holiday Strays

The holidays are approaching quickly, and I want to ignore them all. But Jonathan has other plans and insists we attempt to host a Thanksgiving dinner. He seems to have forgotten that we have zero culinary skills.

"You can't just skip the holidays. You're a mom now. You have to *do* holidays," he says.

"Sure. When Dante's cognizant of them," I say. "I have a few years."

"Yeah, but you're gonna need the practice."

"We don't even have a roasting pan!"

"Exactly my point. Practice. Get the things we need. Be grown-ups and shit."

It's a valid point. Even with the influx of cash from Fat Cat Jack, our kitchen remains woefully basic, a fact that drives David crazy. Because David, of course, can cook. Jonathan reminds me of this to assuage my fears.

"David can bring over what we need. He'll help us. Come on! It'll be fun! We can invite my mom and your dad. And I'm sure I know some strays."

By "strays," he means those in the community that won't – or can't – go home.

Jonathan returns home the day before Thanksgiving with a twenty-five-pound turkey, a roasting pan, a bag of ingredients, and directions from David.

"That's huge!" I protest.

"Leftovers!"

"Are the guests bringing everything else?"

"What else?"

"You know. Sides? Dessert? Forks?"

I don't think we have more than three forks in our kitchen.

"Shit. You're right. Let me make some phone calls."

He disappears into his room, presumably to call David for more help. I read through the directions. They don't sound hard. Surely, if I can build a website, I can roast a turkey.

Of course, there's another reason I don't cook and don't even try. It's not that I'm too busy. It's that cooking reminds me of Shane. His unbridled joy of it has poisoned any potential delight I might find in it. I know now that I'll never make pad thai.

But Jonathan is right. Moms do this shit.

On Thanksgiving morning, David arrives with a box of kitchen tools. He guides us in the prep of the turkey and after it goes into the oven, he starts the task of making a pie.

"You bake too?" I ask.

"He's a real renaissance man," says Jonathan.

Renaissance man. The phrase reminds me of Shane and I'm immediately wistful.

David waves the rolling pin in the air as he defends himself. "I know you're being sarcastic but I'm absolutely a renaissance man."

As he speaks, sirens from emergency vehicles pass our apartment. I close my eyes and try to breathe through them. When I look back to where Jonathan was standing, he's gone. We hear his bedroom door close.

"Was it something we said?" David asks.

"Hang on," I say. I walk to Jonathan's door and knock.

"It's me. Can I come in?" I softly ask.

"Yeah."

He's curled up on his bed and I sit beside him. His hands are over his ears, and he's got a confused, pained expression.

"Hey, baby... you okay?"

I don't think he's breathing.

"Hey... breathe, baby." His eyes are glassy, and he starts twitching, like his skin is suddenly on fire. I hold his shoulders and wait for his breath to come back.

"Fuck. I'm sorry. I don't know what's happening."
"Are your ears ringing?"
"Yes."
"Just try to breathe."
After a moment, he whispers, "It was the rolling pin," he says. "It wasn't a rolling pin. It was... fuck. It sounds stupid."
"It was the bat," I finish.
"Yeah. Has this happened to you?"
"I get flashes sometimes when I see an ambulance or hear a siren. And I've had a panic attack before."
"Right. The séance from hell."
"Right."
"Well, this sucks. Not a fan."
"Does David know? I mean, I know he knows you were hurt... but does he know all of it?"
"I told him it was a car accident when we met. I had to explain the crutches."
I can't really chastise him for the lie.
"You think I should tell him," he says.
"I think you should do whatever you want to do." I kiss him on the cheek and give him a hug. "But it would probably be the healthy choice."
As I start to leave, he says, "Hey. Are we fucked?"
"Oh, yeah. But I'm almost sure everyone else is too."
"Well, shit."

I return to the kitchen where David is rolling out the dough.
"He alright?"
"Yeah. He'll be out soon. Now, what can I do?"
I can tell he wants more information, but he lets me change the subject. I assist with whatever he needs, and the memory of helping Shane with the sushi makes me melancholy.
"You okay?" David asks.
Dante's cries save me, and I excuse myself to tend to him. I bring him to the kitchen where Jonathan re-joins us. But first he stops by the stereo. Music as avoidance but it works. The happy club beat fills the apartment, lifting us up. We continue cooking all day, both

Jonathan and I following David's instructions. When Emily and my father arrive, they take seats in the living room. I put the football game on for them and hand off Dante so I can help finish the dinner.

"We should check the internal temperature of the turkey," David directs us.

"And how do we do that?" I ask.

"We use a meat thermometer. Do you have a meat thermometer?"

Jonathan and I both laugh.

"Well, it's a good thing you have me. Because I do." David digs through the box of supplies and finds the tool. "Just take out the turkey."

Jonathan takes out the turkey and places it on the counter. David hands me the thermometer. "Just put it under the thigh."

I take the thermometer and plunge it into the bird, and we all hear a distinctive cracking sound.

"Uh-oh," I say.

"Did it break?" David asks. "I've never had it break before. Huh."

I pull the remains of the thermometer out of the bird.

"What do we do?" I ask, my voice rising.

"I don't know. Do these things have mercury in them?" David asks.

Jonathan and I both shrug.

"Well, I'm not eating mercury," David says.

"So, what? We're gonna throw this whole thing away?" I ask. "That's crazy!"

They both look at me like I'm the crazy one. Maybe I am.

"I think we gotta throw it away," David says.

I sit at the kitchen table. I'm so disheartened as I watch Jonathan pick up the turkey and throw it in the trash. Of course, it's too big for the receptacle and just sits on the top. This causes both of them to erupt into giggles. I want to join them, but I can't. As they get a trash bag and dispose of it properly, I feel the tears streaming down my face. *Come on*, I think. *It's just a turkey.*

David, ever practical, speaks to Jonathan. "I can tell everyone, and we can just order some Chinese takeout."

"Thanks, baby," Jonathan replies. David goes to the living room and Jonathan comes over and sits with me.

"Hey, it's just a turkey," he says, echoing my thoughts.

"I know!"

"Okay..."

"It's just... I should be able to make a turkey. I want to be a mom that can make a turkey."

"Wasn't your mom's turkey kinda terrible?"

"Yes, but at least it was edible!"

"I'm sure with enough practice, your turkey will be edible too." This gets a weak smile from me. "Remember? Practice? You're getting the kinks out now. It's all good. Come on. Let's get the dining table set up."

Jonathan invited a dozen or so strays to join us but only two accepted. They're both younger than us and just out of high school. Their names are Liam and Jamie. Liam is clearly a boy, but Jamie is androgenous, and I can't get a lock on whether our guest is a boy or girl. Normally, I'd look for an Adam's Apple, but Jamie is wearing a turtleneck sweater. After both guests settle into our apartment, I pull Jonathan into my bedroom.

"Is Jamie...?"

"Is Jamie what?"

"A girl? A boy?"

"Does it matter?"

"Well, no. I just don't want to make an assumption and get it wrong."

"Jamie was a lesbian but is in transition."

"So... *he*?"

"Yes. He."

"Cool."

Jonathan starts to walk out but I grab his hand.

"You know, that's the only reason I'm asking, right? Like, I don't care what's in his pants. I just don't want to look like an idiot."

"I know, babe. And asking is always okay."

Liam is gregarious and Jamie is reserved. Jonathan serves them both wine even though I'm quite sure they're underage. I don't say anything. I remember drinking wine while in France at the age of sixteen. Tonight, we'll be Paris.

Everyone is incredibly sympathetic about the turkey which just makes me feel more incompetent. When the take-out arrives and the boys are busy setting up the feast, Emily pulls me into my bedroom for a private conversation.

"Have you looked at the yearbooks yet?" she asks.

I wasn't ready for this question, and I don't say anything.

"You know how the reporter was getting threats? Now they're calling me too."

"Oh, shit. Did you star69 them?"

"Hell yeah. But no one picked up." She pauses before continuing. "Look, we gotta find these guys. Before they start smashing up *my* car... or worse."

Fuck. She's right.

I walk over to my desk and pick up the yearbook. I show her the circled names and photos.

"Jonathan identified them?" she asks.

"Yes."

"I can't believe it. I have to talk to him."

She turns to walk out, but I grab her arm and stop her.

"No. You can't. He didn't *actually* tell me. He circled their pictures and I found it. We haven't even talked about it."

"Oh. But you're giving this to me anyway."

"Well, I probably shouldn't be."

"No. You did good. Thank you."

She studies the photos of the boys. "This boy seems familiar. And the name. Owens. Why does that sound so familiar?"

"I don't know."

"Hmm... well, it doesn't matter. If Jonathan is sure, then I trust him."

"Are you going to go to the police?"

She thinks for a moment before answering. "I have another option. There's a guy at the casino. He can take care of them for us."

"What? You mean... like *a hit man*?" I ask incredulously. I can't believe I'm saying this. I mean, we're not in Jersey. "Uh... maybe you should give me the yearbook back."

"Don't worry. I'm not gonna do it. Mostly because I can't afford it."

"Well, good. I guess."

"I mean, he said he's willing to make a trade. If you know what I mean…"

I don't immediately understand. Not until she raises her eyes and tilts her head in a knowing look.

"Ew! No!"

"I know. But I thought about it."

"Well, don't. Cuz *ew*."

"Don't worry. I'm going to be a good citizen and go to the police."

"You'll need Jonathan to make the statement."

"Right. And you."

"I don't remember them!"

"So?"

It's a fair question. I obviously have no moral impediment to lying and this would be lying for the greater good.

"Fine. I'll back him up but do me a favor. Just… wait until after the holidays." I appeal to her protective nature. "Let's not ruin Christmas."

"Okay."

The feast is eclectic. Chicken chow mein, eggrolls, mashed potatoes (brought by my dad from the deli), stuffing (brought by Emily), and cranberry sauce and pumpkin pie (David's contributions). I nurse a glass of wine, afraid of a repeat of Halloween.

Before we dive in, David asks, "Would anyone like to say grace?"

Jonathan and I grew up in houses that never said grace. Our group of heathens sit in silence at the question.

"Why don't you, babe?" asks Jonathan. He glances around the table and we all nod, eager to be given reprieve from the task.

"Alright. Well, I just want to say how grateful I am to be here. To have met you all this year. I know this isn't the feast we had planned but it's still beautiful. Because we're beautiful. So, thank you, Lord, for all this beauty. Amen."

Jonathan takes his hand and squeezes. "That was lovely, babe."

Looking around the table, the food is as mismatched as the group, created from both blood and circumstance. But the camaraderie is real and is reflected when Jonathan prompts us all to share what we're grateful for this year.

"Since you already shared, I'll go," he says to David. "This year, I'm grateful for new beginnings." A glance to David. "And for my family." A glance to the rest of us.

I answer as expected, though it doesn't make the choice any less sincere: "I'm grateful for my beautiful baby boy. And all of you. I couldn't do this without you."

My dad: "I'm grateful for my grandson. And take-out."

Emily: "I'm grateful my son is healthy and well."

Liam: "I'm grateful for all this food! And Madonna, of course."

We all take a moment to be grateful for Madonna. Even my father, which makes me smile.

Jamie: "I'm grateful I'm not at home."

And with that answer, the mood slides into somberness. It's a shift that Jonathan won't tolerate. Bless him.

"Sometimes you have to make a new home. And a new family. To the homes, and the families, we create," he pronounces. We all raise our glasses to toast this affirmation. Then we dig in.

When the last guest leaves, David (who by this point is no longer really a "guest") helps Jonathan clean up while I put Dante to bed.

"That went well!" Jonathan assesses, as the three of us plop onto the couch together after our tasks are completed.

"I know," I add. "I feel like an actual grown-up."

"Becoming a mother didn't do that for you?" David asks.

"Yes and no. Mostly I just feel incompetent."

"Well, you're young."

I snort in response.

"What?" he asks.

"Everyone says that. Like it's a compliment but it's really not."

"Sorry," he says, grabbing my hand and squeezing it. "I don't mean it as a dig. I promise."

"I know. I just get sick of hearing it."

"What can I do to make it up to you?"

"Can I touch your hair?"

"No. Freak."

I chuckle because I've been asking him this since we met, and the answer is always the same. I don't even want to touch his hair anymore but it's now just a bit we do.

"What were you and Emily talking about?" Jonathan asks me.

"The... thing," I say cryptically, which sounds ridiculous.

"What thing?" Jonathan asks.

"You know..."

"Oh. That. I told him," Jonathan says, indicating David.

David nods and says solemnly, "That was some pretty fucked up shit."

Jonathan and I nod our agreement.

"I'm going to bed," I announce without further explanation. I almost get away.

"Wait," Jonathan says. "So, what did she want? Emily?"

"She wanted to know if you looked at the yearbooks."

"Ah."

He doesn't tell me that he's looked at the yearbooks. And I don't tell him that I know he has. We just look at each other in a kind of awkward standoff.

"For real now. I'm going to bed." I kiss them both good night and drag myself off to my room. I only cry a little that night before drifting off.

I'm no longer having my anxiety dream but that's only because I never sleep deeply enough. The experts all say to sleep when the baby sleeps, but I've never been someone who takes naps. When I've tried in the past, I usually just lie awake, thinking of all the things I should be doing. If I do manage to finally fall asleep, I wake up groggy as hell and the rest of the day passes in a haze. With Dante, I *can* finally nap but only if he's in my arms and at my side. If he conks out in his carrier or crib, I'm at a loss. And like before, I find myself paralyzed with possibilities. The pressure to be productive is even greater now because the time allotted is so limited. Should I work? Read? Clean? Take a shower? Should I try, in vain, to nap by myself? Usually, I work, a decision based on fear as much as desire.

The fear is the worst part of motherhood. It's constant. I'm scared that I'll never have a proper career, that I've sacrificed any kind of future by choosing to have Dante. I'm scared that if I do have a proper career, I'll miss the most important moments of his life. But most of all, I'm scared that I'll fuck him up in countless ways I can't even imagine.

The second worst thing I discover two nights before Christmas: Motherhood stops for nothing and no one.

I'm watching TV when the commercials come on, every image of food turning my stomach queasy. I lay Dante down on the couch and run to the bathroom where I promptly throw up. (What will I do when he can finally roll over? It's a milestone that's coming soon and one I'm definitely not prepared for.) I haven't had the stomach flu since high school. I crawl out of the bathroom and into the living room. I check Dante's temperature with my palm. He feels normal and I'm relieved. I lay on the floor next to the couch and I realize that I can't call in sick.

I lay there until I hear the front door. I try to stand but I can only sit up. I close my eyes and Jonathan's voice rings out.

"Hey! You're up! Great!"

"Ugh."

"You okay?"

"Stomach flu."

"Ew. That sucks. Can I do anything?"

"Make the room stop spinning?"

"You got it. Hey, I got us something."

He leaves the living room and I hear him talking with David, followed by rustling. The sound wakes up Dante and I drag myself up on the couch to bring him to me. When my eyes re-focus, I see Jonathan and David attempting to put up a Christmas tree in the corner of the room.

"You got a tree!" I say, my voice raw. Expressing enthusiasm is exhausting but I can't help it. I'm delighted.

I watch as they decorate the tree using a box of newly purchased silver ball ornaments. They throw on clumps of tinsel that I'll have to fix later when I can actually stand up.

"We didn't get a topper," David says.

"Topper?" Jonathan asks.

"Yeah. You know, an angel. Or a star. We always had an angel."

"Hang on." Jonathan goes to his bedroom, and we hear him digging around in his closet. He returns with a tiara, a Halloween relic from when he dressed as Laura Palmer. (He wore a ball gown and wrapped himself in plastic.) He walks over and places it atop the tree.

"There." He steps back to admire his ingenuity.

David laughs and shakes his head. "You're crazy."

They sit on either side of me, keeping a little distance, no doubt due to my infectious state. The tree promptly tilts to one side but manages to keep its crown. All three of our heads tilt with it.

"It looks like a drunk prom queen," David says.

I call my father the next day to let him know that I'm sick and that I'll have to forego coming home on Christmas Day as we had planned. I feel guilty but he doesn't seem too upset. In fact, he seems oddly relieved, like he had been looking for a way out of our plans. Jonathan and David are also planning on staying in town and this marks my first Christmas spent only with my found family.

"What's Emily doing for Christmas?"

"Oh, she's going on an Alaskan cruise."

"No shit?"

"Yup."

"And she's not making you go with her?"

"Oh, she asked. But I'm not really a cruise guy. And David is *definitely* not a cruise guy. She's going with a friend."

I still haven't gotten presents for anyone. I had a brief moment of inspiration a few weeks ago, thinking that I would create handmade gifts for everyone. This was before I remembered that I have zero skills in all types of arts and crafts, and no time to make anything even if I did.

So, now I have about twenty-four hours to come up with something, anything. I think about drawing up some coupons like I made for my mom when I was a kid. But I can't even think of what I would offer. Maybe I'll get better at Christmas too. I'd better because this is pathetic. And that's what I'm thinking when Jonathan walks in from getting the mail.

"We got some packages," he says. "What did you order from the Home Shopping network?"

"Oh, shit! Don't look at that!" I yell.

I had forgotten. I was so addled with sleeplessness one night that I ordered gifts being pitched by perky people on late night TV. Though for the life of me, I can't remember what I actually bought. I take the box and walk into my room. I open it up and see a label that reads "Magic Wand."

Wow. Did I get something fun for him and David? But then I look more closely and see that it's just a food processing tool. I sigh in disappointment. A sex toy would have been so much cooler. Just how tired was I?

Christmas arrives and the three of us exchange gifts. Jonathan and Dante give me a gift certificate for a massage and facial. It's so thoughtful I nearly cry. I give them the Magic Wand and Jonathan has the same assumption as me.

"Oooh! Fun!" Jonathan exclaims.

"It's for the kitchen, babe," David deadpans.

"Oh."

"I'm sorry it's so lame," I apologize. "I bought it in a sleep-deprived haze. I'll get you something better."

"It's fine," David assures me. He gives Jonathan an encouraging look.

"Yeah, yeah. It's fine."

"You're both terrible liars," I tell them.

They exchange gifts, a sweater for Jonathan and a bottle of Drakkar Noir for David. And then they disappear and return with a small gift for Dante.

"Oh wow! What did y'all do?"

I open the gift and it's a customized onesie, printed with our company name.

"This is amazing!" I exclaim. "I want one too!"

"Good. Cuz I got us shirts too."

"Shut up!"

"For real."

He disappears again and returns with a box of merchandise, all sporting our company logo.

"Holy shit, dude. What is all this?"

"Marketing!"

"Right. Of course. I knew you'd find a way to go shopping."

By the year's end, Dante is sleeping through the night. I'm thrilled to have more sleep but despondent when the nightmare returns.

It's clear now that I'm running from sirens. I'm packing, I'm in an ambulance, I'm packing, I'm in the ER waiting room. Jonathan is there. Sometimes Shane. Nothing makes sense. Everything is a jumble. The only thing I know for certain is that tragedy is keeping me from going wherever I'm intending to go. As always, I don't know where that is. And what's more unsettling is I don't know what the tragedy is. Do I want to know? No. But I also don't want to wake up in the morning drenched in sweat, awash in anxiety either.

David and Jonathan try to persuade me to join them on their party-hopping plans for New Year's Eve. But all I want to do is stay in, order pizza, and watch Dick Clark. I explain the importance of being in my pajamas. Jonathan snorts his disapproval.

"I won't let you become a crazy cat lady," he tells me.

"Hey! I will *absolutely* be a crazy dog lady."

"You know what I mean. You have to get out there."

"It's only been three months since I've had Dante!"

"You'll have to excuse him," David chides. "Three months is an eternity to him."

"It is an eternity," Jonathan protests.

"I'm not ready."

Jonathan shakes his head. What I want to say is that I'll probably never be ready.

Annie Marie Huber

Another Dead End

Dante is five months old in mid-February and the city streets are back to snowy drudgery. Having been here for a year, the magic has waned a bit. I'm now like the locals, cursing the weather gods and anxious for any sign of spring. I long to take Dante to the park but we spend most of our days cooped up inside the apartment.

One afternoon, I'm lying on my bed half trying to nap and half watching Dante in the carrier. The phone rings and I instinctively cringe as I do every time that happens when he's napping. But Jonathan answers right away and Dante stays asleep. I take a deep breath and try to continue resting. After a few minutes, Jonathan appears at my door. He tip-toes inside my room and gently sits beside us.

"I have to go to LC," he whispers, using our abbreviated term for Lake City.

"Why?"

"Apparently, Emily is at the police station. She's trying to report the guys that attacked us. And she needs me there to confirm who they are."

We lock eyes and I know he knows what I've done.

"I assume you gave her the yearbook?"

"Yes."

"Dammit, Katie. You should have told me."

"Yeah. I know."

He's pissed but shakes his head with resolve. What's done is done. He starts to get up and I grab his arm.

"Wait. I'm coming with you," I tell him. I got him into this; it's only fair I see it through.

"What about Dante?" he asks.

"We can drop him off at my dad's house. He'll watch him."

To my utmost surprise, my dad is a doting grandpa. I wonder if he was ever the same with me. If so, I don't remember.

"Should we bring David with us?" I ask.

"Why?"

"I don't know. He's a lawyer. He might come in handy."

"I'll call him. He'll come. It's what a good boyfriend would do."

"Boyfriend?"

"Focus, girl."

"Right. Sorry."

I can't help being amused. It's the first time I've heard Jonathan give anyone the official label of "boyfriend."

I start gathering the arsenal needed for traveling with Dante.

"Do you know where the police station is in Lake City?" I ask. For all my romping as a teen, I never had to go there. Sometimes I wonder if I wasn't a "cute" white girl, would I have spent my formative years in juvie?

"Yeah. I went with Emily to bail out my dad on a drunk and disorderly once. Festive."

Since his passing, Jonathan now refers to his father as his "dad" regularly. I guess in death comes a bit of respect, if not for the person than for the position.

"I can't believe we're doing this. Remind me to kill you both later," Jonathan says to me as we leave the apartment.

He drives my car, with me in the back seat attending to Dante. We stop at David's office on the way and pick him up. I've never seen David in his work clothes before which feels impossible but it's true. He changes after work before coming over and stops back at his place in the morning to get ready for work. The David I know wears overalls and sarongs. Lawyer David is in a dark gray suit. He's holding a briefcase, and he appears like he just stepped from the pages of *GQ*.

Dante wakes up halfway through the drive and I entertain him with the toys in the diaper bag. He loves riding in the car, so he doesn't fuss much. When we arrive at my dad's house, I run in with Dante. I give my dad a short explanation as to what is happening.

He doesn't seem too surprised.

"I thought she might do that," he says.

"Really?"

"We ran into each other getting coffee the other day."

"Oh." My dad has never had much of a social life, so hearing that he had coffee with Emily is a nice surprise.

"I'll be back soon," I say, kissing Dante on the head and handing him over.

Ten minutes later, we reach the station, a one-floor concrete building clearly marked and with ample parking. The interior of the building feels like all government buildings: cold. Six basic metal and vinyl chairs sit across from the front desk. Emily is sitting on one of the chairs, waiting for us.

She jumps up and approaches the desk that separates the state from the public.

"He's here. He can make the statement now," she tells the officer manning the desk. The sight of the officer (and his gun) makes my chest tighten.

Without a word, he turns around to inform someone of our presence. We all wait, not sure what to do. Eventually, a different officer walks through the side door and approaches us. He's tall with short red hair and a handlebar mustache.

"Hi, folks. I'm Officer Bernard. What can I help you with?"

Emily is the one to answer for us all. "We need to make a statement about an assault that happened."

His gaze travels across the four of us. "Are all of you involved?"

"I'm Emily. And this is my son Jonathan and his friend Katie. They were assaulted. This is David, his…"

"His lawyer," David interrupts.

"You need a lawyer?" the officer asks Jonathan, ignoring the rest of us.

"I have no idea what I need," Jonathan answers.

"Why don't you all follow me? We can talk over here," the officer says, waving us to follow him through the door and down a short hallway. The white walls feature framed photos of decorated officers. We enter a small conference room and take a seat around a table. I realize that I'm in an interrogation room. I feel like I've entered a *Law & Order* episode and I wonder how long before I start sweating.

"So, when did this assault happen?" Again, he directs his question only to Jonathan but it's Emily who answers.

"December 27, 1995."

Two days after Christmas. Memories begin to wash over me, and my breath becomes shallow. *Keep it together.*

The officer's eyebrows come together in curiosity. "That's over a year ago. You're just reporting it now?"

I chime in; I can't help myself. "There was an incident report. I'm sure you have some paperwork somewhere." I wish I had kept the card of the officer I saw at the hospital, but I know it's long gone. "Two officers came to see me at the hospital after it happened."

"There's definitely a report," Emily adds, while digging through her purse for her contact's card.

"The statute of limitations is five years in Indiana, yes?" David asks.

"Two years for a misdemeanor," Officer Bernard corrects. "Where are you from?" The question is directed at David and is more accusation than question.

"Is that relevant?" David responds. He knows what the response will be to the words "New York." There's a subset of people in the Midwest that really hate New York and California. I'm not sure why. And while not one of these people myself, I would bet a million dollars that our officer here is part of that camp.

Before the conversation can devolve into one where the phrase "big city attorney" is thrown about, Emily interrupts. "It wasn't a misdemeanor! They almost killed my son!"

"Alright, ma'am. Well, if it's a felony, you have five years to press charges."

"You're damn right it was a felony," Emily says. She finds the card and hands it over. "I've been talking to Officer Taylor."

"Ah," Officer Benson responds. "Officer Taylor retired earlier this month."

"Well, surely you still have the report," Emily persists. I can tell Officer Bernard is trying hard to exhibit patience.

"I'm sure we do. What is your statement about today?"

"We know who did it," Emily answers.

Jonathan tries to clarify. "We didn't know who they were when it happened. But, after looking at a bunch of yearbooks, I can tell you who did it."

Emily hands the yearbook over. The pages are clearly marked with sticky notes. The officer studies both circled images.

"Is this a joke?" he asks.

We're all dumbfounded by the question. Eventually, David speaks up. "No, sir. It's not a joke."

"Josh Owens? You know that's the chief's son, right?"

Jonathan and I share a look that translates to "fuck."

"I didn't know that. You didn't know that, right?" Emily asks Jonathan and me.

We both shake our heads.

"It shouldn't matter," Emily continues. "Look at the report. They almost killed him," she repeats, indicating Jonathan, who I can tell wishes he were anywhere else.

"And you were assaulted too?" he asks me. I'm suddenly visible and I don't like it.

"Yeah."

"And you can confirm it was these two boys?"

I nod. The lie is easier than I expected.

"Well, let me look into the report and I'll see where this new information takes us." He gets up. The meeting is over.

"Can I get your card?" Emily asks as we're being shuffled out the door.

The officer produces his card, and she takes it, shoving it into her purse. We all walk outside and stand together, collecting ourselves.

"Well, shit," Emily says.

"Indeed," David adds. Emily lights a cigarette and hands it to me before lighting another for herself. I take it without comment.

"Well, that explains the threatening phone calls," she continues.

"The journalist was still getting threats?" Jonathan asks.

"And me."

"*What?*"

"I didn't want you to worry. But yeah, I've been getting calls too."

"Fuck. I didn't know," Jonathan says quietly. "But don't you see?

We need to let this go. It's not a fight we can win."

"No. This is totally unacceptable," she argues and stubs out her cigarette on the ground. "Fuck it. I know where they live." She starts walking quickly to the car. Jonathan and I share a look.

"Emily!" Jonathan calls out.

She keeps walking.

"*Mom!*"

She stops and we catch up to her.

"This is not okay. This is bullshit," she says, her voice rising. "And I know what I'm going to do. I just need to make a phone call and take care of this once and for all."

"No!" I yell, knowing just what kind of phone call she's planning to make. I pull on Jonathan's arm and say to him, "She's going to call *a hit man.*"

"Shut the fuck up," he says, dismissing me.

"No! For real!" I protest. "Ask her!"

He shakes his head at me but does as I demand anyway. "Mom. Tell me you're not going to call a hit man." He mutters, "I can't believe I'm even saying these words."

She doesn't answer.

"Mom?"

"I know a guy," she whispers.

"Mom!"

"I think I should remind everyone here that I'm an officer of the court," David interjects.

We all look at him for a moment before continuing.

"Tell me why not?" Emily asks Jonathan. "Why the fuck not? Give me one good reason these guys shouldn't pay." She's crying now, hysterical.

Jonathan takes her hands in his and answers calmly. "Because we're not like them. Because we're actually *better* than them. And because it won't fix it. You want justice. But there is no justice here."

"I want accountability."

"Well, there's not much of that either." Jonathan looks to David for confirmation. "Hey, officer of the court. What do you say? How are we doing in the great war of good versus evil?"

"Oh, we're definitely losing."

His answer is enough to deflate the tension.

"And really, you gotta let this go," Jonathan tells Emily. "Cuz all I fucking need is for you to end up in jail."

"I just have all this rage," Emily says, defeated. "And I don't know what to do with it."

"I know you do."

"Don't you? Why aren't you angry?"

Jonathan sighs. "Of course, I'm angry. But that's why we drink."

She lets out a sharp laugh.

"In fact, I could use a drink right now," Jonathan states. "Anyone with me?"

We all nod in agreement.

"Foxhole?" he asks.

We all nod again.

Only the desperation of a local dive bar will do.

Consensual Scars

The War Room

The chances of me running into Shane at the Foxhole are zero percent. Jonathan and David go with Emily, and I follow them in my car. When we get there, I find a pay phone to check in with my father. After confirming that all is well with Dante – and warning my dad that I might be returning late – I join the group at the bar. Jonathan has ordered tequila shots for us all.

"He's not going to look into shit, is he?" Emily asks to no one in particular, referring to the officer we spoke to at the station.

"I'm going to guess... no," David responds.

"Goddammit."

We order beers to chase the shots. I haven't eaten anything all day and the alcohol hits me quickly.

"So, now what?" asks Emily.

"Now... we let it go," Jonathan declares.

Emily stirs in her seat as the answer is wholly inadequate.

"Why don't you put all that energy into something positive?" David suggests.

"Like what?" she asks.

"Like running for city council. Make some changes from the inside."

Em observes him like he's grown an extra head.

"I'm serious!" David protests. "You're smart, you've got passion. Why not?"

"I'm a cocktail waitress not a politician."

"Fuck that. You're what you want to be." David looks to me and Jonathan for support. "Back me up, guys."

"I think it's genius," I say.

"I think it's crazy," Jonathan says.

"See? Crazy!" Em agrees.

David shrugs. "It's just an idea."

We all marinate a little longer on the idea.

"It might not be *that* crazy," Jonathan says.

Jonathan orders another round and I excuse myself to use the restroom. Before I make it there, I literally bump into Carlos.

"Oh, shit! Hi," I say.

"Hey girl! Wow! Long time no see! How are you? Where have you been?" His smile is wide, and his demeanor is as charming as ever.

"I'm good. I've been living in Chicago. You?"

"Oh, you know, here and there. Doin' this and that. Hey, do you have a minute to talk?" he asks.

"Sure," I say, hesitantly. I can't imagine what he wants to talk about. We take a seat at a table in the corner, out of earshot of the other patrons.

"Something's goin' on with Shane."

"What do you mean?"

"I don't know, man. When I go over there, the door's always locked. I can see he's home, but he won't open the door. He won't pick up the phone. I thought he was pissed at me. But I don't think he's talkin' to *anyone*."

"What about Matty?"

He shrugs. "Haven't seen her lately."

"What about your *men's group*?" I ask this with more venom than I intend. I'm still jealous.

"Hasn't been goin'. And no one in the group has talked to him either."

"Has he done this before? Cut off contact like this?"

"No, man. It's weird!"

"How long has this been going on?"

"A few weeks. I just know you care about him. Maybe he'll talk to you. I'm really worried about him."

He's not teasing me about my feelings for Shane like he did before. He's serious. And I don't think I've ever seen Carlos serious about anything. Yet, the idea that Shane would confide in me is so improbable as to be laughable.

"I don't know, man. I don't think he'll talk to me."

"You can try though, right? Check in on him?" he persists.

"I'll try," I promise. I don't know if I mean it but it's enough to placate him.

"Thanks, girl. I really appreciate it."

I give him a hug.

"You look different, by the way," he says, taking me in.

"Yeah?"

I can only imagine negative connotations of "different." Exhausted? Heavier? I don't really want him to elaborate but he does.

"Yeah. You look... grounded."

"What does that mean?"

He laughs. "I don't know. You look good." He squeezes my hand and kisses me on the cheek. "Thanks again."

I continue on to the bathroom where I enter a stall and quickly throw up. My head is spinning, my thoughts a whirl of confusion. Hadn't I wanted Shane to be miserable? Wished for it when I spoke to Ellis? And now that I hear that he is, it twists me up just the same.

And what did I just promise? After the past year, can I really go see him? Wouldn't that undo all the work I've done? But it's like putting heroin in front of an addict. The pull is too much, and I know the answer. I desperately want to see him again. And all the reasons I shouldn't are quickly being rationalized away. Surely, I can just check in. I can just say, "hi." I don't have to fall in again. The lies I tell myself are so easy it's scary.

I flush the toilet, wipe my mouth, and exit the stall. I'm mortified to find two other women in the restroom with me. I have no idea when they entered.

"Hey, girl, you okay?"

Shit. They heard me throw up.

"Uh... yeah. Sorry."

I'm sweating and panicking. But then I remember that a women's restroom can be the most supportive environment on earth. Guys are always curious about why women go to restrooms together, but it's not that hard to figure out. They're part war room, part therapist office. It's where we strategize and sympathize.

"Pregnant?" asks the other woman. They're about the same age as me, but I don't know them. They're a bit tipsy, and are dressed in club clothes, ready for more action than this town can possibly provide. One of them whips out a compact from her purse and produces a small vial of white powder. I love how it's still the '80s here.

"No, no," I answer, as she sniffs up a line. "Not pregnant. Actually, I just had a baby about five months ago." I view myself in the mirror and assess my image. "Can you tell?" My insecurities are met with a litany of encouraging words.

"No way, girl! You look great!"

"Five months? You look amazing!"

I'm pretty sure it's a lie but they're so insistent that I let them lift me up. Just because they're high, it doesn't mean they're wrong, right?

"Too much to drink?" the taller girl asks, as she reapplies her lipstick in front of the mirror, before taking her turn with the coke. It takes me a moment to realize she's still trying to deduce the reason for my vomiting.

"No."

"Sick?"

"No."

"Purging?"

"No, no!" I protest a little too much. Then I feel bad, thinking back to my dalliance with knives. Lord knows, I have no room to judge how any girl processes her pain.

"I mean, no. Not purging," I say more calmly.

"Oh, I know," the other girl says and offers me the straw and the compact of coke. "It's about a guy, right?"

I'm tempted to take a line. Wouldn't it be grand to feel fabulous and invincible? But then I remember the messy comedown that awaits and wave the coke away.

"None for me but thanks."

She shrugs. "So… a guy, right?"

I don't answer which is all the answer they need.

"*Of course*, it's about a guy. Duh. I should have known," says the first girl. "So, what's the story? Is he here? Do you need us to smuggle you out of here? Cuz we can do that."

Ah, the unsung heroes in women's restrooms.

"No, he's not here. I just... I haven't seen him in a long time. And now I might." It's weird how easy it is to talk to total strangers. Just like with the message boards.

"*Might?* And you're already throwing up? Yikes."

For sure.

"You love him?" she asks.

"Yeah."

"Ugh. That's the *worst*," says the second girl. I love that she has just enough context to make this assessment. It *is* the worst.

"Well, honey, keep your head up. You're gorgeous and if he doesn't appreciate you, then fuck him."

I want to hug them both but instead I just thank them. They smile encouragingly at me before sending me back to battle. Or in this case, the bar where Jonathan turns to me when I settle back onto a stool.

"Shit, I thought we lost you. Who was that guy you were talking to?"

"Oh, that was just an old friend. Saying hello."

Jonathan knows all my friends except those in Shane and Matty's orbit. I've probably mentioned Carlos to him before but I'm really not up to introductions. Fortunately, he doesn't ask for specifics.

We finish our drinks. The conversation has moved on to lighter topics since my absence, but I never jump in. Instead, I formulate a plan. When Jonathan proposes another round, I cut him off.

"No more for me. I gotta get back to Dante. And, if it's cool with you two, I think I'm gonna stay the night here. Can you guys catch the train back?"

"I was thinking of staying too," Jonathan says. "David, wanna see where I grew up?"

"I would love to," David answers, his eyes wide with curiosity.

"You're staying the night? Oh, that's wonderful!" Emily cheers.

We pay the bill and exit the bar. I hug everyone goodbye and head to my car alone. I stare at myself in the rearview mirror. My blonde hair has grown back since I dyed it. The nose stud is still in, and I wonder if Shane will notice it... if I actually go see him.

Even though I've made my escape from the group, I'm still undecided. I remain that way until I'm driving down his street, the narcotics of him too strong to resist.

The Lion's Den

I sit in my car in their driveway, the autopilot that propelled my body here finally pausing. What am I doing?

Don't think. Just get out of the car. Go to him. Find out what's going on.

The house is dark and quiet, but I can see the landscape in the moonlight. I haven't been here in over a year, and I never expected to see this place again. I love it so much that it hurts. I fight the urge to run into the woods and live there.

Carlos is right. The house is locked up tight. Shane's truck is there so I know that he's home. I knock on the back door. I want to call out, but I can't find my voice. I walk to the front of the house to see if I can see him in the windows. He's nowhere in view, so I trudge back to my car. I drive to the nearest payphone, about five minutes away at a gas station. I call the number I memorized long ago. When the answering machine picks up, I choke out a message.

"Hi. This is Katie. Remember me?" I sound like an idiot. "So, I ran into Carlos, and he's worried about you. I promised him I'd check in. But you're not answering the door. Your truck is there so I think you're home. Anyway, I'm gonna try again. If you are there, can you let me in?"

Let me in. The words echo in my head. Isn't that what I've been begging for since I met him? How can I be here again?

Don't think.

I get back into my car and return to the house. This time when I try the door, it's unlocked. I open it slowly and walk in, delicately like I'm entering a lion's den. It's dark, with only candles lighting the house. I wonder if the power is out again or if this is just a new aesthetic. I take off my boots and walk through the hallway, willing the floors not to creak beneath my feet. I find him in the kitchen, sitting on a barstool. My breath catches at the sight of him. His beard is longer, scruffier, and his eyes are bloodshot, either from crying, booze, or both. I want to run to him, comfort him, kiss him. But that's not my privilege. Instead, I just sit on a barstool next to him. He watches me and tries for a casual greeting.

"Well, well, well. Long time, no see."

He's smiling but it doesn't reach his eyes. The joy that used to radiate from somewhere inside him is manufactured. The attempt at normalcy is an ill-fitting suit that I can see right through. Usually, he would hug me hello and the lack of his touch burns.

"Want a drink?" he asks, as he pours another for himself. He's drinking whiskey and I wonder how many he's had.

"Sure," I answer. I could use a very strong drink right now. I take a too-large sip and it causes me to choke.

"You okay?" he asks.

"Yeah. Just… I don't drink much anymore."

"Really?" I can tell he approves, even in his own liquored state.

"Yeah."

"But you still smoke weed, right?"

"Not so much."

"Now, that's a shame."

"Sorry."

"Still saying 'sorry' all the time, I see. Tell me… just what exactly are you sorry for?"

"Oh honey, we don't have that kind of time."

He barks a laugh, a real laugh, and it's like a balm.

"Where's Matty?" I ask.

"Yoga conference." His eyes drop down as he answers, and he bites his lip afterwards. I've never known him to lie. He's terrible at it. "So, Chicago, right? How's that?"

"It's fine." I have to get the conversation off me. "I saw Carlos," I continue. "He said you won't see him."

"Don't you two have anything better to talk about? I mean, really. Art, music, philosophy? There's a whole world out there and you've got nothing to talk about other than me? How fucking sad is *that*."

It's an echo of the joke that Ellis made, but this time it just sounds mean.

I don't have an answer. His rant has made me small as I sink down in my seat ashamed. I've never seen him angry or cruel and now he's both and I want to die. I'm frozen, staring at the floor. We stay like that forever, him staring at me staring down, my soul shattering.

Stop. Breathe. Think of something else, anything else. This horrible moment will pass.

There are crumbs on the floor where there were never crumbs before. The mess makes me wonder how long Matty has really been gone. The thought reminds me of my mom. Woman's work. It's no safer a thought.

I give up. I can't do this. I'm drowning.

"I'm sorry. I shouldn't have come. I'll go." I get up to leave. I get only a few feet from the kitchen before I hear him, his voice softer.

"Wait."

I stop. When he follows up with "I'm sorry," I turn around and walk back to him.

"Matty's not at a yoga conference, is she?" I ask.

He sighs and smiles, a joyless ironic gesture.

"You were always very sharp," he tells me. It's not really a compliment but a diversion.

"So…?"

"No, wise one. Matty is not at a yoga conference. Matty is in Florida, fucking one of her students."

I don't have an eloquent response to this, so his words just hang in the air, like smoke from a cigarette. I could say "I'm sorry," but I know it'll be as insincere as it is redundant. (Redundant.)

"Marriage, my young friend, is a bitch," he continues, shaking his finger at me so I'm sure to absorb this valuable lesson. It's so condescending that I want to grab his finger and twist it right off.

"Then why do it?" I ask pointedly.

"Because we don't know any better, I suppose."

My anger dissolves as quickly as it showed up. He's broken and I can't be mad at him. Instead, I want to save him.

"What about love?" I ask.

"Love just fucks everything up."

True.

"Ever been in love?" he asks.

"Once."

"Tell me about it."

"Well, it wasn't very convenient. Him being married and all." The words fall from my mouth before I can stop them. Fuck it. Maybe the truth will set me free.

"Yeah?"

"Yeah."

Time stops while we gaze at one another. Slowly, his face transforms as understanding takes hold, his eyes filled with drunken wonder.

"I'm... I don't know what to say."

"You don't have to say anything. I'm here if you need... or want... anything."

The truth has made me bold.

"I'm amazed," he confesses.

"I'm amazed you didn't know."

"Well, I mean... we had that one night. But, I didn't know..."

"That I love you beyond reason?"

And with that, the guise is gone. And the more confessional I become, the more the words are a potent elixir. The spell that's always been around me is widening to encircle him too.

"No. I didn't know that." His voice is so soft I can barely hear him.

He stands up and walks toward me. He pulls me into a hug and his touch is life. I expect him to pull away, but instead he moves his hands from my back to my cheeks. And now he's kissing me, so slowly. He tastes of whisky, woody and dangerous, and I'm dizzy. I know he's drunk, and I don't care. I probably should care. I know I'm taking advantage of him. But he's using me too. I'm pretty sure if any random woman showed up and said the same things to him that I just said, he'd be kissing her. I'm a placeholder, a warm body. But I don't care about that either. So maybe we're even.

All I care about is that he's kissing me.

I take his hand and lead him from the kitchen, past the master bedroom, to the guest room. He sits on the bed, and I move between his knees, pushing him down on his back. I'm on birth control now but I know I should inquire about a condom. I don't though. As a man who's been married for over a decade, I'm certain he doesn't have any on hand. (And if he does, I'd be way too curious about the implications of that fact.)

My reticence to ask for additional birth control is moot though. Before anything else can happen, he passes out. I roll off him and stifle an ironic laugh. I'm disappointed and relieved at the same time. I also feel ridiculous and humiliated though I'm not sure why. Maybe it's because if I was more of a sex goddess, he would not have passed out. But surely that's dumb. I'm sure even Pamela Anderson has had men pass out on her. (Okay, maybe not her.) Nevertheless, I can say that every part of me feels like the exact opposite of a sex goddess right now. What would that be? A troll? I feel like a troll.

I cover Shane with a blanket and return to the kitchen. I find a pad of paper and pen near the phone and write him a note. I tell him to call me, and I put down the number for my father's house. And then I leave to get back to Dante.

Twenty-four hours pass before the phone rings. My father is in the kitchen, and I run past him yelling "got it!" so loudly, he cringes. I pick up the kitchen phone, cursing that I have no privacy. When will my dad invest in a cordless?

"Hello?" I answer.

"Katie?"

My breath catches and I feel weird and exposed. Oddly enough, we've never spoken on the phone before. All of my visual cues are gone. But then again, so are his. Maybe there's freedom in just one sensory overload. His voice, no longer slurring, has lost the sarcasm and false reverie of last night. It's calm and kind, deep and lovely in a way that makes my knees weak.

"I'm sorry about last night."

Shit. What does this mean? Is he sorry about the kissing? Sorry about passing out? Sorry about what, exactly? Normally, I would just crumble under my litany of internal questions. But something about the phone makes me brave.

"What exactly are you sorry about?"

"For passing out on you."

I smile, knowing we've just averted a misunderstanding that would have sent me spinning. He doesn't know that, of course. He'll never know his luck in not needing to dissect every moment of our relationship.

"Did you mean what you said last night?" he asks.

"You remember what I said last night?" I haven't decided yet which answer I want.

"Yes," he answers.

"Then... also... yes."

The word has never sounded more alive.

"I'm amazed," he says, repeating the word from the night before. Amazed is good, right?

"I'm amazed at your amazement."

A short silence settles in while I try to think of something else to say. But he saves me.

"Come over," he softly commands me. "I want to continue where we left off."

My knees nearly buckle beneath me. This phone is a miracle device, forcing specificity and directness.

"I'll be there as soon as I can."

I ask my father if he can watch Dante again. I tell him that I'm helping a friend... which I suppose I am? He agrees to help, and I feel a twinge of guilt. Of course, it's not enough to stop me. I barrel towards my car like a freight train. When I arrive at Shane's house, the back door is unlocked. I come in and remove my boots.

"Katie?" Shane calls out, and I can hear him walking down the hall. I meet him there and like two magnets, we're immediately in an embrace. His lips find mine and we're kissing with an urgency I've only ever imagined. He turns me around in his arms, his lips on my neck and his hand reaching between my legs. I unbutton my jeans and welcome his touch where I need it most.

"You're so wet," he sighs into my ear.

This determination, so blunt and so true, would normally embarrass me. But the way he says it wrecks me. He's turned on by how turned on I am, and it's like discovering a superpower. I boldly

Consensual Scars

spread my legs further apart, moaning in response.

"Come here." He takes me by the hand, and he leads me into the forbidden lair, the master bedroom. We're standing next to the bed, and I help him take off his shirt. My lips travel from his neck, down his chest. I want to do the things I've never done before. I want to give him pleasure in every conceivable way. I drop to my knees. He holds my head gently in his hands as I taste every part of him.

He stops me suddenly, instinctively, pulling my head from him and I know it's because he's close to the edge. He pulls me up and pushes me down on the bed, kneeling between my legs. He tugs my jeans the rest of the way down. Soon, my legs are shaking in response, my breathing ragged. I don't think I can take any more when he stops and slowly, methodically, takes off the rest of our clothes.

"Get on top of me," he demands, laying down on the bed.

I obey, sliding him into me. He groans as I begin to move, finding a rhythm that pleases us both. With every motion, I feel more powerful, more in control than I ever have in his presence. I look in his eyes, see his pleasure, his desire and I'm overwhelmed again. My whole body is shaking as I repeat the only word I can say over and over: "Yes."

Suddenly, he rolls me over roughly. He's a man possessed, fucking me hard and fast. When he finishes, I pull him as close to me as possible, our sweaty bodies bonded together. I kiss his shoulder as he recovers. He stays inside me as long as he can, causing me continuing spasms of bliss.

When he catches his breath, he moves so that he's lying on his side next to me. His fingers track across my body. I cringe when he gets to my fading c-section scar that runs between my hips in the shape of a smile.

"What's this?" he asks, his voice still slightly ragged.

I should be honest. But I can't say anything that will stop his hand from moving across my body. And the truth would surely do much more than that.

"Oh, that. I had my appendix out."

I have no idea if an appendix scar resembles a c-section scar but I'm betting he doesn't know either. Thankfully, he doesn't question it.

"Can you stay the night?" he asks.

Every part of me wants to stay, to sleep in his arms and wake up beside him. But I know that I can't. I have to get back to Dante.

"I can't. I have to be somewhere."

"Okay." He accepts my vague answer and I'm relieved. I don't have a lie ready for any follow-up questions.

He puts his hand on my cheek, turning my head toward his and kisses me. My toes curl beneath the sheets, my whole body instantly on fire.

"Careful," I say, when our lips separate. "If you start again…"

He smiles. "Can you come back tomorrow?" He doesn't need to be more specific. Tomorrow will be just like tonight.

"Yes."

And with that one simple word, my life splits in two.

A Week of (lite) S&M

Jonathan and David return to Chicago the next day on the train. I touch base before they leave and tell them that I'll be staying in town for a few more days. During the day, I'm a proper mom and daughter. I take care of Dante and help my father with chores. I've offered to go through my mom's clothes, a task he's put off again and again. I don't particularly want to do it either but it's a penance. Good deeds during the day so I can be sinful in the evening.

After Dante is asleep, I make my nightly escape. I tell my dad that I'm catching up with high school friends and he's happy to watch Dante while I'm gone. And I know it sounds crazy, but my new extracurricular activities with Shane are actually making me a better mom. Ok, maybe not these *specific* activities. Just getting out for a few hours and having something of my own. Even if that something is... well, this den of iniquity.

Since having Dante, I've spent almost every waking moment near him. The freedom of having a few hours away from his constant care is like getting something I desperately needed... that I didn't know I needed. The guilt still creeps in, but it's no match for how good I feel. Nothing can touch me. Because Shane's touching me. The smile on my face feels permanent even as I'm making piles of clothes to take to the Goodwill.

I only stay at Shane's house for a few hours each night. I take my dad's car when I go, leaving my car with him. This was my dad's suggestion as my car has the child seat for Dante.

"Just in case," he says.

My mind floods with possible tragedies that would make them

need to leave the house unexpectedly, but I push away the thoughts.

"Right. Good idea," I agree.

When I return to my dad's house after my visits, I check in with Dante, shower, and climb into my childhood bed. There, I make myself all kinds of promises. Specifically, that I'll tell Shane the truth. Tomorrow. Surely, I'll do it tomorrow.

However, tomorrow comes and I always chicken out. I rationalize that I have to know what Shane and I are first before I drop this bomb. Unfortunately, definitions feel equally dangerous. Do I really want to know what we are? I fear that defining us will surely make us disappear. And if we disappear, I'll die.

How did I end up here again? Easy. I never left. All he's ever had to do is express even the tiniest bit of interest in me and I would undoubtedly come running. I don't know if he loves me, but I know that he wants me. He's under my spell and I don't know how I did it. (Maybe I didn't do anything. Maybe timing really is everything and we hit the sweet spot.) Right now, all I know for certain, is that we're lovers engaged in a passionate affair that is rapidly getting kinkier each night we spend together.

The slide into our respective roles (dominant and submissive) is inevitable considering my devotion to him. I can't help but ask the question ("How can I please you?") on our second night together. And asking that question is like lighting a match in a room doused in kerosene. He follows up with commands that I dutifully obey. My obedience has unlocked something in him, an innate desire that surprises and delights him. Unlike our first night together, when I needed him so desperately, now he seems to need me. Or he just needs *this*. Either way, I'm happy to oblige.

With each demand, I can feel us daring each other. How far can he make me go? What are the limits? What won't I do to please him? He's searching for the line, and I keep moving it. Honestly, I don't know where the line is or even if there is one. It's a thought that scares me and thrills me. I wonder how much of this is a game and how much is real. My supplication to him feels like an irreversible state.

Meanwhile, he's able to switch from discerning master to gentle lover with ease. The transformation is usually smooth and when it happens, the fire in me is replaced by a love so powerful it terrifies me. Lying together, our bodies spent, he's remarkably tender. We don't talk much in these moments. And really, I prefer the silence. The less words, the less lies I need to tell. When he does talk, his words center around my needs. ("Would you like some water?" "Are you comfortable?" "Do you want to come back tomorrow?" Answers: "Yes," "Yes," and "Yes." Always "Yes.") The one time the shift is abrupt is when I'm on top of him and get a sudden leg cramp. I leap off him, crying out in pain.

"Baby, are you alright?" he asks, dropping character, his voice full of concern.

He's never called me "baby" before and my insides melt even as I'm hopping about the room, trying to rid myself of the cramp. I know I look ridiculous, and I start laughing. He joins in, then takes my hand. I sit beside him, and he massages my leg until the pain subsides.

"Don't hurt yourself," he warns as I climb back on him.

Oh, but I will. I almost say it aloud but stop myself.

While I trust him completely with my body, I know my heart is in imminent danger. I shake the thought away and just focus on the physical. In this realm, at least, I know he'll never break me. I know he'll never ask for anything I'm unwilling to do. (And he doesn't. His demands are all acts I desperately want to perform.) I've always heard that in this particular playground, the submissive is the one with all the real power. I can now attest to the truth of this dynamic. Whenever I please him, I feel this power flow through my veins. I'm a mythological creature, a temptress, a siren – and the metamorphosis is exhilarating.

"I don't know if you're an angel or a devil," he tells me one evening as I'm getting dressed to leave.

"Do I have to be one or the either? Can't I be the Madonna *and* the whore?" I ask, my voice dipping down to a lower register. I want to be both. But I understand the tendency toward binary terms. Because sometimes I feel like this thing between us is a gift from the gods and other times I know it's a curse.

He shakes his head in response, his face full of wonder. I've captivated him with my answer. Right now, it's a gift and I want to freeze time.

One night, after returning to my father's house, I notice a nasty friction burn on my thigh while washing up. I know when I must have got it but at the time, I barely registered any discomfort. Shane and I were on the floor of his den, my leg repeatedly rubbing aggressively against the wool rug. The wound hurts and I love it. I know it'll heal but I wish it wouldn't. While Shane is adept at giving commands, I know he's timid around causing actual pain. (As I witnessed when my leg cramped up.) I wonder how I can get him to be less restrained. Because I want scars, permanent reminders on my body. And that's when I decide that props might be in order.

"Were you ever a boy scout?" I ask him one night, our bodies recovering.

"A long time ago," he answers.

"So, you know how to make knots?"

He laughs. "I know how to make a few knots."

"Good," I say.

On my way home, I stop by our little local sex shop, a longtime staple of our town called Sinful Secrets. (I can't buy liquor in this town on a Sunday, but I can get S&M gear any day of the week. I'll never quite understand the moral delineations of this place.) I've been inside the store a few times with Jonathan. Like with our viewing of porn, these were exploratory missions, a chance to giggle at the inventive merchandise. The only time I've ever purchased anything is when I was attending a bachelorette's party for one of my girlfriends and I needed risqué party favors. This trip is different.

I feel exposed when I enter the store but then I remember: if someone catches me here, I also catch them. I'm only as vulnerable as everyone else. We're a shame collective, really, this store's customer base. But once inside, I can see the shop is nearly empty, with only a few strangers wandering the movie selections. I have no interest in that part of the store and instead browse the disciplinary gadgets.

Most of these devices feel like novelty toys. Handcuffs with pink fur. Silky, soft blindfolds that barely block out the light. Whips that would require a ridiculous amount of force to ever cause welts. If I were in Chicago right now, I bet I could find a proper shop with more serious wares. But this is all I have to choose from, so I examine the most restrictive blindfold I can find. It's pricey and still flimsy so I put it back.

I'm spending way too much time debating the merits of their collection when I realize that he can just use a scarf to blindfold me. After all, Matty has a million of them. I suck in air as I think about her juggling the scarves in the living room. Then I remind myself that Matty is far away and that her actions have made mine excusable. If she doesn't want her husband, I certainly do. But, of course, I don't know how I would get one of her scarves (nor do I know how Shane would react to such brazen borrowing), so I pick up the blindfold again and decide to purchase it. I also take a pair of the handcuffs, with the intent of removing the soft fur that's attached.

I'm about to go to the counter but as I pass by the vibrators, I stop. I've never used a vibrator before, and I want one. Not to use with Shane, but as a replacement for him when I'm not with him. I ache for him constantly. The options are varied, some truly scary in their size. I inspect a modest model that reminds me most of Shane's proportions. (I have no basis for comparison in this department, but I haven't found him lacking in any way.) I purchase the vibrator, the blindfold, and the handcuffs, paying cash for the anonymity.

On the drive home to my father's house, I feel like I'm freefalling out of an airplane but with only the slightest bit of curiosity about the reliability of my parachute. It'll either open or I'll drop dead to the ground. For right now, the fall is so unbelievably good, I don't care. If I've learned anything from Shane, the present is all that matters. Fuck the future.

I arrive the following night and find him standing naked in the master bedroom. The bed is different, higher. He's raised it by at least a foot by putting wooden blocks beneath it. Pieces of black rope are tied to the wooden slates of the frame on each of the four corners. The lights are off, and candles are lit around the room. (I silently hope that he uses those candles on me, my body craving the burning sensation of hot wax.) I walk to him and fall to my knees. I offer him the blindfold like a sacrifice. He doesn't take it. Instead, he gives me my instructions.

"Take off your clothes and lie down on your back, with your head at the foot of the bed. Then put on the blindfold."

I do as he commands as he watches intently. Unsatisfied with my positioning, he adjusts my body so that my neck is at the bottom edge of the mattress, my head tilted backwards and the world (appropriately) upside down.

"Now, stay there."

I lie there, exposed and turned on beyond measure as he leaves the room. The wait for him is agony and he knows it. He puts music on the stereo. I don't recognize the hypnotic new age sounds but they fit the scene he's concocted perfectly. When he returns, he fastens each piece of rope to my limbs. I'm relieved that he takes his time, perfecting each knot, making my restraints tight. When I'm splayed before him helplessly, he leaves again for several more minutes. I don't know what he's doing this time, but I know my role is to stay silent and wait patiently. I'm finally, *finally*, physically in his control as much as I am spiritually and waves of pleasure pass through me before he even returns. When he does come back, he takes his time working my body over, delighting in torturing me, touching me and kissing me everywhere except where I desire him most, until I'm begging him.

"Please."

"Please what?" he murmurs. He runs his tongue across my inner thigh. He's so close that I whimper.

"Please fuck me."

He stops touching me and gets up from the bed. Though I can't see him, I sense him moving toward the end of the bed. When he speaks, I feel his breath on my face. He responds to my plea with conviction.

"No."

I want to implore him to return to my thigh. To touch me anywhere again. But it's a new game now and the more I beg, the more he's going to withhold. So, I stay quiet and pray that his hands, his mouth return to me soon. I know he's watching me, enjoying my hunger for him. After a few minutes, he walks to the foot of the bed. And now I know why he's raised the bed. My head matches up perfectly with his waist. He brushes himself against my lips.

"I will let you do this," he offers.

He gives me strict instructions on how to pleasure him. And that's when I decide to disobey, in the hope that he'll discipline me further. We don't have a safe word though, so I have to trust that he knows this is part of the game and not an actual refusal.

"No," I whisper. The word feels weird in my mouth. I don't know that I've ever said it to him before. I can't see him, so I wait for his reaction.

"No?" He's surprised. The word must sound as odd to him as it does to me.

"No," I repeat, this time with a sly smile to let him know that the word is not really a refusal but a dare.

"Ah." He leaves the room once more. I wonder if he's deciding on my punishment and my nerves are in a state of desperate anticipation. I also wonder briefly what would happen if he just left me here indefinitely. My other life enters the corners of my consciousness. If not for those other obligations, I would surely stay here willingly forever.

When he returns, he stands behind me again.

"You can't control yourself, so I'll control you."

His fingers open my mouth, and he enters my mouth, deep, holding himself there until I gag, and he pulls himself away. He does this again and again until my lips are numb.

"Please," I gasp again.

"Please what?"

"Please fuck me."

Again, I feel his breath on my face as he whispers, "No."

The torture continues until I'm writhing in ecstasy, struggling against my restraints. Eventually, he gives me what I want, and I thank him for the honor. The rope burns on my wrists and ankles the next day are so satisfying, so exquisite, and I wonder again if I truly need help.

The next night, I bring the handcuffs with me, dropping them in the brown, leather purse I found while cleaning out my mom's closet. I was able to strip the pink fur from the handcuffs, and I can't wait to feel the cold metal pressing into my skin. I plan to offer them up in the same way I did the blindfold. I enter Shane's house and quietly remove my boots, my body shaking in anticipation for what's coming. But as I round the corner into the hallway, I bump right into Matty.

"Katie!" She greets me with the enthusiasm of two long-lost friends, embracing me tight. I'm paralyzed with surprise. Finally, I choke out a greeting as I will my arms to reciprocate the hug. Out of the corner of my eye, I see Shane come into view, a look of apology clearly written on his face.

All I can think is I have to disappear.

Terrible Timing

When Matty lets me go, I stumble backwards. I bump into the wall, knocking a frame to the floor. I pick it up and it's a picture of Matty and Shane on the beach, holding hands and looking perfect. I am, quite literally, a homewrecker.

"Oh god, I'm sorry." I pick up the frame and hand it to Matty.

She takes the frame, undeterred by my clumsiness. "Come in, come in!" she says, gesturing towards the living room. "Let's catch up!"

I walk like an inmate to the electric chair. Dead Mistress Walking. Matty takes a seat in the living room, and I sit down opposite her. Shane sits next to her, and I can read his face. *Breathe.*

If I've ever had any chops as a thespian, it's time to employ them.

"How is Chicago?" she asks. Her voice is so perky that I wonder if everyone, everywhere, is acting.

"Great. Living with Jonathan. It's definitely more exciting than here." I don't mean it as a snub and Matty doesn't take it as one.

"I'm sure it is!" Matty exclaims.

"Did you get your website finished?" I ask.

"I did." She then tells me all about the website, her teacher training program, and her classes. I know everything already because I searched online one sleepless night and found the site. (A small lapse back into stalking but it only happened once, I swear.) As she talks, I plan my escape.

"Can I use your phone?" I ask.

"Of course," Matty answers.

I walk into the kitchen and dial the number for the time and temperature. I hold the phone and fake a whole-ass conversation.

"Hey. Just wanted to check in... Yeah... I'll be there soon."

I walk to the living room and announce my untimely departure.

"Sorry, guys. I actually can't stay. I have to go help my dad. He's snowed in again. We can catch up later though."

"Oh no! Well, okay," Matty says. She gets up and hugs me. I feel like Judas.

"I'll walk you out," Shane says.

"No need. I'm fine." I can't bring myself to hug Shane. I just wave goodbye to them both and go back to the mudroom. I put on my boots and coat as quickly as I can, grab my purse, and sprint to the car. Before I reach it, I hear Shane calling for me to wait. *Just go.* But his hold on me has never faltered and doesn't now. I stand in front of the vehicle, the keys pressing into the flesh of my hand, keeping me from screaming. He walks up beside me.

"She just came home. Out of the blue. I tried calling you, but you must have already left."

"Does she know... anything?" I ask.

She obviously doesn't but I fear what she might have walked into if he was waiting for me.

"No. She doesn't know anything. She got here before I..." he trails off and I wish he'd finish the thought. But I suppose it's not necessary. I'm drowning in the disappointment of not knowing what he had planned for tonight. What I will be missing. The loss of just one night is so acute that I can't bear to process the further implications... that we've already had our last night together and everything has changed once again.

I want to ask if he loves me but I'm not that brave. And when I look in his eyes, the only expression I see is a sense of pity that thoroughly humiliates me. No. He doesn't love me. I've cried oceans of tears for this man. As I feel my eyes welling up, I think, apparently, there's just no end.

"Is she... here to stay?"

"I don't know."

"Are you... back together?"

I shouldn't ask this question either. I know I won't like the answer. He hesitates before stating, "She's my wife." He says it like it's the obvious answer and I'm a little dense for asking. And maybe I am.

The answer is a version of "yes," but not the good kind. Not the same "yes" I've been saying to him for the past week. The "yes" I breathe when he's giving me orders or when he's inside me, filling me and making me whole. No, this is a limp "yes." This "yes" isn't about want or desire, but obligation. She will always be his first priority, even if she disappears for months at a time.

"And what am I?"

I want him to say it. Say I'm nothing. Say I'm your mistress, your fuck toy. I'm daring him. Again, not the provocative dares we've been playing. No, this is an ugly dare and one that he won't take up. His eyes lower and he sighs in frustration. Why won't I just go quietly back into my box?

This is another reason I haven't told him about Dante. My silence isn't about some righteous protection of Matty and Shane's marriage. Not anymore, anyway. No, the reason I don't tell him is because he doesn't *want* to know. I'm almost certain that he'd prefer the lie if the lie makes his life easier. For all his reverence around the gray areas of life, I know that he likes his world uncomplicated. While I've been struggling to define us, he's always known exactly what we are. Matty is for marriage. I am for fucking. (And only at his convenience.)

"Right. Exactly," I quietly say, answering myself since he won't. I open my car door but before I get inside, he grabs my arm.

"You're Katie." He says it with kindness and fortitude, and it devastates me because I know just what he means. The words are meant to be inspirational, a fortunate diagnosis, one unworthy of all this drama. I don't belong to him because I don't belong to *anyone*, other than myself. But in this moment they ring hollow. Because whether he likes it or not (whether *I* like it or not), I do belong to him. The fact that he can't see that makes me want to bang my head against a wall.

"Lucky me," I respond, as sarcastically as possible. And then I look at him. He's obviously hurt by my words and the anger leaks right out of me. I've been trying so hard to decipher his feelings for me. But in the end, they don't even matter.

And suddenly, I'm exhausted by it all. I reach for grace, which has never come easily. Especially in a situation such as this. I search for the lie that will make him feel better.

"It's okay," I assure him. *It's not okay.* "Really. I'm fine." *I'm not fine.* "You have no idea what you've given me." This part, at least, is true.

All that power I had been feeling recently is gone. This relationship doesn't extend past the bedroom (or the den, or the hallway, or – once – in the garage). In the end, I'm always going to be the one standing in the cold as I am, quite literally, doing right now. I've always known I was the one to be sacrificed in any scenario.

But *not* Dante. I won't let him reject him too, compartmentalize him, pity him. I can't protect myself, but I can protect him.

I give Shane a kiss on the cheek and get into the car, leaving him standing in the driveway. My stoic mask lasts about ten seconds when the floodgates open. My eyes are blurry as I drive down the icy hill. I'm going faster than I should. The car quickly loses control, plowing straight into a tree just off the road.

One in Three

So much for my graceful exit. The car is dented, not totaled. Like me, I suppose. I momentarily wonder if I caused this by not bothering to put a good tune on the radio. I look in my rearview mirror to see if Shane saw what happened but he's nowhere to be seen.

I restart the car and the engine is fine, but the tires just spin and spin in a snowbank. I go over my options. I can walk back up the hill and face Matty and Shane. Horrifying. Or I can approach one of his neighbors and ask to use the phone. But I don't have anyone to call other than my father or AAA. Neither sounds appealing so, instead, I start walking.

My father's house is about three miles away and the temperature is around 40 degrees. It's only 6pm, but it's already pitch dark out. I'm glad for the sensory deprivation. I don't want to see anything. I just want to walk with the cold air on my face, praying for numbness.

The route is all country roads, no sidewalks. When the occasional car comes along, I veer off the road into either someone's yard or the surrounding woods. I don't have gloves with me, so I keep my hands buried in my pockets.

I probably should feel shame, but I don't. Just overwhelming sadness that whatever the past week was, it's now over. And even as my heart is being shredded, I know I don't have the luxury to fall apart again like last year. I can't wallow in suicidal ideation, cry every day while sprawled across the bathroom floor. I have Dante now. Mothers don't get to do self-destruction. I have to be strong because I have to teach him how to be strong, how to never end up here, walking alone in the dark with tear-stained cheeks. With each step, I become more determined to focus on what should be the real priorities of my life: Dante, Jonathan, my father, and the business. I have so much more to grab onto if I can just let this one thing go.

I pass the gas station from where I called Shane a week ago. The road from here is the path of a million childhood bike rides. A car passes me, going in my direction. A few seconds later, it slows down and pulls over. When I start to pass it, the driver rolls down his window.

"Need a ride?"

I can't see him well. As a child of the '80s, I'm well-versed in stranger-danger and the perils of hitchhiking. I should be scared but I'm not. I'm cold and miserable and tired. Besides, it's a blue Ford Taurus, not a truck with a scary gun rack. How bad could it be? I get into the passenger side.

"Where to?"

"Just up ahead about a mile," I answer.

He doesn't start driving though. Instead, he wants to chat, a decision that has me instantly regretting my choice. "It's a cold night to be walking. What's your name?"

I don't want to tell him my name, so I tell him the fake name I used with Matty at the casino.

"Sasha."

"Sasha. That's a hot name," he says. He turns to face me full-on, studying me. I suck in air as I realize who this is. Crew cut. Gold earring. Chin Dimple. Nick Rivas.

"You look familiar. Do I know you?" he asks, while starting up the car and pulling forward.

"You're Nick Rivas." I say it without thinking.

"So, I do know you!"

"Stop the car."

"Why?"

"Just… stop the car."

"But, why?" He doesn't stop.

"Stop the car!" I shout.

"Fine, fine. Girl, you're trippin'." He pulls over.

I open the passenger door. But before I get out, I take a parting shot.

"You almost killed my best friend in a parking lot last year." He has no reaction, so I continue. "You and your friend Josh. You used a baseball bat."

I get out of the car and slam the door. I start walking. When I hear his door slam, I instantly regret my boldness. He's enraged by my accusation, and I walk faster.

"Bitch, I know you're not out spreading rumors about me!"

He's following me now.

"It's not a rumor," I yell over my shoulder. I search frantically in my purse for some kind of weapon and grasp the handcuffs.

He catches up to me and grabs my arm, turning me around. I take the handcuffs out and swing them wildly at him, but it's a weak effort and he deftly catches them.

"Oooh. Handcuffs, eh? Kinky bitch," he says.

He grabs me by the shoulders and pushes me to the ground. He slaps me hard across the cheek and the effect is immediate. I don't fight any more. I'm frozen. I think he's just going to continue beating me up, but as he gets on top of me, I realize what's actually happening. He shoves himself between my legs, working the button on my jeans.

And all I can think of is *one in three*. It's my turn. I close my eyes and hope it's over quickly.

"Hey!"

Nick stops at the sound of another man's voice. He scurries up and gets back into his car, leaving me on the side of the road. As the car skids away, I button my pants back up. I cover my face with my hands in a mix of terror and relief.

"Katie?"

I know the voice, but the context makes no sense. I move my hand and Shane is standing there like a goddamn guardian angel.

"What the fuck?" I ask. "How are you here?"

"Come here." He helps me up while explaining his miraculous arrival. "I left the house to go to the store and I saw your car at the bottom of the hill. I thought you might be wandering around with a head injury since you didn't come back up for help."

"So, you've just been driving around looking for me?"

"Yes."

I shouldn't be this elated after such a harrowing experience. But he rescued me. I feel like a princess. A bloody, assaulted princess, but a princess, nonetheless. We get into his truck and his eyes take in my state.

"I should take you to the hospital. Or the police."

How bad must I look if Shane is willing to go the police?

"No."

"Why not?"

I take a deep breath and roll up my sleeves to show him my wrists. "These bruises and burns? They're not from this, you know. They're from the consensual sadomasochistic affair we've been having. I really don't feel like explaining them."

The irony hits us both at once and we grimace.

"Did you know that guy?" he asks.

"Sort of. He was one of the guys that attacked me and Jonathan last year."

"Are you serious?"

"Yes."

"Fuck."

"And I accused him. I shouldn't have done that. I need to learn to shut the fuck up." A wave of guilt rolls over me.

"Hey... hey...." His hand is on my cheek, catching my tears.

"Just drive me home."

He looks at me, waiting for more information. I remember that he has no idea where my father's house is. How can two people be so close in one regard and absolute strangers in another?

"It's just a few miles ahead on this road." But I stop him before he starts the truck. "Hold on." I get out of his truck and scour the scene until I find the handcuffs. I grab them and get back into the truck. He watches as I drop them into my purse, raising an eyebrow.

"Handcuffs?" he asks.

I nod. "They were for tonight."

"Ah."

He starts the truck and drives only about a minute before pulling over again and killing the engine.

"What's happening?" I ask.

He turns to face me. "I want to tell you something."

Oh no. I can only imagine. "Maybe... don't," I say. "You know, if it's something bad."

"How do I know if it's bad?"

His question exasperates me because I'm sure, with just a little bit of effort and empathy, he can make that judgment.

"Fine. Just say it," I tell him, bracing myself for whatever cold, hard truth he's about to lay on me.

"I think... I'm falling in love with you," he says.

"Oh."

It's everything I've ever wanted him to say.

"But I'm not going to leave Matty," he continues.

This doesn't dampen his words at all. I know he's never leaving Matty.

"I don't think I've ever asked you to."

He considers this. "So, what do you want?"

"I want you," I answer, before clarifying, "in whatever capacity that's possible."

"I want you too."

"So, what now?"

"I think we should go to my place..."

I shake my head, aghast at the suggestion.

"Let me finish," he says. "I think we should go to my place. Visit the pool house and try out those handcuffs."

"And Matty?"

"Matty took a sleeping pill. She's fast asleep in the house and..."

"Yes."

He turns the car around and heads back to his place. When we pass my car, I'm momentarily deflated.

"Can you take me home... after?" I ask him.

"You can stay in the pool house. Carlos stays there all the time."

"No, I have to get back tonight."

I hope he doesn't ask why, and he doesn't.

"Okay. I can take you home."

"Thank you."

He parks the truck in the driveway, and we walk to the pool house. He turns the light on inside and starts up the space heater. Half the room is filled with the tools for maintenance on the pool and spa.

The other half contains an open futon. The light is bright, so he rummages around looking for candles. He finds a few, lights them, and flicks the main light off.

"I've been trying to find a way to give you a hint about candles."

He stares at me, awaiting further explanation.

"The wax," I clarify.

"Really?"

"Yeah."

He grins. "Good to know."

I take the handcuffs from the bag and hand them to him. He eyes them curiously, apparently weighing his options. He then places them on the table in the corner and walks back to me. I don't know what I'm expecting but it's not the hug he gives me. Then he asks, "What do you want?"

At first, I think we're switching roles, an idea I'm not particularly comfortable with pursuing. But then I realize the question is genuine. We're not playing games.

"I want you take off your clothes. Then take off mine."

He does so, taking his time.

"Now what?" he asks.

"I want you to kiss my neck."

His lips go to the side of my neck. He travels around until he's behind me, lifting my hair to kiss the nape of my neck, causing me to suck in air.

"Mmm," he murmurs, whispering in my ear again. "What next? Tell me what you want."

I take his hand and put it between my legs.

"I think you know what I want."

He turns me around so I can see his face, keeping his hand in place.

"Tell me."

"I want to fuck you."

I've inverted the usual framing ("I want you to fuck me"), giving myself all the agency. Ironically, I do it because I know it's what he wants to hear. Nevertheless, I like the sound of it. So does he, apparently, since his lips take mine hungrily as his fingers work me over.

When he stops, I can barely stand.

Consensual Scars

"Good. I want to fuck you too."

I lay down on the futon and he lays on top of me, sliding into me. We find an instant rhythm, the Goldilocks of rhythms, not too fast and not too slow. Perfect. And then, I will my hips to stop moving.

"Stop…" I say.

"Stop?" He begins pulling away from me.

I grab his hips and bring him back. "No… I mean… stop moving. Just stay. Right here. I want to feel you inside me."

"Baby," he gasps. And that's all it takes. Uncontrollable moans escape me as waves of pleasure flood my body. He tries to remain still.

"Look at me when you come," he says.

He's telling me this because I'm always evasive in this moment. The vulnerability of being tied up is nothing compared to looking in his eyes right now. But I do as he requests, and he can no longer be still. He can no longer be gentle.

"Baby, come with me," I beg.

He groans and does as I ask.

As we recover, his fingers trace the bruises on my wrists.

"I don't know if I should feel bad about these," he confesses.

"You shouldn't."

"You sure?"

"Dude, I just asked you to pour candle wax on me."

He laughs. "Good point."

I can tell seeing the altercation with Nick has spooked him. While his tenderness is wonderful, I never want him to stop being rough with me.

"Would you feel better if we had a safe word?" I ask.

"Yes! We should have a safe word."

"What should it be?"

We both think for a moment.

"All I can think about are the worst possible words," I say.

"Like what?"

"Yes and please."

"Ha! Yeah, those aren't gonna work. I can only think of food words. Like avocado."

"Ugh. No! I want a sexy word. But you know, one we'd never say in that context."

He takes another moment then says excitedly, "Wait. I got it."

"Yeah?"

"Indica."

"That's fucking perfect."

"Right? Like, slow down, baby. Take it easy."

"I wonder what would make me say it."

"I wonder that too."

I get up to get dressed as he watches me. I've been gone for far too long this time, and I need to get back.

"You have to get dressed too, you know. To take me home."

"Oh, shit. I forgot." Before he gets up, I sit on the bed beside him. I need to take this opportunity when I feel strong and sure.

"I have to get back to Chicago."

He nods and I continue. "But I want this to happen again."

"I want that too," he agrees. "When are you leaving?"

"Soon. As soon as I can get the car fixed." I hadn't decided until this very moment when I would be leaving, but it's time. Now that I know he loves me, I have the strength to go. Because I know I'll be coming back. It's not like a year ago when I was so sure I'd never see him again.

"Call me… when you can see me next," I say.

"I will."

And then curiosity gets the best of me.

"What did Matty say about the bed? How you changed it?"

"I'm not sure she even noticed. Amway, if she does, I'm sure she'll see the benefit of it soon enough."

Bile rises in my throat as the implication of his words settle into me. Of course, he's going to keep fucking her. *She's his wife.* I swallow the jealousy but I'm sure he can see it all over my face. In response, he pulls me back into the futon with him.

"You need to get dressed and take me home," I say, half-heartedly.

"I know. But first, let me see if I can make you say 'indica.'"

An hour and multiple orgasms later, we finally make it back to his truck. I direct him to my father's house. On the way, he offers to get my father's car towed to a body shop in the morning. I graciously accept.

"I'll call you and tell you where you can pick it up."

When we pull into the driveway and he turns off the car, he turns to me and takes my hand. He presses his lips to my palm.

"I love you."

I breathe in these precious words and echo them back to him. Then I get out of the car before I can jump him again.

The next day, Shane calls me with the information of when and where to pick up my dad's car (this afternoon, at a body shop in town across from the McDonalds). He offers to give me a ride and I readily accept.

I watch for him to drive up, and when he does, I run to his truck. I've only been away from him for hours since he declared his love and I've been dying for him every second of his absence. I'm not sure how I'm going to survive being in Chicago.

As he drives away, I run my hand up his thigh. I massage him, my intention becoming clear.

"Baby," he says, looking side to side, obviously unsure about our visibility.

"I know a place."

"Tell me."

I give him directions through town toward the lake. We travel the winding roads until we're at the same dead end that Carlos and I vandalized. The spot is deserted, and Shane pulls over to the side of the road. I know it's crazy to return to the scene where I almost got arrested, but the thrill of possible discovery is like an unstoppable wave carrying me forward. At least, this time – if we get busted – I'll actually be doing what the officer assumed I was doing before.

We don't get caught though. And like last night, Shane is gentle until the end.

"Wow," he sighs, recovering. "I don't think I've done that in over twenty years. I mean, in a car. Like a teenager."

My math brain can't help but do the quick calculation. Twenty years ago, he wasn't yet with Matty. The thought that I gave him something that she never has makes me high. I wonder what other acts are ours and ours alone.

"Have you ever tied up anyone before me?" I ask him.

"No."

"Mmm."

He shakes his head, smiling. "You're crazy."

When we park at the body shop, he turns to me and promises to call me tomorrow night. I silently pray that Dante is asleep by the scheduled time and that the phone doesn't wake him up.

"Do you have privacy at your place? Like, a phone in your bedroom?" he asks.

"Yeah. Why?"

His answer is a sly grin and I know what's in store with this phone call. I'm nervous about the idea, unsure if I can satisfy him with just words. Surely, that's a special skill.

"I'm not sure I'd be very good at that," I say.

"I'll teach you."

As an older man, he wins with me either way. If our actions are new to him, I'm thrilled to be his temptress. If he's teaching me, I'm equally thrilled by his experience. Damn, it must be nice to be him.

I desperately want to kiss him goodbye. But we're in public now, so I restrain myself.

And just like that, I realize that we've never been out in public together before now. How is this possible? But I think back, and I can't come up with another instance beyond last night. And even then, we never left his truck.

The rules are different now.

The Bigger Picture

"What the fuck?" I mutter when I enter the Chicago apartment with Dante. While not a crack den, the place is a level of straight-guy messy I've never seen before: trash and dirty dishes are scattered about the common areas. Fortunately, my room and Dante's are both undisturbed.

I call out for Jonathan, but he doesn't answer. I knock on his bedroom door but get no response. I crack it open to reveal a similarly messy tableaux, with the addition of clothes strewn everywhere. The disorder is so unlike Jonathan and I'm worried. I page him. We haven't spoken for a couple of days, and I have no idea what he's been up to.

I clean up what I can while keeping one eye on Dante. When Jonathan fails to call me back, I phone David at work. It's nearly 6pm but he answers.

"Hey, you!"

"Oh. Hey, Katie. Are you back in town?"

"Yeah. I'm back at the apartment and I'm wondering if you know where Jonathan is? The place is kinda trashed."

"We should chat. Can we meet up for dinner?"

I desperately want to get into sweatpants and unwind.

"Ugh. I just got back. Can you just come here?"

"I'm not so sure that's a good idea."

"Why?"

"Jonathan and I broke up."

"Shit. No! I'm so sorry," I say.

"Thanks."

"When?"

"Last night."

"Well, he's not here. Can you come by after work, and we can talk in my room?"

He hesitates but relents, telling me that he'll be by in an hour. When he arrives, he asks if Jonathan is still gone. I assure him that he is.

We settle into my room, me on the floor with Dante and David sitting on my bed.

"What happened?"

He sighs before starting. "Let's just say… I know what it's like to be twenty-three and party every night. I'm just not interested in that anymore."

I'm surprised because I just assumed that Jonathan was the dumper, not the dumpee.

"Wait, you broke up with him?"

"Is that surprising?"

"No… well, yes. A little. I don't think anyone's ever broken up with him before."

Is that what the mess is about? Is Jonathan heartbroken? Feels inconceivable, but maybe?

"Is he… okay?" I ask.

"I don't think he's upset about the breakup. But I am worried about him. I mean, I don't have a problem with taking a hit of E on the weekend. But he's at the clubs every night. And I have, like, a real job. I can't keep up with that."

"He just needs to blow off some steam."

I defend Jonathan, partly out of instinct and partly because I'm not sure I like our company being diminished in comparison to his Very Important Job. But perhaps the condescension is warranted. David is an attorney and we're a fledgling enterprise with two clients.

"I get that. I do," David agrees. "But I can't keep up. And I've seen some shit, you know? I've lost a lot of friends. And I'm not saying he's not careful. But if I'm not with him… well, I just don't know, you know? I have to protect myself here."

I nod because I understand. Even if I am guilty as fuck in this department.

"And I don't want to watch him fall off a cliff. That money you got is a real opportunity. And it's a lot of money. Until it's not."

This statement jolts me. I've only been gone a week. How much can change in a fucking week? But then, I think about my own week. Worlds can be turned upside down in mere moments.

Still, I can't conceive of going through all that money.

"How much has he spent?"

"Oh, I don't know. Maybe not that much," he says, trying to reassure me. "I just know that bottle service ain't ever cheap. And neither are drugs. I just can't watch him blow it all. Not without slapping some sense into him. And I'm not his daddy. That's not my kink."

"Do you have a kink?"

"Yes. Wanting to, maybe, one day, get married."

"That is kinky."

"Right? But he's already married," he says.

Shit. I don't want to be the reason for their breakup.

"It's just paperwork," I say, repeating my mantra about our nuptials.

"Y'all keep saying that. But paperwork is important. I'm a lawyer. Most of my job is fucking paperwork. And that paperwork means something. When it comes to marriage, it means legal rights. Power of attorney. Custody issues. I mean, come on! That's what we've been fighting for."

I hadn't really thought of all that and I feel foolish. He must read it on my face because his voice eases up.

"One of these days, this country just might do the right thing," he says. "And if it does, I'm gonna want the option."

"Jonathan and I can get divorced. Or, shit, maybe even annulled?"

"Then, from what I understand, he doesn't get the inheritance. I don't want to stand in the way of that. I want him to have everything he wants. Except maybe more threesomes. I'm a little tired of threesomes. I just want him."

Wow. Jonathan predicted this shit perfectly. I must remember to commend him.

"Have you told him that?" I ask. "That you want to be exclusive?"

"I don't wanna clip his wings. He's young. You're both young."

I suppress the urge to scream. Instead, I just say, "Oh, come on.

He loves you. He might agree to monogamy."

"Yeah. I know he loves me. I love him. But sometimes, that's just not enough."

Tell me about it.

And then I remember the other part of Jonathan's prophecy and the reason he made it in the first place.

"You have to promise me you're not gonna disappear on me," I plead.

"Disappear?"

"Dude, I don't have a lot of friends right now. It would really suck to lose you."

His face softens as he reassures me. "You're not gonna lose me."

I want to believe it.

Vocal Range

Jonathan doesn't come home until mid-morning the next day. His eyes are glassy and his movements reckless. I know he's rolling on ecstasy, and I have to wait until he's had time to crash and recover before speaking with him.

We need to talk but I pray that he slips back out to the clubs instead. Which I know is wrong. However, I want the privacy. I want to get Dante asleep and wait by the phone for Shane's call. I can feel myself becoming a bad person, choosing Shane over everyone and everything. And the worst part is I can't stop myself. I would sacrifice anything for him. Tell a thousand lies.

So, when Jonathan does wake up and heads out to the club again, I don't try to stop him. I do tell him that I miss him though, before he can make a clean exit.

"Are we breaking up?" he teases, his hand on the door.

"No, *we're* not breaking up. But I did talk to David."

"You talked to David?" he asks, betrayal in his voice.

"Baby, why didn't you tell me?"

"What's to tell? He broke up with me. Whatever. I gotta go. I'm meeting some people."

"Can we hang out tomorrow night? Just you and me?"

"I don't know. I might have plans."

He sees my face fall and he amends his answer. "We can hang before I go out. We can order some take out."

"Perfect." I kiss him on the cheek, and he disappears out the door.

When Jonathan leaves, it's time for Dante's bedtime routine. I've adapted the routine from advice on the AOL mommy message boards: dinner (applesauce), bottle, bath, and *Goodnight Moon*. Usually, he falls asleep soon after and I lay him down in his crib. When he inevitably wakes up an hour or two later, I bring him to bed with me where he falls back asleep instantly. I say a silent prayer that he sleeps for several hours, long enough for my phone call with Shane. How long does phone sex take? I have no idea.

I stand in my room, wondering how one prepares for such an event. I decide to take a shot of vodka to calm my nerves. Then I strip down to just an extra-large t-shirt, get my vibrator from its hiding place, and slide it with me under the covers. I have the cordless phone next to me, ready to grab it before the ringing wakes up Dante. (If that happens, I don't know what I'll say.) When the phone rings at the allotted time, he's shocked by how quickly I pick up. I realize it's exactly what I've been taught, as a girl, not to do.

"Wow. Were you waiting for me?"

"Yes."

"Where are you?"

"In bed."

"Mmm."

"Where are you?"

"The same."

I want to ask where Matty is but that's not my responsibility. He will have determined it's safe to call me.

"What are you wearing?"

I giggle at the trite question.

"What?" he asks.

I worry I just embarrassed him with my laughter but then I remember. He never gets embarrassed. We are so very different.

"I just… never thought I would hear someone say that in all seriousness," I explain.

"Oh. Do you want me to…"

"Just a t-shirt," I interrupt, answering him.

"Mmm."

That little affirming sound from him is everything. The fear I had slips away as his voice leads me where I want to go. I'm just as physically powerless as when he's standing above me, my limbs tied down. But I still have the upper hand somehow. Because the more brazen my words, the more turned on he is. It's the same game.

I can't orgasm until he does. But when he does, I can't stop. Each moan he elicits makes my body tremble. I don't think I'll ever know a more potent aphrodisiac than his pleasure. When we finish, our words are gone and only our ragged breathing remains.

"You alright?" he asks, finally.

"No," I answer.

He laughs and then falls silent again. I know I should get off the phone. But we can't seem to hang up, holding on like lovesick teenagers.

"I want to see you," he says. "I'm going to get a hotel room between here and Chicago. Can you meet me? Next Saturday?"

"Yes."

"Can I call you again tomorrow night?"

"Yes."

The next night, when Jonathan fails to come home and meet up for our dinner, I page him relentlessly. But he never calls. I'm worried, though I don't want to raise alarms by alerting Emily or David. Jonathan's probably lost his pager and is staying with friends. I talk myself into this possibility, in part because I want the solitude at night.

Over the next two nights, I repeat the same bedtime routine for Dante, followed by my own routine of prepping for Shane's scheduled call. By the third night, I don't need the vodka to relax me anymore. I've found a secret skill I never knew I had, perfecting a low purr in my voice that even I'm surprised by. I feel sexier than I ever have. The physical distance between us has created a new kind of intimacy that's only strengthening our desires.

I worry about his phone bill with these long-distant calls. When I mention it, he shrugs it off.

"Don't worry about it, baby. I got it."

When he says that, I feel a bit like a kept woman. And shame on me, because I don't hate it.

I always end the phone calls first, fearful that he'll hear Dante on the baby monitor. His limited access to me is driving him crazy and I hate that *The Rules* is a little bit right. On the third night, he gives me the hotel information. I'm counting the minutes.

Annie Marie Huber

Higher Ground

The next afternoon, when Jonathan finally returns, he's jovial and energized.

"Hey, girl!" he greets me, walking into the kitchen to make himself a drink.

"Hey." I'm sitting at the table with Dante on my lap. He's just woken from his nap and I'm trying, unsuccessfully, to get him to eat a jar of pureed carrots.

"I just had the most amazing time. I met these guys at the club, and we ended up on a yacht. Can you believe that?"

I'm staring at him, waiting for him to realize how pissed I am. But it's not registering. He's in his own tripped-up world. I also wonder how *discreet* a yacht party is. I ask him this and he gets defensive.

"Seriously?" he asks.

"Hey, it's not *my* inheritance. I'm just sayin'."

"Whatever."

I feel like crap and try to think of another way into the conversation.

"I was really worried about you," I say, careful of my framing.

"Really?" He doesn't look at me, just continues to make a 3pm cocktail.

"Yes, really." Less careful now, as an edge creeps into my tone.

He laughs, dismissing the idea as ridiculous. Without saying another word, I take Dante into my bedroom and shut the door. I'm not sure how to get him to listen. Jonathan's energy can feel insurmountable to me. This has always been a plus as he lifts me out of any funk. But I don't know how to bring him down. And maybe I shouldn't? I'm not his mother.

Before I can figure out what to do, he knocks on the door.

"Come in."

"Hey. I'm sorry. I didn't mean to make you worry."

He's sincere and it's a start.

"We had plans."

"We did?"

"Yeah."

"Shit. I'm really sorry."

"I'm worried about you."

"You don't need to worry about me."

"Maybe not. But I do."

"You need to come out with me. Check out this scene before you judge it."

By "scene," he means "ecstasy." I didn't expect this but perhaps I should have. Instead of me pulling him out, he's going to pull me in with him. I look at him like he's crazy, but he just yanks my levers harder.

"Come on. You'll have such a good time. You'll see. You could use a break. We'll find a sitter. It's been forever."

I can feel myself start to give in to his pleading puppy dog eyes.

"Who would babysit?" I ask.

"Emily."

"Fine. I'll go out with you. On one condition."

"Go on…" he says, wearily.

"I'll go out with you if *you* can babysit for me next Saturday."

"Why? Do you have a hot date?"

"Sort of."

"Really?"

"Yeah."

He's waiting for me to expound but I don't. Instead, he's weighing the pros and cons. Is going out with me worth changing diapers for an evening?

"Alright. It's a deal. But we're going out *tonight*."

"You don't want to, I don't know, take a break? You've been out for three nights."

"I slept on the yacht. I feel great! But yeah, I could probably use a disco nap. Let me call Emily."

Emily agrees to come over after work around 10pm. Normally at that time, I'd be in bed, exhausted. I'm going to *need* drugs if I'm going out that late.

When Shane calls at the allotted time, Jonathan is in the shower. I grab the phone on its first ring as always. But this time, I'm not in bed.

"Hey, baby," he greets me.

"Hi. I'm sorry, baby, but I can't tonight."

"Oh."

"Yeah."

He doesn't ask me what my plans are, and I don't offer.

"Should I call tomorrow night?"

I don't know where Jonathan will be tomorrow night. I don't even know where I'll be, to be honest. Possibly trapped on a yacht with a gaggle of gay men? Nevertheless, I need him to call.

"Yes."

We hang up and then the primping begins. It's been so long since I've gone out with Jonathan for a night of debauchery that by 9pm, I'm yawning.

"I don't know if I can do this," I tell Jonathan, as he stares in the mirror, perfecting his coif.

"Don't worry. You're gonna have plenty of energy soon." He turns to me and looks my outfit up and down. "Are you wearing that?"

I'm wearing my usual attire of jeans, a t-shirt, and a flannel shirt. He shakes his head in disapproval. He grabs my hand and leads me to my bedroom. But a quick look inside my closet elicits more disappointment.

"Girl, we need to get you some new things. Don't you have a little black dress? Doesn't every girl have at least one little black dress?"

I do have a little black dress. It's my one go-to nice outfit that I wear when I need something respectable. I haven't worn it since having Dante, but I think it'll still fit. (The fortunate result of motherhood making me too tired to eat.) I dig the dress out from the back of my closet and take it into the bathroom.

The dress fits, just barely, but I can see the bruises on my wrists.

I've been careful since their arrival to wear only long-sleeved shirts so as to avoid questions and concern. I put the flannel over the dress but, of course, it looks ridiculous. I ask Jonathan to find me a sweater to put over it and he obliges, tossing it to me.

"You're not gonna want it though. It gets hot in the club. It'll end up tied around your waist. Trust me."

I put the sweater on and come out to a whistle from Jonathan.

"It's really tight," I tell him.

"Yes. That's what makes it perfect."

Jonathan does my hair, using a curling iron to create a gorgeous updo that I would never, ever have the patience or skill to do. He asks if I have any makeup and I dig out a red lipstick from my bag. I swipe it across my lips and Jonathan nods his head, approvingly.

Emily arrives and I give her the Dante briefing. I feel bad that we're going out so late, but Emily is game.

"Don't worry about it. When was the last time you got to go out?" she asks me.

I think about the stolen hours with Shane and answer carefully.

"Oh, I don't know. I haven't been to a club since before Dante. Actually, not since I got pregnant. Like, over a year?"

"Oh, honey, you deserve a break. Go have a Long Island Iced Tea on me. And don't hurry back. I can stay all night."

Out of the corner of my eye, I can see Jonathan smirk. We're not going to be drinking Long Island Ice Teas tonight.

"Thanks, Emily." I tell her.

"And besides, my hot date cancelled," Emily continues.

Jonathan and I both raise our eyebrows.

"I didn't know you were dating," Jonathan says, surprised.

"Well, I didn't want to freak you out."

"Oh, I'm not freaked out! You should definitely be dating! Who's the lucky guy?"

Emily turns to me. "Well, it's your dad, actually."

My mouth opens but nothing comes out.

"I take it back. I'm freaked out," Jonathan says.

"Why?" Emily asks.

Jonathan and I are both stunned into silence until we leave the apartment. At which point, we both start screaming.

"So, that's weird, right?!" I yell at him.
"Oh my god. It's so weird!"
"It's incestuous!"
"Yes!"

Whatever reticence I had about this evening has been eradicated. I need to get fucked up and pronto. We take a taxi downtown to a nondescript black box of a building. The only giveaway that it contains anything of interest is the line of people outside. We join the ranks. Jonathan is on his heels, bouncing in anticipation.

"I'm so glad you came out tonight. We're gonna have a blast. I just need to find Geoffrey when we get inside."

I presume that Geoffrey is the drug hook-up and I'm not wrong. We get inside the club, and it takes my eyes a moment to adjust to the dim lighting. There's a bar on one end and a huge, crowded dance space, punctuated with platforms where professional dancers, wearing very little, perform. The demographics are about 99.99% male and me. I don't mind the disparity. I always feel safe in a gay space.

(Don't get me wrong. Misogyny exists here too, in the subset of gay men that disparage women constantly. As if the more they disdain our body parts, the more gay cred they have. These men, obviously, suck. Fortunately, they're easy to identify and avoid.)

I follow Jonathan around as he approaches several people and inquires about Geoffrey's whereabouts. They need to shout in each other's ears to be heard over the incessant techno beat. After several tries, we find Geoffrey in a corner of the club near the restrooms. He's like the rest of the men in the club, sexy and sweaty, with his shirt off and tucked into the back of his jeans. He digs product out of his front pocket and makes an exchange with Jonathan.

"Come on," Jonathan says, grabbing my hand and leading me to the bar. "Let's get some water to wash these down."

We make our way to the bar where boys are lined up from end to end. It usually takes forever for me to get served in a gay bar. Which is fair. The bartender is not going to take me home. Jonathan, not having that problem at all, gets a bottle of water for us to share almost immediately.

"Ready?" he shouts in my ear.

I have no idea if I'm ready, but I nod anyway. He places a little white tablet in the palm of my hand. He has one in his hand too and we toast them as if they're wine glasses.

"Cheers!" he says.

I echo the sentiment and we down the tablets.

"Come on, let's dance," he says, grabbing my hand and leading me into the throngs of half-naked men.

I'm uncomfortable and my dancing is stiff. I'm used to dancing to songs that I'm familiar with (gay anthems like *I Will Survive* and *It's Raining Men*). Songs that I know the words to or, you know, songs *with* words. But this throbbing beat rings hollow to me. The guy next to me, tall and beautiful and completely engaged with the music, leans into me.

"It hasn't hit you yet, has it?"

I look at him and shake my head, helplessly. I know I'm being a bitter buzzkill, but I can't help it. I should have stayed home, should have gone to bed. I should have had my phone call with Shane. But I look at Jonathan, who is so happy to have me here, and try to find my groove. And then it happens.

My body becomes light as a feather and starts moving without effort. The music is inside me, like the drums when I was on mushrooms. The lights are mesmerizing, and the joy is unstoppable. Jonathan can see the change as can the gentleman next to me. We lock eyes and he throws his hands in the air.

"Yeah!" he yells.

I yell back in solidarity while Jonathan laughs knowingly. Our bodies are carried away by the waves of the music. When he pulls me back to the bar, I can't form a sentence. I'm just grinning like an idiot.

"Wow!" I yell.

"Right?" he yells back.

Everything is alive. When I go to the girls' bathroom (which is full of men), I wonder who that cool person is in the mirror, not recognizing myself at all. The dress, the hair, the joy... nothing is familiar, but I love it. I feel beautiful and the sensation is extraordinary.

I'm introduced to a lot of other beautiful people, people I instantly adore and most surely won't ever remember. Jonathan, to his credit, never deserts me no matter how many offers he gets (and he gets many). He makes sure that I stay hydrated, buying bottled waters at the bar that we gulp down quickly before returning to the dance floor.

I don't know how long we dance. I'm sure it's hours but it feels like minutes. I'm surprised when Jonathan pulls me toward the coat check and out of the club. The sudden silence and cool air are a shock but not an unpleasant one.

"Where are we going?"

"They'll be closing soon. We don't want to be there when the lights come on. Trust me." Jonathan explains, not answering my question but satisfying my curiosity all the same.

"I love you so much!" I say, hugging him. He's delighted by my amorousness.

"I love you too!"

"Where are we going?"

"There's an all-night diner up here. We can walk there."

The city is so fucking amazing. I spin around like Mary Tyler Moore, expressing my unfettered joy. Jonathan laughs while guiding me in the right direction down the street. When we enter the diner, I almost run back outside. It's too bright. Too real. Jonathan sees my reticence and does his best to reassure me.

"It's fine. It'll be fun. It'll be jumpin' soon."

We get shown to a booth and sit down. Food is the furthest thing from my mind, so I order coffee and Jonathan does the same.

By the time our order arrives, a steady stream of beautiful boys have entered the diner. The party has moved here and the milieu melds into something just as wonderful as the club. It feels, impossibly, even more wonderful since we can actually hear one another.

"So, this is what you've been doing?"

"Guilty."

"I get it."

I'm still sweaty from the club so I absent-mindedly take off my sweater. Jonathan quickly notices my wrists and his face becomes concerned.

"What's this?" he asks, holding my wrists and examining them.

"You didn't..." He trails off, not asking the question that's on his lips.

"No! No, not at all. Shit." I quickly pull the sweater back on but it's too late. I'm going to have to provide some sort of explanation here.

"These are consens...." I can't finish the word. What's the damn word?

"Consensual?" he asks.

"Yes! Consens..." I still can't quite say it which causes us to giggle uncontrollably.

"Girl, what have you been doing? Or... should I ask, *who?*"

"Who?"

"Yes."

"Who... what?" I can't follow.

"Who... who..."

"You sound like an owl."

We erupt into giggles again.

"Oh, I know!" he says, excitedly. "Who... are you *doing?*"

"Oh shit. Yeah. Um. Shane."

This drug is like a truth serum.

"Really?"

"Yeah."

"Does he know about... you know?"

It takes me far too long to figure out that he's talking about my son.

"You mean... Dante?"

"Yeah."

"No."

"Why not?"

I can't possibly articulate a reason in this state, so I simply shrug my shoulders.

"Do you think he'd be bad for him?"

"Who?"

"Shane... do you think he'd be bad for Dante?"

"Oh. Well, I'm sure he's bad for me."

I want to take the words back as soon as I say them. They might be true but why give them oxygen? I'm not going to stop.

"You're like a mistress."

"Yeah."

"How does that feel?"

"I kinda like it. Shhhh." I put a finger to my lips. "I'm a bad..." I can't find the word.

"Person?"

"No!"

We stare at our coffees until the word materializes.

"Feminist!" I yell.

"What?"

"I'm a bad feminist."

"Ah. Well." He shrugs.

"Hey, what's the word for the guy?" I ask.

"What?"

"I'm the 'mistress.' What's the name for the guy?"

He thinks for a moment then says, "Adulterer?" I'm impressed with his ability to come up with that, as Scooby-Doo'd as we are.

"Yeah, but that's for both. The guy and the girl."

"Right."

"So, no word for the dude. Man, that's fucked up."

He laughs at my righteous indignation.

A steady stream of Jonathan's club posse stops by our booth. Introductions and small talk take place, with exchanges feeling weightier than they are. Every word is drenched in a deeper meaning even if we can't quite articulate what that meaning is.

"What do you do?" The question comes from a guy named Kyle who has joined us in our booth.

"We are the future. We build websites," Jonathan tells him.

"That's so cool."

"It is *very* cool," Jonathan confirms.

Of course, we've only built three websites at this point. (One of them being our own to market the company.) Right now, though, we're existing in the realm of infinite possibilities where our little company is thriving.

Eventually, I start to yawn. I notice the sun coming up in the windows and I can't believe we've stayed out all night. I wonder how long it will take me to recover from this. I won't have the luxury of spending the day in bed and a tiny bit of regret seeps in.

Jonathan notices the yawning and suggests we head home. I nod gratefully. Outside, we search for a cab but find nothing, so we start walking toward the 'L.'

"Emily can stay a little longer so you can crash," he tells me.

"That would be great."

"You might get a second wind. It's not like coke. It has an easy come down. You'll see."

Again, he's right. When we get back to the apartment, I have energy again. Which is good since Emily and Dante are crashed out in my bed. I shut the door after checking in on them and re-join Jonathan in the living room. He's starting up the stereo.

"Keep it low. They're asleep."

"Sure."

He puts on a CD and the music that comes out is transcendent even at a low volume.

"Who's this?" I ask.

"Robert Miles."

We sit down on the couch. The drug is wearing off, but I've still got a perma-grin.

"I can't wait for the revolution," he says, enthralled in the music. "It's coming."

I laugh. "So you say. But after tonight, I can see why you want it so much."

"Right? So, other than the music... what do you think?" He means the E.

"I love it. Obviously. It's scary good."

"Scary?"

"Well, I'm worried about you."

He grunts in frustration.

"I know. I'm sorry. But I talked to David, and I just want to make sure you're okay. Maybe all the partying is... I don't know, a way to hide?"

"Hide from what?"

"Me?"

"That's crazy."

"Maybe from something else then?"

"I don't think you're in a position to really criticize anything I'm doing."

It's a fair hit.

"It's not a criticism... it's... I'm just worried is all."

"Well, *don't* be." His exasperation is replaced by tenderness. "I'm alright. Really."

We're quite for a moment, just long enough for me to start yawning again.

"Shit. I don't know how I'm going to stay up for the rest of the day."

"Want a line?"

"Oh, no. No, no, no, no."

"You sure? Just a bump?"

"I can't do just a bump! You know that."

"How about some coffee then?"

"Hell yeah. Some coffee would be wonderful."

He gets up to make a pot and returns ten minutes later with a cup for me. We haven't chatted over coffee in ages, and I love this kind of intimacy even more than the club.

"He also told me he's sick of threesomes," I say, continuing our conversation about him and David.

"Why is everyone so obsessed with monogamy?"

"I don't know, man."

"It's an unrealistic societal expectation."

"You're preachin' to the choir, baby."

"Right."

"So, that's it? Monogamy or bust? No compromise possible?"

"Oh, I don't know. Maybe. I just don't like ultimatums, you know?"

"Are you two going to stay friends?"

"Are you asking for me or for you?"

"For me," I admit.

"I want to stay friends. We'll see how it goes."

"Good. Cuz I only have the two of you, you know."

"Baby."

"It's true!"

"You could go to some Mommy and Me shit. Make some other mommy friends."

I grunt in reply. The thought is terrifying to me. All those well-adjusted moms. And me.

"David thinks I should get a financial planner," he says, changing the topic.

"That sounds smart. How do you find a financial planner?"

"He knows a guy."

"He always knows a guy."

"Right? Anyway, David already told me what he's gonna say. Real estate."

"Buy a big place. We can start a commune."

I'm only half-joking. Part of me wants the commune, a big house with friends coming and going, like what Shane and Matty have. (Or had? Who knows?) Part of me wants to live in a single apartment, just me and Dante.

"We should move to the island," he suggests.

"The island!"

The island is a dream, a magical place for us and all our friends. Jonathan and I have been referencing this imagined utopia since we met.

"If you get Jack's inheritance, you could probably actually buy an island."

"Right?"

"Should we talk about your mom and my dad?" I ask.

"No!" He buries his head in his hands as if to hide from the reality. "It's so fucking weird!"

"I know it's wrong in all kinds of ways..."

"Yes!"

"But... hear me out. Maybe it's not so bad, you know, for them to have each other."

He sighs. He knows I'm right but doesn't want to concede.

"If they get married, what would that make us? Step-siblings?" he asks.

"Well, that would be *really* weird considering we're married."

"Ha! I forgot all about that."

I love that our marriage of convenience slips his mind. It does for me too.

"I hope you'll come out again. To the club," he says.

Fatigue is setting in even with the coffee and my eyes are starting to water. Nevertheless, I want to go out again.

"What is sex like on E?" I ask.

"Oh, girl. It's intense. Amazing. Though some guys have trouble getting an erection on it. Not that I have that problem. But some guys."

"Bummer."

"Total bummer. You want some for you and Shane? I can hook you up."

I'm tempted until I remember that he no longer does psychedelics. Plus, I think the drug plus Shane would probably kill me.

"Nah, I'm good."

"So, when can we go out again?"

"When can Emily babysit again?"

"How about Saturday? I can ask her."

"I can't on Saturday, and neither can you. Remember? *You're* babysitting."

And then he puts two and two together.

"Oh! *That's* your hot date. Shane."

"Yeah. We're meeting at a hotel."

"Oh, wow. That's so… affair-y."

"I know."

Jonathan then wants to know everything about me and Shane, and so I share all the dirty details. The story, of course, leads to the incident with Nick.

"You really said that to him? What the fuck were you thinking?"

"I wasn't. I just wanted him to know… that I know."

"Jesus. You and Emily. What am I going to do with you two?"

"I'm sorry, baby. What can I say? I'm a mad woman."

"I'm sorry too. What a dick."

"I'm okay."

"Me too."

Probably neither of us are okay.

Cracking the Safe

Dante can't quite crawl yet but can roll almost anywhere. I spend a few days babyproofing the apartment. Jonathan is the opposite of handy, so he just watches as I screw safety latches everywhere. I move everything out of reach in the living room and gate off the hallway.

"Am I going to be able to manage these things when I'm fucked up?" Jonathan asks.

"Probably not. Practice sober, friend."

When Saturday arrives, I have visions of *Trainspotting* running through my head. I hand off Dante to Jonathan with a good-hearted (yet serious) warning.

"No parties. No drugs."

"You say that like you don't trust me," he says.

"I trust you with *my* life."

"We'll be fine."

I must believe him because I practically sprint from the apartment to my car.

I follow Shane's directions from the highway to the motel. He's waiting for me in the parking lot, key in hand. I'm worried that it's going to be a rat trap but it's not bad. (I've stayed at a lot worse on road trips with Jonathan.) We enter the room together and I wonder if we should be more covert in our actions. But the motel is an hour outside Lake City, and he must feel it's far enough away from prying eyes.

I set my bag down on a chair and survey the room. He digs out a pipe, takes a hit, and offers me some. I haven't had pot in so long and I gratefully accept.

We both know why we're here and so it doesn't take long before we're in the bed. I didn't bring any toys this time. He doesn't seem to miss them, nor does he need them. He knows by now that I'm in his control, with or without restraints.

As we catch our breath afterwards, he asks if I can stay the night. I tell him that I can.

"Really? Great. I didn't think you would. You're always running off. I think you have a secret life." He's not complaining, just acknowledging the mystery I've inadvertently constructed around myself. If I tried to conjure these enigmatic airs deliberately, I'm sure I would absolutely fail. But circumstances have made parts of me unattainable. (Damn. *The Rules* win again.)

"Baby, *this* is my secret life," I respond, gesturing around the room.

He nods, conceding the point.

"How do you spend your day?"

"Well, Jonathan and I are starting a web development company. Well, we're trying, anyway. We have a couple of clients."

"That's exciting. What you were doing with Matty?"

Hearing her name, in this position, is strange. I feel guilty for my lack of guilt.

"What is your favorite flavor of ice cream?" he asks in a sudden change of topic.

This innocuous question does more than anything else to convince me that he does, indeed, love me. I remember how I looked through those photo albums in his house, searching for answers to questions I couldn't even form. Just an unquenchable thirst for the details of his life.

"So, what, we're playing twenty questions now?" I tease.

"I just want to know everything about you."

His words make me swoon.

"Chocolate chip mint," I answer. "You?"

"Butter pecan."

"Does this mean I can ask you random questions?"

He appears confused, as if permission for an inquisition is ridiculous. But he's always been somewhat guarded, preferring only to ask the questions.

"You can ask me anything," he says.
"And you'll answer?"
"Yes."
And just like that, it's like I've cracked the safe.

I only have about a million questions for him. (Are you still sleeping with Matty? Is she still sleeping with other guys? Does she have any idea about me? Does anybody know about me? What in the world are we doing? And on and on.) But the only question that escapes my lips is the one that is, perhaps, most pertinent.

"Did you ever want kids?"

"Oh…" He seems taken aback. Perhaps I should have started with something as trivial as ice cream flavors.

"I'm sorry if that's too personal…"

"No, no. It's fine. Well, Matty and I tried for a while. But it just wasn't happening. She wanted us to go to the doctor to find out why, but I just… I don't know. I think if it's supposed to happen, it happens."

I mull over his answer which is more specific than Matty's response but nevertheless lands in the same place. "The universe" decides for us when we can't or won't. I wonder if he would apply this logic to Dante. He exists and therefore, by that fact alone, he is *supposed* to exist. I mean, I certainly feel this way. But would he?

"I bet you'd be a great father… if you wanted to be one," I say, ever cautiously. I'm getting too close to the flame again.

"Eh, maybe," he says. "But I kinda like being selfish."

I can attest.

Then his body stiffens, and he asks the question I've been wondering if he would ever ask.

"You're on the pill, right? I mean, I've just been assuming…"

"Yeah."

His body relaxes as mine tenses up. He instantly notices.

"You alright?"

"Yeah. Can I have more of that pot?" I ask. He obliges, getting the pipe and filling it before handing it over. I take a couple of hits and pass it back to him. He places it on the nightstand without smoking any.

"You want to watch TV? Or sleep?" he asks, wrapping his arm

around me as my head returns to the nook of his chest.

"I don't want to sleep. If I sleep, it'll be morning and then I'll have to go."

"Baby."

"What do you want to do?"

He shrugs and smiles. "I could sleep."

I laugh at his opposing view. Of course, he can sleep. Everything is easy for him, even missing me. If he misses me.

I expect him to unwrap his body from mine and roll over to the other side of the bed. But he doesn't. He turns and spoons me from behind and I know this is heaven.

I wake up before Shane, his body still intertwined in mine. I need to get home and relieve Jonathan. I get up to get dressed but his grip on me tightens.

"Not so fast," he whispers in a morning raspy voice I've never heard before.

I want to brush my teeth before he kisses me, so I tell him that I'll come back once I do that.

"You don't need to worry about your breath for this," he says, diving under the covers.

He's right. When he's satisfied that I'm satisfied, he gets up from the bed. I can barely move, so I just lay there while he goes to the bathroom. When he returns, he grins at my state.

"You okay?"

"No."

"Well, when you're able to get up, I want you to write your address down for me."

This gets my attention. I rise up to a sitting position.

"Why?"

"So I can send you something," he explains.

"Oh. Sure."

"Your birthday is coming up, right?"

"Right." I'm shocked that he remembers.

"Does Jonathan know about us?" he asks.

"No." The lie is quick because I know it's what he wants to hear.

"Good," he confirms. "I just think it's better if no one knows."

He gets back into bed with me. By now, I'm wide awake and

ready to reciprocate. I start kissing his neck.

"What? You don't want anyone to know about this?" I purr, my lips traveling down his body.

"Baby," he groans.

When we finally get up from the bed, we prepare to leave the hotel. We plan to exit separately, with an understanding that we will meet up again as soon as possible. I tell him to call me at our allotted time.

"You like our phone calls, don't you?" he asks playfully.

"You know I do."

"Good."

Up until now, I've only been comfortable engaging in our calls when Jonathan is out of the apartment. But now that he knows, I'm sure I can tell him to stay clear of my room when the phone rings. Or put a sign on my door like we're in college. It's an upside to having a best friend who is unfazed by deviant behavior.

"Your voice makes me crazy." I punctuate the statement with a kiss on his neck.

He groans. "Stop. I have to go."

I stop and pick up my bag to leave first. But now he's the one who can't leave. He takes the bag from me, puts it back on the floor, wraps me in his arms and kisses me deeply.

"I love you," he says, pulling away only slightly, his face so close to mine. I repeat the words back and then leave, before they can be tainted by saying anything more.

The drive back to Chicago is fraught with worry. I imagine all sorts of scenarios, all of them proving wild and untrue as soon as I walk into the apartment door. Jonathan has Dante on his lap and they're watching TV. He seems more tired than if he had done drugs all night.

"Girl, thank god you're back. I almost called Emily."

"Oh no! Was he difficult?"

"I mean, not particularly, I guess. I just don't know how you do it."

"It's the attention thing. It's exhausting," I say, repeating my theory on parenthood. "Go to bed. I'll take him." He doesn't argue, just waves back at me as he slumps off to his bedroom.

Shane and I continue our affair in this way. We talk every night on the phone, from a few minutes to a few hours, depending on circumstances. We see each other once a week. When we meet at a motel, I leave Dante with Jonathan so I can stay the night. When we meet at Shane's house, I leave Dante with my father, and only stay for a few hours.

I don't know where Matty is during these times, only that she is nowhere near us.

On my birthday, Shane sends me a strawberry pie. I'm delighted by the gesture and tell him so on the phone.

"I can't believe you remembered."

"You're… what? Twenty-four now?"

"Yup."

"Still so young." He sounds wistful, as if remembering when he was twenty-four.

When we talk on the phone, he tells me about his day, omitting mentions of Matty. And I tell him about mine, omitting mentions of Dante. (Which is a feat since my day revolves around him.) Endless questions both trivial and probing explode from his boundless curiosity, and he hangs on my every answer. This reflection, seeing myself through his bedazzled eyes, is the most enticing drug of all. He's hungry for me and it's exotic and wild and I feel marvelously, naturally high all the time.

"What was the worst day of your life?" he whispers into the phone one night.

"The day my mom died."

"Right. Of course. You wanna talk about that?"

And it's crazy because I do. For the first time ever. I tell him about the day, driving home from college in a haze, not knowing what awaited me. I tell him about the ER and my broken father. He listens, his responses perfectly empathetic and kind. I ask about his own worst day, and he echoes my memory.

"When my mom died."

I give him the same opportunity to share in detail but instead he moves on to more questions.

"What was your best day?" he asks.

"The day I met you."

"No, really."
"Really."
"Mmm."

My questions for him are just as infinite. And to my delight, he answers them all now. I know his favorite things and every choice feels revelatory, a key to understanding him more deeply. I know his life choices and his regrets, his desires and his fears. I know the boring details of his day that never seem boring at all because they're his. I know his secrets and his habits now.

I know he stays up way too late and wishes he would stop but never does. I know he keeps a dream journal. (His dreams are nothing like my anxiety ones. Instead, they're delightful, first-person, heroic adventures that he recounts to me in detail.) I know how to kiss his ear in a way that makes him crazy and that his toes are ticklish. And I know that I'll never feel like this with anyone else.

I know he loves his life in Lake City even if he still resents his mother for guilting him to come back. (I also know he'd never use those words.) While he misses California and wonders what that path could have been, he loves his house, the woods, and this world he's created. I know that Matty is a part of that world, and he loves her too. It's a truth I've reconciled in my head by accepting that people can love more than just one person. And that's okay. (Sure, honest polygamy would be better but some people just aren't ready for that.)

And then one night on the phone, he breaks the unspoken rule.

"I never loved her… like this."

He means Matty and I'm shaken. Partly because I'm so enraptured with his love for me and partly because it means every thought I've ever had about them has been wrong.

"Timing is everything," I say, repeating the philosophy that never stops feeling relevant.

"Yeah," he says.

I collect all these facts about him, file them away, and know I'll never forget them. They've been imprinted on my otherwise faulty memory. I know if I hear his favorite song twenty years from now, it will wreck me. Because I know that this is, just like during the summer we met, just like *always* really, a temporary moment in time. I'm dancing on the edge of a dangerous cliff (again). And (again), I push it to the back of my mind. But I know it's there, always.

The worst thing about love is knowing it can disappear in an instant.

Indica

Like so many things, the shift starts slowly and then happens all at once. About six weeks after our first trip to the motel, his interest wanes. Our conversations become halted. We stop making plans to see one another. He stops asking questions, no longer curious. I compensate by talking more. I ask anything I can think of to try to get his words flowing, but I only get vague one-word replies. The door to his inner life is closing and I'm throwing myself in the way of it.

"How was your day?" I ask, one night on one of these tortured calls.

"Fine."

"Well… want to know about my day?" I try a teasing tone, one meant to entice although I have nothing interesting to say.

"Sure." But there's a sigh. I can hear the goddamn sigh.

The breath of pleasure has been replaced by one of exasperation. He's bored with me, which means I'm boring. I want to ask what changed but don't know the right words to use. When I try, my thoughts get muddled until I'm the one apologizing. And when I do, he doesn't stop me. He doesn't reassure me the way he once did.

"Are you okay?" I finally ask after a minute of uncomfortable silence. I want to ask if *we* are okay, but even after all that's happened, I still don't know if the two of us can constitute a "we." How pathetic is that? But these are the terms I agreed to.

"I'm fine."

"Really?"

Frustrated sigh.

"Sorry."

Frustrated sigh.

And so on.

I know that if I could manage the words, the precise question to ask, he would placate me with platitudes of ever-constant change and the foolishness of expectations. I replay every word he's ever said to me in my head on a loop, my fickle memory so perfect when it comes to him. When I review the declarations, I'm forced to acknowledge his lack of promises. He was always careful, like a criminal who doesn't leave a trace. He never said "forever." Should I protest, should I do a post-mortem, I'm quite sure I'll find that all my wounds are self-inflicted.

One night, he doesn't call at all. It's the first time since our affair began in earnest and I wait with the phone in my hand for hours, willing it to ring. I would call him but that's not the deal. The next night is the same and I'm left clueless and desperate. The days are interminable, the nights intolerable. I focus on Dante but it's like running a marathon with a broken heart. Absolutely doable, just ridiculously agonizing.

On the third night, he does finally call. I answer too eagerly.

"Hey. I thought you forgot about me," I say, trying to keep my tone light.

"I've been busy." He sounds defensive. Already.

I don't say anything.

"Don't be mad," he says in an exasperated tone.

"I'm not mad," I say, even though I clearly am.

"Good. Because I didn't do anything wrong."

"I know."

Do I? No. But when I push him on anything, I end up in this same stupid maze. I'm caught in a web of his intentions (obviously all good) and my impressions (apparently all wrong). I doubt my reality and it's a fight I can't win. He's older and wiser, and he's played these games before.

"What were you busy with?" I say, cautiously, weary of the quicksand in which I flail.

"I've been planning a birthday party for Matty."

"Oh."

It's like a dagger in my heart.

"When is that?" I wouldn't ask, but like a defendant on the witness stand, he's opened the door to this testimony.

"This Saturday."

"Oh."

This conversation is painful but, of course, it can get worse. It can always get worse.

"I just think I need some time on my own," he says softly. His tenderness has the opposite effect. By treating me like a crazy woman, one he needs to tiptoe about, he's made me one.

"Okay."

"You understand?"

I don't, so I don't say anything.

"Say something."

How can I? It's a trap. But he's so goddamn patient. Always. So, he just waits for me to say something. To absolve him, I suppose.

I just want this to stop. I want him to stop hurting me. I want *me* to stop hurting me. How do I get it to stop?

"Indica," I whisper.

"What?" he asks. He either doesn't understand or didn't hear me. Clarifying would be devastating so I don't.

"Nothing," I mutter.

"Well, I gotta go. I have some phone calls to make."

"Right."

"Bye."

"Bye."

When I hang up the phone, I just stare at it until a giant sob erupts from my chest. Did he just break up with me? I replay the conversation and I'm pretty certain that I just got dumped. I cry uncontrollably until I notice the lights on the baby monitor. It's like a switch. The tears stop and I go to Dante. I pick him up, snuggling him to me.

"Hey," I whisper. "Don't cry." And then I realize how hypocritical that sounds. "Or, you know, cry all you want. Life is a bitch." My tone is still comforting even if my words aren't. I take him to bed with me. He stops his crying and I start mine again. I cry soundlessly until we fall asleep.

When I sleep, I have a dream of watching a sunset on an unfamiliar beach. Waves crash into the shore and the predictable motion is like a restorative massage on my psyche. I'm alone, sitting in the sand, but not lonely. It's peaceful and beautiful and strange, the antithesis of how I feel when I wake and remember.

Mad Woman

I become obsessed with Matty's birthday party. I imagine him planning it. He's calling all their friends. He's creating a menu. Maybe he's booking a band. I can't help but wonder about the other universe, the parallel one where I'm invited as a guest, as a friend and nothing more. But then there would be no Dante, so I banish the thought.

When the night of the party comes, I go to Lake City. I drop off Dante with my father and I take his car to the liquor store. I want to drink like I did in college. Carelessly. I buy a bottle of Strawberry Hill and take it back to the car. But instead of returning to my father's house, I go to Matty and Shane's. The right side of the street leading up the hill toward their house is lined with cars. I park behind the last one. I'm too far away to see anything but I can hear the revelry. He did get a band, one that's playing the type of music I always associate with Shane. Classic, bluesy rock 'n roll, the kind that makes it impossible to stand still within earshot. (Can anyone stand still to Stevie Wonder's *Superstition*? Ah, but I can. Tonight, I can.)

I take the bottle and sit on the hood of my car. And I start drinking. Boone's Farm is not like Scotch. It takes some work to get a buzz, but I'm determined. Because fuck it. Fuck everything.

A truck drives by, slowing down as it passes. I panic when I realize that it's Shane's truck. But when the window rolls down, I see it's Carlos at the wheel.

"Hey, girl! What are you doing down here? Come up to the party! I was just getting ice, but it sounds like the place is jammin'."

"Oh, I'll be up later."

I wave him away and it works. I have no intention of moving from this spot on this car with this bottle. Unless it's to live in the woods where I can haunt them forever.

I'm halfway done with the bottle when I see Shane walking down the hill. He takes in the scene and his disappointment in my behavior is evident.

"Carlos said you were out here."

"Fuckin' Carlos."

"You can come to the party. You know, if you're not gonna be crazy."

"Ha! Well, I am crazy. So, I should probably stay right here."

"If that's what you want." His tone is dismissive.

I might be buzzed but I can still read him. No matter how much he closes himself off to me. I can tell he's concerned. It's just different now. He's determined to do the good thing, the right thing. The fierce love is gone, replaced by an obligation. Obligation to a mad woman who is doomed to love him. I feel sorry for him, though not nearly as sorry as I feel for myself.

I really hate his forced kindness even more than his dismissiveness. At least that shit's honest. I wish I were a witch and could make him turn around and walk back up the hill.

Leave.

Don't leave.

A car pulls up behind us and a woman gets out. She's familiar to me but I can't place here until Shane calls her by name.

"Vicky!"

"Shane! Good to see you."

She's the woman who dropped by while I was housesitting. I hope she doesn't remember me. Whether she does or not, she ignores me.

"You comin' up?" she asks Shane.

"Yeah, I'll be up in a bit."

She starts walking up the hill. Shane and I stay silent until she's out of earshot.

"Well, I need to get back to the party," Shane says.

"Wait! I need to ask you something."

"What?"

"You did dump me, right? Like, I've never been dumped before.

That sounds like a brag but it's not. I've never dumped anyone either. So, I just want to be sure."

His face is pained. He doesn't like the expression. It makes him the bad guy. And he's the nice guy, the good guy. I slide from the hood of the car, falling on my knees hard. The ground tears a hole through my jeans and I'm immediately bleeding. I don't feel it. I'm reminded of Jonathan's joke about UPBs (unidentified party bruises), the black and blue spots you have after partying with no memory of their origin. I hope this is one. I'd like to forget everything. I get up, trying to steady myself.

"Okay, so I'm just going to assume you did dump me. Otherwise, this is even more horrifying than it already is." I slur the words, cursing my inability to exhibit grace under pressure. Why do I have to be this drunk, disgusting mess? I hate me. But I can't stop talking. "Can I ask why though? Is that in my rights?"

He sighs, wishing this whole conversation would end. But I won't let it go. I can be patient too. I stare at him, demanding an answer.

"Well, I am married," he finally answers.

"Ha! Well, so am I!"

"You're drunk."

"I *am* drunk. And I *am* married."

He doesn't know whether to believe me or not. For all he knows, I could be married in the same way he's married. I expect him to ask more questions about my confession, but instead he expounds on his reasons for dumping me.

"And, you know, it's complicated."

I'm drunk outside his wife's birthday party. Yes, it's complicated. I can't argue the point. I'm fulfilling every negative expectation here and it's frustrating as fuck. I start to cry, and he puts his sympathy cap back on.

"You're going to be okay. Everything is going to be okay."

Does he know how stupid that sounds? Nothing will ever be okay again.

"Right," I say, giving him a sarcastic thumbs-up. "Everything will be fine. Except that you destroy me."

"You destroy you."

The sentiment is infuriating even if he's right. Nevertheless, I'm almost certain I didn't get here alone. I will forever be envious of his infinite ability to absolve himself. If I could bottle that shit, I'd be a millionaire.

"You're so young."

Yes, it's my defining fault, the one used to invalidate every emotion I have. I throw the bottle on the ground where it shatters spectacularly. The childish action is momentarily satisfying, then awfully indicative of his assessment of me. Goddammit. I want to tell him to stop making me crazy and maybe, just maybe, I can stop acting crazy. It's a cyclone that I can't escape. Instead, I just whine.

"Do you know how tired I am of hearing that? 'You're so young.' Fuck that. Cuz I don't feel young. I feel fucking ancient. It's just an excuse to treat me like a child. Which is such bullshit. I mean, how can I *be* a child when I *have*..." I stop myself just in time.

"When you have what?"

"Never mind," I mumble. I really don't know the value in lying anymore, but it's become such a habit I can't stop. Lying isn't going to save anything if there's nothing left to save.

He patiently kicks any shattered glass away from the road, so it won't damage any vehicles. His good Samaritan behavior guts me. It reminds me of why I love him, how kind and considerate he can be. And how much easier this would be if I could just hate him. He takes my arm.

"Come on. I'll take you home."

He leads me up the hill towards his truck. The party is louder here but the people are still out of view. Worlds away.

He opens the passenger door for me. I climb in as he gets into the driver's side. I wonder if he remembers where I live but I don't ask. I'm way too busy crying quietly, wiping tears away with my shirtsleeve. I let out a grim laugh.

"What?" he asks.

"Just thinking about what a sex goddess I am right now."

He doesn't find the thought as amusing as I do. Or he just doesn't ever want to laugh with me again. We sit in silence for the drive. Shane never listens to music in his car, which I used to find quirky but now I think might be a genuine character flaw.

As we get closer to our destination, the silence is replaced with sirens. I'm used to the sounds of sirens in the city. They're part of the tapestry of sound. But here they seem louder, with nothing else to absorb them.

When we take the turn towards my father's house, I see the flashing lights. An ambulance and firetruck are right in front of the house. I stop breathing. I sober up enough to think terrible thoughts. Shane pulls up behind the emergency vehicles and I'm out the door before he can even stop. I run across the lawn to the front door where my father is on a gurney. He's being wheeled out by firemen, and he has a respirator over his mouth.

"What's going on?"

"Are you the daughter?"

"Yes."

"We're taking him to the ER. You can ride along if you want. Or follow us there."

My body is frozen. I can't go in the ambulance. I have to find Dante. I run inside the house, frantic, looking for my son. I scan every room in seconds but he's nowhere. I run back outside, where the firemen are loading my dad into the ambulance.

"Katie!"

It's Emily, appearing out of nowhere.

"Emily! Where's my son?" I shout frantically at her.

She points to Mrs. Tucker's house. My neighbor is on the porch holding Dante. She waves to acknowledge me. I start to run in their direction, but I'm torn between my dad and my son.

"Go. I'll go with your dad," Em says.

"Right. Thank you." I grab her hand and squeeze it. As she starts to climb into the ambulance, I run towards Dante.

"I heard the commotion, so I went to see if everything was ok," Mrs. Tucker explains. "I thought I should take him until you got here."

"Oh, thank you. Thank you so much."

Before I can take him, he utters his first word.

"Mama."

Everything stops if just for a moment. I'm transported from everything around me, amazed at the milestone.

"Did you hear that? He's never said that before!"

"Was that his first word?"

"Yes!"

I plant kisses all over Dante's face. "Yes, I am your mama. And I'm so glad you're okay."

"I can keep watching him if you need to go to the hospital," she offers, her hands out to accept him back. I'm slammed back to the current crisis.

"Shit. Yeah. That would be amazing. Do you know where everything is? You know, diapers, food…"

"I can manage. You go. But…" She pauses, taking in my disheveled state and my still bleeding knee. "… maybe you shouldn't drive?"

Even though I feel perfectly sober now, I know she's right.

"I'll drive."

The words come from behind me where Shane has been quietly observing this whole scene.

Collision

"Let's go," I tell Shane.

I walk past him, back to his truck. I get into the passenger side once again and wait. But he's just standing there, shell-shocked by what he's seen. I close my eyes and try to prepare for the oncoming storm. There's no hiding anymore.

When he does get into the car, he doesn't start the engine right away. Eventually, he speaks.

"How old is he?"

"Almost eight months."

I can see the slightly befuddled look on his face, the one he makes when he's trying to do calculations in his head.

"Don't bother with the math. He's yours."

He sits staring ahead and I have the urge to get out and walk to the damn hospital.

"Look, I know this is… well, big. And we need to talk. But my dad might be fucking dying so can we table it for now?"

As always, saying the words aloud make them all the more real.

"Right. Tell me one thing. What's his name?"

"Dante." I say it softly, like a prayer.

"Dante," he repeats, just as softly. He starts the car and drives us to the hospital. And all the way there, all I can think is that it's happening again.

Shane walks with me into the ER. I tell the nurse at the front desk that my father was brought in by an ambulance and they shove some forms at me to fill out on his behalf. Because, obviously, that's the kind of thing I should be doing right now. Forms.

I take them and sit down but the pages in front of me are blurry and my hand is shaking. I put the clipboard on the empty chair next to me and I excuse myself to find the restroom. It's a small lockable room and I'm glad for the privacy. No amount of cocaine cheerleaders could move me now. I try to throw up, but I only produce dry heaves. I have no idea when the last time I ate anything was. I'm sweating and I'm dizzy, so I splash some water on my face. I look down at my knee and it's a bloody mess.

I exit the bathroom and take my seat next to Shane.

"You don't have to stay," I tell him.

He ignores me. He won't let me be the martyr. Fine.

The smell of the ER doesn't do anything for my nausea. I look down at the tiles and remember counting them the last time I was here for Jonathan. How many were there? I could count them again. It's just some simple multiplication. But my head is throbbing too much to try. I close my eyes. And when I open them, I see Matty coming in through the automatic doors.

Shit. I look at Shane and follow his gaze. He sees her too. As she spots us and walks our way, the interior doors also slide open. As Matty approaches us on one side, so does Emily on the other. But while Matty is taking both of us in, Emily is staring straight at me. And I don't need anything more than her tear-stained face to know what's happened. I get up and she hugs me.

"I'm so sorry."

I don't hug her back. I'm too stunned to move.

"He had a heart attack. A big one," she continues. "They tried so hard to save him."

My dad is dead.

Matty is here.

Shane knows.

It's just too fucking much. I sit back down.

Emily sits on the other side of me. Matty backs away, registering this part of the drama in which she has no part. Emily takes note of my injury.

"What happened to your knee?"

"Oh. I fell." A million years ago.

"You need stitches. Let's get you looked at." She gets up and approaches the front desk. Always a mom.

Shane gets up and takes Matty's hand. He leads her out of the ER, and I wonder if I'll ever see him again. A wave of despair washes over me and I start to sob. I run back into the restroom to grab some toilet paper to blow my nose. When I come out, Emily is looking for me. A nurse is calling my name. I follow her to a room where she assesses my knee. She proceeds to wash the injury and stitch me up. It's quick but I'm not allowed to leave. She tells me to wait for my discharge papers before she exits the room. I look at the clock, but I have no sense of time. And then Shane walks into the room. I barely got to mourn his absence. I feel like a yo-yo, my emotions swinging every which way. Despair when he leaves, relief when he returns, over and over and over.

"Hey," he says, taking a seat next to me, cautiously, like I'm radioactive. Maybe I am.

He sits quietly, having the decency not to ask how I'm doing.

"How is Matty here?" I ask him, staring at the wall.

"Vicky thought we looked suspicious. She followed us. First to your house, then to the hospital. Then she called Matty."

"Jesus. I really don't like that woman."

Just a week ago, he might have been interested in my opinion, but now he just judges my judgment of her. He should hate her too, the nosy bitch. But no, the problem is me.

"And what did you tell Matty?" I ask.

"The truth."

I almost laugh.

"Which truth?"

"That I drove you home because you were drunk. And the ambulance was there so I drove you here."

"Ah. That truth. Convenient for you that my dad died."

It's a fucking horrible thing to say and I regret the words immediately. He lowers his face, expressing a tiny bit of shame. The first I've ever seen in him.

The nurse returns with the discharge papers. "Your husband is here," she tells me, as Jonathan appears in the doorway.

"Baby," he says, coming over to me. He kisses me on the head and takes my hand. "I can't believe it. Papa." The word sends me into such sadness I choke. He hugs me. And then he notices Shane. "Oh. Hey."

"Hey," Shane says, equally awkward.

If Shane wants to ask me if it's true, he doesn't. Thank god. I don't have the energy to explain my marriage to Jonathan. I may not have the energy to stand.

"How did you get here so fast?" I ask Jonathan.

"Emily called. David drove us."

"You must have been flyin' to get here so quick."

"Pretty much."

"Are you and David…?"

I'm sure it's not the appropriate time for such a conversation but fuck it. I need normal, unthreatening words like I need air.

"We're talking," he hedges.

"Good." All hail something good. Not all is lost.

I sign the discharge papers and manage to push myself up. I follow Shane and Jonathan back to the waiting room where Emily and David join us.

Jonathan offers to take me home, but I don't know where he means. Does he mean my father's house…. which is now no one's house? Or our apartment back in Chicago? I don't know where I want to go. It doesn't seem to matter much.

"Let's go to our house," Emily suggests. "Is that alright?"

"Dante," I answer. I want my son.

Shane's eyes meet mine, a reminder of unfinished business.

"I'll call Mrs. Tucker," Emily says. "I'm sure she can watch him until tomorrow."

I want to argue but I don't have the will. I just nod numbly. We all walk outside where Shane wraps me in a hug. I'm caught off guard by the sudden affection. And then he's saying good-bye. The yo-yo swings again as he walks away, towards his truck. We walk in the opposite direction towards David's car, my eyes still on Shane's back. I can see Matty sitting in the passenger side of the truck waiting for him. I wonder how much she knows, how much she believes.

"Who was that?" Emily asks, as we all settle into the car.

I don't say anything, so Jonathan gives me a look. I know he's asking for permission, and I give it to him. Never let tragedy get in the way of good gossip.

"Go ahead," I tell him.

"That was the father."

The father. Like he's a holy man or something. Maybe he is. Maybe all fathers are. I close my eyes, the thought too heavy to hold.

Annie Marie Huber

Fallout

Everyone is right. I'm not a grown-up. Not only that but I'm now an orphan. *Orphan.* The word conjures up visions of the destitute girls of *Annie.* Am I too old to be an orphan? Is there an age when that word no longer applies? Surely, middle-aged people don't refer to themselves as orphans when their parents pass.

When my mom died, my father took care of everything. Now it's my turn. I know I have to get my shit together for Dante's sake and it's the thread that's keeping me from utter despair.

A few months after my mom passed, my father brought me into the garage. He wanted to show me an all-important file cabinet. The "just in case" file, he called it. I understood what he meant. With Dante perched on my hip, I pull out the file folder of paper and bring it inside. I spread the contents across the kitchen table. As I look at it all, I realize just how right David is. This paperwork, put together so carefully by my father, is here to save me. I don't have long to analyze the papers before I hear a knock on the door.

I answer the door, Dante still on my hip. It's Emily. Also here to save me.

"Hi, sweetheart. I thought I'd come by to see how I can help."

I direct her to the kitchen table where she sits and looks over the papers.

"Thank you for helping," I tell her.

"You're lucky. Your dad really did his work."

Lucky. Funny word but I know what she means.

"Yeah?" I ask.

"He has a burial plot all paid for. Next to your mother. Have you called on the life insurance yet?"

"No."

"Let's do that now. You can use a portion of that for the funeral expenses."

She gets the phone and calls a number from one of the forms. She puts it on speaker, and we wait for someone to answer. Before they do, I hang up the phone. All this paperwork, while lifesaving, is also a trail to the truth.

"What's the matter?" she asks.

"If they're going to send me a check, they need to send it to my married name."

"Your *what?*"

"Um… Jonathan and I are kinda married."

She stares at me like I'm talking Klingon. It feels good to let this secret go. I want all the secrets and lies gone. I don't have the strength for them anymore.

"We did it for his grandfather. He wants an heir. It's a whole thing."

She takes the phone and calls another number, putting the receiver to her ear. I know she's calling Jonathan. I take Dante to his room to change his diaper. When I come back, she's off the phone.

"I'm going to have words about this," she says. "But not right now."

"Thank you."

She calls the insurance number again, putting the phone back on speaker. When someone answers, she takes the lead. I jump in on cue when necessary. The next hour is filled with more phone calls. To the funeral home, to the newspaper, to the social security department. It's not long before I realize that Emily's skills are wasted as a cocktail waitress. She should be the project manager for a Fortune 500 company. I tell her this.

"Well, actually, I'm planning something. I know this isn't the right time…"

"No, tell me. Distract me."

"I'm going to run for city council."

"No!"

"Yes."

"Wow." I grasp at the news, hungry for something good. "Congratulations." I hug her.

Emily stays with me throughout all the planning and execution of the funeral. No one could ask for a better mother-in-law. I tell her this and she smacks me playfully on the head.

"Mother-in-law! I'm going to kill the two of you."

"Cool. Then you can plan those funerals too."

She makes a face at my macabre joke.

"Seriously," I say. "You have a skill."

"What a shitty skill to have."

"No doubt."

When she asks if I want to hold a wake, I laugh out loud.

"I can hold one at my place," she offers.

"Ugh."

"Got it. No wake."

We didn't have one for my mother either. Personally, I don't understand the post-funeral party.

On the day of the service, Jonathan slips me a one-hitter at the funeral home. I hand off Dante to Emily and go to the bathroom to take a hit. I'm immediately regretful. I want to be numb, but the pot just makes everything too vivid. Too real. Too *sharp*. I crave a sensory deprivation tank, away from everyone and everything.

More people have come than I expect. Our neighbor is here, along with a parade of old men who offer their condolences to me. They are men from his work, strange men in dark suits, who assure me how much I was loved by my father, words that ironically he never said but I know to be true. Emily and Jonathan are like pillars, standing by my side, keeping me upright and on script through it all.

The service begins with me, Emily and Jonathan sitting in the front row. I've got Dante on my lap. I didn't want to bring him. I wanted to protect him from this. Fortunately, he's too young to understand. I'm given the opportunity to speak but I can't, my mouth full of cotton. Jonathan rescues me, going to the podium in my place.

"Good morning. My name is Jonathan. I'm best friends with Katie. I just want to say that I called him 'Papa.' Because he was more of a father to me than my own."

Someone makes a sobbing noise and then I realize it's me.

"I know Gene was technically a Boomer. But I always thought of him as more a part of the Silent Generation. Stoic and proud. And how unfair it is that someone that found grace in silence got stuck with us loudmouth kids."

Subdued laughter ripples through the room. Thank you, Jonathan.

"But no matter how uncomfortable I made him, he never made me feel unwelcome. Oh, he'd grumble sometimes. But like a bear without claws. And then, when I left for Chicago, he took me aside and said, 'You're my kid, now.' I'll never forget that." Then he turns to address the casket. "Oh, and I promise to never spend more than thirty percent of my income on rent. Love you, Papa."

Jonathan sits back down next to me, and I squeeze his hand in gratitude. The rest of the service passes with generic words of condolences, offered up by a minister I've never once met. Which is fine, since I'm counting the seconds until it's all over.

At the gravesite, the sun shines. Again.

After my mom's death, I was able to go back to college. I long for the insular, safe space where expectations of me were so clearly defined. Because right now, I don't know what I'm supposed to do. Now that the rituals are complete, I'm left in this house. Surrounded by the familiar things that are not mine, but also somehow now mine. I find the energy to care for Dante but not without regular crying jags. They occur most often when I read to him. (*We're Going on a Bear Hunt*, an insightful book with the refrain "we have to go *through* it" whenever the protagonists face an obstacle, breaks me every time without fail.)

In the midst of my confusion about next steps, I call the smartest person I know. The person who can make sense of the remaining paperwork.

"Hey, David. Help."

"Hey, Katie. Sure, whatcha need?"

"I think... all this is mine now? Like, my responsibility?" I say, referencing the walls around me and all the things they hold. He can't see my hand gesture though, so I can only hope he understands.

"Do you have a copy of your father's will?"
"Yeah."
"I'll come by tonight."
"Thanks."

When David comes over, his pragmatic approach is a salve for my soul.

"So, you were right," he confirms. "Everything goes to you. What do you want to do?"

"I have no fucking idea."

"Cool. Got some coffee?"

Over coffee, he lays out a number of options regarding my new status as homeowner. By the time he leaves, I have detailed pro-con lists and much to think about.

I've been waiting for Shane to make an appearance since the night he found out about Dante, but I suppose he's giving me space. So, when I hear someone at the door the next day, my body goes on high alert. I pick up Dante and answer the door, bracing myself for what's to come.

I inhale in shock. It's Matty. Standing just behind the screen door. I stare at her, but she stares only at Dante.

"So, it's true," she says.

I open the screen door to let her come in. She does but it doesn't do anything to alleviate the awkwardness. I walk with Dante and put him in his electric swing for his nap. (His electric swing is the greatest invention ever.) I sit beside the swing as Matty comes over to the sofa. She sits on the edge of the cushion, not truly committing. She's still watching Dante, her face inscrutable.

"So, it was me. All along it was me."

It takes me a moment to understand what she means. She continues, "I was the defective one."

The word shakes me, and I say, "You're not defective…"

She interrupts me. "Please, don't try to make me feel better."

I put my head down, chastised.

"I'm more upset about the lying than the cheating. And you know what's ridiculous? I wanted an open marriage. He wanted a traditional one."

My mouth opens in response, but nothing comes out.

"I guess traditional *is* fucking a twenty-two-year-old," she continues.

I almost correct her on my age, but it hardly seems like a pertinent point.

"You're so young," she says.

For once, I don't fight it. Where once she said this with enthusiasm, this time, her tone is one of sadness mixed with a bit of contempt. As if to say "young *and* dumb." I can't contest it.

"Do you love him?" she asks.

"Yes."

"Does he love you?"

"I don't know." He did. I know he did. For a moment. Until that love seemed to evaporate into the ether. But I don't say any of that. She can ask him for the answer. Hell, then she can come back and tell me.

"Okay," she says. She stands with the clear intention of leaving, having gotten all the intel she needed. "What are your plans?" she asks as she heads toward the doorway.

"I don't know."

It would be cool to have another answer to this question. Just once. I've been assuming that I'd just go back to Chicago whenever this treadmill of trauma is over. But now I truly don't know. I feel like I'm at a crossroads. I feel like it's time to make an actual choice.

"You don't have any siblings, right?" she asks.

"No."

"I'm sorry about your father."

"Thanks." I don't deserve her kindness, but she gives it anyway. I may be better than the assholes that assaulted Jonathan and I, but Matty is indeed better than me. Maybe she's better than all of us.

Neither of us know how to end this meeting. The usual hug and kiss are now unthinkable. So, she just nods her head and walks out the door. I watch her get in her car and drive away. Only then do I have time to process her words and roll my eyes dramatically.

All this torture was a *choice*. Damn.

Annie Marie Huber

Conciliable Differences

The next person that comes to see me is Jonathan. He arrives with a bag of fast food, a trunk full of boxes, and several rolls of packing tape.

"Where'd you get all these?" I ask, helping him unload the trunk.

"Well, the nice thing about big box stores... they sell boxes."

"Right. Of course."

Once inside, we dig into the food. I put Dante in his highchair next to us and feed him a jar of pureed pears.

"Thanks for the boxes."

"You talked to David?"

"Yeah. He put me in touch with a real estate agent."

"You're definitely selling?"

"Yeah." I can't stay here. I've thought about it, but the ghosts are too much.

"I have something to tell you," he says.

"I have something to tell you too," I echo.

"You first," we say together and laugh.

"Okay, okay. I'll go," he says. "I want a divorce."

I didn't expect this. I jump up and hug him. "That's wonderful!"

He grins ironically at my response. "Gee, I don't know how to take that."

"Well, it has to do with my news. But first, what about your inheritance? You're letting it go? Don't you want that 'fuck you' money?"

"Oh, I absolutely want that money. But I want David more." He seems a little sheepish at the cheesy sentiment. But I love it. So much that I hug him again.

"Have you spoken to Jack?"

"Not yet. But I've put a message through to Mr. Anderson. I expect to be summoned any day."

"Need me to go with you?"

"Nah. I'm pretty sure I can tell him to shove off on my own."

"No doubt."

"Now you. What's your news?"

I take a deep breath. "We're moving to California," I say, indicating Dante. "Once I sell this house." It's the first time I say my intention aloud. It makes me feel high. The dream I had about the beach at sunset has replaced my anxiety dream. The west coast is calling me.

"Oh." He's disappointed but not surprised. "Shit. No, I'm sorry. That's good. Great. But, you know, shit."

"We can still make the company work. That's the beauty of what we're doing. We don't need to be in the same place."

"Yeah. I'm not worried about that. I'm going to miss you!"

"Yeah. I know. And I'm going to miss you so fucking much. But I have to get out of here. *Far* away from here. And, I don't know. I feel like, if I do this, I'll be going *towards* something. For once. Instead of just running away." Or maybe not. Maybe it's both. Maybe it'll always be a bit of both.

"Los Angeles?" he asks.

"Yeah." The city of angels.

"Talk to David. He has friends in West Hollywood that can probably put you up until you get settled."

"West Hollywood, huh? Isn't that, like, gay mecca?"

"Yes and I'll be so jealous."

"You could come too. You and David."

"Maybe one day," he says, before changing the subject. "What about Shane? Have you heard from him? You know… since he found out."

"No."

"Wow."

"I saw Matty."

"*Wow*. So, she knows? About Dante? And you and Shane?"

"Yeah."

"Was she pissed?"

"She was… stoic. And kind."

"Damn."

"Right? It's infuriating."

"Ha."

"I'm so glad you want a divorce. I'm so done with secrets and lies."

"And you're going to *Los Angeles*?" he laughs.

It's a good point but I think the artifice is part of what's drawing me there. While I've forsaken outright lies, I *want* my reality in soft focus. I need beauty. I need angels.

Gravity

Boxes are everywhere. Dante loves them, crawling around them and in them like a curious cat. My plan is to go through every room in the house. I make three piles: one for refuse, one for charity, and one for things to take to California. Eventually, I find myself making a fourth pile, for things that I don't particularly want but can't part with, nonetheless. These include my father's tchotchkes, like his small wooden paintings of antique cars and his framed photo of the Cubs historic 1908 World Series win. They've been on the walls as long as I can remember. And while I'm not going to put them up wherever I land, I can't toss them either. When I survey the garage, I notice the boxes of my mother's things that my father and I had recently packed.

"Ugh," I groan.

While not hoarders, my parents nevertheless collected an impressive amount of junk in their nearly three decades in the house. And paper. File cabinets filled with the stuff. Why my father thought saving the power bill from 1983 was important I'll never know. As I make my way through the cabinets, I long for the day when everything is an email.

I keep moving no matter how overwhelming it all seems. And soon, the boxes that I'm swimming in start to feel like walls surrounding my heart. I imagine laying bricks around my fragile soul, reinforcements against all the world can throw at me.

When I hear someone knock, I steady myself still expecting Shane to come by. But it's Emily, checking in, a habit she's adopted and for which I'm wildly grateful. I ask if I can store a few boxes in her garage until I get settled in California.

"Sure. Want me to take him for a stroll?" she asks, indicating Dante. "Give you a break."

"Hell yes. Thank you."

I carry the stroller down the front porch steps and get him settled. When they start walking down the sidewalk, I collapse onto the step. I want to lay down, but I know if I do, I'll never get back up. I should use the opportunity to make more coffee and continue working.

Before I can rally myself, a familiar truck approaches and parks on the side of the road. Shane is finally here, and I want to run away and hide. But I'm paralyzed as he walks from his truck. He sits next to me. I can't meet his eyes, instead focusing on the grass in front of me.

"I thought you'd show up sooner," I confess.

"I wanted to stop being angry first."

"And did you? Stop?"

"Yes."

Relief spreads through my body.

"I'd like to see him."

"Em is taking him for a stroll. He'll be back soon."

"Em?"

"Jonathan's mom."

"Ah."

"She's been checking in on me. Since, you know…"

"Right."

A wave of grief washes over me, but I don't get to indulge it before Shane is asking the big question. The one I've been wrestling with since the day I discovered I was pregnant.

"Why didn't you tell me?"

Where to start?

"Well, at first, I didn't want to blow up your marriage. I realize how ridiculous that sounds now. Then, when things between us changed…" I trail off because I don't know how to explain myself. The secret was like a snowball, growing bigger and more dangerous with every passing moment. Secrets gain momentum if you let them.

So, I just say the most honest reason I can muster. "I didn't want you to hate me."

"Were you *ever* going to tell me?"

"I don't know." My go-to answer for everything. "Matty was here. Did you know?"

He shakes his head. It's the answer I'm hoping for as if to prove that we're all liars of omission, even his saintly wife. But I know the situations don't compare. Maybe if I believed in moral absolutism. I don't though, so I silence my point.

Part of me wants to bring up the revelation that Matty shared. I'm pretty sure I have a valid complaint for all that has happened.

"Matty said…"

"What?"

"Nothing."

This answer frustrates him, but I watch him let the emotion go in seconds. It feels like magic to me, the way he can shake everything off him. If only I wasn't part of "everything."

"I'm concerned that you're not up for this," he says, quietly. "And if you're not, Matty and I can take him."

I've been preparing for this. For the past few days, I've been running every possible conversation with Shane through my head. And while I want to shout ("oh, hell no!") at his offer, I know I have to be calm. No more mad woman.

"Thank you for the offer. But no thank you. Not on your life."

I used to torture myself with images of the three of them as a happy family, with me banished like some monster in a fairy tale. But these fears have always been irrational. What is he going to do? Sue me for custody? Tell the courts all about his income? He can't take Dante from me. And that realization is everything… since I have no idea how to qualify myself as a mother. Who can? My son is happy and healthy, meeting all the benchmarks established by the pediatrician. My report card will come much later, and it will be Dante who does the grading.

"I know you haven't seen me at my best," I continue. "But in my defense, I like to think there's been a few extenuating circumstances."

"Your dad."

"Yes. And us. Whatever we are."

We. Us. It's the first time I've ever used these pronouns when speaking to him. My bravery, however, has no reward as he doesn't add anything to the comment.

I don't want to apologize but I know I need to.

"I'm sorry I didn't tell you."

He doesn't absolve me, nor do I expect him to.

"So, what now?" he asks.

"Dante and I are moving to California."

Tell me to stay. Tell me to stay and I'll stay.

He doesn't tell me to stay.

He doesn't say anything. And now Emily is turning the corner and heading our way. For the first time ever, Shane appears nervous. I introduce Emily and Shane. Dante is sitting up, with his hands around a bottle.

"Formula?" Shane asks me.

Well, that was fast. Three seconds before judgment. This should be fun.

"Don't start," I warn.

"What?" he asks innocently.

Dante calls out to me ("mommy!"), his arms reaching out. I unstrap him and pick him up. Emily, perhaps sensing the scene to come, takes off while the rest of us file inside.

"I tried to nurse him. It didn't work," I explain, placing Dante on his playmat in the living room. "I also wanted a natural childbirth. That didn't work either. And maybe that's another reason I didn't tell you. Because I'm not fucking perfect."

It's an argument with him that I've had enough times in my own head that I'm fast on the offense. He's taken aback.

"Okay…" he says. I can hear the subtext: "Calm down." Is there a way to make a woman crazier than telling her to "calm down," even if the direction is only implicit?

I want him to apologize to me. For all the slights against me, real and imagined. For breaking my heart. But he doesn't do that. I remember when he encouraged me to stop apologizing. It sounded so wise. But surely, that doesn't mean to *never* apologize. There has to be some fucking middle ground.

I make a promise to myself to always apologize to Dante whenever I fuck up. If I do one thing as a mother, I will teach him this: Don't hurt people. And if you do, apologize. No matter your intentions. Fuck intentions. They're as capricious as rationalizations.

Of course, I'm just as guilty. All the excuses I've held up to guide my behavior line up in my head like witnesses against me. I have to change my own behavior first. Like, did I even apologize to Matty? No? Shit.

Okay... starting *now*.

I'm suddenly desperate to push Shane from the pedestal I've placed him upon. In doing so, I see all the attributes I love in him as tragic flaws. With just a little re-framing, his altruism is an opportunity to judge others. His confidence becomes arrogance. And the fierce love I felt from him is now a casualty of his transient nature.

"Huh," I say, lost in my thoughts.

"What?" he asks.

"Nothing. I just... I always thought you were, like, holy. And you're not. Like, *super* not. You're fucked up too."

"Okay..." (Translation: "What the fuck?")

His bewildered response makes me chuckle. Not getting the joke (and why would he?), Shane turns his attention to Dante, who is crawling around, playing with an empty box in lieu of all his other toys. Shane sits down on the floor beside him, watching him intently. Dante, fearless, crawls over to Shane. Seeing them together is heart-wrenching. I get up to make a pot of coffee to distract me from the tender scene.

When I return to the living room, I've steeled myself again.

"So, California..." Shane says.

"Yeah."

"Los Angeles?"

"Yeah."

"You're gonna love it."

"Hope so."

"Jonathan going?"

"No."

"So, you're not really married to him then?"

"Oh, we're married."

"*Why?*"

"Remember how I thought Jonathan's grandfather was setting a trap? Well, he was. He wanted Jonathan to be straight. And in exchange for that, he'd get an inheritance."

"Wow. And what was in it for you?"

"It was good to not be alone."

"You wouldn't have been alone."

"And money," I say, eager to move on from his kind words. "I was getting money too."

He grins, pleased by my selfishness.

"But he's not going with you?" he asks.

"Well, as it turns out, being straight isn't worth it."

"Ha."

"And he's in love."

"Good for him."

"You must not have heard me. He's *in love*. It's quite terrible. Or, you know, will be. Give it time."

"I don't think California admits bitter people. Better change your tune."

"Ha," I echo.

I pick up Dante to put him down for a nap in my old bedroom where the crib is set up. Shane waits for me in the living room. As soon as we're alone together, my body pines for his touch. Even after my epiphany, I know that if he were to initiate anything with me, I wouldn't resist. My desire for him is like gravity.

"When are you leaving?"

"Soon as all this shit is done," I say, waving my arms around the room.

He seems sad at the prospect. If it were only enough.

"I want to be part of his life."

"You can be part of his life. You can't be part of mine."

I can't believe I'm saying the words. I want to take them back immediately.

"Ouch. And how is that going to work?" he asks.

"Matty can be our go-between."

He raises an eyebrow at me, and I give him my reasoning. "I know it sounds crazy, but she's the only one of the three of us that I trust. Ironic, ain't it?"

After everything that's happened, I know I can deal with Matty.

I understand Matty. At least, I understand her better than I do him. And I can't spend one more minute trying to decode him.

"So... this isn't a gray area," I tell him, referring to Dante. "This is one plus one equals two. You're either in or out."

"I'm in."

I want to believe him. But it doesn't really matter. One benefit to moving two thousand miles away is that he'll have to actually try. I'll know soon enough what it's worth to him.

"Great. Just have Matty contact me."

He rolls his eyes at this extra step, but I hold my ground.

And then he hugs me. He doesn't let go until my arms lift to embrace him back. Damn him. The sooner I get to California, out of his orbit, the better.

Revolution

"You won't believe what happened!"

Jonathan is running from his mom's car. He's shouting at me as I meet him on the front porch. Emily and David follow behind him.

"What?" I ask.

"So, I went to see Jack, right? Went there to tell him to fuck off. And I did. Very politely, of course. As soon as we were settled in the sitting room…"

"Drawing room," I correct.

"*So* not the point."

"Right."

"As soon as we were seated in the *drawing* room, I told him. I said, 'I want the money, but I want to live my life more.' And you know what he did?"

"What?"

"He laughed. I mean, *roared*. Then, he jumped up out of his chair and shook my hand."

"What the fuck?"

"Apparently, the whole thing was some sort of game. He wanted to see how far he could push me. I was never gonna get any of his inheritance *unless* I told him to fuck off."

"So… he *wanted* you to tell him to fuck off. From the very start."

"He said he was 'testing my character.'"

"Dude. Rich people are sick."

"Right?"

David and Jonathan have decided to make the cross-country

drive with me and Dante, and fly back once we're settled. David does have, in fact, a friend in West Hollywood who has a small guest cottage for rent.

As David and Emily go inside to retrieve more items for the car, Jonathan and I sit together on the front steps. "I can't believe you're moving to West Hollywood," Jonathan says for the millionth time.

"I know. I should switch teams." After all that's happened, the idea is tempting.

"So, what's the verdict with Shane? Is he in or out?"

"He says he's in. But, you know, I've decided to not have expectations anymore."

"Less chance of being disappointed that way."

"Exactly. And you and David must be good... if you're braving this road trip together."

"Frighteningly good. Let's just say I'm starting to have expectations."

"Ah. Scary. My condolences."

"Ha. Speaking of scary, you think your car is going to make it?" he asks.

"We'll see."

"This should be fun."

"Relax. I have AAA." I get a little wistful when I say this, as it's always been a gift from my dad that I'll have to renew myself from now on. The list I have of tasks like this is long. Grown-up responsibilities and no supervision. If I think too hard about them, I'll feel a panic attack coming on. And then I remember to focus on my breath which makes me wistful again. Around and around. The only way to stop the spinning is to look at Dante.

Emily has come over to see us all off. She's wearing a t-shirt that says "DOMA is DUMB."

"DOMA?" I ask.

"The Defense of Marriage Act. We need to get that repealed." She's in campaign mode, having made her platform one of fighting LBGT discrimination. I doubt her success in this little conservative town, but I admire the effort.

I hug her tightly. "Thank you, Em. I would not have survived the past year without you."

"Oh, honey. You're my kid, now." I choke up and hug her again.

The road trips that Jonathan and I have taken have always been spontaneous with no clear destination. But David is a planner and has created an itinerary, mapping out all our rest stops, hotel stays, and worthwhile landmarks. Even though we tease him relentlessly for his meticulous planning, we're grateful for the constraints. We're going to see the Grand Canyon.

David does his share of teasing too. As a native New Yorker, he has an inherent disdain for the west coast. He doesn't so much hate it as he distrusts the smiles on everyone's faces. I explain to him how much I need these smiles, no matter how fake.

We pile into the car, with David taking the first driving shift. Jonathan sits in front, and I climb into the back beside Dante. The trunk is packed tight with luggage. I'm not bringing much, opting to buy another stroller, highchair, and other necessities once I arrive. It's a daunting task but I really want a fresh start. Everything here feels tainted with grief. My childhood house is still on the market, Emily having agreed to field offers for me. And I have enough money from my father's life insurance to get us through the first few months of our new life.

"So, if Chicago is the blues and New York is jazz… what is Los Angeles?" I ask David as he starts the car.

"Well, I'm glad you asked. I was just thinking about that. Ever hear Enya?" he asks, producing a cassette from his jacket pocket. He pops the tape into the cassette player.

"No!" Jonathan and I yell together but not in time to stop him.

"Oh. Shit. Is the tape player still broken?" David asks.

"I hope we like it," I say, breaking into giggles.

Ethereal sounds fill the car. But before I can be transported by the music, Jonathan objects.

"Oh, hell no," Jonathan declares, offended by the lack of a beat. "No. Just no." He digs around for a pen to jimmy the tape back out. David starts driving but Jonathan stops him.

"No! We need a good song first. For luck."

David stops the car while Jonathan gets the tape out. He then searches the radio for something acceptable to launch our journey.

"No… no… no…." he says, flipping through the stations. "Wait!

Consensual Scars

What's this?" He turns the sound up. "Oh, shit! This is Robert Miles! On the radio!" He turns to David and me.

"You haven't heard this yet?" David asks.

"Not on the radio! I don't listen to the radio if I can help it. Why didn't you tell me?!"

"We were broken up."

"Oh. Right." Jonathan's excitement is only dampened for a few seconds. "Do you know what this means?"

David and I both laugh because we know exactly what it means. This is clearly a sign that Jonathan's prophecy is coming true.

"The revolution is coming. It's a new day, my friends," Jonathan pronounces.

It is, indeed.

"Can we go now?" David asks Jonathan.

"Onward!"

I wave to Emily and lean into Dante.

"Ready?" I ask him.

He smiles at me as he grabs my hand. His face is all trust and excitement. I take a deep breath and watch the house behind me disappear.

Annie Marie Huber

Acknowledgements

While this book is fiction, the people that inspired it are very much real and awesome. Shout-out to my beta readers, who held my heart in their hands (Christian Huber, Jenn Stithem, and Jess McNeil-Estes), to my parents who raised me with the confidence to write this (Mary Cummins and Don Cummins), to my MC peeps with whom I found great debauchery in a small town (Jason Matheson, Michelle McNally, and Angela Fisher), to my college peeps who invented the impromptu Laundromat road trip (Heather Conlon and Elaine Campbell), to my LA peeps who caught me when I wandered far from home (Wes Ferguson and Jerome Singletary), and to my yoga gurus who taught me to live by "lovin' it all" (Don Wenig, Marsha Wenig, and Sue Beres). Thank you all for your love and fuckery!

Made in the USA
Monee, IL
21 December 2024

74921549R00194